BOSNIAN DAWN

BOSNIAN DAWN

Peter Dyson

Cover design: @MaxDesign
Editorial: Richard Leslie@richardeditorial.com

Our Greatest Glory Is Not
in Never Falling,
But in Rising Every Time We Fall

Confucius

PROLOGUE

Chapter 1
Babonavic
November 1992

Ana Poborski lay marooned between the outer edges of sleep and wakefulness, as the bitter, ashen light of a Bosnian dawn crept in through her bedroom window. Then reality thundered in and fear took hold. The sound of gunfire in the hills had ceased, as her mother Katerina, said it would. Ana heard footsteps coming up the stairs and peered out from beneath the duvet, her heart racing. The door swung open and her mother entered the room, as Ana's fear drained away. She traced the lines on her mother's face, searching for a sign that said everything was okay.

'Come on, sleepyhead. It's nine o'clock. Time you were up.'

Her mother kissed her on the cheek, then Ana listened to the footsteps as her mother descended the stairs. She climbed out of bed and looked out on the street below, onto the scene of last night's exodus. The suitcase the Pleva family had left behind in their haste to leave still stood on the pavement. Their dog, Rodin sat abandoned next to it. Ana pulled on a jersey and her red skirt, she would shower later, and went downstairs to the kitchen.

The scene that met her was reassuringly familiar. Katerina was preparing breakfast while her Aunt Zara sat in the big armchair reading.

'Good morning Ana,' Zara forced a smile. 'How are you today?'

'Still sleepy,' she replied climbing onto her aunt's knee. 'Can we finish reading the book we started yesterday?'

'Yes of course we can, and we can do some drawing after lunch if you like.'

Ana finished the last of the bread for her breakfast, before showering and returning to the kitchen to read with Zara.

There had been no school for weeks, so ten-year-old Ana had kept up with her schoolwork at home with the help of her mother and Zara. Her mother's younger sister was a language teacher in nearby Banja Luka. Katerina prepared lunch as Ana's morning passed quickly enough, reading and drawing, until Zara tired and had to rest. Katerina finished chopping the vegetables for the soup and placed them in a pan on the cooker.

'We ate the last of the bread this morning. I'll go for another loaf while the soup is cooking. Erik said he would bake fresh bread today.'

Katerina collected her purse from the kitchen dresser and stepped outside. Her footsteps echoed in the eerie silence. As she made her way down the hill towards the bakery, old Mr and Mrs Pleva came out of their house and walked slowly towards her.

'Hello, I see you're still here?'

'Yes, in the end we decided to stay after our sons and their families left late last night,' said Mr Pleva.

'Have you heard from them since? Have you any news?'

'No. Nothing. Not a word. Well at least not yet. They'll be okay. I know they will.'

***

Katerina pushed open the door of the bakery as the bell jangled to summon Erik from the back of the shop. The vacant shelves behind the counter stared blankly back at her. Erik arrived; his customary greeting appeared to be hidden beneath a tangle of his own thoughts. Erik was a man in his sixties, but still had an eye for a good-looking woman and would always flirt with Katerina when she came into the bakery.

'Am I too late, should I have come earlier?'

Eric turned theatrically towards the empty shelves, and then reached nimbly beneath the counter to retrieve a freshly baked loaf.

'You are never too late.'

Katerina opened her purse to pay, but he raised his hand in a gesture of refusal.

'It's free. I fear this is the last loaf I will bake here in Babonavic.' He paused, 'I have just heard the Serbs could be on their way.' The words took Katerina's breath away and the blood drained from her face. 'They are members of the Communist Serbian Democratic Party. They have already razed two nearby villages to the ground. Babonavic is directly in their path. Tonight, we should all go to the church. I think it may be our only hope.'

2

'Is there no one who can save us?'

'Where are Boris and Leo? Are they still defending Sarajevo with the militia?'

'Yes, but there is no way of contacting them, we've tried. It's almost three months since we've seen them. There must be someone who can help?'

'There'll be no help from the UN. They're on the outskirts of Srebrenica, at least a day away from here, maybe more. Perhaps the Pleva's sons were right to leave.'

After lunch Ana spent the rest of the day with Zara, absorbed in her schoolwork as time slipped pleasantly by. Katerina went upstairs and sat staring out of the window watching the light flee from the winter sky, as night seeped into the village. She agonised what, if anything, she should say. Perhaps they'd be alright, perhaps the Serbs wouldn't come after all. She went downstairs to the sitting room where Ana and Zara sat quietly reading.

Then all the lights went out and they heard the thud of shells as they landed nearby. Katerina brought Ana's warmest clothes.

'Come on,' she said. 'We must dress quickly.'

Ana pulled on her anorak and Katerina snatched hurriedly at the zip, jamming it in Ana's jersey. She tugged at the zip, but it refused to budge. She tried again but her fingers wouldn't work.

'Here, let me help?' Zara struggled with the zip. 'There that's got it.'

Zara zipped up the anorak and Ana pulled on her fur-lined boots. Finally, when Katerina was dressed, she fastened Ana's hood and they were ready.

'Come on, hurry up, we're going to the church.'

Her mother's words just burst out. Ana waited for an explanation, but none came. She took her mother's hand, and as their eyes met, Ana grasped the need to escape from an evil her mother could not explain. They left their home as it began to snow, joining other villagers on their way to the church. They ran through the night, the sound of their footsteps the only witness to their flight. They held each other's hands as they tried to keep together, but Zara struggled to keep up. Through the darkness they could see the reddening flush from their burning homes as it bled across the sky. Ana tripped and fell to the ground, and as she rose to her feet, she heard the crackle of soldiers' voices close behind her. Wild-eyed, she watched as Rodin skittered past, to be lost in the chaos of the night.

Inside the church they sat down in front of the altar as they fought to regain their breath.

Ana looked up at Jesus on the cross. The Crucifixion always terrified her. It was such a powerful image of a cruel death, yet a path to heaven. Father Benjamin stood in the pulpit and raised his arms aloft.

'Gather round and we will pray.'

Ana's anxiety subsided as they prayed together. Then hymn books were given out, and the congregation joined the young priest in the singing of a hymn. It was a song of love and death. As the singing continued, Erik led the way as a handful of villagers barricaded the doors and windows with the wooden pews in the hope that they could keep out the Serbs.

The small band of white-faced women, young children and old men defended the church for less an hour. Then the Serbs battered at the church door, and there was an anguished scream as the door was torn from its hinges and the snow swept in. The Serbs were in the church, the house of God. A great silence descended on the congregation as they waited for the drama to unfold.

Four gunshots rang out and another layer of panic and terror gripped the congregation, draining from them everything but fear. In the confusion that followed, Katerina searched for a hiding place for Ana. Then she saw the cassock box. With the advantage of a child's suppleness, Ana contorted her body within the confines of her hiding place. Her chin pressed hard into her shoulder, while her legs were twisted back beneath her body.

'Be quiet Ana. Hide. Stay here until I come for you.'

Ana grasped her mother's hand for a moment as she lay in her refuge, trying to understand the danger that now consumed her. Then her mother was gone. Ana repeated her mother's words over again in her head. *"Be quiet Ana. Hide. Stay here until I come for you."*

Ana remained still and silent for what seemed forever, as she tried to stay detached from what was happening in the church. Her thoughts, incarcerated in a headache of confusion, ebbed and flowed but would not settle. She peeped out through a crack in her tomb.

She could see a soldier. He had thick rugged hands and salt-and-pepper coloured hair. From the far side of the chancel, another man whom Ana could not see called over to him.

'Roman.'

'Over here, Milo,' answered Roman in reply, as he walked over to sit on the cassock box, Ana's hiding place.

Ana held her breath and bit her lip, making it bleed.

'There are twenty-five Bosnians, eight old men, ten children and seven women. What are we to do with them?'

'Kill the men and the children,' said Roman.

Milo came over to where Roman sat, as Ana squinted through a crack in the cassock box. She could see Milo's face. He had a deep scar above his right eye.

'And the women?' Milo continued.

Roman stood up and placed his hands firmly on his hips, then thrust his groin violently forward.

'What are women for?' he sneered.

A sexual frisson brought a sparkle to his eyes. With that, both soldiers walked away in the direction of the women. It was then the screaming began again.

***

Nightmarish visions overwhelmed Ana. What must she do? In her head, she heard her mother's voice *'Be quiet Ana. Hide. Stay here until I come for you'.* As the cries for mercy died away; exhausted, Ana gave into sleep as she waited for her mother. She slept, for how long she didn't know, but when she woke it was light. She had to move. Her whole body ached. She peered through the crack in the cassock box. There was no sound, no movement. She opened the lid and looked out.

She could see her mother. She looked so beautiful lying there. Ana crawled on her hands and knees to where she lay. Katerina's clothes were torn, and blood caked her long black hair. Her face of brittle ice-white displayed no pain. She held her mother's hand and knelt to kiss her cheek. Tears sped down Ana's face as she looked up at an unseeing Messiah, and her emotions froze.

Ana's mouth was dry, and her tongue kept sticking to the roof of her mouth. She left her mother's side and foraged through the carnage. She could see Zara lying nearby. The chain that carried a gold ring still hung around Zara's neck. The bodies of the congregation were scattered amongst the wreckage of the church. The young priest, a red gash below his sleeping face, gazed up through the eyes of a man already in Heaven.

Ana was able to take respite from her thirst by sipping holy water from the font. Then footsteps shattered the silence as they echoed through the nave. Heavy, purposeful footsteps, heading straight towards where she stood. Quickly she retraced her steps to the cassock box, passing the Pleva's, locked in each other's arms amongst the hymnbooks. She squeezed in, closing the lid behind her, the footsteps hard on her heels.

The footsteps stopped nearby, as silence once again flooded the church. Ana clenched her eyes tightly together and held her breath. In an instant the lid to her hiding place was wrenched open. Wide-eyed Ana sought an escape as she stared up into a face. It was the face of her father.

'It's okay, Ana. You're safe now. You're safe.' Boris Poborski's voice floated down, enveloping her in a blanket of well-being. Ana held her father's hand as she left the church, pausing for a moment where her mother lay, reliving the memories of the night before—memories that would never leave her, not even in her sleep, and with her memories Ana took a promise. The promise that she would never hide again, she would always fight.

***

The rain beat down on the funeral cortège as it carried Katerina and Zara to their final resting place. Dying floral tributes stained the freshly dug earth of so many new graves. Ana held her father's hand, her head down to deflect the worst of the rain as it lashed spitefully in her face.

Boris tried to hide his grief. He had to be strong for Ana. Zara and Katerina's older sister Marija and her husband Jan, followed behind. They'd travelled down that morning from the safety of Banja Luka. Marija couldn't stop crying as Jan helped her to the graveside.

'It's my fault. I failed her,' said Boris. 'I should have been there, Leo. I should have saved Katerina.'

Leo turned to face Boris. 'How could you? You weren't to know. We were defending Sarajevo. We have to fight for Bosnia. You can't blame yourself.'

Katerina and Zara were laid to rest, as Boris looked out on a world of a thousand shades of black. Leo Illic stood by his side, silent and still.

'Here you are, Ana,' Boris said softly, handing her a small bouquet of winter pansies.

She stared down at the bouquet for a moment as she held it in her hand.

'These were Mama's favourite flowers.'

'I know,' he said.

Ana knelt on the wet earth and laid the winter pansies on her mother's grave. Then Boris said farewell to Katerina, his childhood sweetheart, before lifting Ana up into his arms.

'I have to leave you now. I have to go back to Sarajevo with Leo. I want you to go with Jan and Marija to Banja Luka. They'll take good care of you there.' He kissed her gently on the cheek. 'Goodbye Ana, it won't be for very long.'

Marija took Ana's hand as the rain swept in, and as Ana left the graveyard her grief was slowly buried beneath the weight of her promise. The promise that she would never hide again, she would always fight.

After no more than an hour in the car, they drove down the tree lined boulevards of Banja Luka. It was still raining as they arrived at the home of Jan and Marija, not far from the university.

***

Jan parked the car close to the door, but they were all soaked by the time they'd made it into the house. Ana looked around the room, taking it all in. The kitchen was a good size, though not as big as the one at home in Babonavic. Stairs in the far corner led to the first floor bedrooms. Ana liked the curtains and the big table that stood in the middle of the room. The table was set for the evening meal. She noticed the knives and forks were different to the ones at home. The spoons looked much bigger and she wondered why. A fire burned brightly in the grate, though Ana felt no warmth from it. Family photographs in ornate frames hung on one wall. There was one of Ana. Several condemning gaps stared blindly out, evidence that some photographs had recently been removed. Marija saw Ana looking at the empty spaces and pulled her away.

'Come on, let's go to your room.'

Ana had lost everything in the fire at Babonavic and Boris had packed the new clothes he'd hastily bought in Sarajevo, into a small case. Jan took it upstairs to a bedroom at the back of the house.

'This will be your new bedroom,' Marija announced, her voice was warm and welcoming. Ana nodded, but said nothing. The room had been decorated in a pretty shade of pink. Floral curtains complemented the duvet cover and pillowcases. Even the lampshade was coordinated, and a soft beige carpet covered the floor. Marija straightened the duvet and plumped up the pillows. Ana was pleased there was a desk in the space beneath the window where she could sit and read. On a chair in the corner of the room, three teddy bears waited, a testament to the children Marija and Jan had planned but could never have. Ana looked around the room. She didn't like pink and she'd never liked teddy bears. She much preferred her old room in Babonavic.

Together they unpacked the clothes that Boris had bought. Most of the outfits were unsuitable. Some were the wrong size, others the wrong style or colour. There was a large hideous tee shirt and a pair of purple leggings. Regardless, Marija made complimentary comments as she placed the clothes carefully in the chest of drawers.

In the morning Ana was up early. She came downstairs into the kitchen dressed in the hideous tee shirt and purple leggings. The tee shirt had been her first choice.

***

Jan was there. Ana waited for him to speak. She was confused by his bewildered look, he seemed tongue-tied. She was still waiting when Marija came in from the sitting room.

'Morning Ana, how did you sleep?'

Ana thought for a moment before answering as silence filled the room, leaving Jan and Marija looking uneasy.

'Good, thank you,' she replied nodding her head, 'and you and Uncle Jan, how did you sleep?'

Both began to speak at once, contradicting each other. Ana burst out laughing and the tension was broken.

At first Boris wrote a letter every week, never to Ana, always to Marija. The letters contained a message for Ana and money for her board. He hoped she was well and was enjoying the good weather, but as the weeks and months slipped by, the messages dwindled and then finally stopped. The envelopes contained only the money. It was left to Jan and Marija to invent the messages and remember Ana's birthday. Ana wasn't fooled and Jan and Marija knew it, but the charade had to continue; all three were complicit. Ana never occupied herself with the reason for her father's omission. Innately she understood. Her father blamed her for her mother's death.

Chapter 2
Sarajevo
April 1995

On the Bosnia Serb front line in Sarajevo, Leo Illic stared out through the darkness from behind a jumble of bricks that had once been a school. A noise in the rubble over to his right drew his attention, and he turned to see Savo Stanisic on his hands and knees crawling towards where he knelt.

'Anything to see?' Savo whispered.

Leo shook his head. His eyes were focused on the buildings that surrounded what had once been a bustling, living square. The château opposite had taken a direct hit from a Serbian mortar earlier that week. The entrance had been blown away and the contents of the château scattered across the cobbled square. Leo's attention was drawn towards the empty dilated doorway. To one side of the square, a splintered telegraph pole stood at an angle, half buried in the remains of someone's former home. Telephone cables carpeted the cobbles like crazy spaghetti. Savo indicated his intention to move up the front line and take cover behind the rubble. Leo tried to stop him, but before he could, Savo was off, crouching low and running hard. Leo turned, training his Agram machine gun to cover the château. Savo was only halfway to the brick and concrete rubble when deep within the doorway a machine gun spat out a hail of bullets spraying the square.

There was no way Savo could avoid them. He took a hit to his left thigh but limped on, propelled by adrenaline and his momentum. The second burst took him down and he lay where he'd fallen, one metre from the safety of the rubble parapet, as Serb gunfire strafed the square. Leo opened up with his Agram, directing a stream of bullets towards the doorway, as other Serb guns returned fire from the upper windows of the château. Boris Poborski joined Leo and took out one of the insurgents, but another Serb took his place. Two more Serb guns opened up, peppering the surrounding rubble. The noise was deafening as gunfire lit up the square.

'Cover me.'

Leo was almost to Savo before Boris opened up with his Kalashnikov and a second Serbian gun fell silent. Three more militia joined Boris as Leo threw himself headlong to where Savo had fallen. He picked him up, slung him roughly over his shoulder and made off under Boris' covering fire. He raced back across the cobbled square, as the sound of gunfire filled his head and another Serb took a direct hit. He was almost there. Almost safe. Leo was no more than five metres from where Boris knelt, when a trailing loop of telephone cable became entwined around his boots lassoing him in a noose, bringing him down. Leo scraped through the rubble, tearing the flesh from his knees, before staggering to his feet to make the last few strides. He dropped Savo at Boris' side; the cables still knotted around his boots.

After last night's firefight, Boris was taking no chances. The Serbs had withdrawn from their forward positions. They were out of sight, out of range of his Kalashnikov, but never out of mind. Boris rubbed his stubby beard as he viewed the pockmarked façade of the three-storey château away to his left. It reared up, ghostlike, as the predawn light struggled out through the mist. All the windows were broken, the glass scattered on the ground, like jewels in the dirt. Boris found the fighting cathartic, an anodyne to help him deal with his grief. He picked through a collage of thoughts as they tumbled around in his head. Why had he not been there for Katerina and Ana when they'd needed him most? Now he was fighting back to atone for his guilt. Boris wiped a single tear from his cheek as he scrutinised the wreckage for any Serbian insurgents.

Engulfed by the deafening silence, he watched as a gust of wind chased a flotilla of garbage across the square. Then as he turned his head back towards the enemy positions, Boris' piercing brown eyes looked directly down the barrel of a submachine gun.

'What the f...? Leo, thank God it's you. I never heard you. How's Savo, any news yet?'

'He's fine. The news is he'll make it.'

Then Leo was gone, moving through the front line to check on the other positions of his unit. Boris thought he was becoming feral.

Chapter 3

Ana looked out of the window and over to the nearby mountains. The blue sky was sprinkled with white fluffy clouds. With no schools open in Banja Luka to occupy her time or her mental energy, Ana had made the mountains her refuge. Aunt Marija's approach to fostering was gentle and caring, but Ana was drowning in an oversweet, crushing love. She missed her mother. Ana longed to be free. Her happiest memories of life before the war were climbing in the mountains with her father and mother.

She was tying up her walking boots as Marija came into the kitchen.

'Climbing again?' she asked. To Ana it was obvious Marija knew the answer. Ana nodded a silent reply but said nothing. She avoided conversation without purpose.

'Are you going alone again, or are you taking Dagma with you?'

'Alone. Dagma is away with her family.'

Ana was envious of what Dagma had – a real family.

'You be careful, dinner is at eight,' Marija called as Ana closed the door.

Ana was glad of Dagma's friendship. She was the only friend she'd made since arriving in Banja Luka. Today Ana would climb alone in the mountains. She'd be able to talk aloud to her mother without Marija rushing to her side.

Returning from her climb, as the setting sun stained the roof tops, Ana turned to face the mountains, as memories of her mother lingered in her thoughts.

'I was so lucky to have you for my mother,' she said. 'Even though it was for a short time. But I know you're still here. Still with me.'

Ana was home for eight, and after dinner she sat at her desk studying a textbook on mathematics until Marija brought her a hot drink. By now the room had been redecorated and the teddy bears exiled to the back of the bedroom cupboard.

Chapter 4

On Friday morning one week after the firefight, Leo sat by Savo's hospital bed as he slept. His eyelids blinked for a moment as he woke.

'Leo, it's good to see you, really good.'

'You're looking well. Better than the last time I saw you in the square. How do you feel now?'

'Absolutely bloody awful, I feel as if I've been shot up the arse.'

Leo chuckled. 'You have, but you're lucky to be alive.'

Savo managed a weak smile as he reached up and gripped Leo's hand. 'I know,' said Savo. 'I know I owe you my life.'

Leo made his way through the war-torn, jagged streets of Sarajevo after visiting his friend. He passed huge piles of garbage as he made his way back to the barracks. It was too dangerous to collect and impossible to dispose of. Shellfire could be heard close by. He had to report back to his unit before twelve noon. He felt good now that he knew Savo was going to be okay. Too many lives had been lost in a conflict Leo could only accept as an appalling mistake. No one would have instigated the war knowing the grotesqueness of its consequence.

Boris greeted him on his arrival.

'You made it all right. I was concerned. We've had a report the Serbs were bombing the hospital again.'

'Yes, I'm safely back, although there was some bombing. About ten or twelve shells fell close by and a few mortars, but there were no direct hits on the hospital this time.'

'And Savo, how's Savo doing?'

'Savo should be back with us in a couple of weeks, he sends his regards.'

'So, he could make it back to witness the end to this ghastly war. I'll be glad when we're done with the wretched thing. Then I can see Ana again.'

'At least you know she's safe with Jan and Marija. It won't be long now.'

'I know, that's what I told Ana when I left, but it's been nearly three years. She must think I've forgotten all about her, but getting out of Sarajevo has been far too dangerous.'

***

Shortly after noon Leo received his orders and gathered his unit together.

'Okay, listen up. We're detailed to cover the zone down by the Energoinvest building, so we can expect both sniper fire and mortars. Stay sharp and look out for each other.'

The seven-man unit made their way out of the barracks and across the Miljacka River, towards Sniper Alley.

'It appears very quiet today, we've heard nothing for the last two hours, perhaps the Serbs have gone home,' suggested Boris.

'I doubt that very much,' laughed Leo.

As Leo finished speaking, a Serb mortar exploded over towards the Energoinvest Building to their right. A huge plume of smoke and dust rose high into the air, and then hung in the pale blue sky. A second landed a few metres away, shaking the ground. The windows in the house opposite, just off Kolodvorska, shattered, showering the street with shards of glass and fragments of window frame. It was followed seconds later by two more mortars and then another, completely demolishing the house.

'They're aiming for the Energoinvest Building, but they haven't found their range yet,' Boris yelled above the noise.

'True, but they're getting closer to us,' shouted Leo. 'Keep your head down and start running.'

Leo rounded the corner and threw himself into the doorway of the Café Bosna. Boris made up ground and dived down beside him, the rest of the unit close behind. The mortars continued uninterrupted for almost an hour and then the apocalyptic roar of a United States Air Force F-16 filled the air, blotting out every other sound. The F-16 came into view, low and menacing, its silver wings shimmering in the dying rays of the sun. Unheralded, it took out two of the Serbian mortar positions with its precision guided missiles. The touch of a button, it was simple, clinical, and final. Then as quickly as it came, the F-16 was gone. The mortar bombs ceased, and an unnerving silence descended. Leo crawled warily out from the safety of the café doorway, Boris and the others followed, as two British Jaguars swept the area, rupturing the fragile silence.

'Well, if that doesn't convince the Serbs to sign the peace agreement, nothing will,' said Leo.

'What's happening at the peace talks in Dayton, why have the accords not been signed? Why has it not been sorted out?' asked Boris.

'I don't know but we must be nearing the end of the war by now.'

The next morning, as Leo briefed his unit before patrolling the zone down by the Energoinvest Building and Sniper Alley, a cease fire was announced.

Chapter 5
September 1995

Ana left her aunt Marija's house and took the narrow lane towards the church, passing piles of rubble on the way. Schools had just reopened in Banja Luka and this was only her second week back. Her first week had not gone well. As she neared the church, Ana paused and reaffirmed the promise to her mother. She would never hide. She would always fight.

Ana had discovered in that first week, there was a huge gulf between the making of a promise and being able to keep it. Crossing the street, she reflected on last week's stand-off. What would be her chances if it came down to a fight? Her adversaries were all boys, there were three of them and being a year older, they were much bigger than her. No one else had stood up to them during that first week. In her head Ana calculated a number of probabilities as well as possible outcomes. Her conclusion was that in a fight, she'd have no chance. So, where did that leave her promise?

Ana had delayed her arrival in the hope she could avoid any confrontation, and so she entered the schoolyard with less than ten minutes before classes commenced. The tactic was doomed to failure. She was the only student not to submit to the gang's demands for money, and all three boys were waiting for her.

'Well if it isn't little Miss Smart Arse.' Danko, the leader of the gang, sneered. Ana held his gaze as she bit her lip making it bleed. She could taste the blood. 'Are you going to give us the money we want. Or do we have to take it off you?'

A crowd quickly gathered in the schoolyard. Ana waited at its centre, as if considering her options but under the circumstances she knew she had only one.

'I'm not giving you the money, so I guess you're going to have to take it off me.'

'Are you sure you want to fight me and my soldiers?'

Danko laughed out loud, as the rest of the crowd joined in nervously. He turned his back on Ana to acknowledge his companions standing behind him, as they echoed his laughter.

'Yeah, I'm sure,' she replied, picking up a brick from a nearby pile of rubble and as Danko turned to face her she stepped purposely forward. Then with all her strength she hit him in the face with the brick. At the point of impact both her feet were off the ground. Danko dropped in a heap on the broken tarmac and Ana kicked him twice in the groin. He did not get up. The crowd was stunned into silence as Ana disappeared into its midst. The gulf between the promise and being able to keep it had just been bridged.

***

On Sunday morning Ana and Dagma left for the mountains. On their return Dagma confided she'd received demands from Danko for yet more money. When she'd refused to pay, Danko had delivered his customary threats. It was over a week since the battle of the brick.

On Monday evening, Ana chose two chemistry books from the Banja Luka library and with some difficulty squeezed them into her overstuffed satchel. She made certain both buckles were securely fastened and then left for home. Outside in the street it was much colder now that darkness had drawn in and she pulled her beret down over her ears as she descended the wide stone steps. She crossed the street and entered the narrow lane that led down to her aunt's house. Towards the end of the lane, almost opposite the butcher's shop, someone waited. As Ana drew level, Danko stepped out into a pool of light shed by the shop's window.

'Well if it isn't the girl with the brick.'

Ana retreated a couple of metres back from the point Danko had chosen for his ambush as her eyes darted up and down the lane. Was he alone? In the darkness it was hard to tell. She placed her satchel down in front of her on the rutted lane. Then she carefully repositioned it, as she directed her gaze towards his face. His left eye was almost fully open now and some of the bruising had faded, but his face was still badly swollen, and Ana could see that the deep cut on his top lip had bled recently. He tried to smile.

'You haven't got your brick to play with this time,' Danko announced matter-of- factly.

'Is that right?' replied Ana, biting her lip. 'I see you've no toy soldiers to help you,'

'So, we're quits,' he said.

'You think?'

Danko came towards her and aimed a solid punch. Ana was ready. She quickly sidestepped and the blow only glanced her left eye. As he readied himself for his next attack, Ana moved deftly to her right and picked up her satchel by the strap. Then with both hands she swung it in an arc above her head. The satchel hit home, smacking Danko in the face. The boy staggered backwards, but he did not fall to the ground. Ana dropped her satchel and aiming for the blood on his top lip, landed a vicious blow with a wide sweep of her right fist. Bullseye. She felt a searing pain in her hand as the blow hit home. Then Danko fell to his knees holding his face and Ana kicked him to the ground, where he lay concussed.

Danko opened his one good eye as Ana brushed an errant wisp of hair behind her ear, then she emptied out the contents of the satchel in front of him. There were two chemistry books fresh from the library, an exercise book, three pens, a packet of paper tissues, some small change and a brick. Nonchalantly she picked up the brick and showed it to Danko.

'The brick,' she announced. 'I brought it especially for you. I hope you appreciated it. The punch in the eye was for Dagma. Leave her alone.'

Simply by calculating probabilities and possible outcomes, she had been prepared.

Ana made her way home; her eye was throbbing and the pain in her right hand was intense. She wondered if it might be broken, but she didn't care. She'd kept her promise to her mother.

The following evening after tea, with some difficulty, Ana finished writing up the chemistry project from her library books, and then put the notebook in her satchel. Her hand was much improved, but her left eye still throbbed. She looked in the mirror and checked it out. It was still red, and her face was bruised, a small price to pay. Aunt Marija came in with a hot bedtime drink.

'How's your eye after I bathed it?'

'My eye's fine. It's my chemistry I've had a problem with,' Ana lied. 'But it's done now.'

'Will you get the top grade like the rest of your chemistry projects?'

Ana took out the notebook from inside the satchel and reviewed her work. She flicked rapidly through the neatly written text that was punctuated by meticulous sketches.

Finally, she nodded. 'Yes, I'll get the top grade.'

'Now, do want to talk about your eye. About the fight?'

'There was no fight. Some one hit me. So, I hit them back. They didn't get up. At least not for some time.'

'Are you a victim of bullying, is that it?'

The hairs prickled on the back of Ana's neck and her eyes narrowed.

'No way, I am not a victim.' She spat out the word 'victim' as if it held a bitter taste. 'But my friend Dragma is. I mean was. In trying to stop the bullies, one of them hit me so I hit them back.'

'Ana, you know you shouldn't fight with the other girls.'

'I don't fight with the girls. It was a boy I hit.'

Chapter 6
February 1996

Leo Illic and Savo Stanisic watched as the Serbian aggressors withdrew from the city of Sarajevo. Boris Poborski took out a prayer book from his tunic pocket, knelt down on the earth he had defended for so long, and prayed. Then together they could only look on as the Serbs plundered and burnt everything possible as they left the city of Sarajevo. Walking away from the front line for the last time, they passed through the Bare Cemetery and then into the overflow graveyard that had once been the soccer field. They embraced when they reached the Parliament Buildings before Savo made his way home. Leo and Boris stood in a bubble of their own, in the noisy, crowded square, as hundreds of Bosnians celebrated their victory, while others dealt quietly with their personal grief.

'So that's it. The war's over, four years of our lives gone,' said Boris, still holding Leo's hand. 'Now we can return to normality and I can have Ana back.'

'I guess so,' agreed Leo. 'Now all I have to do is deal with the hate.'

As the city returned to normal, Boris began to contemplate Ana's future and his own life as a single parent. Still guilt-laden, he was not ready to deal with the emotion their reunion would bring, or to cope with a teenage daughter he barely knew. He put Ana's return on hold.

***

Five months after the war, Boris was invited to attend an interview with Georg Komikosovitch at the offices of the new Bosnian Ministry for Industry, in Sarajevo. He had hoped to retain his previous position as a Director at Bratsvo Steel. To his surprise, only a week later Komikosovitch offered him the position of General Director in total control of the steel complex. The previous incumbent, Lenord Stanislav, had not met with the approval of the United Nation's High Representative, who had vetoed his reappointment. The reason proffered for his demise was that he would be unable to adapt to the free-market strategies imposed on the fledgling industries of the emerging Bosnia–Herzegovina. The truth was that Western intelligence had identified Lenord Stanislav as too hard-line Communist for the palate of the Western-backed regime.

Boris sat in his office at Bratsvo Steel, gazing down at the paperwork that carpeted what had once been Stanislav's desk. The new Bosnian Ministry for Industry had spewed out the paperwork. He knew he could run a steel works; of that he had no doubt. Coping with the paperwork would be an entirely different matter.

As a new dawn painted the Sarajevo skyline, nothing but the rumble of the city's ancient trams invaded the surreal post-war silence. Leo Illic walked down Alipasina to the tram station on his first day back. He'd been happy to accept the offer to return as chief engineer when Boris Poborski offered him the position. Leo knew the task of recommissioning the giant steel plant would take many months. He stepped down from the tram as it stopped close by the steel complex, and walked the rest of the way through the outskirts of Sarajevo. Leo looked up at the Bratsvo Steel Works, its dirty silhouette stabbing the dawn sky. So, this was normality, the new normality.

Initially Bratsvo Steel had received start-up finance from the Bosnian Ministry of Industry to recruit forty-four staff, including a thirty-four-man engineering team. Additional funding would be released in instalments and made available as the commissioning work progressed. In the past weeks, Boris had sought out many of the key workers who had made it safely through the war. Stefan Matic the accountant was one of the first back.

Boris, as the newly appointed General Director of Bratsvo Steel, gathered his team together. As they entered the canteen, he recognised his own anxiety reflected on their faces and when they were all present, he opened the meeting.

'Welcome. Welcome back. The task we have before us is a difficult one. I cannot hide this fact from you. If our country is to have a future, we must generate the funds to deliver that future. Simply put, we need work. Not work as in the past, but work where everyone has a job to do, a role to play, all working to a shared agenda, all adding value. We cannot afford to carry passengers as in the old days under Communism, and we cannot simply unload our steel onto other Comecon partners as before. There is no Comecon. We have start-up finance from the Bosnian Ministry of Industry and the Interim Government. It is enough to make a new beginning. After that, we are capitalists, operating in a free economy in a global market. We must secure finance from one of the international banking consortiums, based on sound commercial and economic strategies. It is a world where only money talks. Our government is bankrupt, and unlike the past, cannot extend loans to us. Without international finance, Bratsvo Steel is finished, and so is Bosnia-Herzegovina. I look forward to working with you to achieve our goals. Together I know we can do it. Thank you for listening.'

The resounding applause that followed brought a tear to his eye, and as Boris looked around the room, he realised others shared the way he felt.

Chapter 7
February 1997

As Boris made his way to Banja Luka, ghosts from the past invaded. Surrounding him everywhere, were buried tormented memories, stabbed through with sadness and regret. He was unsure how his news would be received by Jan and Marija after all this time. It had been one year since he and Leo Illic had watched the Serbs as they left Sarajevo.

Lost in a world of his own, Boris became confused. How did he get here? This wasn't right? Where was he? Disoriented, he brought the car to an abrupt halt, the car's front wheel colliding hard against the kerb. Then he realised his mistake. For the first time since before the war he was outside the wreckage of his former home in Babonavic. Boris sat for several moments, puzzled and bewildered. Then he left the car by the kerbside and walked up the drive to survey the empty shell. It bore no resemblance to his family home. Inside, the debris from a broken door littered the sitting room floor. Over by the fireplace, in what had been the kitchen, a flash of colour caught his eye. He stooped down, pulled a child's book from beneath the broken armchair and gazed down at the cover. He opened up the book, and on the first page Ana had written her name, so neat, an echo from another life. Boris slid the book into his pocket. How would she be after her trauma?

***

Boris arrived at Banja Luka unannounced, to be met by Jan and Marija.

'How's Ana?' he asked, as Ana ran towards him.

'She's fine,' said Marija.

'My, look how much you've grown.'

Ana hugged her father. Her embrace carried a message Boris could not evade.

'Now that Sarajevo is slowly getting back to normal, and with the schools and colleges open, I've decided we should move to an apartment in Sarajevo, so Ana and I can be together again. I think it will be best for Ana.'

Boris saw the impact of this unexpected news on Marija's face in spite of her effort to control it. Marija's role as a foster mother was over. She packed Ana's clothes into the small case while Ana collected her textbooks and notepads.

'We'll miss you both, but Jan and I will come and visit, and Ana can come and stay during the school holidays,' said Marija. She held Ana in her arms as they said a long goodbye. Jan carried her case to the car.

'Thank you for taking such good care of Ana.' Boris forced a smile. 'It's been such a long time, much longer than I ever thought, but I'll take good care of her from now on.'

Ana had no time to say goodbye to Dagma. Ana would have to find some other friend. So would Dagma.

Chapter 8
May 1997

Boris pushed open the bedroom door, with Ana close on his heels, as they viewed the vacant apartment. He walked over to the window that looked out across the park and rested his hands on the windowsill. A frown wrinkled his brow.

'This is our fourth visit to this apartment. I know it better than our rooms at the Grand Hotel and we've been there for three months now. It meets all the criteria we set for our new home. It's in a nice area and it's close to your new college. The rooms are a good size. You've chosen your new bedroom, I'm happy with mine, we like the kitchen and the lounge.'

Ana nodded, but the sign of consensus was not visible on her face. Boris saw in her brown eyes what he knew the apartment lacked. It was the absence of her mother's warmth. The realisation rattled around his head, jangling in the empty rooms.

'Okay, that's it, we'll take it. You can choose a new colour for your bedroom if you want to.'

Boris' enthusiasm sounded synthetic even to him.

'Can I have the same colour as I had at home in Babonavic?' she asked.

Boris swallowed hard.

'Of course, you can, that will be lovely.'

Chapter 9

Olga Lukic lay in bed enveloped in her duvet listening to the trams as they trundled past her bedroom window on Obala Kulina bana in Sarajevo. She glanced at the alarm clock. It was five minutes to six. She had to be at work before eight. Without waiting for the alarm, Olga gritted her teeth, threw off the duvet and jumped out of bed as the freezing temperature took her breath away. She burrowed into her tracksuit bottoms, pulled on the baggy jersey she'd placed judiciously on the chair next to her bed and finally stuffed her feet into her slippers. She hurried into the kitchen, the only room she could afford to heat, scraped the ice from the inside of the windowpane, and peered out across the Miljacka River. An electric fire stood in the corner, starved of the electricity she could not afford.

Taking a bowl, she filled it almost to the brim with muesli, and then drowned it with milk heated on the small wood-burning stove that had remained on throughout the night. Olga simply couldn't face the shower until she'd had breakfast. She finished her drink of hot water, washed her bowl, cup and spoon and returned them to the cupboard in the kitchen of her one-bedroom apartment. She looked up and surveyed the peeling paintwork as she warmed herself in the tepidity of the stove. The apartment was a start, she thought, that was all, because now she had a job and money coming in. She made her way to the bathroom and turned on the taps that worked the shower and waited, listening to the cacophony of clanks and coughs. At last the water gurgled through, cleansing, invigorating, freezing cold. The water had been off the previous week, prompting a noisy local protest, and when it returned it was a disgusting muddy colour. It could have come straight from the Miljacka River. Olga showered and rushed through to the kitchen to dress. She dried her body and her mop of short, jet-black hair, with an enormous bath towel relinquished by the apartment's previous owners, as the colour returned to her cheeks.

An elderly couple had lived in the apartment at the start of the siege. Now they were no longer welcome in the home they'd shared for thirty years. They'd fled to Dubrovnik in Croatia to live with their eldest son—innocent victims of ethnic cleansing. They'd left many of their possessions behind, such had been their haste to leave the home they'd loved. The most haunting relic was a photograph taken as they posed with the children. Their eyes gazing out from their picture frame prison from a world that used to be. All these things, their things, would have to go, but in time.

Many of Olga's friends had left Yugoslavia, left for Holland, Austria or Germany, some for the United States of America. Most of them had gone. Gone for good. But not Olga, she belonged in Yugoslavia and intended to carve out her future here.

In her younger days, Olga's parents owned a big house in the smartest part of the city, as well as a château in the mountains, where the family took frequent vacations. In the winter she would ski, often off piste, and climb in the surrounding mountains. She was the youngest in the family and her father's favourite.

Olga gazed into the mirror as she brushed her hair. She was smooth skinned, with high cheekbones, dark brown eyes and a figure to die for. She never needed to wear make-up. Olga took her new business suit from the wardrobe and the white blouse that she'd ironed the night before and dressed. She took one final look in the mirror before putting on her overcoat. Yes, she decided, she looked the part.

Olga closed the door behind her and descended the wide marble stairs of the Tito-era apartment block where she'd lived for the last four months. She reminded herself that it was her turn to wash the stairs next week. Mrs Svestka had washed them the day before. The black and white tiled squares now gleamed in the early morning light. Olga stepped out cautiously onto Obala Kulina bana, the Miljacka River visible close by, a fast-flowing swathe of brown water on its way to meet the Bosna. Walking quickly towards the cobbled streets of Stari Grad, passing other commuters as they began their trek to work, she felt the pavement shudder as the trams clattered by. Towards the end of the street she went into Sarajka and bought a large cheese butha, she would eat it at her desk at lunchtime. Nearby she could hear the wailing of the loudspeakers on the minarets calling the faithful to prayer, a practice Olga had studiously avoided.

Olga entered the steelworks' general office and hung up her coat. The office was as she'd left it the night before, as usual she'd been the last to leave. She passed the clerk's desk that had been hers since her first day only six months ago and made her way to her office in the corner and unlocked the door. The spreadsheets she was preparing for Stefan Matic lay on her desk in a file marked Sarajevo Steel. The company had to become independent and change its name from Bratsvo, in an attempt to secure international consortium finance. The door to the general office opened and Olga looked up as three of her team entered and a new day began. Olga refocused on the spreadsheets as she came alive with the buzz. Yugoslavia was on the way back and she was going to be part of it.

Chapter 10
September 1997

That night, after Ana changed from her school uniform into the hideous tee shirt and the purple leggings from Banja Luka, she and Boris sat around the big coffee table in the lounge of their new apartment playing chess. In his university days, Boris had considered himself an accomplished chess player. None of his circle of friends had ever defeated him in a match over three games. Only Leo Illic had managed to win a single game on more than one occasion. Then he met Katerina, the university chess champion, and Boris' chess supremacy came to a sudden end.

Like Katerina, Ana played so quickly, she gave Boris no time to think, no space to visualise his next move, or to speculate on her counter move. Boris moved his queen from e7 to e6 and waited.

'Are you sure you want to do that?' asked Ana.

'Absolutely,' replied Boris. His voice carried a confidence he couldn't justify.

'You can take it back, if you want to. It's up to you?'

Boris' eyes quickly scanned the chess board, as his brain followed, only more slowly. Why would I want to take it back?

'Come on, it's your move,' he said.

After two more moves Ana moved her knight from f4 to e6 and captured her father's queen. She swept it off the board with a flourish.

'Checkmate,' she said.

Oh no, not again, he thought, but said nothing.

'Come on you, it's time for bed.'

Ana kissed her father on the cheek and skipped over towards her bedroom, the queen still clutched tightly in her hand.

PART ONE

Chapter 11

The winter sunshine struggled in through the stained-glass windows of the Monastery of Saint Jerome on Via Tomacelli in Rome, shedding pools of light on the grey slab floor. No sound emanated from the world outside through the ancient walls. Monsignor Bernarez sat at the long oak table in a room just off the nave. His long white fingers formed a steeple in front of his gaunt, thin-lipped face. The Monsignor sat deep in thought as he waited for the eldest son of a Croat farmer who had travelled to Rome from Sarajevo. The Monsignor knew him to be a devout Roman Catholic and a fierce supporter of an independent Croatia.

A knock on the door brought Monsignor Bernarez sharply back to the here and now. The door opened and the postulant stepped into the room, head lowered. The Monsignor heard his confession, and then they knelt together in silent prayer.

'Arise.' The Monsignor's voice broke the silence and the postulant rose to stand before him. 'Do you swear before God that you will observe the doctrine of the Holy Order of the Sword of Saint Jerome and execute without condition every command?'

'I do swear.' The postulant responded, his voice level and clear.

'Do you swear to preserve the secrets of our Holy Order?'

'I do swear.' His steel grey eyes burned out a clear message of intent.

'Do you swear to fight for the Order and accept death as the penalty for any failing?'

'I do swear.'

Monsignor Bernarez knew the postulant accepted every word of the oath, every single syllable.

'This day you fulfil the pledge preordained by your father at your birth, you are now a Knight of the Holy Order of the Sword of Saint Jerome, may you be truly worthy of our glorious dead. Have you chosen your nom de guerre?

'My name of war is to be Bleiberg.'

'You have chosen well, my son.'

The Monsignor handed a small river pebble to the newly initiated Knight. The iconography portrayed Saint Jerome beating his breast with a stone and this had become a symbol of the whole order, a metaphoric sword, humble and unassuming, the ideal monk's talisman. The Knight looked down at the Val Susa blue-green pebble inscribed with a small ornate letter 'J', which he held in his hand. He bowed, turned, and left the room, closing the door silently behind him.

Chapter 12

The sun ceased to shed its pale, yellow light through Olga Lukic's office window. She'd been in her office from ten minutes to eight that Friday morning, an hour before the rest of the office staff arrived at Sarajevo Steel. Now she watched as they filed out at ten minutes past six. She could hear their chatter drifting into where she worked, rechecking the information requested by the Deutsche Bank Consortium, the selected international financiers, in response to the meeting held two days ago. She knew how important it could be. The office chatter focused on various weekend activities the other girls were considering. No details of these social events had reached Olga over the last three months; such was her history of rejecting earlier invitations. Olga walked through to the boardroom and handed a copy of the completed spreadsheets to Boris Poborski, as Leo Illic came into the room.

'Still at it?' asked Leo.

'We certainly are,' sighed Boris, rubbing his brow.

'But not for much longer please,' contended Olga as she reflected on the wisdom of those rejected invitations.

'Are you and Ana still okay to go climbing tomorrow?' enquired Leo.

'Oh yes,' replied Boris, as a suspicion of a smile blinked across his eyes. 'First thing in the morning, Ana is really looking forward to it. Come to think of it, so am I, it's ages since we've climbed, it must have been before the...' His words stalled, then they continued, strangled by sadness and regret. 'Well a long time ago.' His smile now washed away.

'I know,' said Leo. He looked across at Olga. 'We used to climb with Katerina and Zara. Ana would come too. We always said she'd be the best climber. Ana's nearly sixteen now, so we'll see.'

'Where will you go?' asked Olga massaging the back of her neck.

'Oh, to Romanija,' replied Leo. 'It provides good climbing throughout the year.'

'That's my favourite crag,' said Olga. 'I love it there, I was a member of the Climbing Club at the University of Sarajevo, we went there a lot.'

A splash of surprise registered on Leo's face. Olga displayed more than a hint of athleticism, but he'd no idea she might be a climber.

'Would you like to come with us?' invited Boris. 'You're more than welcome, you can meet my daughter Ana.'

'I'd love to,' said Olga, without hesitation. 'What time do we go?'

Stefan Matic, the accountant, entered the boardroom to drop off a report for Boris.

'We're going rock climbing tomorrow Stefan; would you like to come along too?' asked Leo.

'Me?' said Stefan, his face cloaked in mock alarm. He pressed his index finger hard into his sternum as he spoke. 'I don't think so. I get vertigo if I wear thick socks. I can't deal with heights.'

That evening, Olga finished her meal of fresh pasta and winter vegetables, washed and tidied the dishes, then went to her bedroom. She opened the cupboard in the far corner to unearth a large canvas bag and emptied the contents onto the floor. Then she sat back to admire the panoply of climbing gear. There was everything a climber could need, ropes, slings, karabiners, crampons and ice axes. Olga selected some slings, her climbing shoes and harness, a belay device and a pair of double ropes and packed them in her rucksack. Then she returned the rest of the equipment to its hiding place, along with a Gucci handbag and a pair of Jimmy Choo satin stilettos.

***

The following day, dressed in Lycra pants and an orange mountain jacket, Olga was waiting on Obala Kulina bana, as the winter sun fought to break through the early morning haze. Boris drove straight past before Leo recognised her waiting there. Boris stopped and reversed back, then Leo opened the boot of the car and put her rucksack in with the others. Then they drove through the sporadic city traffic and into the open countryside.

In the city of Sarajevo, the visible pain of the siege was familiar to Ana, now she looked out onto countryside decorated with the wreckage of war. As they approached a point where a vast section of road had been blown away by a landmine, Boris slowed the car. Ana held on to Olga as

33

the car bumped along over the temporary diversion, while nearby a burned-out tank and a battered armoured car looked sullenly on. Boris headed towards Pale, a Serbian stronghold during the war. He turned north up a narrow mountain track and soon arrived at a level clearing in the woods beneath the towering rocks. Boris and Leo shouldered the rucksacks and made their way to the crags a short distance away. Ana and Olga followed behind chatting. Boris scrutinised the crag and chose a safe route for Ana to climb.

'Here's a route that's okay, Ana.'

She turned and looked over to where he stood, as Leo adjusted her climbing harness.

'I don't think so,' she replied. 'I'd like to start farther up, on the harder route. The one Olga just showed me, if that's okay?'

Even from some distance Ana read the muted message of concern written on her father's face. Boris and Ana climbed the pitch he'd chosen, while Leo belayed for Olga.

Leo watched Olga climb. Her fast-flowing moves and perfect balance took her quickly up her fourth route.

'It must be lunchtime by now,' suggested Boris, after Ana climbed the route that had been her first choice earlier in the day.

They shared the food they'd brought, and then made ready to climb again, as other climbers joined them on the crag.

'Do you want to climb now, Boris? Olga can belay for Ana,' enquired Leo.

'No thank you, we're fine, I'll look after Ana.'

'Come on, Boris you have to let go sometime,' said Leo. Taking the rope that was tied into Ana's harness, he handed it to Olga.

'Boris and I are going to climb now. Are you and Ana okay to climb together?'

'Yes, Ana and I will be fine.'

'Don't worry,' Ana called over to her father. 'Just watch me go.' She was determined to better Olga's achievements of earlier in the day.

Nearby, two starlings engaged in a noisy fight over a bread crust fed to them by another climber as he assessed his next route. Olga walked over to chat as Ana waited and Leo looked on.

'A friend of yours?' asked Leo.

'Yes, from my time with the university climbing club.'

'Come on then, Boris,' Leo encouraged. 'Show me what you can do. Where do you want to start?'

Boris and Leo climbed for over an hour before Boris sat down on the grassy bank.

'I have to confess I'm a little out of condition for this,' sighed Boris.

'What do you mean, a little?' laughed Leo.

'Okay. You're quite right, I mean a lot, and I've noticed I've put on some weight recently. You never seem to tire, and you're as fit and strong as ever.'

***

Ana climbed the glassy rock, melding into the smooth vertical face, as the sun dropped over the rim of the crag and the light began to fade. Boris traced her route up the face of the crag. The crux was a tricky overhang. Ana arrived at the crux as a warning mobilized in Boris' throat, but somehow, he managed to suppress it as his anxiety sped on. Ana pulled herself up the overhang and stood victorious at the top of the crag. She held her arms outstretched above her head, hands clasped together in triumph, like a boxer who'd just won their bout. Ana looked down through a hazy splash of sunlight and her mother, Katerina, waved back, bathed in the glow of a mother's pride. Ana turned to wave to her father and when she turned again to her mother, it was Olga who waved back.

Chapter 13
November 1997

Luka Haas stood in the kitchen staring down at the envelope that had arrived in the post that morning. The typeface heralded the importance of its contents. She tried to control the excitement its arrival had brought and prepare herself for the disappointment that would surely follow. The old wooden stairs creaked, announcing her grandmother's arrival. Luka greeted her with a customary hug. Then her grandmother noticed the envelope in Luka's hand.

'At least this time you've got a reply.'

Luka opened the envelope as if it were a precious thing. Then she unfolded the letter and read it slowly. It did not begin by saying, 'We are sorry to inform you,' and it was this contradiction of her expectation that confused her. Then the word, 'interview' featured twice, along with, 'Wednesday the nineteenth of November at four o'clock.'

Luka re-read the letter and then again more slowly, to be sure she had understood. She looked up from the letter.

'I've got an interview, with the Production Manager, Mr Dragan Merz, of Sarajevo Steel,' she announced.

'And about time too,' said her grandmother. 'Could I see the letter, please?' she asked.

Luka handed over the letter and her grandmother put on her spectacles and began to read.

'What will you wear?' she asked.

Silence filled the kitchen, flooding the room. At first it threatened to melt the warm glow of satisfaction and success.

'I'll find something, don't you worry about it,' said Luka.

'I know you will,' her grandmother replied. 'But what?'

In preparation for her interview, Luka went to her bedroom and took down a large cardboard box from the top of her wardrobe. In it, spawned by collateral damage were the few relics that remained of Luka's former life. She unpacked the box and laid the contents, on the faded bedcover and inspected them, resisting the temptation to stroke the collar of the grey jacket. Her brother Petra's jacket had been almost new at the time of the tragedy and was still in pristine condition. Luka tried it on. The bedroom mirror told her the cut of the jacket did her no favours, it hung from her shoulders like a pair of old curtains. She could see that the buttons being on the wrong side, were the condemning evidence that the jacket wasn't hers and never could have been. Still, she determined, keeping the buttons fastened might help to deal with that. Nothing else suited her purpose, and she replaced the box back on the top of her wardrobe. Next, she selected her best clothes from which to choose the rest of her interview ensemble. In the end, she chose a light pink blouse and her black trousers. Then she dressed. None of the items she'd chosen matched in any way, but they would just have to do.

Chapter 14
Monday 10th November 1997

At ten o'clock Leo made his way to Boris' office for the management meeting.

'Come in,' invited Boris. 'I've confirmation on our finance situation. I'm just waiting for Stefan to join us.'

Stefan arrived and knocked gently on the door; his pale grey eyes searched for a sign he was not intruding. At twenty-seven, Stefan was an accomplished business accountant, but Boris knew the budgets he'd prepared would come under the closest scrutiny as Sarajevo Steel's bid for finance progressed.

'It's November now, and we are coming to the end of the government finance. So, when do we receive our final payment?' asked Leo. 'Do we know yet?'

'Yes, the next payment is due in twenty days' time on the first of December. It will include the additional finance to pay for the workforce to start steel production. That will be the final payment. There will be no more. Further finance will have to come from the Deutsche Bank Consortium. In a little over fourteen weeks the finance granted by the Bosnian Interim Government will simply run out, and unless we can secure international finance, we will be left to rot. Our failure would bring about the collapse of this major political and financial initiative, a cornerstone in the economic recovery of Bosnia. It will cause total demoralisation, especially here in Sarajevo. Without finance Sarajevo Steel will face immediate closure. There will be a complete loss of confidence in the Western-backed Interim Government. We cannot, we must not fail.'

Chapter 15

One week later, Luka returned from her interview to find her grandmother waiting.

'How did it go?' Luka's grandmother asked as she hustled nervously around a triumphant Luka.

'I am pleased to announce,' said Luka mock formally, 'that your favourite and only granddaughter, has been granted a second interview with the Chief Engineer, Mr Leo Illic, on Wednesday the twenty-sixth of November at five o'clock.'

'How many other candidates are being invited for a second interview?' asked her grandmother.

'Six including me,' Luka was pleased to have the opportunity to take on the others; she would have been disappointed had there been any fewer candidates.

'So, you may be in with a chance, a one in six chance,' proffered her grandmother.

Luka didn't answer.

'What I need now is power dressing,' Luka asserted. 'Now if I had that trouser suit. You know the one I showed you in Stepinac's shop window on Saturday, I'd knock them out. Wham.' Luka punched the air knocking out all the other five candidates with a single blow. 'But I haven't, so I'll just have to do it with what I've got.'

***

Luka was on her way home from the library on Friday afternoon. Her route didn't take her past Stepinac's shop window, but she decided to go that way. She gazed at the suit in the centre of the window display. The neatly tailored suit had a navy stripe and a single button. The jacket sported a patch pocket on each side. It was a really nice suit, but it was not her suit. Her suit had gone.

On her arrival home, she took the library books straight to her bedroom and lay them down on the bed and as she did, she saw it. It was hanging on the outside of the wardrobe. It was a suit, her suit, together with a blue blouse. She dashed downstairs into the kitchen and into the arms of her grandmother.

'They've no chance now,' she said. 'The others need not bother turning up, the job's as good as mine.'

'Don't build your hopes up too much,' said her grandmother.' She raised a hand to brush her silver hair from her forehead and as she did Luka noticed a flash of white on her grandmother's finger that was out of place, awkward and unfamiliar. Luka reached out and gently held her grandmother's left hand in hers.

'Grandmother,' Luka said quietly. 'Where is your wedding ring?'

'I sold it,' her grandmother said proudly. 'It was only a trinket after all, a symbol of your grandfather's love for me. His love is still with me, still inside, nothing will ever take that away from me.'

Chapter 16

On Sunday morning, Boris sat preparing for the meeting with the Consortium. He made copious notes as he scrutinized each document supporting Sarajevo Steel's finance application. The notes covered the dining room table. Only one meeting remained before the final submission.

Since moving into the apartment six months ago, Boris had been sensitive in respect of Ana's past trauma, diligently avoiding the issue of her bedroom décor. He looked across at her to see if he could detect anything that would give him a clue to her emotional state of mind, some sign that said she was okay. Ana saw him looking and challenged his motives.

'Why are you giving me the *look*?'

'I'm only checking you're still awake,' he joked. 'Come on, you need to change into your school uniform and get ready for church, no way can we be late. We've been late the last two weeks. I've made your favourite lunch for when we get home.'

Boris and Ana walked to the old Orthodox Church on Mustafe Baseskije. With the service over, Boris saw Mira Kucsan, the mother of one of Ana's college friends, in the row behind him. Her husband had been killed during the early days of the siege. She had befriended Boris and Ana when they first moved to their new apartment.

'Good morning, Boris, are you well?' she smiled.

'I'm very well. How are you and Ena keeping?'

Ana and Ena drifted away, absorbed in a conversation of their own.

'We're fine, Ena had a cold but she's over it now. What about Ana, is she all right?'

Boris checked to make sure Ana was out of earshot.

'I really don't know. She never seems to go to sleep until midnight, later sometimes. She spends hours in her bedroom on her own, doing goodness knows what. I must confess it worries me at times.'

'Don't be concerned. You've just described the behaviour of all the teenage girls I know. It's nothing to worry about.'

'It's normal? Oh, thank you. Thank you for reassuring me,' he said. 'You've put my mind at rest.'

'Ena is no different. Ana will be fine.'

'That's great, thank you so much.'

Drawn towards the statue of Jesus on the cross, Ana stood fixated as the screaming began. She looked over to where her mother lay, as the memories of Babonavic came flooding in. The screaming. The blood. The stench of death. Boris looked around in search of Ana, then turned back to shake Mira's hand.

'I've left lunch in the oven. I must dash now and find Ana. Goodbye—we'll see you again soon.'

Boris left the church with a smile on his face. Ana was going to be all right.

Chapter 17

Leo Illic tapped on Dragan's office door and entered to find him buried beneath a mountain of schedules and reports. There were material schedules, labour costs, energy requirements and spreadsheets on every conceivable aspect of steel production.

'You have more paperwork in your office than Stefan,' joked Leo.

Dragan smiled. 'You're probably right. But I make money with my paperwork. Stefan only accounts for it.'

'I've seen all the candidates for our vacancy in Production Control, except for one,' said Leo. 'On paper this candidate doesn't appear to be a possible contender for the position. They are the least qualified compared to the others and have no experience in our kind of work.' Leo handed the applicant's employment history and personal details to Dragan. 'How did she make the list for a second interview?' asked Leo.

'I felt sorry for her,' he said. 'I didn't have the heart to reject her. I guess I've left that for you to do.'

'Come on Dragan, this is not a charity, even if this girl, Luka Haas, happens to be a charity case. You know how difficult it is to get funding for the people we really need. We can't use pity as a recruitment criterion.'

'I can get rid of her if you want me to. She's my problem after all.'

'It's no problem. I'm ashamed to say rejecting job applicants is something I'm quite used to by now. She's the last on list you gave me for a second interview, so I might as well see her. It won't take me long to get rid of her anyway.'

Chapter 18

In one of the smartest parts of Sarajevo, Roman Drasko surveyed the entrance hall of the apartment block of his newly acquired home. His attention was drawn towards the staircase where the broken balustrade reclined against the wall. The very sight of this sacrilege caused him to grimace. Roman climbed the stairs, breathing in the air of abandonment that clung to every wall. The ornate door surround to his apartment lay where it had fallen when looters forced their way in. He walked down the hallway and into the bathroom where he added to his burgeoning list.

The indisposition of the former owners had made the purchase of the apartment somewhat protracted. Ivan Krznaric had been queuing for water when a sniper from a tower block on Skenderija, across the Miljacka River, shot him through the head. He died instantly. Roman knew how accurate the Serbian sniper fire had been after their new German rifles were delivered. Ivan's wife, Sara, was one of the fatalities when a mortar hit the Markale Market, leaving sixty-eight dead and one hundred and forty-four wounded, an event that made world news. Their daughter, almost penniless because of the siege and still mourning the loss of her parents, had been persuaded to sell the apartment at well below its true value.

A knock at the crudely repaired front door announced the arrival of Mijat Garvic, a joiner and Communist Party member. Mijat knew Roman had held high government office in the old Socialist Federal Republic of Yugoslavia, enjoying a reputation as a shrewd hardliner who surmounted whatever problems came his way. Mijat did not know that Roman had undertaken extensive training with the KGB in Moscow, or the part he'd played in Yugoslavia's civil war and the war crimes he was guilty of. He greeted Roman warmly, delighted to be acquainted with such an important figure from the old guard.

'Good morning sir, how may I be of service?'

'I have a list of work prepared, please come this way and I'll explain.'

Mijat busied himself with tape measure, pencil and notepad, as Roman looked on, redolent of an expectant father at the birth of his first child.

'How are the family, are they settling into their new home?' asked Roman.

'Yes. Fine thank you. Your help in getting the new apartment was very much appreciated. We're slowly getting everything sorted out. But there is a big job to be done here in Bosnia-Herzegovina now the war is finally over,' said Mijat. 'It's good to know we still have people like you, people we can trust to make sure we progress in the right direction.'

Mijat's perception was unchanged from before the war. Roman almost smiled. It seemed he'd successfully enamelled over his recent past.

'I know how you feel, I'm afraid the country has become bankrupt due to an infestation of Western capitalist doctrinaire.'

'What can be done about it?' Mijat asked.

'We need to go back to basics, back to Marsala Tita and Brotherhood and Unity, back to the good old days. Mijat my friend, we need a People's Revolution to bring about a new regime, where all Yugoslavs live together under the guiding hand of Communism just like before.'

Mijat left with an undertaking to complete the work to the highest standards within two weeks. A favour or two from old friends would enable Roman to carry out his renovation plan and no doubt a little speed money here and there would help.

As night drew in and the shadows lengthened Roman made his way to the Café Bosna on the corner of Maršala Tita and Šenoina. Milo Tolja sat in the far corner. He was drinking his second cup of strong black coffee. Roman was more than a few minutes late, a point not mentioned by Milo. Roman had been delighted to renew his acquaintance with Milo after the war. They'd met several times since their first reunion, to reminisce over their war exploits and what might have been, what should have been. The café owner brought Roman's coffee and Roman thanked him.

'Where next?' asked Milo, without preamble.

'Mostar,' replied Roman. 'As you know the city has suffered power failures for almost three weeks now and the Interim Government is struggling with the war-damaged power plant. On Thursday night, I want you to orchestrate a 'spontaneous' protest of local residents on the streets of Mostar. It should cause the Interim Government some difficulty and a great deal of embarrassment. It will be a small part of the preparation for our People's Revolution.'

The following evening Roman left the comfort of Milo's apartment just off Adema Buoća in Mostar and made his way to the main square. Milo had gone ahead to coordinate the small number of Communist party activists who were now infiltrating the noisy crowd of almost six hundred residents who had rallied to the cause more easily than Roman could have hoped. Roman joined Milo after two hours, as the demonstration broke up and the chant of 'Tito, Tito,' faded away. Roman knew the people of the former Yugoslavia would love to see the back of the Western led Interim Government, and welcome the return of 'Marsala Tita,' but Tito was buried in Belgrade where Roman had laid a wreath at his mausoleum.

Roman however, knew the perfect replacement for his beloved Tito. This man possessed all the necessary presidential credentials and was respected throughout the Communist world. He was a man who commanded the support required to get rid of the Western Powers. The weeks ahead would entail much planning, hard work and patience, but for Roman, no sacrifice was too great to achieve his ultimate goal, the return of Brotherhood and Unity to a reunited Yugoslavia. In three months, February 1998 at the latest, the Communists would show their hand and with support from Communist countries throughout the world already assured, a new and glorious era would begin. Marsala Tita would rise again.

Chapter 19

Leo gazed out at the raindrops as they smacked against his office window. Then he watched them as they raced at breakneck speed down the windowpane. It was five minutes to five. Luka Haas had arrived for her interview at four-thirty and was waiting in the outer office. He looked again at her neatly written application form. It was clear she was wholly unsuitable for the vacancy in the production office.

'Miss Haas?' He sighed; his voice betrayed his lack of interest.

At five o'clock, he opened his office door to greet Luka.

'Good afternoon, Miss Haas, please come in.'

Luka entered, then waited for Leo to invite her to take a seat. She wore a smart trouser suit and a blue blouse, her hair, short cut and impeccably groomed, was jet black and shaped to the nape of her neck. As they shook hands, Leo felt a real warmth from her smile, from her hazel eyes and her friendly disposition.

'I see you live here in Sarajevo, have you lived at this address very long?'

'I live with my grandmother,' Luka smiled back. 'It's nice there, my grandmother and I make a great team, we get on really well. I moved in with her when my parents and brother Petra died two and a half years ago,' she continued.

'I have to ask,' said Leo. 'Though I do not wish to be intrusive, how did your parents and brother die?'

Leo felt the need to understand her emotional journey and measure it against his own.

'Our house was just off Kolodvorska and on the last day of the siege it was hit by a Serbian mortar bomb. It was a stray mortar bomb. It was an accident. They were aiming at the Energoinvest Building. No one was to blame,' she concluded.

Leo vividly recalled the events of that day during the siege when he took refuge in the doorway of the Café Bosna but said nothing.

'You deal with it very well,' said Leo. 'In similar circumstances, I would be very bitter. Are you not bitter?'

'Bitter? Oh no, if I were, I would have failed my family. I loved them so much and they loved me. My grandmother says I must live my life in their memory. I must be happy for all of them, especially my brother.'

Leo's jaw dropped open as Luka finished speaking.

'But surely you must be full of hate for the people who did this?' Leo pressed.

To his amazement, Luka laughed.

'Of course not,' she chastised. 'How could I be happy if I had hatred in my heart?'

'So how did you cope?' asked Leo.

Luka said nothing at first as she tried to find the right words.

'I forgave them,' she said. 'I forgave them all.'

Leo took a moment before he could continue with the interview and then he brought it to an abrupt close.

'I can tell I haven't got the job,' Luka announced candidly. 'But I do appreciate you seeing me. It means a lot to my grandmother and me.'

'A decision has not been made, but we've had some excellent candidates. Excuse me?' said Leo. 'I have someone I must see.'

Luka rose from her seat to leave but Leo reached out to her, indicating she should wait. As he did, his hand touched hers and for a moment he held her hand, not wishing to let go. Luka sat down and Leo left her waiting at his desk.

He entered the paper-strewn office of Dragan Merz, his Production Manager and sat down, his heart racing, unable to think rationally. Dragan could see that Leo was flustered.

'I guess you've seen Luka?' he said.

'Yes,' said Leo as if in some pique. 'She is not qualified in any of the aspects we require.'

'I agree, I should not have troubled you. Do you want me to tell her she hasn't got the job?' asked Dragan. 'I guess it is my problem, not yours?'

Leo ignored the question as he surveyed the office. It was a riot of boxes and files. A stack of reports and a score of other documents covered the floor. Leo picked up one of the reports and scrutinised it.

'This just needs filing,' he said testily. 'This report should be kept for twelve months for audit purposes, why has it not been the filed?'

Dragan looked perplexed.

'But you know why. I'm working all the hours God sends and I'm doing the jobs of at least three people. I know you are too, so I'm not complaining.'

Leo turned to Dragan.

'You need an assistant,' said Leo. 'See to it at once.'

'Luka,' said Dragan, smiling broadly.

'Good choice,' said Leo. 'You can go and tell her now. She's waiting in my office.'

Leo sat alone in Dragan's office. He felt challenged by Luka's contradiction. How could she forgive them? Forgive them all? Leo felt only hate towards those liable for an outrage he must deal with on his own. All he wanted was revenge in his search for peace.

Chapter 20

It was just past midnight and Ana lay on her bed, as her thoughts dwelt on the first weeks at her new college.

Ena Kucsan had been ever-present since Ana's first day. Always close, always ready to express an opinion, always eager to offer help that Ana didn't need, and certainly didn't want. It was becoming claustrophobic. She needed to establish some distance between herself and Ena, but after her encounter with Danko and his gang, Ana was reluctant to dismiss any potential ally, and that included Ena. Ana's short-term strategy in those early weeks at her new college, was to identify any threats, while blending into an undergrowth of neutrality. As yet she hadn't needed the assistance of the brick.

***

Only one student appeared on her radar as a candidate for concern. Jozef Kiska, a boy in the same year as Ana, was almost as big as Danko, but with an affable disposition. Jozef had started at the college at the same time as Ana and seemed to be struggling with much of the basic work. Ana became aware of him looking directly at her on a number of occasions. She'd noticed how quickly he'd look away when detected. On one occasion she thought he was going to come over and speak to her, but he changed his mind at the very last minute. Ana finally concluded Kiska was no threat and her situation was safe. Two weeks later she retired the brick.

***

Ana made her way from college to Marsala Tita. She had to collect a textbook she'd ordered from a bookshop there. She crossed the bridge that spanned the Miljacka River and walked west along the riverbank. Turning right at the junction of Obala Kulina bana and Gimnazijska, she approached the small square where a group of men were playing chess on the oversized, open-air board. She paused for a moment to watch. It was clear to Ana the white knight was about to take the black bishop. As she continued through the square, she heard footsteps running up behind her. To her surprise it was Jozef Kiska. Ana never considered the option of flight, but she did question her decision to retire the brick. She dropped her school satchel and quickly made both hands into tight fists. Then with fists up in front of her and weight evenly balanced on both feet, she readied herself for the fight. Then Jozef froze.

'What are you doing?' He asked in a faltering voice. Ana said nothing. She shifted her weight a little more onto her back foot and waited.

'I only want to talk,' he said. 'Want to ask you something?'

Ana bit her lip as she waited for his first move. Keeping up her guard she took a step towards him. Jozef took two jerky steps back and tripped over his own feet. Ana gazed down at him as he lay sprawled out on the pavement. He was quite helpless. She was pleased she hadn't hit him with the brick. Ana helped Jozef to his feet, and he dusted himself down.

He looked embarrassed. 'I only want to talk,' he repeated. 'Want to ask you something.' Jozef followed Ana into the square where the game of chess was being played. She noticed the white knight had captured the black bishop and checkmate was only one move away. They sat down on an empty bench.

'So, talk. Ask away.'

'Chemistry,' he said half under his breath, as if it was a word he'd been punished for using inappropriately in the past. He tentatively held out his exercise book and Ana opened it.

'I was going to ask you before but didn't like to. You seemed...' Jozef paused as if searching for the right words. 'Superior. You know, too clever to help the likes of me.'

Jozef's opinion came as quite a shock. Ana shuddered, and her mouth opened in disbelief. She let the book slip from her grasp. How could he possibly think that of her? She quickly bent down and picked up his book.

'It's my chemistry project, I must hand it in tomorrow, but I'm just lost, I don't have a clue. Will you help me, please?'

'Well yes, of course I will. Let me see, what have you actually done?'

Ana checked out his exercise book and his chemistry project. Jozef was right. He didn't have a clue. She took out her own chemistry notebook from her satchel and opened it at the project that was so troubling Jozef.

Half an hour later Jozef understood. A smile, like dawn breaking on a bright winter's day, flooded his face.

'Thank you, Ana, you've saved my life.' Ana shuddered again.

As she returned Jozef's exercise book, their hands touched. Ana had a new friend. The question was, would she lose this one like she'd lost Dagma?

***

On Sunday morning the church choir and the congregation sang hymn number one hundred and fifty-seven. They were in good voice. Despite knowing the words and the tune by heart, Ana stood miming the words. Her mind was elsewhere. Was she really as unapproachable as Jozef had said? But that had not deterred Dagma. Ana accepted that she had been somewhat insular and defensive in her outlook. Had that affected her ability to socialise effectively? It hadn't been a problem up till now. She thought of Ena's attempt to befriend her. Ana realised she was shunned by the other girls and avoided by the boys.

Things would have to change. Ana would make friends with Ena and Jozef and this time she would not lose them. Not like Dagma.

Chapter 21

At the start of her first day Luka took a seat in reception and waited for Dragan Merz. She was thirty minutes early.

'Welcome to Sarajevo Steel,' Dragan greeted her warmly.

'Thank you, it's really good to be here.'

Luka followed Dragan down to Production Control and stood in the middle of the office and looked around. She hung her coat on a peg by the door.

'This is your desk. Sorry, it's a bit untidy.'

'Not to worry, I'll soon sort it out.'

An avalanche of paperwork covered Luka's desk.

'You can have this filing cabinet. I emptied it last night. It was full of memoranda from our former General Director, Lenord Stanislav. We don't need the memoranda anymore. Come to think of it, we never did. I'll give you a tour of the steel works after I've shown you the kitchen. The kitchen is the most important room in the whole works. If we don't get our coffee by ten o'clock, everything comes to a standstill. Mr Illic likes his coffee strong and black. He'll be back in the office soon. Would you mind making him one? That's if you can find a clean cup.'

The tiny kitchen was a riot of dirty cups and empty coffee jars. A tattered tea towel hung from a cupboard handle like a flag of surrender.

'I'll wash up first, shall I, before I make the coffee. Would you like one too?'

'Yes please, mine's white with two sugars. I can see we're going to get on great,' he smiled.

At ten o'clock Luka put a steaming cup of black coffee in front of Leo Illic and placed an ancient cake tin down on his desk.

'I hope you don't mind Mr Illic, but my grandmother made this fruit cake for you. It's fresh, she baked it yesterday.'

Leo removed the lid and took out the cake.

'Wow, it looks fantastic, does your grandmother need a lodger?'

'I'm sorry we've no room,' Luka laughed. 'Not unless she gets rid of me and she'd never do that.'

After coffee, Dragan gave Luka a tour of the steel works.

'As you can see the place is enormous. It'll take some time to get your bearings.'

'There are so many corridors, but I'll soon find my way around.'

'Okay, in that case you take us back to the office. That is if you think you can.'

Luka headed back down the corridor. She retraced her steps and in no time, she was back in the office.

Chapter 22

The midnight tide lapped at the harbour walls, as four men descended the steps to the water's edge and boarded the high-speed motor cruiser Marco Polo, as she lay anchored in the shadows. With the collusion of the Harbour Master, they evaded the travel restrictions imposed on all nationals residing in the former Yugoslav Republic. Soon the coast of Croatia dissolved into the darkness, and the lights of Split began to sink over the horizon as they crossed the Adriatic towards Italy's east coast. At the small port of Ancona, they slipped ashore, to be met by a black Mercedes Benz that waited at the harbour entrance.

***

The following day, dawn crouched behind the Mausoleo Augusto, as the Mercedes drove through Rome's ancient piazze and crossed the Ponte Cavour to the Monastery of Saint Jerome. Monsignor Bernarez, in a room just off the nave, welcomed all four men. Two Knights of the Holy Order of the Sword of Saint Jerome, accompanied by their Longa Manus bodyguards, stood before him.

'Good morning, I trust you had a good journey, my sons?'

'The journey was fine, thank you, Monsignor,' replied Lupiana.

A slight trace of apprehension hung on his words. A point not missed by Monsignor Bernarez.

Each Knight took out a small inscribed Val Susa blue green river pebble and presented it for validation to the Monsignor.

'What brings you to the Monastery of St. Jerome?'

'There is a new threat to Croatia, not war or assassination. The threat we now face is an economic one. We need help in our bid to secure international finance for Croatia's Zelejezara Steel in Split. We are in a battle with Sarajevo Steel and we know only one bid can be successful.

The Bosnian's proposal is marginally superior to ours, but it is the status of Poborski that will make them favourites. With the breakup of Yugoslavia, Croatia will have its independence, and so we need to rebuild our industries or become masters of a wasteland, while the Orthodox Christian Bosnians enjoy the economic success that truly belongs to Croatia and the Catholic Church. Is it possible you have influence within the Deutsche Bank Consortium? It is they who will decide the outcome of our funding application.'

'We have influence,' replied the Monsignor. 'Over the centuries our diaspora has been our great strength. Our Knights remain buried in antiquity, waiting to defend our Holy Order when summoned. Anything that is of benefit to the Orthodox Christians of Bosnia is a concern to the Order. The Catholics of Croatia suffered enough at the hands of Tito at the end of World War Two in nineteen forty-five. The Order will act to influence the outcome of the finance decision. It is an important matter. We will not stand idly by while the Bosnians take what is rightfully ours.'

Chapter 23
Friday 19th December 1997

Boris, Stefan and Leo were shown politely into the elegant reception room at the Deutsche Bank offices in Sarajevo. Two leather settees and four armchairs were arranged geometrically on the dark brown carpet. Boris crossed the room to sit in one of the armchairs, his shoes sinking in the thick pile.

'Evidently the war in Yugoslavia has not affected the profits of western bankers,' he observed.

The door opened and a woman dressed in *de rigueur* office garb greeted him.

'Good morning, I'm Bernadeta Banja, personal assistant to Herr Becker. Thank you for waiting.'

Boris struggled to escape the embrace of the armchair.

'No, no, we are early, thank you for seeing us so promptly.'

'Do come through,' she invited. 'Herr Becker is waiting for you.'

Confronting them as they entered the oak panelled room were the Consortium members, along with a brigade of industry-specific consultants. Boris counted sixteen adversaries in all, more than enough to find fault with their finance proposal. Boris subdued a laugh. Even so, he could not prevent a wide grin racing across his face.

'Good God,' he whispered to Leo. 'Why do they need so many people to make a decision?'

Bernadeta introduced Herr Becker, the newly appointed Chairman of the Deutsche Bank Consortium. He surveyed Sarajevo Steel's three-man delegation like an actor appraising his audience. Herr Becker opened the meeting from behind a pair of rimless spectacles and introduced the others present. Boris had identified him as the alpha male long before the introductions began. Herr Becker welcomed them and outlined the process the board wished to follow.

'First I must advise you Sarajevo Steel is not alone in their endeavour to secure finance for the production of steel in the former Yugoslavia. You have a competitor. I can confirm Zelejezara, the Croatian steel company in Split are also applying for finance from the Consortium. There can only be one winner.'

Then the reason for the legion of acolytes suddenly dawned on Boris. Herr Becker had not risen to high office without having someone else to blame if things went wrong.

Boris opened his presentation as the board members shuffled the contents of their submission packs.

'Gentlemen,' Boris began. 'We are well placed to profit from the supply of steel in the former Yugoslavia. Since the cessation of hostilities, no rebuilding has taken place, and with substantial international aid now available, the demand for steel is very strong, as the forecast in the submission pack shows.'

Herr Becker looked up from the columns and graphs that covered more than a dozen meticulously prepared spreadsheets.

'I assume you have used the guideline figure of one percent above World Bank Base Rate for interest in your submission. Although, depending on the amount underwritten by national governments we anticipate the rate could be a shade less.'

'Yes, Herr Becker,' said Boris. 'One percent above the Base Rate is the figure we have used. The interest rate is pivotal in Sarajevo Steel's ability to meet the Consortium's financial criteria.'

When the interrogation commenced, most of the early questions were financial, which Boris and Stefan fielded with confidence.

Boris studied the faces marshalled across the table, trying to work out the likelihood of support from individual Consortium members. Directly opposite sat Roger Arlington from the office of the High Representative. He was gazing intently at his spreadsheet. Boris toyed with a number of contradicting scenarios, none of which seemed to fit. Arlington was dressed in a sad brown suit, an almost white shirt and a dark blue tie.

Suddenly Arlington blundered into speech, directing a barrage of questions in Boris' direction. Boris responded at once, as a game of verbal ping-pong broke out, enthralling the audience. Trend sheet challenged graph, while averages and standard deviations countered percentages.

At one point, Boris paused and intoned politely, 'Mr Arlington, I do believe you can find angles in circles.'

This seemed to disarm Roger Arlington and eventually Boris took the honours.

Next, Georg Komikosovitch from the Ministry for Industry tabled a number of questions on behalf of the Interim Government. Boris had analysed Georg during their earlier meetings and reckoned he had the measure of him. Georg was a sallow faced man of about thirty, who seemed self-conscious of his receding hairline. Dressed in a smart blue pinstriped suit he was the epitome of a man who had never had a girlfriend despite strenuous efforts. Georg thanked Boris for his answers, after which four of the specialists asked questions relating to furnace output and rolling mill speed that Leo judged to be irrelevant. Nevertheless, he answered the questioners in a polite and ceremonious way that impressed the Board.

Herr Becker questioned Boris regarding the phasing of the production targets and the soundness of the assumptions he'd made to justify the sales forecasts and gross margins. Boris was truly magnificent. He emerged banner held high as the legion's paladin.

Then Signor Gianluca Botticelli, Senior Vice President on the Deutsch Bank Main Board in Frankfurt, rose to his feet to address Boris. The others had asked their questions while seated and Boris feared the worst as he reflected on this deviation from protocol. Signor Botticelli seemed to be fulfilling the role of *éminence grise*. He was immaculately dressed in an Armani three-piece suit and a handmade silk shirt. Gold cuff links winked seductively beneath his coat sleeve and his tie complemented the outfit perfectly. In Boris' view, all this lent Botticelli the persona of a Brooklyn Hood. Not that Boris had ever met a Brooklyn Hood, he'd never even been to Brooklyn. Botticelli's beautifully trimmed moustache and his manicured fingernails did it for Boris, this man may not be from Brooklyn, but he was a Hood.

'Could I just bring to your attention a number of anomalies in your presentation?'

Botticelli had a surly attitude, and for a while, he and Boris traded words across the table. As his verbal diatribe continued, he smiled vindictively, believing the initiative was sliding his way. It was at this point that Boris rose to his feet to counter the perceived advantage that Botticelli had up to now enjoyed. For a moment Boris surveyed the other board members as he prepared to conclude his presentation. His soft brown eyes raked the battlement of sombre faces, searching for the eye contact that he knew could make all the difference. Botticelli met Boris' stare darkly from the other side of the table. His small anonymous eyes gave no echo back as to what he might be thinking.

'Gentlemen,' Boris paused momentarily to ensure he had their full attention. 'Thank you for the interest you have shown in Sarajevo Steel, and the many helpful comments you have shared with us. Your observations have been much appreciated. We have discussed the financial aspects of this important undertaking. However, it is our people who will deliver the hard work and the passion for excellence that will make your financial investment in our business an unqualified success. Once more, thank you for your time.' Boris took his seat. Herr Becker and his associates nodded approvingly, all bar one.

Boris, Stefan, and Leo left the meeting with an agreement that Herr Becker, on behalf of the Consortium, would respond to their application within six weeks and confirm the final interest rate. Bernadeta Banja was there to see them out.

'Stefan, you were fantastic, absolutely marvellous and of course Leo, you always are. You never let me down,' said Boris once they had left the outer office.

'You were pretty good yourself,' said Leo.

'The question is,' posed Boris, 'were we good enough?'

Chapter 24

The eighteenth-century Thomas Way table clock, looted during the siege, struck seven, as Roman Drasko wiped a speck of dust from one of the brass feet. He went to his bedroom and changed into a tailored grey suit, white shirt and revolution red tie. Despite the expensive cut of the suit, it failed to disguise the figure of an ageing overweight autocrat. In contradiction to Yugoslav custom, Roman had never dyed his hair. It gave it a distinguished salt and pepper colouring. He pulled on his fur-collared overcoat, then left the apartment by a side door.

Roman walked the short distance to the Zetra Arena, the venue of the 1984 Winter Olympics where Torvill and Dean performed their interpretation of Ravel's Bolero. Heavy bombing during the siege had engulfed the Arena in flames so hot the copper roof melted, destroying the auditorium. Ignoring the main entrance, he threaded his way between dozens of shipping containers abandoned by the many international humanitarian organisations after the siege of Sarajevo had finally ended. He made his way to the service entrance at the back of the building, and then disappeared into the labyrinth of passages. He paused for a moment to confirm he'd not been followed, then took the unlit stairs to the rooms the outlawed Bosnian Communist Party were secretly using.

Dmitri Simvnic, the leader of the Sarajevo cell, had petitioned Roman, the General Secretary of the Party, for an emergency committee meeting at short notice. Simvnic was an intense beady-eyed man who had held a number of junior ministerial positions in the former Communist Government under Tito. Roman knew Simvnic had ambition and suspected his motives may be conspiratorial. Roman agreed to the meeting only after lobbying the other cell leaders. He knew he must proceed with the utmost caution. Nothing could derail the party's plans at this critical stage. Roman now held a high-level administrative position in the recently formed Interim Government and so he was aware of the information Simvnic wished to discuss. It had been circulating in the corridors of government for some days. All twelve members attended the meeting from all parts of Bosnia. Roman opened the meeting and invited Simvnic to speak. Simvnic rose to his feet. His voice was razor sharp and carefully focussed.

'Poborski is giving the people of Sarajevo and Bosnia new hope.' Simvnic announced earnestly. 'Subject to receiving the necessary finance, Sarajevo Steel are to recruit a further two hundred workers before the end of January. The more people Poborski employs, the fewer will join our cause. Poborski must die or our plans for a People's Revolution will fail and with them all hope of re-establishing Communism and our values.'

There was silence and Dmitri Simvnic sat down. Everyone waited for Roman Drasko to speak. Before embarking on his response, he turned and acknowledged the presence of Lenord Stanislav sitting opposite. Stanislav was a gaunt looking man with a pale complexion and a thick mop of black hair. There were strong rumours circulating during his tenure as General Director of Bratsvo Steel, that he had a deviant sexual appetite. Eventually, Roman responded. He was ready to reveal the plans for the Communist coup d'état, or at least some of them.

'Comrades,' he began as he mentally elevated his audience to the dignity of the Politburo. 'Our dream is to rid ourselves of Capitalism, this slime that is strangling Bosnia and our people. We cannot win by military force or embark on some wild terrorist campaign to purge ourselves of these Western Capitalist invaders. To remove Poborski now in the time-honoured way would be fatal to our cause. He is becoming a champion of the people, almost an icon. When the time comes, we will need all the people of Bosnia on our side. Kill him? No, definitely not. Giving the Western Powers a martyr is not the answer. We do not need forever to deliver our solution. Only a few more weeks are required to fully execute our plans.' He paused and briefly looked around the room. 'Do we have a comrade, a friend on the inside at Sarajevo Steel?' he asked, already knowing the answer.

'Yes,' replied Lenord Stanislav, the former General Director of Bratsvo Steel. 'Yes, we do.'

'A simple delaying tactic is required. An accident will occur,' announced Roman. 'Sad, very sad.'

He looked across at Stanislav. 'I will leave you to deal with it.'

Lenord nodded.

Failing to disguise his anger, Simvnic leapt to his feet. His face said it all.

'That simply will not do,' screamed Simvnic. 'We need firm and decisive leadership. Poborski must die.'

Roman nodded, seemingly to acknowledge the point that Simvnic was making. The other committee members drew back from the table as Simvnic made his move to oust Roman Drasko from his position as General Secretary of the Party. 'It is clear you are unable to provide the leadership we need to rid ourselves of this Western filth. Look at you. You've become fat on the excesses of your capitalist paymasters. For the sake of Bosnia, stand down and let me show you real leadership, someone who remains a loyal Yugoslav and a true Communist.'

Both men vied for the high ground, unaware that a Knight, commanded by the Holy Order of the Sword of Saint Jerome, sat in their midst. Bleiberg's own thoughts remained unspoken as Simvnic continued. Finally, his tirade ended, and he sat down.

Roman scanned the committee to assess those in his favour. His furtive glances around the gallery of dirigible, expectant faces told him Simvnic had no support. His recent covert lobbying had paid off.

'You are of course quite correct, Poborski must indeed die, but only when the time is right. We will do this when we are in our rightful place, as the Communist Government of Bosnia-Herzegovina and Sarajevo is firmly established as a bridgehead to return the rest of Yugoslavia to the guiding hand of Communism. The social unrest that is about to occur will bring Bosnians everywhere onto the streets to support our People's Revolution. A new Bosnian Dawn will sweep us into power, as the Interim Government falls. I promise you we will not be alone in our efforts to rid ourselves of these corrupt Western invaders. I can guarantee we will receive support from Communist governments throughout the world. Comrades, we cannot fail. There is, as ever, one hostile faction that will object vociferously. They have been a thorn in the side of Communism for far too long. I know their eradication from our country will be pleasing to you all. I am of course referring to The Holy Catholic Church and their murdering Croat assassins. When the time comes, we will deal with them both. We will deliver our final solution.' Roman laughed. 'As the Americans say, no more Mr. Nice Guy. There are risks of course, but then risk is one of life's few certainties.'

The other members of the committee nodded back their tacit acceptance. Dmitri Simvnic did not re-engage in his altercation. Roman made eye contact with Milo Tolja, the leader of the Communist cell in Mostar, and Roman's oldest friend. Although an engineer by profession, he had earned the sobriquet 'The Undertaker.' Milo knew he had another victim for his amusement.

Bleiberg, the Croat Knight, noted the declaration of war on the Holy Catholic Church. Monsignor Bernarez and the Holy Order of the Sword of Saint Jerome must be informed at once.

Chapter 25

After lunch Luka returned to filing the production report summaries. In the first week she'd almost finished filing every report for the last six months. Already Dragan's desk was clear, and on the floor patches of brown linoleum were becoming visible between the piles of reports. The telephone rang in Leo's office and Luka walked through and picked it up.

'Hi, it's Olga Lukic in accounts. I'm looking for Leo. Have you seen him? It's quite urgent.'

'No. You've just missed him. He went to check on some work being carried out on the furnaces. I don't know when he'll be back. Dragan isn't here either. I'm afraid I'm not much use.'

'No not at all, you can help. Do you think you could find Leo for me? I'd be ever so grateful.'

'I'll try. I'll go down now. I think I know the way.'

Luka left the office and made her way down the back stairs and through the corridors that led to the furnace room, the way Dragan had taken her. As she approached the entrance to one of the tool rooms, she heard voices, muffled and low. Something about a meeting and an accident at midnight. She continued down the passageway that led to the furnace hall. As she entered, Dragan walked over to meet her.

'Are you looking for me?'

'No. I have a message for Mr Illic from Olga Lukic, have you seen him?'

'Yes, but you've missed him. He's just gone back to his office.'

Luka returned to find Leo on the telephone talking to Olga. Dragan returned minutes later, as Luka looked up from the filing.

'Well done, you've beaten me back,' he said.

Leo ended his phone call and joined them in the production office.

'How are you settling in,' he asked Luka. 'If there's anything you're not sure about just ask Dragan or me.'

65

Luka thought for a moment. She was still trying to make sense of the fragment of conversation she'd overheard when she'd approached the tool room, minutes earlier. She was about to mention the incident but was interrupted by the telephone ringing in Leo's office. Leo walked through to his office to take the call.

'Go on Luka, what is it, you can ask me,' said Dragan.

'Well there is one thing. I heard two men talking when I went down to the furnace room just now to find Mr Illic. I didn't see their faces or anything like that. I heard the first man ask, what time do we meet to set-up the accident, and the other one said, we meet tonight at midnight? Or something like that. Is it important?'

Chapter 26

At midnight Leo stood in the shadows of the second floor office block surveying the perimeter fence, as yesterday shrank unnoticed into a new day. Far below, two men slunk through the darkness. Leo relinquished his vantage point and made his way silently down the fire escape. Under cover of darkness two figures huddled around the personnel door that gave access to the steel furnaces. Leo watched as they disappeared through the unlocked entrance.

Luka hadn't understood the significance of the conversation she'd overheard earlier in the day. Dragan however was quick to grasp its importance, and to Leo it made perfect sense. He pushed his hand deep inside his coat pocket and felt the Luger cold and hard. Then he pursued the two men, the first carrying a rucksack, as they made their way to the first furnace room. Only their footsteps broke the silence. Then the footsteps stopped. Leo recognised Rudolf Markovitch, one of Sarajevo Steel's first recruits. He watched him as he put down the rucksack and took out a coil of cable, along with a small parcel.

'Semtex,' Leo whispered half under his breath.

The word ricocheted around his brain. Months of work would be lost in a moment, the hopes of so many blown away. Nervous whispers drifted over to where Leo waited. He moved towards the two crouched figures, a ghostly shadow in the predawn light. In a moment he was on them. His strong hands gripped the head of the kneeling Markovitch, his fingers digging deep into his eye sockets. An instinctive twist of Leo's wrists broke Markovitch's third vertebra with a crack, snapping the spinal cord. Markovitch slumped to the floor, the life rent from his body. He had no time to cry out. Then his accomplice felt Leo's embrace before his head smacked the concrete and he lay there motionless. Leo moved the still warm bodies into a nearby packing case, and then knelt to examine their handiwork. He located the Semtex. It had been expertly placed. The resulting explosion would probably look like a fault in the plant's heat exchanger, an accident, just an accident. He knew the heat from the fire that resulted would destroy any trace of sabotage.

Chapter 27

Walking over the grey cobblestones, Firenze ran the rosary through his fingers as he recited the Paternoster. Rome always made him nervous. *'Pater noster, qui es in caelis, sanctificetur nomen tuum.'* Then turning into Via Tomacelli, where the monastery of Saint Jerome had stood for more than four hundred years, his prayer continued. *'Adveniat regnum tuum, fiat voluntas tua in terris sicut est in caelis.'* He gave a sigh of relief as he checked his watch. He was twenty minutes early and thankful for a few moments repose. Collecting his thoughts, he tried to calm his nerves. He'd not slept at all the night before his flight to Rome and now felt the barbed prickle of fatigue dance painfully between his eyes. He checked his watch again. It was time.

Firenze made his way into the monastery through the cloisters and entered the nave. He knocked on the door, and when summoned, entered head bowed in the fashion he knew Monsignor Bernarez was accustomed to and expected. Firenze presented a small inscribed Val Susa blue green river pebble to the Monsignor.

'Welcome, welcome once more to the Monastery of Saint Jerome, my son. Come please, you will share a glass of red wine with me? The grapes come from the monastery's own vineyard.'

Firenze had chosen the place of his birth as his nom de guerre, the capital of Tuscany, one of the world's artistic and cultural centres. Florence was the only city in which Firenze felt at ease. At the Monsignor's invitation, Firenze took a seat at the oak table and took a sip of red wine from his glass.

'Over the years our order has elevated you to a place of advantage and power at the very heart of the financial and political world. Firenze, you were instructed to challenge the commercial expediency of granting financial backing to Sarajevo Steel, yet still their application has not been rejected.' Firenze's brow glistened with sweat, as the Monsignor continued. 'I understand the Americans are lobbying hard for the finance to be advanced to the Bosnians. This must not occur. The interest rate is the Achilles' heel. The rate your bank will propose on behalf of the Consortium will ensure they are unable to meet the financial criterion that has been set. The funding must go to Zelejezara Steel in Split. There is a debt of honour to repay to our Croatian Catholic brothers as a consequence of the carnage of May nineteen forty-five. You will attend to it.'

Firenze pushed his chair back from the table and rose. Then he bowed and left the room, making no response. He knew no response was required.

Chapter 28

Bernadeta Banja welcomed Boris and Stefan for their meeting with Herr Becker at the Deutsche Bank office in Sarajevo. Stefan joined Wolfgang Spitzel, Herr Becker's accountant, in the waiting room, while Boris and Bernadeta chatted. At two o'clock Bernadeta showed them through to Herr Becker's office. The meeting was to respond to a number of issues raised by the Deutsche Bank's main board, and to confirm the interest rate, before final submission to the International Consortium. Each point was discussed in a convivial and business-like atmosphere. Finally, they came to the issue of the interest rate. Herr Becker looked at his watch.

'I should have received a facsimile by now confirming the final interest rates.'

He got up and walked to the door. As he did Signor Botticelli the Deutsche Bank main board Vice President walked in unannounced. He had not been scheduled to attend this particular meeting. Herr Becker was taken aback. Botticelli's arrival was clearly unexpected. Herr Becker handled the intrusion well.

'You all know Signor Botticelli,' said Herr Becker. Boris nodded, and forced a weak smile that failed to reach the corners of his mouth. Herr Becker flashed Botticelli a question that invited an explanation as to the reason for his arrival. None came. Botticelli pushed in between Herr Becker and Wolfgang Spitzel, to sit directly opposite Boris. Botticelli engaged Boris in a steady gaze as Wolfgang rescued his papers to make way. Clearly Wolfgang knew his place in the hierarchy.

'As to the matter of interest rates, we need written confirmation,' Boris began. 'Our deadline for securing the finance is fast approaching. We need to conclude this agreement. From the outset, the figure of one per cent above World Bank Base Rate was mandated by the consortium for submission purposes. However, after factoring in the guarantees promised by a number of Western Governments, it was understood the figure would be less. Somewhere between zero point seven five and zero point eight five per cent. The rate was to be confirmed in writing by today's meeting.'

Herr Becker turned to Wolfgang Spitzel, who was now on Botticelli's left.

'Check with Bernadeta to see if we've received a facsimile from head office in Frankfurt confirming the interest rate.'

Senior Botticelli snatched a single sheet of paper from his briefcase and thrust it towards Boris.

'I can help you with that,' he announced. 'It is to be two point three per cent above World Bank Base Rate.'

'Say again,' said Boris, confused by Botticelli's response. 'There must be some mistake.'

'The rate is two point three per cent above World Bank Base Rate,' repeated Botticelli in a pompous, obnoxious tone.

'No, no, we understood the interest rate would be no more than one per cent above, and both sides anticipated the final figure would be less. The figure of two point three per cent above leaves our proposal in ruins, Sarajevo Steel could never meet the financial criteria, and so the deal would be dead. Are you sure there's no mistake?'

'There is no mistake,' said Signor Botticelli. 'That is the rate I personally have authorised for you.'

'But that's robbery,' said Boris.

'What do you take me for?' snapped Botticelli. The words Brooklyn Hood formed on Boris' lips then dissolved unseen. 'That is our final offer,' said Signor Botticelli. 'It is immutable.'

'This it is outrageous,' retorted Boris. 'We will not accept it.' The room fell silent.

'Where else can you go?' smiled Signor Botticelli. 'I suspect you have no alternative.'

'Herr Becker,' said Boris politely, 'perhaps you would like to rethink your proposal and submit the consortium's final offer to me in seven days' time. Good day.'

Boris bowed courteously and left the office with Stefan.

After Botticelli left, Herr Becker contemplated a number of behind the scene moves. People owed him favours. It was time to call them in. He knew investing in Sarajevo Steel was low risk and with a man in charge of the calibre of Boris Poborski, it made sound business sense. The Zelejezara Steel proposal was nowhere near as convincing. Herr Becker had to get Botticelli's decision on interest rates changed. He just didn't know how.

Chapter 29

The leader of Sarajevo's Communist cell, Dmitri Simvnic, moved slowly towards the Latin Bridge in Sarajevo. He didn't feel the warmth of the pale winter sun, as he kept pace with the pedestrians scurrying along Obala Kulina bana. As he neared the bridge, a small crowd of onlookers gathered, as if to welcome him on his arrival. Dmitri was unaware of both the onlookers and the bridge, as he floated face-down in the freezing turbid waters. Fighting to avoid the great stone arches that supported the bridge, the Miljacka's current seized his waterlogged body. It dragged Dmitri into a maelstrom of black clawing water, sucking his lifeless body to a watery grave, and in a moment, he was gone. Dmitri Simvnic's body was disgorged at the confluence of the Miljacka and Bosna Rivers the following day.

The subsequent post-mortem concluded Simvnic had accidentally fallen into the River Miljacka and had drowned. The funeral that followed was a quiet affair, with just a few very close relatives and Milo Tolja.

Chapter 30

Herr Becker was still smarting over the way his old adversary, Botticelli, had outmanoeuvred him, and was amazed that he'd managed to coerce the Main Board into supporting his unilateral decision on interest rates, a decision based on Botticelli's own financial risk assessment of Sarajevo Steel. It was a narrow, pessimistic assessment that Herr Becker had not even been privileged to see until now. The word in the corridors of power must have some credence. Botticelli was the Main Board Chairman in waiting.

Sitting alone in his office, Herr Becker tried to build up the courage to telephone Boris after their meeting had shattered so acrimoniously almost a week ago. He stared down at the notes he'd made as prompts and rehearsed them in his head, but without conviction. Finally defeated, he gave in and decided to have Bernadeta contact Boris to make a new appointment.

Chapter 31

Olga waited at Boris' desk for the month-end cheques to be authorised. As Boris signed the last one, the telephone rang, and he was pleased to discover it was Bernadeta on the line.

'Good morning Bernadeta, I hope you are well today?'

'Yes, I'm fine, thank you, and how are you after your battle with Botticelli? You know we are all rooting for you down here at the Deutsche Bank.'

Boris smiled at her candour.

'Thank you, that means a great deal to me.'

'Herr Becker has asked me to arrange a meeting as soon as possible. Is tomorrow at nine o'clock too short notice for you?'

'No, not at all, but under the circumstances I'd be obliged if the meeting was held in my office.'

'One moment while I check with Herr Becker.' Almost immediately, Bernadeta came back on the line. Boris concluded Herr Becker had been standing by her side listening throughout the conversation. 'Yes of course, Herr Becker will see you at your office, with Signor Botticelli and Wolfgang Spitzel, at nine o'clock tomorrow morning.'

Boris replaced the receiver a great deal happier than when he'd picked it up.

Chapter 32

Herr Becker opened the meeting by trying build a position from which to justify the consortium's flawed interest rate proposal, but Boris interrupted.

'May I suggest we put the previous proposal down to an honest error and move on?'

Stefan smiled and nodded, as a gesture of approval. Wolfgang Spitzel looked blankly at the ceiling and avoided any comment.

'Very good,' agreed Herr Becker. 'But I must tell you the interest rate is now based as much on political criteria as financial ones. The Americans have agreed to underwrite fifty two percent of the loan, and based on this and the support of other Western governments, our Main Board met yesterday afternoon to approve the new rate of zero point seven nine per cent above World Bank Base Rate. The agreement is now ready for submission to the full Consortium for approval.' Signor Botticelli sat apathetically studying the wood grain on Boris' desk.

Boris breathed a sigh of relief and looked across at Stefan. Stefan winked back, as Wolfgang distributed copies of the documents that detailed the new rate of interest. Signor Botticelli sat staring at the wall. He said nothing.

Chapter 33

Luka checked her change as she left the small supermarket in Stari Grad and walked the short distance into Bascarsija. She'd never spent so much money in one week, let alone in one single morning. She glowed. Opposite the fountain in the main square, she ascended the stone steps with a sense of purpose and pushed open the door. Mr Zimen entered from his sitting room at the back of the shop and greeted her warmly. He handed over a small box and Luka paid him, then she put the box in her bag with the rest of the shopping.

Luka returned home and placed her shopping bag on the kitchen table, and her grandmother began to unpack it while Luka sat down to read her library book.

'What is this?' Her grandmother asked holding up a large jar of honey. 'And this?' She continued as she picked up a slab of cheese. 'These are my favourite biscuits. We couldn't even afford these at Christmas,' her grandmother added as she unpacked the rest of the shopping. 'Have you picked up someone else's shopping bag by mistake?'

'Yesterday was my first payday. I thought you deserved a treat. Is that everything? Is there nothing left in the shopping bag?'

Her grandmother looked again into the tired old shopping bag and at the bottom of the bag was the box Luka had collected from Mr Zimen.

'What is this,' she asked. 'Is it for me?'

Luka stepped forward and took hold of the box. Removing the contents, she held its secret hidden for a moment, before slipping the well-worn wedding ring onto her grandmother's finger. Luka nursed her grandmother gently in her arms. She thought the tears would never stop.

Chapter 34

Bernadeta Banja surveyed the chaos of her bedroom. Dresses, blouses and skirts, many she'd never worn, were strewn over the bed. A pile of shoes lay in a corner after their rejection. It was decision day for Sarajevo Steel. Bernadeta wanted to look her best for Boris.

She picked up the navy skirt and the crisp white blouse, her usual office garb. This was definitely her final choice. It had been her first choice more than forty minutes earlier. They were the only clothes she felt safe in. Bernadeta's long-held convictions dictated that nothing else felt right.

Chapter 35
30th January 1998

Boris, Stefan, and Leo arrived at the Deutsche Bank in Sarajevo and were ushered into the waiting room by the usual receptionist.

'How can you stay so cool?' Boris challenged Stefan.

'Easy. The one hundred and fifty million dollars will be approved, no problem. Banks lend money, that's what they're about. Our proposal is watertight, there's no problem.'

'Well I'm not so sure. We're in a political arena now. The Deutsche Bank is supportive, but they only front faceless fund managers from across Europe and the United States. I feel we are in God's hands now.'

The thought of failure gnawed away at Boris as he attempted to second-guess the decision. The door opened, interrupting his thoughts. Bernadeta came into the room and walked over to where he stood.

'Are you well today?' she enquired.

Bernadeta tried to make eye contact as she spoke, but Boris looked away in the direction of nothing in particular. His torment was bitten deep into his face.

'Yes, oh yes, very well, thank you.' He failed to notice the crispness of her white blouse or her figure-hugging navy skirt.

As she left his side, she gently squeezed his hand saying, 'Good luck.'

Herr Becker greeted them enthusiastically. Boris thought he'd lost something of his despot image during the time they'd been working together.

'Congratulations,' he beamed. 'All your hard work has paid off; Sarajevo Steel has a future. Western Governments have now underwritten a total of sixty percent of the one-hundred-and-fifty-million-dollar loan. The finance has been approved. The funding from the Interim Government comes to an end on the twenty-eighth of February, and so the Deutsch Bank Consortium finance will be released on the second of

March, after the agreement is signed in England on Sunday the twenty second of February. The Ministry for Industry and our Frankfurt head office are making all the arrangements, Georg Komikosovitch will inform you of all the details in due course.'

'Yes! Yes! Yes!' shouted Boris as he hugged Leo. Stefan stood back. He was not the hugging kind. 'We could not have done it without your considerable help, Herr Becker. 'You were with us every step of the way. Your help and advice have been pivotal.'

'I thank you for those kind words,' said Herr Becker, as he reflected on his battle with Botticelli over the interest rate. 'I do believe some of them are actually true. There are strings attached of course, but no more than required, no more than we discussed. You, of course, Boris, are seen as Sarajevo's biggest asset and you are to hold the position of General Director, and are mandated to remain on the board as a condition of payment under clause 83.1.' After all, we are investing in you as much as Sarajevo Steel.' Boris nodded. 'The US in particular emerged as strong supporters. They are anxious to provide employment. They know capitalism brings with it economic and social stability. A thought flashed through Boris' brain. Had the US prosecuted the war simply to introduce Yugoslavia to the benefits of capitalism and expel Communism?

'The office of the High Representative has approved the rest of Sarajevo Steel's proposed board members, though only after the War Crimes Commission completed their detailed investigations.' Herr Becker continued. 'One proposed board member, however, will not now be taking up his appointment as planned. Signor Botticelli was to have been one of the Consortium's non-executive board members. It seems Gianluca has lost the support of those at the top. He has stepped down and been replaced.'

'Who by?' Boris ventured.

'By me of course,' laughed Herr Becker.

Chapter 36

La Repubblica
Roma Italy
31st January 1998

Late News

The Polizia di Stato discovered the body of Gianluca Botticelli in the vicinity of the Ponte Cavour Bridge near the Tiber, during the early hours of yesterday morning. All available evidence suggests that he had hanged himself. As Senior Vice President of the Deutsche Bank, Botticelli was pivotal in the refinancing of Sarajevo Steel in Bosnia. Botticelli had been confidently predicted to be the next Chairman of the Deutsche Bank. He leaves a wife, a daughter of twenty and a married son of twenty-seven. There appears to have been no suicide note.

During the autopsy examination, the contents of Gianluca Botticelli's stomach, revealed he'd drunk a small amount of red wine one hour before his death, in which a high level of barbiturate was present. Botticelli had not eaten that day.

However, the redacted autopsy made no mention of the presence of barbiturates or that hanging had occurred post-mortem. No suspicious circumstances were reported.

Firenze had failed to deliver on his oath. He had accepted death as the penalty. Bleiburg, the Croatian farmer's son, could be satisfied with a job well done. The Order of the Sword of Saint Jerome's oath had been honoured.

Chapter 37
Sarajevo
2nd February 1998

'England! We're going on holiday to England!' Ana's enthusiasm overwhelmed her father when she heard the news. It buried Boris in a barrage of exuberance.

'You're not listening, Ana.' His face was authoritarian, unyielding. Boris held up a hand to stem the storm of excitement that headed his way. The stratagem failed to derail Ana's onslaught. Smiling broadly, she walked purposely towards him.

'You can't go without me. You know you can't.'

'I'm going to England. No one said us. I'll be involved in meetings the whole time, lunches, dinners, that sort of thing. It's a trade mission, a boring business trip for Sarajevo Steel. Certainly not a holiday.' Although the words, '*I won't have any time for you,*' were poised on his lips, Boris evaded the obvious rejoinder. He fell silent for a moment. Ana moved closer; her brown eyes resolutely fixed on his face.

'You know you can't go without me,' she persisted.

'Watch me,' were the only words he could find to say, as he tried to avoid her gaze. Ana turned to stand in front of her father. Boris saw in Ana the image of Katerina, she had her mother's face, her eyes, her hair.

'But I've never been to England. Never.' Ana went back on the attack, mindful to keep her voice respectful. 'As a matter of fact, I've never been out of Bosnia.'

The night was drawing in and as a means of escape Boris rose from his armchair and walked over to close the curtains at the far end of the lounge.

'Oh, please father.' Ana came closer, entwining her arms around his neck. She kissed him hard on the cheek. She was almost as tall as Boris.

Almost a woman. He smiled down at her and Katerina smiled back as his resolve melted away.

'We'll see,' he sighed.

'Thank you, your munificence.'

Defeated, Boris picked up his newspaper, sat down in his armchair and began to read. Ana had been here before. She curtsied low and headed for her bedroom with a sense of purpose. She was anxious to start packing for her trip to England.

Boris finished reading, put down his newspaper, and rubbed his eyes. Despite the elegance of the apartment, the new furniture and the expensive décor, loneliness crouched in every corner. He walked over to his bedroom, turning off the lounge lights as he went. A photograph of Katerina stood on his bedside table. It had been taken in Sutjeska National Park, in the mountains below Maglić, the summer before they were married. The photograph meant everything to him. It was the only one he'd managed to salvage from their home in Babonavic.

Boris Poborski had been a senior figure in the Bratsvo Group of companies before the war. A successful man, a man with vision, he had energy and real ambition. But since that dreadful day in Babonavic when his world had been ripped apart, changed forever, his vision and energy was fading, his ambitions eclipsed. He should be feeling good with the progress at Sarajevo Steel, excited by the future, but Boris realised without Katerina success meant little to him. He'd even begun to question if there was any point in going on.

***

Sitting on the bedside, with his head in his hands, he heard a gentle tapping on his bedroom door. Then the door swung slowly open. It was Ana. It was Ana's fashion show. Apart from her school uniform she'd had no new clothes since moving to Sarajevo. Ana had emptied her wardrobe searching for any clothes that she thought might be suitable. She was wearing her favourite pink blouse and her best jacket. The cuffs of the jacket exposed her wrists and her lower forearms, the blouse so tight across her chest. Two pale ankles peeped out from beneath her trousers. How had he failed to notice as she'd grown? Then a blinding flash of the obvious struck him. He'd simply not been there. Buried in his work, he'd been sleepwalking as Ana slipped through his fingers.

'How do I look?' she asked. 'Will I do for England, good sir?'

'Wow,' exclaimed Boris. 'You look fantastic.'

Boris held out his arms as Ana came and sat down on the bed beside him.

'I love you,' she whispered.

Boris wiped a tear from his eye. Now he knew the point of going on.

Chapter 38

Georg Komikosovitch, the Bosnian Under Secretary to the Minister for Industry, sat waiting in the reception area of Sarajevo Steel, his penetrating eyes interrogating the surroundings. His slim frame was topped by a bald head. He wore a dark grey suit, white shirt and sombre tie, giving him the appearance of a suited clone. Someone who you could live next door to for a lifetime and never notice.

Boris welcomed him and they made their way to the boardroom. Georg started speaking before Boris had sat down.

'I have requested this meeting to familiarise you personally with the details and timings of our business trip to the United Kingdom for the signing of the Cooperation and Finance Agreement.'

Boris nodded his understanding as Olga joined them to take any notes that may be required. Georg glanced at Boris and Olga to confirm he had their full attention. 'We will fly from Sarajevo to Manchester International via Munich. Then together with our Ministerial Delegation we will travel the short distance to Kermincham Hall, in Cumbria, England, where on Sunday the twenty second of February, the finance agreement will be signed.

'I myself was involved in selecting this venue. Given the international makeup of those involved, it has been difficult to get agreement on a location, one that fits in with the busy itineraries of both international financiers and politicians. Kermincham Hall provides all the facilities required, in a pleasant and beautiful location. While there we will be obliged to comply with a strict security protocol.'

Georg handed Boris five security passes, including one for Ana. 'Here are your travel itineraries. The necessary visas have been arranged by my office. There is one for each member of the Sarajevo delegation. Our Ambassador, Ivan Bobic, will be present in England throughout the weekend proceedings. We are therefore required to be on our best behaviour. As well as the importance to Bosnia, this is significant world news. It indicates clearly that Bosnia is returning to normality, and that Western Governments and international financiers have the confidence to invest in our country, as we embrace our future as capitalists.

'All charges will be met by the Ministry for Industry.' He paused to acknowledge Boris' thanks. None came.

Georg continued. 'I see Boris, from your itinerary, you have very little free time over the weekend. One meeting follows another, all fitted in between official functions. You will observe,' he turned to Boris with a sad pantomime face, 'Ana, your daughter, and Olga are omitted from these official functions. I know you will understand.' Olga Lukic nodded her understanding as she scribbled down some notes. Georg turned to Olga as he drizzled on. 'I believe you and Ana have some outing or other organised. An expedition climbing in the mountains. I hope you will have a nice day.' Georg paused and smiled in Olga's direction. 'Any questions?' asked Georg.

There were none. How could there be?

Olga returned to her office and unlocked the top drawer of her desk. She removed the Tag Heuer watch from its box and slipped it on her wrist. Then she pulled her cuff down to conceal it and left the office for her lunch appointment.

Chapter 39

When Lenord Stanislav reported the failure of Markovitch's sabotage mission, Roman immediately convened a committee meeting in the Zetra Arena for the following evening. All those who attended on the previous occasion were again present—all bar one. Though no one dared to mention the absence of Dmitri Simvnic or his failed coup d'état.

Roman opened the meeting. His mien, as ever, portrayed a quiet confidence that gave his followers the impression he knew more than anyone else, and much more than he was prepared to share. He invited Lenord Stanislav to present his report on the attempted sabotage. In this way the blame for the failure would fall at Stanislav's door.

'Shall we try again?' Stanislav asked obsequiously, as he concluded his report. 'This time Poborski was lucky, that's all. He needs to be lucky every time. We only have to be lucky once.'

Stanislav failed to hide his animosity for Boris Poborski, the man who had taken his job. 'We must act quickly,' urged Stanislav. 'By now the whole world knows that the finance has been approved. They are to get millions of dollars from Western Banks.'

Stanislav was tempted to suggest they blow up Poborski. He looked at the empty seat where Dmitri Simvnic usually sat, then at Milo Tolja and thought better of it. Roman rose to his feet in response.

'Of course, there can be no money without a signed agreement and as yet, this agreement is unsigned. We have one comrade who is close to the negotiations, one who knows all of the details. They know the agreement will be signed in England on the twenty fifth of February, close to the city of Manchester. This is not as convenient as Sarajevo, but we have friends there, and they are prepared to help. Every faction involved in the Consortium felt they should have the prestige of hosting the signing ceremony. It transpires the Germans would not consent to the signing of the agreement in the United States or London, the UK's financial capital, and the Americans could not accept any venue on mainland Europe. So, comrades, there is much to do. We must make our plans carefully. I myself will go to England. It is a country I know well. What I propose will lay the failure to secure Western finance firmly on Poborski. It is the only possible way to avoid a people's backlash against our plans. Boris Poborski will refuse to sign the finance agreement and will immediately resign from his position as General Director of Sarajevo Steel.'

'He will never do that,' gasped Stanislav.'

'Oh, he will. Believe me he will.' Roman continued in a dry voice that he judged conveyed a thread of humour. He looked at Milo. 'You know how persuasive I can be when I try. Leading members of the Interim Government will be in England during the signing. Out of sight, out of mind, and certainly out of Bosnia. Poborski's refusal to sign will bring about the collapse of this major political and financial initiative, a cornerstone in the economic recovery of Bosnia. It will cause complete confusion, especially here in Sarajevo. The Western powers' covert attempt to supplant communism with capitalism will fail. Without finance Sarajevo Steel will face immediate closure. There will be a total loss of confidence in the Western backed interim government. At the height of the confusion, the Communist People's Revolution will take to the streets of Bosnia and the interim government will resign. Everything is in place. The world knows that this failure will deter any similar Capitalist attempts to usurp Communism in the future. Our new President will take over, and Bosnia will be like home again. Then our work can begin.'

Sitting directly across the table from Roman and slightly to the left of Milo, Bleiburg carefully thought through his travel itinerary and mentally prepared his report for Monsignor Bernarez and the Holy Order of the Sword of Saint Jerome.

Chapter 40

Two Knights and their Longa Manus arrived for an audience with Monsignor Bernarez. Lupiana, the senior of the two Knights, lost no time in expressing his displeasure at the Order's failure to influence the financing decision. Sarajevo Steel had won. Zelejezara of Split and the Catholics of Croatia had lost out. Monsignor Bernarez sat unmoved by their pejorative despite the hostile edge conveyed by Lupiana's words.

'We may have lost the battle, but we have not lost the war. With so many foreign litigants influencing the process, failure was always a possibility.'

'You issued no counsel to that effect; we feel badly served. A way to stop Poborski must be found. The Catholic Church cannot fail the Croats again.'

The Monsignor thought deeply before speaking.

'The Communists are taking an unhealthy interest in Sarajevo Steel. I would never have believed symbiosis could prevail between the Communists and the Catholic Church. However, in moments of crisis we are compelled to recognise we do not operate in a vacuum. The Communists are scheming to bring misfortune to Sarajevo Steel, while our Knight, Bleiburg sits unnoticed at their table. Perhaps, with his watching brief, the Communists may yet provide a solution, and deliver recompense for the events of May 1945.'

'Monsignor,' the Knight Lupiana ventured. 'You will, I hope, have a backup plan should the Communists fail?'

The Monsignor made no reply.

Chapter 41

On Friday morning, Boris' telephone call was put through to Bernadeta's office as she prepared for Herr Becker's trip to England with the Consortium. Smiling broadly, she closed her office door for a little privacy, before greeting him with the formality mandatory for her position. Though her voice carried the desire to share a more cordial relationship with him.

'I have a personal favour to ask of you, Bernadeta.'

She was stunned at first, then thrilled.

'I need a female chaperone for a shopping trip in the morning. My daughter, Ana, needs new clothes for our visit to England. I wondered; would you be good enough to help? I know it's short notice.'

Although the invitation was not what Bernadeta hoped for, it was a step in the right direction. It gave her aspirations the encouragement to grow.

'Why yes, of course, what time should I be there?'

'Let me have your address, and I'll send a car for you at ten o'clock, if that's all right with you?'

'Yes, I'll be ready at ten, I'll see you tomorrow.'

Boris had asked Marija, Ana's aunt in Banja Luka, if she could help, but found her out of sorts and in bed with flu. He did not share this information with Bernadeta.

As they waited for the arrival of Bernadeta, Boris studied Ana. She had always been a precocious child, now she was sixteen going on twenty-three. He had almost lost her once, now he promised himself he would never lose her again, he'd always be there for her. The doorbell rang and Ana rushed to greet Bernadeta, as Boris joined them from the lounge.

'Ana's all set for her shopping expedition, she's been up since before seven.'

'So,' said Bernadeta, 'do we know exactly what you want?'

Ana produced a neat handwritten list and handed it to her father. It ran to two pages. He made a face.

'Ana, I said you could have anything you wanted, not everything you wanted. I'm not a walking wallet,' he laughed. 'Well, all right I guess it is a long time since you've had any new clothes, apart from your school uniform.' With that, he dug his hand into his pocket and handed Bernadeta an envelope. 'It shouldn't be any more than this, if it is, just let me know.' Bernadeta took the envelope and put it in her handbag.

'I need a few things myself. Herr Becker needs secretarial support while he's in England, someone who's familiar with the work of the Consortium, so I'm going too.'

It was just after ten o'clock in the morning when Ana kissed her father goodbye. It had been dark for more than two hours when she and Bernadeta arrived back. Boris held the door open as Ana struggled into the lounge with five carrier bags and several boxes.

'Well, you're back at last, I was getting worried. Did you manage to get what you wanted?' Boris helped Ana with her bags.

'Just about,' sighed Ana as she collapsed on the settee.

'We did fine. We're all fixed up, thank you Boris.'

'I can't thank you enough for your help.'

'Not at all, I enjoyed it immensely.'

'Let's do it again next week,' ventured Ana with a smile.

'Come on now,' said her father. 'Say thank you to Bernadeta.'

Bernadeta's help was worth more than a simple thank you. Ana thought it was worth a hug and to Bernadeta's delight, Ana duly delivered. Bernadeta returned Boris' unspent funds, as Ana disappeared into her bedroom, weighed down with her new ensemble.

'I'm quite looking forward to being in England.' Bernadeta hesitated as Boris walked her to the car. 'Being there with you.'

***

Boris received a blow-by-blow account of the previous day's shopping trip over breakfast the following morning.

'So that was it,' announced Ana in conclusion. 'Everything sorted. Bernadeta bought some really nice stuff. She's never married you know. As a girl she was a novice in a convent in, Italy. That's where she learned Italian. But she wasn't cut out to be a nun, so she left before she took her vows.'

'Come on Ana, finish your breakfast, we're going to be late for church, get a move on.'

Chapter 42

The early morning light filtered lazily in through the monastery's stained-glass windows, as Monsignor Bernarez opened the large buff file that Bleiburg had placed before him. He recharged his glass with red wine, and took a sip of the potent draught, before spreading the contents of the file on the long oak table. Diligently he scrutinised each item in turn. He took his time. His attention was first drawn to a photograph of Milo Tolja.

'You say Tolja was responsible for drowning the Communist Dmitri Simvnic in the Miljacka River.' Bleiburg nodded. 'And is it confirmed that he is to go to England?'

'Yes, Tolja flies to Birmingham International via London Heathrow on the evening of the nineteenth, arriving there on the twentieth of February, using a forged passport supplied by the KGB.'

'And Drasko, what about Drasko? I know you said he too was to go to England.'

'Yes, he crossed into Hungary then took a flight from Budapest to Moscow. He arrived in London three days ago.'

'So, neither flew to Manchester as their airport of choice, yet still you are certain the Communists show an unhealthy interest in the business of Sarajevo Steel?'

'Yes, I know it.' Bleiburg replied.

'The location is convenient. It suits us well. We will have all the support we need from Charles Borromeo.'

***

Bernarez placed Milo Tolja's photograph, together with Roman Drasko's, to one side of his now half-empty wine glass and picked up the photograph of Leo Illic.

'Tolja and Drasko will present the main armed threat from the Communists, though they will not be without support. There will be many others. As for Sarajevo Steel, only Illic is a concern. The part he played during the Sarajevo Siege identifies him as a serious threat. This man is dangerous. They will have no one else. Only Illic and perhaps Stanisic. Poborski's genius lies in finance and industrial management; he is no danger.'

Bernarez placed the photographs back in the file, along with the autopsy confirming the cause of Firenze's death was from a cocktail of barbiturates an hour before the sham hanging took place. This was the official autopsy that the Holy Order of the Sword of Saint Jerome had suppressed. Bleiburg handed Bernarez a copy of the Cooperation and Finance Agreement between Sarajevo Steel and the Deutsche Bank Consortium. He pointed out clause 83:1. It had been highlighted in yellow and then this too was placed neatly in the file.

'Is everything ready?' asked Monsignor Bernarez.

'Everything is ready,' replied Bleiberg.

'Are you prepared to deliver against your oath?'

'I am prepared.'

PART TWO

Chapter 43
Snowdonia
Sunday 15th February 1998

Dan Kennedy waited, secured by a sling and two camming devices that bit into the rock face. High above him, Tom's voice rang out. 'Safe.' Tom called again to be certain he'd been heard. Dan felt the tension in his shoulders drain away. He'd been waiting for Tom to reach the top of the final pitch for what seemed like an eternity.

Dan glanced down to where the rock melded with the yellow tufts of coarse mountain grass three hundred and five feet below, as he waited to climb. Trying to stay focused, he transferred his weight onto his right foot.

'Off belay.' Tom untied the lead rope from his harness.

Now knowing Tom was okay, Dan removed his belay device that had held Tom safe during his ascent. Then he scoured the rough, black rock for possible handholds, searching for anything to cling onto. Tom set up a belay at the top of the pitch to bring Dan up, then took up the slack in the rope that would hold Dan in case of a fall.

'That's me,' called Dan as he felt the rope go tight.

'Climb when ready.'

Tom's command kicked in and Dan released the two cams that held him to the vertical rock wall and clipped them onto his harness. Then he began his ascent.

'Climbing.'

Dan gazed up, following the thin blue-green rope that secured him to the belay. This was the crux of the climb, the most difficult move. He looked up at the big rock overhang that bulged out into nothingness. Dan clung onto the mass of rhyolite, searching for a hold. His progress was slow. Halfway up he felt a tiny crack at arm's length high above his head. No more than a finger hold. Then he secured a knife-edge foothold and tentatively transferred his weight to his left foot. Next he jammed his left hand into a narrow fissure, the rock biting into his flesh as the hand jam took his weight. Praying the soles of his climbing shoes would stick to the tenuous footholds, he smeared them speculatively across the rock face. He was over the crux. The following moves came easily as self-belief pushed him on, leaving a final mantle-shelf move to gain the top of the crag. One big heave and one big grunt and he reached the spiky summit to stand beside his son, a boy of sixteen.

'What took you so long?' asked Tom quizzically.

'I was admiring the view.'

'What, in the dark?' said Tom, grinning broadly.

Dan laughed out loud. He'd completely failed to notice that the gathering gloom had turned to inky black as he'd scaled the final pitch. A coal-washed backdrop had replaced the view down the Pass of Llanberis. They un-roped in the pitch-black, packed their climbing gear into their rucksacks, and began the trek down over the most dangerous crags in Snowdonia.

Tom stowed the climbing gear in the Range Rover, then Dan pulled onto the narrow mountain road that threaded down the Llanberis Pass, the headlights blazing the way. They travelled quickly on the deserted roads, northwest at first through Gwastandnant towards Llanberis and home.

'Well done, that was a good climb. A good session. We just need our final workout next weekend before we go to Chamonix in March,' said Dan.

Silence descended, then continued unbroken. Dan looked over to find Tom asleep. Llanberis was soon behind them and once onto the A55 they headed east through a sleeping Wales. Chester came quickly and minutes later Dan turned into the sweeping drive of Harrowdene Hall. Tom yawned and turned to his father.

'Are we home already?' he asked, rubbing the sleep from his eyes.

'Right on cue,' said Dan. 'Just as we pull up outside the door, you simply resume life. You go from comatose to fully conscious in one move.'

Tom sprang out of the car and began to unload the climbing gear. The front door to the Hall opened and Jane greeted them, dressed in a long denim dress, her light blue eyes signalled her anxious wait was over. She gave them her customary welcome home hug, which masked the relief she felt on Dan and Tom's return.

'How was the climb?' she enquired.

'Fine,' replied Tom. 'I've just realised I can catch The Simpsons if I'm quick. Can I have my meal in my room?' He called back as he disappeared upstairs with the last of the climbing gear. Tom pushed open his bedroom door and crashed out on his bed to watch Bart and family.

Dan went upstairs to shower. He felt reinvigorated by the hot water as it soaked his body, his muscles honed by the years spent in the mountains. He let the water flow over his tanned, line-free face, as he re-climbed Crib Coch in his head. Dan returned to the kitchen and opened a bottle of wine.

'What have we got?' Dan asked, as Jane joined him from the lounge.

'To eat or think about?' asked Jane.

'Hey,' replied Dan with a big smile. 'You know me, I can't think on an empty stomach, no way'.

'Okay, we have vegetable lasagne. It just needs serving up,' replied Jane.'

'I guess that's to eat,' said Dan.

'Well done you, but I am afraid that's the easy part,' she added, brandishing a sheaf of holiday brochures.

Tom swooped in, grabbed his plate of lasagne from the kitchen worktop and made his getaway to watch the conclusion of The Simpsons.

'Yes, I was afraid it might be.' Dan poured two glasses of wine. 'The pile of brochures was a bit of a giveaway.'

Dan finished his lasagne and poured the last of the wine into his glass, then flicked idly through the brochures.

'More wine?' he asked.

'Yes, please, if you are. I'll have another glass.'

Dan went over to the fridge for another bottle of wine, as Tom came into the kitchen for some ice cream. Tom stood blocking Dan's path to the fridge for a moment, vying for position, before he gave way.

Tom loved climbing, rock, ice and mountains, even onto the roof of the college gymnasium when challenged by his peers. He didn't love the detention that resulted from his gymnasium route, which he graded 'Extreme 5 b,' and in keeping with climbing tradition, as the first to climb the route, he christened it 'Misdemeanour.' The crux was a dynamic move, up and onto the overhanging roof, aided only by a tiny finger hold on a high narrow ledge. Of course, he had to accept the challenge. It was a matter of family pride.

Chapter 44

Milo gazed at the photograph in his new Italian passport as he waited for his car to take him to Mostar Airport. It was a good likeness, jet-black piercing eyes stared back at him. He'd always taken a good photograph. He had granite-like features, with a broad brow and a deep scar above his right eye. Milo peered through the curtains and down Adema Buoća, but there was no sign of his car. He turned his attention back to the photograph. He had worn well, there was little in his features that gave any hint of the passage of time. He tried to remember when he'd last had his photograph taken, but could not bring it to mind. Then Milo smiled. Now he remembered.

It had been on a warm August day on the steps of the University. He was in his gown and proudly holding his engineering diploma. Other students were having their photograph taken, while some relaxed in the warm summer sunshine. As he walked down the steps, he caught the eye of a girlfriend. She smiled a big happy smile and blew him a kiss, and he smiled back and waved.

Delighted with his photograph, he read out his new name from the passport, Angelo Moretti. He'd chosen the pseudonym himself. Moretti had been his mother's maiden name and he felt it had a contemporary ring to it. Milo checked the plane tickets Roman had provided, one way to Birmingham via London to avoid heightened security at Manchester. He put his passport and ticket, with the reservation for the Wast Water Inn, into his inside jacket pocket. Then the car pulled up and Milo Tolja left his apartment and Angelo Moretti climbed into the waiting car.

Chapter 45

Stefan Matic knelt in the hallway of his apartment just off Marsala Tita, where he'd lived alone since the death of his parents during the siege of Sarajevo. It was two minutes after seven o'clock. Stefan never thought his trip to England would begin on his knees, the position for prayer. With his suitcase on the floor, he tried again to encourage the last of his possessions into the bulging suitcase. He found a tiny space in one corner, then triumphantly squeezed his toilet bag into it, pulled up the zip and secured it with a small padlock.

The embassy car arrived and the driver, Josip Budach, introduced himself to Stefan. They drove down Marsala Tita and onto Obala Kulina bana to follow the Miljacka River, arriving at Olga Lukic's apartment a little more than five minutes later. The driver pulled over to the opposite side of the road to avoid parking on the tramlines. He crossed the road and rang the bell, as the trams rumbled by.

Almost at once, the door opened and Olga stepped out onto the wide pavement, leaving the bags for Josip to carry to the waiting car. She crossed the road, avoiding the deep ruts scoured by the tank tracks of the UN Protection Force during the siege. Olga reached the safety of the pavement and glanced across the Miljacka River, and up towards the distant hills. She knew the Serbian snipers had gone long ago. Only their ghosts remained in the memories of the people of Sarajevo. The driver put Olga's luggage into the boot of the Mercedes and set off towards Butmir and Sarajevo Airport, on the western outskirts of the city.

'Are you looking forward to the trip?' enquired Stefan.

'Yes, of course I am,' Olga replied. 'Although I know it's simply something we need to accomplish if we are to attain our goals.'

'Quite so,' he replied smiling. 'Quite so.'

Stefan detected Olga was a little different today. She looked almost radiant. He looked out of the window, leaned back in his seat and made himself comfortable.

The car left the confines of the city centre and continued west, passing white minarets as they pierced the grey blue sky, like accusing fingers pointing to heaven. Nearing the airport, the number of UNPROFOR vehicles increased. Olga watched the distinctive white Land Rovers travelling at great speed, flying an array of multi-coloured flags from long willowy aerials. The Mercedes passed through several checkpoints, its diplomatic plates ensuring unhindered progress to the front of the terminal building. On arrival, two UN soldiers, accompanied by a ministerial aide, escorted them to the diplomatic lounge, where Georg Komikosovitch welcomed them from behind a façade of diplomacy that failed to hide his anxiety.

Chapter 46

Gazing out from their apartment not far from The Café Paris, Ana waited with her father for their car to arrive. Then she began pacing around the lounge again. She returned to the window and looked out, constantly willing the car to arrive.

'It's late.' She announced, turning from the window and continuing to circle the lounge. 'We are going to be late.'

'Sit down,' pleaded her father. 'The car will come in its own good time. Wearing out the carpet will not get you to England any quicker.'

Ana sat down for a moment, but soon she was on the move again, this time in the direction of her bedroom. With her head to one side she consulted the wardrobe mirror. A beautiful face with high cheekbones smiled back, her black hair swept up in a short ponytail. An icy shiver came from nowhere, forcing Ana into the past. If only her mother could see her now. She felt a searing burn of guilt, a feeling of wrongdoing. Was she to blame for her mother's death? Keeping her promise was the only way Ana could forgive herself. She would never hide again; she would always fight. She pushed her thoughts behind her, turned from the mirror, and walked back to the living room.

'Well, how do I look?' she demanded as she posed in the doorway. Boris considered his answer. The new black trousers and suede jacket made her look more of a woman than he thought she should at sixteen. His reply feigned a deep disinterest.

'Not bad I suppose.'

'Not bad, not bad, what do you mean not bad?' Ana challenged.

'Okay,' Boris conceded. 'You look absolutely fantastic.'

Ana rushed forward and gave her father a hug. Only part of the hug was a thank you for the compliment.

'Do you have everything you need for your climb with Olga? How are the new walking boots?' he asked.

'Fine,' she replied, 'Bernadeta helped me choose them. All of my stuff is pretty good. I've a new hat and the new fleece you bought me last year for my birthday when I was still living in Banja Luka.'

It was a birthday present Boris couldn't bring to mind, owing to the fact he'd only paid for it. It had been Jan and Marija who bought it.

'Why don't you find something to occupy yourself until the car comes?' suggested her father.

Ana returned to her room and took out the maps of the Cumbria Mountains from her satchel and laid them out on her bed.

'The Corridor Route,' she announced aloud. 'Southeast from Stockley Bridge to Sty Head.' She traced the route with her finger. 'Pick up the Corridor Route then south to the Scafell Pike summit. No problem,' she concluded. In her mind, Ana was already in England, already climbing in the Cumbrian Mountains of the Lake District. She returned the maps to her satchel, along with a textbook on Robert Doyle, the seventeenth century alchemist.

'Come on Ana, the car's here! Come on!'

Ana returned to the living room as her father carried out their cases. She took a final look around the room before stepping out into the breaking day.

Leo sat in the front passenger seat beside Savo Stanisic. Savo was now a driver with the Bosnian Embassy, having fully recovered from the injuries he sustained while serving in Leo's unit during the siege. They chatted together as they waited. Savo saw Boris emerge from the apartment and went to help with the luggage, followed by Leo.

'Thanks for that, it's good to see you again Savo.' Boris shook Savo's hand. 'How are you keeping now?'

'I'm fine thank you, and you Boris, are you okay?'

'Never better, thank you, Savo.'

'These suitcases are heavier than they look,' said Savo.

'Yes, they are, I really don't know what Ana has packed.'

Ana made no reply as she climbed into the car, then the car pulled away, bumping over the potholes in the road.

'Good morning Ana, you look very smart this morning, are you looking forward to your visit to England?'

'Thank you, Leo. You look very nice yourself,' replied Ana. 'And yes, I can't wait, I've heard so much about England.'

Ana looked out of the window as the car left the city centre and made its way towards the airport. She could see burned-out houses, the scars of war and the cancer of ethnic cleansing. They stood out like angry wounds demanding attention. Saddened, she turned away from the bruised spectacle and as she did, her father met her gaze.

'I know,' he said. 'But we cannot vandalise our country and not expect to live with the consequence.'

Ana could only nod in sad agreement.

***

On arrival at the airport Boris entered the diplomatic lounge to find Stefan and Olga already waiting. So was Georg, who was standing with his clipboard, checking through the list of delegates again. Stefan walked quickly over to greet Boris.

'Thank God you're here,' said Stefan in a stage whisper. He looked across at Georg. 'This man is driving me mad, please keep him away from me. Please.'

Boris smiled sympathetically at Stefan, and then walked over towards Georg and Olga. Two airport baggage handlers collected their luggage, the diplomatic labels denying any right of search or X-ray. Stefan wondered if he would ever see his case again, as his mind drifted towards lunch. He hoped there would be food on the flight to Munich. The difficulty with his case that morning, meant he'd missed his breakfast.

***

Georg immediately ticked Boris, Leo, Ana and Savo off his checklist.

'Good morning Georg, everything seems to be going according to plan. Everyone's here on time.'

'Oh, thank you for that,' replied Georg. He shook Boris' hand. 'I can't tell you how important this operation is to me. I know that its success is crucial for our future, I'm really proud to be playing a part, albeit a mere cameo role compared to you.'

'You're doing a great job,' said Boris. 'Everything will be fine, you'll see. We're all in this together. You're not on your own, you know.'

Georg's visage lightened and a smile spread tentatively across his face.

'You're right of course, Boris. I'm not alone on my mission. I know I have plenty of help to call on if needed.'

Outside on the tarmac, bee-like, khaki-coloured military vehicles shuttled back and forth between the planes and the main terminal building, and as Ana watched, flakes of snow began to fall.

'Does it snow in England in February?' she asked.

'No, I shouldn't think so. Though I do remember reading somewhere that it's always foggy in November,' said her father.

'Yes,' said Ana. 'We learnt that at college. Also, at four o'clock everything stops for tea.'

'Is that true?' asked Boris, quite surprised.

'Oh yes,' confirmed Ana confidently. 'We had a visit from the British Commission. They told us a whole load of stuff about England.'

***

When their flight was called, Ana pushed her way to the front of the line. Squeezing past Georg, she turned and apologised for standing on his foot. Ana located her seat and settled down to enjoy the flight to Munich. She had a clear view out of the small round window. The plane taxied out to the end of the runway and paused for a moment. Then with a roar that set Ana's heart pounding, it set off down the runway, and glided effortlessly into the sky. Ana peered down at the forests and snow-speckled fields far below, which were interspersed with tiny, red roofed houses. Rivers and roads snaked their way through the rolling countryside. The plane rose to clear the Sarajevo Hills, banked to the south, and then as they disappeared into the chaos of white fluffy clouds, her view was lost. Once above the clouds, Ana smiled down on a sea of cotton wool. She was on her way to England.

***

Stefan's stomach rumbled. One ham baguette, a small slice of fruitcake and a cup of coffee had not been enough for Stefan. So, by chance he'd managed to secure an extra baguette from the stewardess by employing what he mistook for charm. Looking around as he ate, he could see only Ana was awake. He peered out of the window. The short flight was nearly over, they were coming into land at Munich Airport.

***

Inside the terminal building, everything was soaked in dazzling white light. They passed a bewildering array of shops on the busy concourse, as airport officials chaperoned them directly to Gate H30 for the waiting Lufthansa Flight LH 2506 to Manchester. Their departure was on time, and after just over an hour into the flight, Ana heard the tone of the engine fall away as the Canadair 100 began to lose altitude. Looking out of the window, she could see a maze of yellow and white lights far below. Mile after mile of straight, bold white lines criss-crossed the city of Manchester, while others arched out in vast curves to disappear below the dark horizon. Brightly lit tower blocks poked up through the urban sprawl. Then the runway lights came into view, and their plane touched down. Ana was in England, it was three twenty, and soon everyone would be stopping for tea.

Chapter 47

Milo's flight touched down at Birmingham Airport from Geneva with the first flush of dawn. Roman had taken care that Milo entered England in possession of nothing that could connect him with Bosnia, the Communists, or to Roman himself. It was Friday, the twentieth of February. The Wast Water Inn in Cumbria was not expecting 'Angelo Moretti' until after lunch.

He walked over to the pay phone on the far side of the concourse and dialled the mobile phone number Roman had given him. His call was answered after the first ring.

'I'm here, come and get me.' He repeated the words precisely as Roman had instructed.

Milo replaced the receiver to find a man standing at his shoulder. He was the epitome of average, with an anonymous face like ten thousand others. The man nodded, turned to his left and walked towards the exit with Milo following. Neither of them spoke. They slalomed through the busy concourse, arriving at the short-stay car park adjoining Terminal One. Avoiding the lift, they climbed the four flights of concrete stairs to stand beside a dark blue Ford Focus on the fifth floor. Milo's companion was slightly out of breath. Milo opened the car's rear hatch and stowed his suitcase in the empty boot as the driver started the engine. Leaving the car park, they drove out of the airport complex in the direction of Birmingham city centre. Sitting in the passenger seat, Milo reflected on the contrast between the city of Birmingham and war-torn Sarajevo, but soon New Street Railway Station came into view and Milo's driver pulled over to the nearside curb, parked and then exited, leaving a map on the driver's seat. Neither goodbye nor thank you accompanied his departure.

Milo consulted the map and familiarised himself with the car's controls, then headed north out of Birmingham towards Ashbourne and the Peak District. Dropping down into the Goyt Valley, he stopped to re-examine the map his taciturn driver had left him. Circled loudly in red ink was a grid reference marking the car park at Errwood Reservoir and nine fifteen, the time of the morning rendezvous. The car park was less than three miles away.

Milo checked his watch on arrival. It wasn't quite nine o'clock. He had fifteen minutes to spare. Nettled by a sensation of vulnerability in the deserted car park, Milo left the car, and walked east to reach the calm of Errwood Reservoir. Rows of jaded trees stood black and stark, their gnarled branches stretching skywards like the fingers of a drowning man. Suddenly something unseen clattered noisily in the bushes behind him. Milo's eyes searched for a fight, but the only adversary was a blackbird startled by his arrival. He made his way back to the car park to find a black BMW parked next to his Ford Focus. It was nine fifteen, exactly. He opened the boot of the BMW and took out a heavy red suitcase, which he placed with his own in the boot of the Ford Focus. Then Milo drove out of the car park heading south-east to his next rendezvous in Buxton.

**

He parked the car at the far end of Buxton Station and walked in the direction of the platform. Crossing over the railway footbridge, he paused as if to check his watch as he observed those waiting on both sides of the track. It was five minutes to ten. Three middle-aged women chatted on the station platform. None were equipped with anything more intimidating than a shopping bag, while a young mother on a nearby seat waited with her son. The remaining passengers were teenagers. There were six of them, all were carrying sports bags, and decked out in tracksuits. One held a football.

An overture of squealing brakes accompanied the arrival of the train, and a number of passengers disembarked and scurried towards the exit. As those waiting boarded the train and challenged for the few remaining seats, Milo entered the first carriage. Once on board he continued through the three-carriage train, then left from the final carriage, stepping out onto the empty platform as the train moved off, leaving the station silent and abandoned. Satisfied he'd not been followed, he re-crossed the footbridge to the station car park, where Helmut Jorgen was standing by the Ford Focus. He was reading Der Spiegel. The time was ten o'clock.

**

Helmut, as German protocol demanded, was precisely on time. Helmut had arrived with his driver in the Mercedes Benz that Milo could see nearby. He and Helmut shared a mutual respect that went back to 1992, when Helmut supplied German rifles to Milo for the Serbian snipers. Milo unlocked the car and they both climbed in. Milo drove north out of Buxton on the A6, shadowed by Helmut's Mercedes Benz, to ensure they were not followed. At Fairfield Common, they parked in a small, secluded lay-by just off the main road.

'So, to business,' announced Helmut. 'I now have available everything you requested. All is arranged just as we agreed. I will deliver the munitions to the Zetra Arena in Sarajevo on the agreed date. I give you my word.'

Without warning, Milo turned and deftly made a grab for something on the back seat of the car. He showed no trace of his intentions. Milo saw a look of horror flash across Helmut's face, then waited as Helmut's heartbeat returned to normal. Milo recovered his jacket and unzipped the inner lining to remove a thick wad of U.S. Treasury Bonds that had been packed in the red suitcase, as Helmut's heartbeat slowly returned to normal.

'It is the amount we agreed. There is no need to count it.'

'Thank you so much,' said Helmut. Then on his signal the Mercedes Benz pulled up close by. 'May your God be with you,' he said as he opened the door to leave.

'And yours with you,' said Milo.

Milo drove out of the car park, north towards the A6 and the Wast Water Inn. He would arrive before the night drew in. Everything was going to plan.

Chapter 48
Wast Water Inn
Cumbria

Ted Baker descended the stairs, straightening a couple of pictures on the wall as he went. He tugged up his slacks. They'd become loose since he'd lost weight on his diet. Since his fifty-seventh birthday, Ted had worked hard on his fitness, after there'd been a veiled threat to retire him from Wasdale Mountain Rescue. Despite his weight at the time, his position had never been in doubt. Ted was the team's most experienced climber and an accomplished medic.

Thursday night had not been particularly busy. There'd been five or six regulars in the bar from nearby farms and cottages, a handful of residents who were staying at the Inn and a dozen or so walkers and climbers. During the week, the car parks around the shores of Wast Water stood almost empty, the few cars reminiscent of dinghies washed up on a deserted beach.

Ted made his way through the bar towards hotel reception.

'Good morning Rachel, is everything okay?' Ted asked.

'Everything's fine,' she replied. 'You haven't forgotten I'll be leaving straight after lunch today? I'm bridesmaid at my sister's wedding in Keswick tomorrow.'

'Course not, I'm all organised, just take me through the weekend room reservations before you go.'

Eleven of the Inn's twelve rooms were already booked. Two rooms were booked for Friday night only, regulars and Ted's climbing partners for Chamonix. Nine rooms were booked until Sunday night and one single room booked for Friday and Saturday.

'Not bad for this time of year, not bad at all,' said Ted.

'I won't see you now before Monday, so keep up with your training.'

'No worries, my training is going really well. I'll be running down to Wasdale Hall as usual in the morning, come rain or shine and then spend an hour on the weights.'

'Body Magic, that's what we call it at Slimmer's World. I'm pleased your running is helping. It certainly gives the regulars a laugh.'

Ted laughed out loud.

'Just give me their names and I'll ban them.'

A car horn sounded outside. Ted sauntered out into the clear crisp morning air to meet the postman.

'How's it going Ben?'

'Decidedly cooler,' Ben handed Ted the post. 'Cold enough for snow,' he added before jumping in his van and heading back towards Nether Wasdale.

***

Milo looked out of the window of his room in the Wast Water Inn. He could see across Wasdale to the mountains of the Scafell Pike Massif. The footpath to Sty Head was clearly visible. The path threaded its way intricately up the southern flank of Kirk Fell and Great Gable like some grey prehistoric worm. Milo made himself a cup of coffee before unpacking his belongings. He thought through his plans for the next day, his excitement mounting. Tomorrow would be an eventful day. Game changing. After dinner he'd have an early night. He was unsure when his next chance to sleep would come.

Chapter 49

Luciano Magiera looked up at the grandfather clock at the top of the staircase. The time was twenty-five minutes to midnight and there was still much to do. Luciano's day had begun at five on the morning of the twentieth of February, which was unusual for this eminent Front of House Manager. But then it was unusual to have some of the most influential politicians and financiers of the Western world descend on Kermincham Hall, not to mention the world's media. Three housemaids completed the dusting in the Great Hall, as Luciano put the finishing touches to the floral arrangements. He inspected their work, nodded his approval to the housemaids, and then went to check on reception.

Chapter 50

The Lufthansa flight from Munich landed into a freshening breeze at Manchester Airport. Once inside the terminal building Stefan followed Leo along the busy concourse. Stefan thought he was back in Munich, so alike were the design of the two airports and their facilities. Officials of the Bosnian Embassy in London met the party in the arrival hall of Terminal One and took them to their waiting cars. Within minutes they were out of the airport on their way to Kermincham Hall. Ana and Boris shared Josip Budach's Mercedes E500 with Olga. Georg followed behind with Leo and Stefan in the Mercedes ML350 driven by Savo, much to the annoyance of Stefan. Six more cars carried the rest of the delegates, including members from the Bosnian Embassy.

Bright streetlights penetrated the darkness, as they headed away from the airport towards the M6. Ana gazed out of the window, as their Mercedes Benz drove through the sprawling urban jungle. She watched as houses and office blocks glided by. One thing they all shared played on her mind. None of the buildings carried the scars of war.

The traffic was light along their route and after leaving the M6 motorway, they made good progress on the A66 towards Keswick. Passing the village of Troutbeck on the old Roman road, the silhouette of the Cumbrian Mountains came into view over to the west, and then out of nowhere the outline of a mountain summit rose up out of the gathering dusk.

'Is that Scafell Pike?' Boris enquired. 'The one you're going to climb?'

'No,' replied Ana. 'That's Blencathra. You won't be able to see Scafell Pike from here. It's southwest of Derwent Water and Keswick.'

Her father smiled and took her hand in his. Then as the time approached ten minutes to six, the cars pulled into the drive of Kermincham Hall. Boris looked at his watch. They were precisely on time.

Luciano Magiera waited at the top of steps and greeted them as they arrived in front of the magnificent hall and disgorged a mountain of luggage. A drove of scurrying porters hurried in the direction of the pile of suitcases. As Ana entered the lobby, her eyes dwelt on the wide marble staircase that wound its way between ornate balustrades. Gold brocade covered the walls, on which portraits of former owners hung—High Sheriffs, Lord Lieutenants, Dukes and Duchesses, and their descendants. Overhead hung a beautiful chandelier, from which a thousand rainbows cascaded, sending rills of light to every corner of the lobby. As tired delegates besieged the reception desk, Luciano's experience told, and guests were quickly shown to their rooms. Leo and Olga waited patiently for their room key with Ana and Boris, as the throng buzzed around them. Josip Budach, the driver of the second diplomatic car, squeezed past Leo and Ana and approached Olga holding a small leather case.

'Excuse me, I think you must have left this in the car.' He stepped forward and handed Olga the case.

'Oh sorry, thank you very much,' she apologised.

***

Stefan immersed himself in the surroundings. They were the embodiment of his dreams. He received his key from the receptionist behind the desk, as a young woman dressed in a pale blue blouse and a smart grey business suit approached him. Stefan thought the suit complemented her hair colour and complexion perfectly.

'Can I show you to your room sir?' she enquired, smiling radiantly.

There was a message in her smile that Stefan was unable to decipher.

'I'm Julie Hardy. I will be on hand throughout your stay, to be of assistance in any way I can.'

Stefan's eyes followed her as they took the lift and then walked to his room.

'Here we are, sir.' She pushed open the door of Stefan's first-floor room. Stefan began to feel completely at home. 'Your luggage will be with you shortly. Will that be all sir?' she enquired.

Stefan didn't answer. He was deep in thought.

***

'Good evening sir, good evening, madam.' Luciano draped a heavy Italian accent over his welcome, especially on the word "madam". 'I trust your journey was not too tiring. Here are your keys, two adjoining suites on the first floor.'

A porter in his late teens stepped forward to escort Ana and her father to their rooms. The young man unlocked the door to Ana's bedroom and went in.

'Is everything okay? Will you be able to find everything?'

'Yes, at least I think so, but I'm not sure what should be in here.'

He showed Ana and her father around the room and the facilities, smiled and left.

'I'll be fine now, Dad. You look tired. Why don't you go to your room?' said Ana.

Boris kissed her on the cheek.

'All right, if you're sure you'll be okay. I'll see you in half an hour, and we'll have a late tea in my room.'

Ana hung her new clothes in the wardrobe and explored the dressing table drawers, before neatly arranging her new lingerie in them. Next, she investigated the lotions in the bathroom, before meeting her father in his room for tea.

When she returned to her bedroom, she noticed the flowers on a side table near the door. She caressed the purple and gold petals as she held the small bouquet in the palm of her hand. She was back in Babonavic, back in the graveyard with the rain lashing down. The winter pansies were a sad reminder of that cold and painful day. She looked around the room, as if her mother should be there, and as she closed her eyes to sleep that night, she saw her mother's face.

Chapter 51

Tom Kennedy wiped his feet on the mat, pushed open the door and walked into the kitchen.

'Hi, you're back early from college.' His mother opened the oven door and took out a tray of freshly baked flapjack.

'Things to do, you know.'

'I know. Your dad was up till one o'clock this morning sorting out his rucksack. He tells me you're planning the route for this weekend, is that right?'

'Yes, I can't afford to make mistakes, and I still need to pack my rucksack. I didn't get time last night, I had to finish some history homework. Is that our flapjack you're baking? It doesn't look enough.'

'That's the second tray. The other tray is cooling over there on the worktop.'

Tom breathed a sigh of relief.

'I'll just take a slice for quality control purposes,' he said as he made his exit and headed for his room.

Tom sat cross-legged on the bedroom floor and looked up at the framed poster his father had given to him a month ago on his sixteenth birthday. He read it out, half under his breath.

'The Seven Ps, proper planning and preparation, prevents piss poor performance.'

He lay out the two Ordnance Survey maps of the Lake District on the floor, as he devoured his flapjack, showering Scafell Pike with crumbs. He located Wasdale Head and followed the path up Great Gable, and then down to Sty Head on the way to their overnight campsite at Hollow Stones. Then he traced their return route back to Wasdale Head. They would reach the Inn on the second day just as darkness was falling. Tom rechecked the route. He knew he couldn't afford any errors. As the scion of the family, he was painfully aware of his father and grandfather's achievements, and he knew a mother's love could never be a substitute for a father's pride.

Tom took out the list of equipment for the weekend climb and ticked off each item as he packed it in his rucksack. Then he went down into the kitchen.

'Is this our food?' he asked.

'Yes. Your father always jokes I cater for twelve climbers, not just for the two of you.'

'There hardly looks enough, are you sure it's all here?'

Returning to his room, he finished packing his rucksack and took it downstairs. Satisfied he'd delivered against the requirements of the seven Ps, he could now look forward to the two-day climb, and to seeing his godfather, Ted Baker, at the Wast Water Inn.

Dan arrived home at seven, showered and changed before sitting down to dinner with Jane and Tom.

'How was your day?' he enquired.

'Fine,' replied Jane, 'I spoke to Alice, she and a few others are coming for a girl's night in tomorrow. It's her birthday on Wednesday.'

'Sounds good,' said Dan.

With dinner over and their equipment on board the Range Rover, Dan and Tom were ready to leave.

'Stay safe, take care of each other.' Jane held Dan close.

'No problem, we'll be just fine.'

Dan kissed her hard on the lips.

'Now your turn, come here you.'

Jane kissed Tom and then slowly released him.

'We'll be fine, Mum, see you Sunday.'

***

They negotiated the narrow lanes of Cheshire and were soon travelling north up the M6, before heading west to Duddon Bridge, then along the maze of single-track lanes to Eskdale and finally down into Wasdale. The road dropped down sharply from High Birkhow, shrugging off the last vestiges of light pollution as they caught their first glimpse of Wast Water and The Screes. Tom felt a shiver down his spine, even though he had witnessed this scene a hundred times before.

'There are The Screes,' whispered Dan reverentially.

Through the shimmering lunar hue, they could see the near vertical screes as they slashed deep into the black icy waters, to whatever lay below. They followed the lakeside road north before arriving at the Wast Water Inn and sanctuary. It was ten-thirty and the number of customers in the Inn had dwindled. Ted came around from behind the bar and greeted them both. They had supper. Tom was starving, but he always was. Then after checking the weather forecast together, they were both in bed by eleven o'clock.

Tom flopped down on the big double bed, gazing up at the low ivory ceiling. He lay awake anticipating the climb, ritually searching for an omen that foretold his failure, until he drifted into sleep.

Chapter 52

Milo searched for sleep, tossing and turning, until sleep found him. Then as night receded and dawn broke over Wasdale Head, he felt the unbearable weight of a man's body crushing down on him, forcing him into the earth. Straining every muscle, he tried to rise from his makeshift grave, but he was not strong enough. He fought to pull himself free, clawing at the earth that entombed him. But he couldn't move. The body of a man pinned him down. Then he saw the blood. Blood covered his hands and face. Confusion and panic took hold of him, then he realised it was not his blood. He felt no pain. Milo struggled to escape, as the earth began to fill his mouth and nostrils. He couldn't breathe. Finally, he twisted and turned beneath the lifeless body until he broke free, to wipe the bloodied earth from his face.

Milo turned on the bedside light as he battled to reconfigure the real world. He sat bolt upright, trying to comprehend his recurring nightmare, before shadows swept it away.

Chapter 53

Ana woke in the early hours of a new day, anxious to start her adventure in England. She sprawled out on the four-poster bed waiting for dawn to break. After what seemed an eternity, she could wait no longer, and jumped out of bed to hurry over to the window at the far side of the room. The ghost of a pale moon looked down from an empty sky. Its eerie presence radiated a soft glow over the wooded grounds that encircled the hall. In the distance, Ana glimpsed a man standing sentinel-like in the trees, his body a mere shadow in the moonlight, but when she looked again, the shadow melted and was gone.

***

Messengermire Woods were now behind him. Only the dirge of the wind in the treetops broke the silence. Satisfied the mountains to the north held no threat, Leo returned to Kermincham Hall through a service door in the northeast prospect to avoid security. He moved silently, making a mental note of entrances and escape routes, as the guests slept in the stillness of the early hours. After the failed sabotage attempt in Sarajevo, Leo tried to assess from where the next attack might come and how best to counter it. He would not get a second chance.

***

Ana retreated to the comfort of her bed, drifting in and out of sleep, then a noise from outside her bedroom disturbed her. Instantly, Ana was wide-awake. She sat up, trying to detect any repetition of the slightest sound. Had she been dreaming? Her room was at the end of a long blind corridor. No one would be passing. At first, there was nothing, then she heard footsteps. She wouldn't hide. Not this time. She'd made a promise to her mother. Her fingers dwelt for a moment on the door handle. Then with a violent jerk she wrenched open the door to confront her adversary face to face. She stepped out from the safety of her room and scrutinised the dimly lit corridor as it disappeared around the corner en route to the lift and the stairwell. There was no one. Unfazed, Ana returned to her room. She'd kept her promise, and as dawn broke, she prepared for her great adventure.

Chapter 54

Dan and Tom Kennedy came down for breakfast. They chose a table with views towards Wast Water.

'Are we okay for time?' asked Tom.

'I think so. We should be able to leave before eight-thirty, if your rucksack is packed?'

'Yes. Everything's packed, my new crampons and ice axe, rope and harness. I have the stove, food and water. We have two torches. You have the new mountain tent and the sleeping bags. We each have a full load of around fifty pounds for the two days.'

'The plan is to put the new equipment to the test before we go to Chamonix with Ted,' said Dan.

Tom knew the real test would be of him. He was aware of an unspoken expectation that he would take over the family business, as his father had before him. Climbing was a mere overture to the rest of his life, a precursor to the test that lay ahead, waiting.

Dan finished his breakfast as Tom attacked the toast.

'An army marches on its stomach,' announced Tom through a mouth full of toast and marmalade.

'If that's the case you should go far,' said his father.

Ted came in from the kitchen.

'You nearly ready for the off?' he enquired.

'Just about,' replied Dan. 'Tom just wants to finish his second round of toast, and then we're ready. We don't call him Hovis for nothing, you know.'

'I wish I was coming with you. The weather forecast looks good and my training is going really well, but it's my weekend on. I'll be ready for Chamonix though, you'll see.'

'We know you will,' said Dan.

Chapter 55

Leo joined Stefan in Kermincham's Great Hall for breakfast at seven-thirty. Stefan had begun with a bowl of porridge and was now finishing off his third, and Leo hoped, his final bowl. Boris joined them, as Leo attempted to prevent Stefan from ordering a fourth bowl.

'Good morning Leo, I trust you slept well?' said Boris.

'The toast,' said Stefan thoughtfully. 'I'll just have some toast.'

'I slept really well,' replied Leo, trying to ignore Stefan, who had attracted the attention of a waiter. Stefan ordered toast while Boris ordered a full English breakfast.

'You should have had the porridge,' suggested Stefan.

'I doubt if there's any left,' said Leo dryly.

Stefan's toast came just as Georg arrived.

'May I join you?' he asked.

'But of course,' said Boris.

Stefan excused himself and made his way out of the restaurant. The toast was left untouched. Stefan had been looking forward to the toast, but not that much. He was anxious to put as much distance between him and Georg as he could.

'Stefan need not have left,' said Georg dolefully. 'I'm not going to talk business. All the arrangements have been made.'

Chapter 56

Olga finished packing her rucksack, looked round the room one last time, then stepped purposefully out into the corridor. Arriving at reception, she found Julie Hardy and the other receptionist busy with new arrivals. Luciano was speaking on the telephone, so she waited for him to finish.

'Good morning madam, how may I help you?' Luciano intoned, exuding charm.

'Good morning, Luciano, a car has been arranged to take Ana Poborski and myself to Seathwaite. It needs to arrive at eight-thirty as agreed. We are climbing Scafell Pike from Seathwaite and must start our climb no later than nine o'clock. I believe our driver is to be Josip Budach.'

'I understand completely. Excuse me for a moment while I check the driver's logbook for Josip.' Luciano retrieved the logbook from the back office, then ran his finger down the page of bookings. 'Ah yes, here it is, everything is in order, be assured your car and Josip will be ready to leave at eight-thirty.'

***

Kermincham Hall reverberated with a carnival atmosphere that morning. There was a buzz of excitement that bubbled along the corridors, spilling over into the Great Hall, as the delegates met over breakfast and old acquaintances were renewed. The hard work of negotiating the agreement had taken place in Sarajevo and in the board rooms of financial institutions across the world. Now the signing ceremony was for media manipulation, and a celebration of a job well done.

***

Ana stood up from the table and waved as Olga entered the Bassenthwaite Restaurant, a huge log fire crackling in the grate. Ana had already ordered her breakfast.

'Good morning Ana, I hope you slept well after the flight?'

'Yes, I slept really well, though I did wake up rather early.'

'We need to leave directly we've had our breakfast,' said Olga. 'Will you be ready?'

'Yes, I'm so looking forward to this climb.'

'Me too, we're unlikely to get another chance to climb the highest mountain in England. We need to make the most of it. Eat well,' advised Olga, keeping one eye on her watch. 'We have a demanding day ahead of us.'

***

Boris enjoyed a hearty breakfast in the company of Georg and Leo, and at eight-twenty, all three left the Great Hall to go their separate ways. As a matter of protocol, Georg intended to introduce himself to the most influential of the delegates. The American Ambassador to the European Union, Joe Brown, was high on his list, and of course Ivan Bobic, the Bosnian Ambassador to the UK, was Georg's priority. On checking with reception, Georg was informed by Luciano of the delayed arrival of Ivan Bobic. He had been detained on important business and would not arrive until later that morning. Boris went to find Ana and Olga to see them off. Leo disappeared into a bright new day.

Boris spotted Ana and Olga leaving the restaurant.

'Are you ready to go?' he asked Ana.

'Almost, we have our lunch box to collect from reception, then we'll be leaving.'

'Have you any idea what time you'll be back? You know, just a rough idea?'

'I'm not really sure, but it won't be before four, perhaps later.'

Boris took out his diary and checked his itinerary for the day.

'I'm in a meeting with officials from the Consortium and Herr Becker at four, so try and make it earlier. That is if you can?'

'Well that's unlikely, but we'll try.'

Ana looked across to Olga, who smiled and nodded back.

'Yes, we'll try,' she said, but Boris thought Olga sounded doubtful.

'What about later?' asked Boris.

'Well by the time I recover from the climb and have a shower, it will be at least five o'clock, maybe six.'

'I'm meeting Ivan Bobic, at five thirty, for drinks. It's something Georg has arranged. I daren't miss that. You haven't forgotten I'll be at the official dinner from about eight o'clock this evening?'

'No, I haven't forgotten.'

'I'll reserve a table for you and Olga, for eight o'clock, in the Bassenthwaite Restaurant, but I won't be able to join you. Is that all right?'

'Yes, that will be fine. Look, don't worry about me. We'll catch up with each other sometime during the evening. That's if I don't just crash out when I get back. If I do, I'll see you in the morning.'

Boris walked with them to reception, where they both collected their lunch boxes, mountain jackets and rucksacks from the porter's office. The porter helped Ana with her rucksack and offered to help Olga with hers.

'No thank you,' Olga declined. 'I can manage.'

'Oh, and don't forget your security pass, Ana, or you may not get back in,' Boris laughed.

'Yes, I have my security pass.'

'Me too,' added Olga.

Boris gave Ana a great big hug.

'Take care, Ana. You too, Olga,' he said.

'No problem, we'll be fine,' said Olga. 'I've never been known to fail,' she added.

Chapter 57

Monsignor Bernarez clicked open his email and shifted the cursor down the list of messages that populated the in box. Highlighting the name Bleiburg 1945, he left clicked the mouse and smiled. Bleiburg was in position at Kermincham Hall and had made contact with his Longa Manus and Charles Borromeo. He was awaiting further orders.

Chapter 58

Dan came out of the Wast Water Inn, and clearing his mind of incidentals, focused on the first day's climbing. He knew the route well enough, having climbed it several times before, but no route was ever the same, as changing weather conditions meant the demands on a climber varied every time. He drank in the scene, raising his eyes to the mountains. Tom joined his father and they hoisted their rucksacks on to their backs, as Ted came out to wish them luck.

'We'll see you Sunday evening,' said Dan, adjusting the waistband on his rucksack with a grunt.

'Any idea what time?' enquired Ted.

'No later than four, five at the most,' was Dan's reply.

Tom added his goodbye, and at twenty-five minutes past eight they headed northeast through the small, stone-walled fields that surrounded Wasdale Head. The aperitif to Tom's Alpine expedition began with a familiar question rattling around his head. *Would he be good enough?*

Leaving the Inn, a chorus line of crows moved stealthily across one corner of the field, harvesting insects to serve up a scrawny early morning snack. Sheep were everywhere, brought down from the mountains with the onset of winter. Leaving the farm lane at Burnthwaite, they joined the Moses Trod path, as the sun radiated a pale watery light that surrendered no warmth. For a while they followed the course of Lingmell Beck as it tumbled down the rocky mountainside, flooding and then escaping from small alluvial pools. After crossing a small tributary and heading north towards Beckhead, they steadily gained altitude. As the terrain steepened, Tom engaged 'Yak' mode. He slowed down, matching his stride pattern to his breathing. Dan adopted the same technique and they kept pace with each other, stride for stride as they ascended Great Gable. Ahead, the narrow track carved its way up the shifting scree, and as their route became more exposed, they felt the bite of the raw north wind as it raced down from Kirk Fell.

'Getting draughty,' called Dan.

'Certainly is,' shouted Tom in reply. 'What's happened to all our blue sky?'

Chapter 59

At eight thirty Josip Budach arrived driving the Embassy car and Ana and Olga climbed into the Mercedes E500 saloon. Boris waved as it pulled away from the splendid portico of Kermincham Hall and disappeared down the long, tree-lined drive. He waved long after he knew Ana could no longer see him, but something told him she knew he was still there, still waving. He stood for a moment in deep thought, taking in the view of Bassenthwaite Lake and Skiddaw Mountain in the distance. As he made his way back to rehearse his speech, he met Bernadeta. Most of the male delegates had relinquished their workaday pinstripes for new tailored business suits, whereas Bernadeta still wore her customary office clothes.

'Hello Bernadeta, I didn't see you at breakfast.'

'No, I missed breakfast. I was helping Herr Becker prepare his speech for tomorrow. I'm going for a coffee now; would you like to join me?'

'That would be really nice,' said Boris. 'I have a little time before the Consortium meeting at nine fifteen.'

'How's your speech going'? asked Bernadeta.

'I'm on my way to go over it now.'

'Would you like me to go through it with you later, I could if that would help?'

'No, no I could not possibly impose. I'm sure Herr Becker has work that is far more important.'

Apparently, Herr Becker did not have work that was more important, at least not according to Bernadeta, and Boris in the end decided to impose.

Chapter 60

The sun shone high above Scafell Pike and Lingmell Crag, shedding its cold silver light down the mountainsides and into Wasdale Head. Milo had been up just before dawn. He unpacked the suitcase he'd collected from the BMW and laid the contents on the bed. He reassembled the Kalashnikov and cradled it in the palms of both hands, welcoming the return of an old and trusted friend. He picked up the Glock 17 pistol. He was familiar with the name Glock but had never had the chance to use one until now. It had a nine-millimetre calibre and a magazine capacity of seventeen rounds. The weapon, solid yet light, was comfortable to hold. Milo checked out its finer points, beginning to like it. Next he examined the rest of the suitcase's contents. There was a rucksack, along with three hundred rounds of ammunition for the Kalashnikov and two hundred rounds for the Glock. A smug smile washed over Milo's face, accentuating his scar. He considered there was more than enough ammunition to kill all the inhabitants of Wasdale Head and most of the tourists, but he reminded himself he was not here for fun, he was here on business.

Milo opened the brown envelope that accompanied the formidable arsenal. There was a compass and a sheet of notepaper, on which in scrawly handwriting, appeared a grid reference together with the name 'Timbersbrook Cottage,' and today's date, Saturday the twenty first of February. A Yale key was securely taped to the note paper. Finally, there was an Ordnance Survey map. He opened up the map to show Wasdale Head and the full length of Wast Water. He located Timbersbrook Cottage using the grid reference. He would pay a visit to the cottage after breakfast.

Milo chose a corner table facing the door in the dining room, a position from which he could best defend himself if danger threatened. The waitress brought his meal, and he settled down to enjoy a leisurely breakfast. He finished off the toast, drank down the last of his coffee, and returned to his room. He consulted the map again, this time in minute detail. The obvious route to Timbersbrook Cottage was south down the single-track road along the west shore of Wast Water. Milo chose instead a narrow, indistinct thread of a path, barely visible from the road that traced a thin line across the foot of The Screes. The path started at Keeperswood, on the east side of Wast Water, before emerging into the trees at Eastwaite.

From here, Milo's path led westward for little more than a mile to Timbersbrook and the safe house. Milo scrutinised the topography on either side of his route for points that could present danger, as well as for escape routes. The farm at Wasdale Head was his main concern, but it could be avoided by taking a more easterly route if detection threatened. Escape to the west presented a problem, as the grey turbid waters of Wast Water, the deepest lake in England, formed an aqueous divide for most of his route, its deepest point being below sea level.

Milo loaded the Glock and packed it in the rucksack. The map and compass followed. Then trembling with anticipation, he put the penknife he'd owned since a boy, into the pocket of his mountain jacket and zipped it up. He felt the intoxication of war flooding back. Milo couldn't wait for the action to begin. He whistled as he finished fastening his rucksack, and as he left his room for breakfast, he began to sing the chorus of his favourite Ray Charles. song.   'Let's get together and let the good times roll.' Milo loved Ray Charles.

Chapter 61

The Mercedes Benz reached the end of the drive and squeezed into the narrow lane that led from Kermincham Hall. Ana looked out of the window as they headed south. The narrow road twisted and turned, hugged between high bare hedgerows, to arrive at the A66. Now they travelled south to Keswick, the old Cumbrian market town on the shore of Derwent Water.

'The guidebook we were given by Mr Komikosovitch says Keswick is a great place to shop,' announced Ana. 'I'd like to go there tomorrow morning, would you come with me?' she asked Olga.

'Sounds like a great idea. There's so much I want to buy while I'm in England. I wouldn't miss a chance like that. So that's confirmed then.'

The car made its way through the cobbled streets of Keswick, past The Moot Hall and south along the east side of Derwent Water. Ana pressed her face to the car window, as dark mountains and cathedral-like cliffs rose all around them. They reached the end of the lake and skirted round the hamlet of Grange, where the mountains tumbled down to the narrow road, as it squirmed into the northern end of Borrowdale.

'It's very beautiful,' said Ana.

Olga smiled and nodded in agreement. Turning left down a single-track road before the tiny village of Seatoller, the driver made his way to Seathwaite. He pulled over to the side of the lane and parked on the narrow strip of muddy earth that served as a lay-by. Then leaving the car they walked towards Seathwaite Farm.

'This is it,' announced the driver as Olga consulted her map. 'This is the place you asked to be dropped off.'

'Yes, I can see it on the map, this is perfect, thank you.'

'I'll come back here and pick you up, you can phone from there.'

Josip pointed to a red telephone box opposite the farm buildings. 'Do you have the number for Kermincham Hall?'

'Yes, I do,' said Ana. 'Can I phone? I've always wanted to use a telephone box like that.'

'You may need to. Mobile phones sometimes struggle to find a signal in the mountains. I'll see you later.'

Ana stared at the iconic bright red telephone box and hoped she'd be the one to make the call that evening. She checked her watch. It was nine o'clock.

'Scafell Pike, by the Corridor Route, takes three to three and a half hours in ascent and no more than two and a half hours in descent,' Olga announced didactically. 'We should have no difficulty in completing the climb in that time. Our bearing is one hundred and eighty degrees south. Are you ready to go?'

Olga looked up from reading her map to find Ana already on her way towards Scafell Pike. Olga followed, making her way past the neat farmhouse and through the farmyard, where cattle stood ruminating in their rickety pens. Two black crows hung on the wind high above the farm, weaving a graceful tango across the sky.

Ana, bedecked in her birthday fleece, new hat, and mountain jacket, was glad of the warmth they provided. She pulled her hat down over her ears.

***

They followed the valley as it rolled south, protected from the worst of the icy blast by Base Brown to the west, to arrive at Stockley Bridge, a beautiful stone arch perched on enormous boulders. The beck from Grains Gill thundered beneath it. They paused, taking in the views down the valley to Seathwaite. Over to the east, evil-looking clouds scurried by, wiping the sun from the sky. As Olga and Ana moved off, a sprinkle of snowflakes bustled down the gill, from the saddle at Styhead. It passed in seconds and was almost forgotten. Heading west, they climbed steadily to reach Greenhow Knott and Taylor Gill Force, as silence descended. From here, Olga took a compass bearing to a point at the north end of Styhead Tarn, which nestled below Great Gable. All around, black rock rent the earth, thrusting jagged spires towards the sky.

'We continue on 222 degrees until we reach Styhead Tarn,' she called to Ana, as the wind suddenly increased in ferocity.

'It's now ten-thirty,' shouted Ana. 'How are we doing for time?'

'Okay,' replied Olga checking her watch. 'Perhaps a little slower than I'd planned, but okay.'

Chapter 62

After breakfast, Milo slipped out of the Wast Water Inn and into the nearby woods. He crossed the fields, to join a green lane leading south to the ribbon of road that drilled its way down Wasdale. In a clump of silver birch trees, he waited to ensure the road was clear before crossing. Then skirting the campsite, a faded sign proclaiming it closed until Easter, he headed southwest towards Keeperswood. Wasdale Head Farm came next, his eyes scanning the outbuildings as he made for the path that would take him to Timbersbrook. Milo crossed the wooden footbridge as the sparkling waters danced below and black clouds raced across the mountaintops. He zipped his jacket up, to keep out the biting wind. Emerging from a lakeside spinney, The Screes came into view. They were barren and unforgiving.

Milo negotiated the skinny path as it clung to the steep scree slopes in a most precarious way. Nothing grew. It was a desolate, god-forsaken place. Beyond The Screes, the terrain softened, and a few scrubby trees fought an endless battle for survival. The narrow path wormed its way towards the woods, slitting open the waist-high swathes of weather-beaten bracken. A small, black-faced sheep stood defiantly on the path in front of Milo, blocking his way. No fear showed in its eyes, only a mild curiosity. Milo smiled, amused at this display of disrespect. He took out the Glock and pointed the gun at the little black face, then Milo watched as it trotted off to disappear into the bracken, its insolence unpunished.

Leaving the hamlet of Easthwaite, the outline of Timbersbrook Cottage emerged through a stand of beech trees north of Flass Tarn. He watched the cottage for some time before judging it was safe to approach. Taking advantage of the available cover, he approached the cottage with caution and arrived at the front door. He took out the Yale key and held his breath as he slid it into the lock. Then turning it quickly, he pushed open the door. He stood just inside the low oak doorway, listening, waiting for any sound. Silence drowned the musty rooms and Milo breathed again. He walked through the sitting room and into the kitchen. There was no one there. He checked the bedroom. It was empty. The cottage was deserted, and Milo relaxed.

'Good morning comrade.' The voice came from over his right shoulder. In an instant Milo turned, Glock held menacingly in his hand.

'Are you not pleased to see me?' asked Roman as he stepped out from behind a heavy curtain that screened a low door.

Chapter 63

Tom stopped to change his hat and gloves for warmer ones, and Dan did the same. When they started off, a scatter of snow appeared out of nowhere. It didn't last long, perhaps a minute, two at the most, but it changed the complexion of the climb completely.

'This is a bit unexpected,' said Tom. 'But it could get interesting.'

'I hope so, this needs to be a real test,' was Dan's response. 'So much for this morning's weather forecast.'

The path cut its way between towering crags towards the summit of Great Gable, as storm clouds queued to bombard the peak, which was fast disappearing behind a shroud of black. It was shortly after ten minutes to eleven when Dan and Tom breached the skyline, and within minutes they reached the summit. The wind was colder here, and their arrival was welcomed by a flurry of snow, harder this time, whipped up by the wind as it scoured the mountaintop. It lasted longer too, five or maybe even ten minutes. The two climbers lost no time in vacating their lofty perch and descended to the southeast. Passing Raven Crag, the snow began to fall, not as wildly as on the summit, but it lasted almost forty minutes and did not subside until they reached Sty Head at eleven forty-two.

Chapter 64

Georg Komikosovitch approached the full-length mirror again, this time from a slightly different angle. He stood for a moment, studying the reflection that stared back at him. His mother had always told him he was no picture. Dressed in the blue business suit he'd bought for the occasion, he thought at best he looked okay. The *piéce de résistance* was his new viridian tie. He adjusted it again for the third time to ensure perfect symmetry. At last he decided he would do, it was not wise to look too smart, or appear too clever, not on this type of operation. As a child, he'd survived an austere and pious life, to achieve high office. He knew his father and grandfather would be proud of him. Finally, he polished his spectacles until they sparkled and after checking that everything in his room was just so, he made his way downstairs to the Georgian Suite.

***

Boris was late for lunch. The meeting with the principal members of the Consortium had gone on much longer than planned. He knocked on Leo's door just before five minutes past twelve, but there was no reply. Boris joined Stefan as he waited for the lift.

'We're late,' Stefan announced.

'I know,' said Boris. 'Georg won't like that. He won't like it at all.'

As they left the lift on the ground floor, Stefan saw Bernadeta coming towards them. At first, he did not recognise her. A very smart tailored suit that was both appropriate for the occasion and very fetching, had replaced her drab office garb. A scalloped blouse that tantalisingly exposed an emerging cleavage, complemented the cream suit. The hemline of the skirt revealed an exceptionally fine pair of legs. Bernadeta had taken advantage of Kermincham's beauty salon, her hair that had been long and brushed back, now bobbed gently on her shoulders. The fringe, short and spiky, revealed an attractive, delicate face that required little makeup apart from lipstick, which had been expertly applied. Stefan had never seen Bernadeta with lipstick on before.

'I think that's called sex on legs,' muttered Stefan, nodding in Bernadeta's direction.

'What was that?' said Boris who had not recognised Bernadeta.

Boris continued walking, as Stefan stopped to talk. Then realising he was on his own, Boris turned in search of Stefan and came face to face with Bernadeta.

'Bernadeta, I didn't recognise you. It's just that you look so different from this morning. You look fantastic.'

The words slipped out before he could stop them, but he didn't want to take them back. Bernadeta blushed and was hungry for more.

'Oh, thank you, thank you very much,' she said. 'I'm pleased you like it.'

Stefan walked on, leaving them in an invisible bubble of their own, as life zigzagged around them.

Chapter 65

At Styhead Tarn, Ana and Olga watched as fluffy snowflakes transformed the steely blackness of the mountains with a blanket of glistening white. Now on level ground, they quickly left the Tarn behind them to arrive at Styhead, as the storm gusted down from the north. After continuing west towards Sprinkling Tarn for four hundred meters, they turned south on the Corridor Route to Scafell Pike.

For the best part of an hour, they followed the path as it dodged and weaved to avoid the huge boulders that littered the mountainside. They passed Greta Gill in the shelter of Broad Crag as the wind dropped and they became enveloped in an eerie calm.

'I could do with some lunch now, if that's okay. This seems a good place,' suggested Ana.

'Yes, the wind has dropped. Are you okay to carry on after lunch?' asked Olga.

'Yes, I feel good. We should go on. We'll never get another chance to climb Scafell Pike.'

'Fine. I don't want to fail. I have experienced much worse conditions on winter climbs in Bosnia.'

With their lunch over, the two climbers followed the Corridor Route, as the wind, rising in strength flayed the mountaintops. Despite a cover of snow, they were able to follow the path by tracing the depression formed by thousands of boots that had climbed the route before them. As they claimed altitude, the snow became much deeper, concealing the direction their path took. In the eerie stillness Olga scrutinised the map, picking out their course, as head-down against the wind, she climbed through a curtain of snow. Then a piercing scream splintered the air.

'Stop!'

Ana's scream brought Olga to an abrupt halt, as she realised where her next footstep would have fallen. There was nothing there. Nothing but vertical blackness for one hundred and ten meters from which there would be no way back. Olga looked down into the abyss, took a step back and consulted the map.

'We have found Piers Gill,' she announced calmly.

It was forty-five minutes past twelve.

Chapter 66

The Georgian Suite was a large room with gilded windows looking out over the lawns to the west. Ornate curlicues worked their way elaborately across the lofty ceiling, terminating in the centre where a splendid chandelier glittered. Rich velvet drapes, secured neatly in place by golden holdbacks, towered from oak floor to ceiling, and beautiful flower arrangements bedecked the room. Georg was already on parade when Boris and Stefan arrived. He walked briskly over and welcomed them.

'I have been here since before eleven o'clock, to give me over an hour to ensure everything was in place and just so for our guests. Where's Leo, why is he not with you?'

Before either of them could reply, Georg disappeared to greet Herr Becker, who had arrived with Bernadeta. Herr Becker was the paradigm of the Teutonic culture he was so proud to represent.

'George is nothing if not thorough,' said Stefan. 'It must take him ages to tie his shoelaces.'

Joe Brown, the American Ambassador to the European Union, entered the room, accompanied by a chorus of aides. Joe Brown had played a crucial role in persuading US financiers to back the Consortium. He was here to ensure maximum world press coverage of the event. The US wanted to highlight the transition from Communism to Western style Capitalism. There was still no sign of Leo. Georg introduced Joe Brown to Boris and Stefan. The Ambassador looked every bit the all-American boy Stefan thought he should. He was tall, well over six feet and had to weigh in at over ninety kilos. He had a gentle face and wore a pair of rimless spectacles. He was unassuming and softly spoken as well as amazingly polite. Stefan's image of the all-too-loud, overly brash American took a dive. Accompanying Joe Brown was a mountain of a man, who Stefan guessed must be Joe Brown's minder. He ambled up to Stefan and shook his hand.

'Pleased to meet you, I'm Jon White,' the mountain said. He sat down on the three-seater sofa and offered Stefan a place.

'I'm with the US Diplomatic Service now, but I was out there in Sarajevo with the UN. We did our best for everyone, you know. I guess it just wasn't good enough?'

'I know you did,' said Stefan, quite taken aback. 'It wasn't easy.'

'Well, we're all hollering for you folks now, you ought to know that.'

'Thanks, that means a lot,' said Stefan.

***

Georg was doing an excellent job circulating with the other guests, not too formal, not too personal. Herr Brandt, representing the EU Economic Development Council entered the room surrounded by his acolytes. Georg welcomed him warmly. Stefan marked Herr Brandt down as the archetypal political acrobat that organisations like the EU bred in the hundreds. Stefan recognised Roger Arlington from the meeting in Sarajevo, standing alone over by the window. Arlington was dressed in the same sad brown suit he'd worn when they'd crossed swords during Sarajevo Steel's finance presentation. He seemed to be observing Boris. Stefan moved to confront him but was diverted by the arrival of Ivan Bobic, the Bosnian Ambassador to the UK. Stefan was pleased the Ambassador was not late. He was ready for his lunch. After all he'd missed his toast.

***

Ivan Bobic was a highly respected member of the Bosnian Diplomatic regime. Stefan knew he'd been born into a wealthy family and brought up by his beautiful mother, the daughter of an influential Austrian businessman with an apartment of her own in Vienna. As a boy, she had taught Ivan to play the piano, and they would ride together each morning. Soon he became an accomplished horseman. Well educated, with enviable linguistic skills, Ivan Bobic's rise through the diplomatic ranks had been spectacular. He had never met his father but was proud of his father's achievements and what he stood for. Ivan Bobic had been the Yugoslav Ambassador to the UK since before the Sarajevo Siege. He played a key role during the peace process and was involved in the political restructuring of the former Yugoslavia. Stefan was proud to meet him.

At one o'clock, they sat down to lunch. Stefan turned to speak to Boris, and as they chatted, Stefan caught a glimpse of Leo sitting next to Joe Brown. Stefan had not even been aware of Leo's arrival. It was as if he'd been there all the time. Leo and Joe Brown were talking together like old friends, while the rest of the party chatted amiably over a very fine lunch, Luciano presiding adroitly over the whole affair.

After lunch, Boris, Leo and Stefan went their separate ways. Stefan decided he would need to rest if he were to do justice to dinner. He was asleep in his room by three fifteen. Boris needed some fresh air. He envied Ana climbing in the mountains. He went to look for Leo, but Leo was nowhere to be found. Boris collected his coat from his room, and then walked down towards the shore of Bassenthwaite. It was snowing quite hard. He was pleased Ana had Olga as company. He knew she'd be okay.

Chapter 67

Milo surveyed the room and its furnishings, as the winter light drained in through the dirty windowpanes. Timbersbrook Cottage was not up to Roman Drasko's customary opulence.

'I trust your trip was uneventful?'

Roman's welcome was calm, without emotion.

'Yes, my journey was uneventful.'

Milo flopped down in the big armchair in the far corner of the room, as a broad grin spread across his strong granite features.

After Milo escaped from the carnage of his childhood, he was befriended by Roman, who sponsored him when he read engineering at the University of Sarajevo. Roman stood in the open doorway, administering his own brand of psychological analysis. Behind his impenetrable mask, nothing spilt out to indicate what he might be thinking.

'You flew from Mostar to Geneva and then to Birmingham?'

'Yes,' said Milo, 'It was a good flight,' Milo added. 'I picked up the car as arranged and collected the suitcase.'

'The toys, they are to your liking?' asked Roman.

'They are perfect,' replied a beaming Milo.

'Your meeting with Helmut Jorgen, did it go according to plan?'

'Yes, the guns are being delivered on the agreed date to the Zetra Arena, where the SDP will ensure their safe receipt.'

Roman's questions were to confirm the integrity of the mission had not been compromised.

'Well done, it's pleasing to know everything proceeds as planned. The armaments will smooth the way for the People's Revolution. It will be the trigger for Operation Bosnian Dawn and the prelude for the Communist world to reunite the countries of Yugoslavia.'

Milo was aware this form of debriefing was standard practice in the KGB and that Roman would be calling on his KGB training as the mission unfolded. Milo took off his mountain jacket and threw it over the other armchair and waited as Roman considered his next question. 'The Wast Water Inn, is it to your satisfaction? None of the guests give cause for alarm?'

'The Inn is fine. There is no one who causes any concern.'

Roman appeared satisfied as he produced a bottle of Speyside Aberlour Malt whisky and filled two tumblers that sat on the slate-topped coffee table, almost to the brim.

'And now, my friend, let us share a glass of something to keep out the cold before we get down to detail.'

'To Marsala Tita and Operation Bosnian Dawn,' toasted Roman.

'To Marsala Tita and Operation Bosnian Dawn,' echoed a smiling Milo.

Milo knew of Roman's love of a fine glass of whisky. He'd always been relentless in his pursuit of pleasure. He handed Milo a small brown envelope and a mobile phone, along with a rusty key for a mortice lock.

'You already know what the key is for?'

Milo nodded.

'Programmed into the phone, you will find the only contacts you will need. They are as follows: *Control*, is my number; *Inside* is the number of one of our comrades who is observing Poborski and the Bosnian entourage at Kermincham Hall; and finally, *Escape* holds the contact number for the snatch squad that will provide immediate transport home for you when your mission here is concluded. No other calls will be made on this telephone, do you understand?'

Milo understood.

'Our plan is already in progress,' announced Roman, refilling both of the empty glasses as he continued. 'As the next twenty-four hours unfold, we will persuade Poborski to refrain from signing the finance agreement and convince him to resign his position as General Director of Sarajevo Steel. No doubt you recall our success in the employment of persuasion during the war, as well as the pleasure it afforded?'

Milo smiled, Roman had evoked memories of the war during which they'd sated their desire for lubricious recreation, committing unspeakable acts that elevated bloodshed to the realms of ritual sacrifice. Milo took another drink of whisky, almost emptying his glass, as memories from the past spun around his head.

'Then at noon on Sunday,' Roman continued, 'you will contact *Escape* and receive full instructions regarding your immediate return to Sarajevo, where with support from the SDP Militia you will prepare for our People's Revolution. Is that clear?'

Milo finished off his whisky before answering.

'Crystal,' he replied.

Milo left as the snow was falling gently and headed for The Screes. He was a happy man. Let the good times roll.

Chapter 68

Dan and Tom searched the craggy mountainside for an escape from the biting wind. At the far side of the tarn they found a cleft in the rock that afforded some respite. Relieved to take shelter from the gnawing gale, they enjoyed an early lunch.

'I suppose it will be colder in the Alps,' said Tom between mouthfuls of flapjack.

'Yes, it will indeed,' Dan agreed, 'but a very dry cold, unlike here.'

The snow began to fall again before lunch was over, and as they climbed southeast the wind increased, whipping the snow into their backs. They cut up to the saddle between Great End and Broad Crag towards their goal, the summit of Scafell Pike. At this point, the wind threw everything at them, bursting up spitefully from the valley below. At this higher altitude, the snow had been falling for some time and showed no sign of relenting. In blizzard conditions, they stood on the wide summit plateau of Scafell Pike and surveyed the polar landscape.

'Where did all this come from?' quipped Tom.

'I've no idea, but this is going to be a real test, and it looks as if there's a lot more to come,' shouted back Dan. He checked his watch. It was five minutes to three.

Chapter 69

Two guests arrived back at Wast Water Inn from their walk to the lake. Ted invited them to sit beside the roaring log fire.

'What can I get you folks?' he asked.

'A rum and blackcurrant please,' the man replied. 'What about you?' he asked his wife.

'Yes, and the same for me please, and can you make them both doubles.'

Ted came around to join them by the fire, having helped himself to a glass of rum, but only a small one.

'It seems quiet for a Saturday afternoon. I guess it's the snow?'

'You're quite right,' said Ted. 'The lunchtime weather forecast reckoned we should expect snow before night, and quite a lot of it, by all accounts. There was no mention of it on last night's weather forecast, or this morning's. I checked in particular.' Ted looked out the window, as the snow fell unremittingly. 'The good news is it will only last a day, two at the most, according to the forecast. The bad news is, if it keeps on snowing like this, the road from High Birkhow through to Nether Wasdale could be blocked. You'll have no chance of getting any further south than the end of Wast Water. Not without a big four-by-four. I'm not expecting any more customers today, but I stay open no matter what, so I can be here to help Wasdale Mountain Rescue if need be.'

Ted threw another log on the fire, and it blazed up brightly.

'Do you think they'll be needed?' asked the man's wife.

Ted turned to welcome another guest, before replying.

'Let's hope not, but you never know.'

Ted left the couple by the fire and walked into reception. 'Yes sir, what can I get you?'

'My room key please.'

'Here you are Mr. Moretti, is there anything else?'

'No thank you, not at the moment.'

Chapter 70

Dan and Tom fought their way across the summit plateau of Scafell Pike, at the mercy of the storm. Without warning, a great gust of wind hurled Dan to the ground. He lay there spread-eagled in the deep snow, waiting until the wind subsided. As he rose to his feet the gale blasted the peak again, bringing both Dan and Tom to their knees.

'We need to get down off the plateau as quickly as possible. Which direction takes us down? Come on Tom, it needs to be now.'

'Yes, I know that Dad. We need to find the summit trig point first. I need to take a compass bearing from there to navigate from the plateau down into Mickledore.'

Visibility had dropped to less than five metres. It took more than ten minutes of methodical searching to find the trig point.

'Two hundred and thirty degrees southwest,' Tom shouted, trying to make himself heard above the gale as it howled in his face.

Tom set his compass bearing on two hundred and thirty degrees. Dan did the same. He knew two navigators had a better chance of a positive outcome. Even a small discrepancy could lead them blindly over Pike's Crag to an unwelcome vertical descent.

'Distance to Mickledore?' shouted Dan. Just then, the wind dropped, and an eerie silence descended.

'Eight hundred meters,' Tom shouted back, surprised how loud he was shouting now the wind had dropped. 'Vertical descent is one hundred metres. I won't be sorry to get off the summit.

'Me neither,' said Dan, now talking normally.

Then without warning, the gale resumed. Head down, they struggled over the piles of jumbled boulders, concealed beneath the deep snow. Conditions made a rapid descent impossible and they picked their way carefully over the rocky terrain to reach the saddle at Mickledore. At this point they took another compass bearing and turned to follow a course three hundred and seventeen degrees northwest that would take them down into the natural amphitheatre of Hollow Stones.

Tom looked down from the top of the scarp into the steep couloir. The way down into Hollow Stones was obscured by drifting snow, making it a treacherous and dangerous descent to their overnight campsite. He searched for the tiny ledges and footholds normally used, but the snow had buried them all. Dan signalled to Tom to move to a narrow ledge above the couloir that offered a degree of safety.

'We need to rope up,' shouted Dan, but Tom, having assessed the danger, already had the rope out of his rucksack, along with crampons and ice axe. After putting on their harnesses they tied on to the rope using a figure-of-eight knot. With crampons on, Tom held his ice axe in the self-belay position in readiness for his descent. Dan tied into a large rock flake, then took in the rope's slack and prepared to belay Tom down into Hollow Stones. Tom lowered himself off the ledge and disappeared into the blizzard and out of sight. Dan kept the rope tight throughout. After twenty-five metres, Tom saw a rock that offered the ideal belay stance and tied in, to bring his father down. He gave three hard tugs on the rope as a signal he was ready for his father to join him. Dan moved out onto the icy, snow-covered couloir, aware that any fall would take some distance to arrest. Dan reached the belay stance that Tom had set up around a projecting rock that poked out of the snow. Dan now led the descent down the precipitous mountain couloir, continuing a further thirty metres, to set up a second belay point on a rock outcrop. He slipped once, but Tom held him firmly on the rope. Tom joined his father, before continuing a further twenty-five metres down the snow-glazed rock. At this point he tied into the third and final belay stance, and with care they both arrived at the point where the slope softened and they un-roped. They stowed the rope in Tom's rucksack and moved off towards Hollow Stones to find a campsite for the night out of the teeth of the gale.

As they descended, the wind dropped, and then together they scoured Hollow Stones for a suitable site. Tom found a place beneath Pulpit Rock and pitched the yellow, two-man mountain tent, while Dan dug boulders from the snow to secure the guy ropes that would hold the tent to the mountain. They squeezed into the tent and zipped up the door. After taking their boots and waterproofs off, they took a long drink of water to combat dehydration and shared the pasta that they cooked on the small stove.

'Well done, Tom, you were brilliant up there on the summit, I was proud of you.'

'Hey, you were pretty good yourself. It's just a shame Ted missed out.'

'Yeah, next time in Chamonix, he'll be there. Get some rest, Tom, even if you can't sleep.'

They burrowed down inside their sleeping bags as the storm raged. It was twenty-four minutes to four.

Chapter 71

Boris welcomed the warmth of Kermincham Hall as he arrived back from his walk, and dusting off the snowflakes from his shoulders, he made his way to collect his room key. He had fifteen minutes before his next meeting, at four o'clock.

'Here is your key sir.'

'Thank you, Luciano. I just wondered if my daughter Ana or her friend Olga had telephoned for a car to pick them up?'

Luciano checked the driver's logbook for Josip Budach.

'No sir, she hasn't. Not yet. There is a note to pick them up when they telephone, with an estimated time of four o'clock this afternoon.'

'That's fine, thank you. Oh, and I'd like to reserve a table for two, at eight o'clock in the restaurant this evening. It's not for me. It's for Ana and Olga.'

'Very good, sir. So that's a table for two in the Bassenthwaite Restaurant. We'll look forward to seeing them both at eight o'clock.'

As expected, the Deutsche Bank meeting finished precisely on time at five fifteen, and Boris made his way for drinks in the Garden Room, with Georg and Ivan Bobic. He'd touch base with Ana before he went into dinner.

Chapter 72

Olga edged slowly back from Piers Gill, a deep ugly scar that starts its journey east of Flass Knotts on the south side of Lingmell Beck, to end abruptly, close to the summit of Scafell Pike. Olga's heart never missed a beat. Unperturbed, she consulted the map, and continued as if nothing had happened.

'After five hundred meters we change direction to the southeast. From that point the distance up onto the Scafell Pike plateau is no more than four hundred meters, but it is a considerable ascent. The route we take will be very steep.'

They paced out five hundred meters and turned southeast to find a shallow depression gouged out of the mountainside. Here they shared a drink and rested for a few moments at the foot of the ascent that led to the summit plateau.

'Are you okay to go on?' asked Olga. 'It looks very steep and the snowfall is reducing visibility.'

Ana put her thumbs up.

'Ready when you are,' she replied.

They set off up the snow-filled gulley for their final assault. Olga led the way and Ana followed five metres behind in Olga's tracks. At one point Ana lost her footing but managed to regain her balance as her left foot wedged against a rock hidden beneath the snow. Relieved at her good fortune, Ana continued upward, searching carefully for each foot placement in the fading light.

Then a warning cry came from high above Ana's head. She looked up and saw Olga sliding down towards her, out of control. Ana had no time to take avoiding action. Olga hit her hard. The impact took Ana's legs out from underneath her and together they skidded down the gully, accelerating towards the edge and the sheer drop below. Olga grabbed hold of Ana's mountain jacket, while Ana pulled Olga towards her. Both searched for somewhere to jam their feet as they sped down the slope. Then something hidden in the snow dug into Ana's rucksack, jerking her back. She clung on to Olga, wrapping her legs around her waist.

'Hold on!' she screamed. 'Hold on!'

Olga's fingers tightened around the straps on Ana's rucksack that had snagged on a flake of rock protruding above the snow. Breathless, they came to a sudden stop. Ana and Olga lay there, sprawled out on the icy face of the mountain, not daring to move.

'Are you okay?' asked Olga as she rose to her feet, her voice laced with concern.

'Yes, yes, I'm fine.' Ana reassured her. 'But I don't want to do that again, thank you.'

Olga smiled as she tried to compose herself. 'We've had a lucky escape; it could have been much worse.'

'What about you?' asked Ana.

'Yes, no problems, let's get going.'

Ana's confidence dissolved as the gravity of their situation began to dawn on her. She saw the same concern reflected on Olga's face. After the fall they were almost at the bottom of the gully and with care, they continued down towards the depression. Olga spoke first.

'The time is twenty-seven minutes past four. We cannot make it to the summit now. We must go down as quickly as we can.'

'Yes, I agree, as quickly as we can,' echoed Ana.

They rested for a moment and confirmed they'd sustained no more than a few cuts and bruises. Then they returned to the shallow depression they'd left earlier.

Chapter 73

Milo loaded the Kalashnikov and placed it in the rucksack with the Glock and the head torch. Additional ammunition followed. He felt a shiver of excitement. This was not as good as the Sarajevo Siege, but it was the next best thing. He looked out of the window as the snow fell, covering the car park at the Wast Water Inn. Next, he packed a small amount of food, followed by a litre of water. The dramatic weather conditions had altered the landscape. Though the circumstances had changed, Milo knew the objective had not. Regardless of whether the roads were passable, the package would be delivered to the safe house one way or another. Milo would do whatever it took. Putting the mobile telephone and the key that Roman had given him into his mountain jacket pocket, he zipped it up. He stepped outside into a world of white. He was battle-ready.

Milo followed the route he'd taken earlier that day, in the direction of Timbersbrook Cottage, before turning off towards the deserted campsite.

He circumnavigated the campsite buildings at a safe distance. The area seemed sterile, but he could take no chances. Crouching low to avoid detection, he made his way through the trees to the door at the rear of the main building. He took the rusty key and placed it in the mortice lock. It slid in without difficulty. A noise behind him drew his attention and he turned around; the Kalashnikov eager for action. Sweeping down the mountainside, the wind had become entangled in a huge oak tree, its branches creaking eerily in the dying light. Milo turned the key, gently at first, then with increasing force. It would not turn. He tried again. This time it moved, but only a fraction. He pulled the door's handle hard towards him to take the weight off the locking mechanism. He tried again, more firmly this time. He didn't want to break the key. There was a loud crack and the lock grudgingly surrendered and, in a moment, he was inside. He was safe.

Milo checked out the interior of the building. It contained showers and toilets, as well as a small storeroom that served the campsite. It was clean, dry and completely deserted. Windows on all four sides made the building good to defend. He checked to ensure the windows opened; he may be in need of an escape route. Next he switched on his mobile phone and found he barely had a signal. Milo looked out onto the path that came up from the Wast Water Inn, his Kalashnikov trained on the point where any attacker would emerge. A noise drew his attention and his muscles tensed. Outside something moved. In an instant he was back on the streets of a ruined and bloodied Bosnia. Milo took out his penknife. He was ready for his next ritual sacrifice.

Chapter 74

Olga checked their position on the map before plotting a compass bearing to take them down an escape route. They drank the last of the water and shared the food that was left in their lunch boxes. Then as the snowstorm raged, they retraced their steps to where they'd left the Corridor Route three hours earlier. Progress became painfully slow as they headed northeast towards Lingmell Col. Ana missed her footing in the darkness and fell to her knees. She knelt for a moment, watching the snowflakes fight to fill the folds in her mountain jacket. She blinked a snowflake from her eyelash as she struggled to her feet, to be swallowed up in a world that had now turned a sooty black.

The realisation they may not have the strength to make it down to safety dawned on both climbers at the same time.

'We have to try and make it down. Every metre of descent will help reduce the effect of the cold.'

'I'll do my best, Olga. You know I will.'

With visibility down to no more than a few metres, Olga set off to find shelter, closely followed by Ana. Thirty-five minutes later, Ana collapsed in the deepening snow.

'I can't go on, I need to rest,' she blurted out, in between taking great gasps of freezing air.

'No, we must keep going, you have to make it down. You just have to,' insisted Olga as Ana rested on her knees.

'Just give me a minute, then I'll be okay.'

She stood up, but by now she had lost all feeling in her hands and feet. As Ana led the way down, she caught sight of a yellow pallid smudge. She looked again. It was a light. Olga saw the ghostly blur and gasped more in disbelief than hope. Through the snowflakes she could see a young man standing next to a small brightly coloured mountain tent, no more than ten metres away. He saw them as they moved slowly through the deep snow. He stooped down and disappeared inside the tent before re-emerging with a bigger, much brighter torch, which he shone in their direction.

'Hi there!' he called, walking towards them. 'Do you guys need any help?'

Ana made no reply. She staggered forward and collapsed in his arms. The time was three minutes past five. Ana felt Tom's body as he held her in his arms. Her face, tightly framed by the hood of her mountain jacket, was bathed in the light of his head torch. He helped her into the doorway of the small tent to where Dan watched and waited.

Needing to keep the inner tent dry, Dan removed her boots, jacket, and waterproof trousers. Next, he removed her wet gloves and socks, but left her hat on, which had remained dry under her hood. He knew it would help conserve any heat her body had retained, though Dan thought there was precious little of that. He worked quickly, aware that time was of the essence if Ana was to cheat death on the mountain.

'What's her name?' he shouted as he bundled Ana's waterproofs into the tent's entrance that served as a small porch.

Dan realised Olga couldn't hear above the howl of the gale. He called again, louder this time.

'Ana,' she called back, as she crouched outside the tent. 'Her name is Ana. Is she okay?'

Dan made no reply.

'Ana,' Dan's voice was direct and penetrating. 'Ana, you're safe now, you're safe.'

There was no response from Ana. She lay there in Dan's arms, lifeless. He felt her hand, it was as cold as marble. Concerned that Tom and Ana's climbing partner remained outside, and still subject to the worst of the elements, Dan began to ascertain the medical help Ana might need. Until then he would move her as little as possible, in case she had sustained injury. 'Has she fallen?' he asked.

'Yes,' came back Olga's reply.

Dan searched his memory to recall the sequence of emergency first aid checks, as the windswept frantic snowflakes down the mountain and hurled them at the tent, while Olga and Tom tried to take shelter in the entrance porch.

He began by confirming there was no restriction in Ana's airways. As he did his hand touched her face. It was ice cold. An audible gasp escaped from Dan's lips. She was cold enough to be dead already. Then he checked her breathing. At first, he could hear nothing above the wind. He felt her chest. There was a gentle, but distinct, rising and falling of her chest cavity.

'Her breathing's good,' he said. The comment was for his own benefit rather than anyone else's. 'Come on, Ana, you're going to be fine,' he encouraged. Dan could find no sign of a pulse on Ana's wrist. He searched again. Still nothing. He feared the worst. 'Okay Ana, I'm going to check the pulse on your neck. 'Are you okay with that?' he asked, not waiting for a reply.

Dan unzipped her fleece to expose Ana's neck, a flash of milk white skin, soft and yielding. He felt a faint pulse. Barely at first, then he moved his fingers a mere fraction on her neck. 'Ana has a pulse, but it's very weak,' he called out to Tom and Olga. 'She's so very cold, if her temperature continues to drop, she could lapse into hypothermia.'

Suddenly the storm grew in ferocity and the teeth of the gale tugged at the tent and the guy ropes that secured it tenaciously to the mountainside. Tom looked across at his father, Dan read the question on his son's face. *Will it hold?*

'Is she going to be all right?' begged Olga.

'She's going to be just great,' reassured Dan. 'Just great!'

Tom helped Olga remove her boots and waterproofs, and they both squeezed inside the tent. Then after pulling the rucksacks into the porch, Tom zipped up the outer door.

'You say she fell. Did she injure herself in any way?' asked Dan.

'After her fall we walked four, or maybe even five kilometres in deep snow, she seemed all right. Just really tired.'

Dan carried out a full body check on Ana, gently feeling her legs, arms, chest, and pelvis for any deformity. There were no apparent injuries, no broken bones, no bleeding or swelling. 'We need to make sure Ana knows she's being taken care of. Tom, tell her she's going to be all right and keep telling her. She may be able to hear you, but most of all we need to get her warm. Help me lift her into your sleeping bag.'

Tom nodded. 'Ana, we're going to lift you into my sleeping bag, is that okay? You can get nice and warm in there.'

'The bag will stop her getting colder,' said Dan. 'But that's not enough, she needs more heat, you'll have to get in beside her.'

'I'm going to get in with you Ana, just to warm you up. Just move over a little, that's fine.'

Tom manoeuvred Ana's body down inside his sleeping bag, and then carefully wriggled in to wedge himself next to her. Tom held Ana close;

162

his life-giving warmth would drive the deathly chill from the core of her body.

Dan turned to Olga.

'Hi, I'm Dan Kennedy, and this is my son, Tom. What's your name?'

'Olga. Will Ana be all right, please, I must know?'

'Yes,' replied Dan, 'she'll be fine.'

Olga gave a sigh of relief.

'Are you okay Olga, have you sustained any injuries?'

'No, I'm unhurt, just worn out and very, very cold.'

Dan felt her hand. She was not nearly as cold as Ana, but Olga was indeed cold. Cold enough for concern, thought Dan, as he zipped up the door to the inner tent, shutting out the storm.

'Get into my sleeping bag. Is it okay if I join you?'

'Anything to make me warmer,' she replied. 'But first, is my rucksack in the tent?'

'No,' answered Dan. 'It's in the entrance porch. It's all right in there. There's no room in the tent with the four of us in here. It's only a two-man mountain tent.'

'I must make sure it's okay.' Olga's voice carried an element of anxiety.

'Later,' insisted Dan. 'You need to rest.'

'No, now.'

But Olga didn't have the strength to argue any further. She fell back and gave into her exhaustion. Dan helped her into his sleeping bag, and then leaned over to check on Ana. Tom was still engaged in a one-way conversation with her. She was still breathing, still cold, still alive. Dan squeezed down into the sleeping bag with Olga and into the welcoming warmth.

***

After only four hours of fractured sleep, Dan lay awake in the confines of his refuge. He could hear nothing inside the tent above the power of the storm as it raged outside. Suddenly, a gust of wind collided head on with the tent, forcing it towards the ground, as it struggled to stay secured to the mountain. Then, as abruptly as it began, the wind died away, as if its life was over, and an uncanny stillness descended. Dan tried to reason how the weather on such a beautiful morning could transmogrify into a killer storm by nightfall. He checked his mobile phone for a signal, but there was nothing, and any hope of summoning Ted Baker and Wasdale Mountain Rescue immediately floundered.

Dan twisted his upper body and squirmed out of the sleeping bag to check on Olga, propping himself up on one arm. Olga's breathing was no longer laboured, but regular and rhythmic. He counted each breath while she slept.

'Twelve breaths a minute,' he whispered. Dan felt Olga's hand. She was warm. He checked her pulse for thirty seconds, slowly counting each beat. 'Thirty-one, that's sixty-two beats a minute. Good girl, you're going to be fine.'

Dan freed himself from the sleeping bag and retrieved his head torch from the storage pocket in the side of the tent. Then, with trepidation, he leaned over to where Tom and Ana lay, their bodies melded together, hungry for warmth. Ana was young, her chance of survival should be high, but her mental strength would play a vital role in her life and death struggle. Dan could see no discernible movement in the beam of his head torch. He hesitated, afraid to confirm his worst fears. Why had he persuaded himself Ana would pull through, rather than face the possibility that she might not make it down to safety? He wondered if other climbers would lose their lives before the storm blew itself out.

Tom and Ana lay face down, tightly pressed together in the sleeping bag. He searched for her wrist, but at first could find only Tom's hand. He moved closer, plunging deep inside the cramped sleeping bag, searching for the evidence that could shatter his fading optimism, wreck all hope. He found Ana's hand. It was soft, yielding and warm. He felt her pulse. She was alive.

Chapter 75

After drinks with Georg and Ivan Bobic, Boris checked his watch as he took the lift to his room on the first floor. It was twenty minutes past six. Dinner was at eight. Boris had more than enough time to change before checking on Ana. He entered his room and removed his shoes then lay down on the big double bed. Staring up at the ornate ceiling, he languidly reflected on the events of the day. Finally, he began to relax.

***

Boris woke with a start. He felt refreshed, so much better for his impromptu sleep. He checked his watch. It was twenty minutes past seven. He was late.

He hurried over to the window and drew the curtains to close out the night. It was still snowing, but Ana would be down off the mountain by now. He'd look in on her before dinner. Boris showered and dressed and then at seven fifty, he went to see Ana. *Had she enjoyed the climb?* He knocked gently on the door. There was no reply. She must be at dinner with Olga. The table had been reserved for eight o'clock. He knocked again, as Georg approached from the far end of the corridor.

'Come on, Boris, we don't want to keep our guests waiting, do we now?'

'I just want to say hello to Ana, I haven't seen her all day, not since this morning when she left to go climbing with Olga.'

'She's probably fast asleep, recovering from her climb. All that fresh air, I know it makes me sleepy. Ana won't thank you for waking her up.'

'You're probably right. She said she might just crash out. I'll pop back a little later when she's had time to recover.'

Georg and Boris were the last to arrive. As they entered the room, the guests rose to their feet and welcomed Boris with a round of applause. Then followed by the others, Ivan Bobic raised his wine glass.

'Gentlemen, I give you a toast. I give you Boris Poborski. A great industrialist, a great Bosnian, but first and foremost, a great man. One of our elite on whose shoulders the economic future of Bosnia depends. Gentlemen—Boris Poborski.'

Boris was still blushing as the first course was being served. He'd not anticipated such an accolade from someone as prestigious as Ivan Bobic.

The French onion soup was superb, the sirloin steak wonderfully tender, and the tiramisu so delicious. Both Stefan and Herr Becker requested an extra portion of tiramisu. Leo couldn't help noticing how bright and sociable Boris was. Just like the old Boris.

Chapter 76

On the mountain Dan Kennedy focused on three credible choices. Stay put until help arrived. Attempt a descent together. Or send for help. Staying put was dependent on how much food and water they had between them, and what medical attention Ana and Olga may require. The option of attempting an escape rested on the physical shape of all four climbers. Ana's fitness was pivotal. Then there were the weather conditions. Finally, he contemplated the question, if help was to be sent for, who should stay and who should go for help, Dan or Tom? Dan was an accomplished mountaineer having honed his skills in the Alps where he'd bagged all the classic routes with Ted Baker. He knew Tom was strong and by working as a team their chances of a safe descent were high. He turned his thoughts to Ana and Olga as the storm outside abated. Chaperoning two climbers of unknown ability and poor physical condition added an unwelcome dimension. He checked his mobile phone for a signal, but there was nothing. It was five past nine. The others had slept for just over four hours. It was time to check out the options.

Dan squeezed past Olga and shuffled to the doorway. He unzipped the inner tent door and pulled Tom's rucksack towards him, as the others slept on. There was no room for the rucksack in the overstuffed tent. With the rucksack still in the porch, he foraged deep within it in as best he could. He found some nuts and two apples, the cereal and milk for breakfast and the remainder of the flapjack. Dan reckoned they had enough food, carefully rationed, for two days. What they were short of was water. Both Tom's water bottles were empty, and Dan knew he had less than half a litre left. The frozen streams lay deep beneath the snow and the option of melting snow was a last resort.

He checked out Ana's sack for possible food supplies but found none. Both water bottles were empty and a crumpled lunch box from Kermincham Hall was the only evidence of food. There was nothing else in the rucksack apart from a spare pair of gloves and two Ordnance Survey maps. Next he dragged Olga's rucksack towards him. There was no water in either of the bottles and no food in the lunch box. There was a torch, which Dan thought could be useful, a small first aid kit and a green sponge, which Dan could think of no use for, and a spare pair of socks. He was about to return the rucksack to the porch, when he noticed a bulge in the zipped pocket on the top of the rucksack.

His son was waking. Dan signalled for him to be quiet. Tom looked down at Ana as he moved to free himself from the sleeping bag.

'She's going to be okay.' Dan whispered.

'Yeah I know, that's great.' A big smile flooded his face. 'How's Olga, is she all right?'

'Yes, Olga's fine. I'm going outside now to have a look at the weather. It's still dark, the moon's a good four days away from being full, but I should get some idea of what it's like. The good news is the wind has dropped and it's stopped snowing.'

'I need something to eat. I'm starving,' said Tom.

'We have some flapjack, but go easy, we may have to ration it.'

Dan turned on his head torch and zipped up the outer door behind him as he left the tent. He needed to maintain the temperature inside to improve Ana and Olga's chances. In the darkness that flooded in with Dan's departure, Tom located his rucksack in search of his head torch and the flapjack.

Dan emerged on all fours from the confines of the tent, to be greeted by an Arctic vista. Looking back at the tent, half buried in the snow, it looked so pathetic, yet so utterly incredible. Dan couldn't believe it had survived the storm. All around him, the wind had chased and bullied the snow, sculpting great white curves at the foot of the rock walls. Drifts had formed, some over two metres high, while in other places, patches of black igneous rock devoid of any snow poked through, naked and raw. Dan arrived back at the tent happier than when he'd left, to find Tom and Olga sharing some flapjack.

'Olga's well into flapjack,' declared Tom. 'She thinks it's cool.'

'Olga said that?' asked Dan.

'More or less,' Tom replied.

Olga could only smile back through a mouthful of flapjack.

'Keep the noise down,' whispered Dan. 'You'll wake Ana.'

'It's too late for that.' It was Ana. 'Any chance of some flapjack?' she asked.

***

As Ana pushed herself out of Tom's sleeping bag, her elbow made contact with the ground and she winced. Dan examined a graze on her left arm, sustained during her fall as she ascended the gully.

'That's a nice one. Let me have a look at it.' Dan pulled out his first aid kit and dressed the wound. 'You'll do.' He declared, as Tom offered her some flapjack. The colour had returned to Ana's cheeks; even her eyes sparkled.

'Are you okay to attempt the descent, Ana?' Dan asked.

'I think so. Apart from wet socks where the snow came into my boots, I'm in quite good shape.'

Tom and Dan went outside to assess the weather and the snow conditions. Dan tried his mobile phone again. There was still no signal. It was time to abandon any hope of rescue and focus on the remaining choices. Olga joined them as they tried to get a fix on their position and agree the best route down. Their best way to safety. Alone in the tent, Ana searched for the spare pair of socks she thought she had somewhere in her rucksack.

The sky was clear, their head torches cutting through the blackness with ease. Tom felt they had to make a run for it now, a view he now shared with his father.

'We have to get down quickly. Before the weather changes.'

'I agree, my preferred route is straight down into Wasdale, but I guess it all depends on our two strays. What do you think Olga, can you make it down?' asked Dan.

'I'm fine now after the rest. I feel good, almost fully recovered. I think we can make it down. Anyway, we must try.'

They returned to the tent, to find Ana changing her socks for a dry pair.

'Where did you start climbing from?' enquired Dan, his breath hanging in the beam of Tom's head torch.

'Seathwaite in Borrowdale,' responded Olga.

'We need to get back there as quickly as possible,' Ana interrupted, as she finished tying up her boots. 'My father will be very worried. When can we start down to Borrowdale?'

In the light of the torch, Dan examined the Borrowdale route on the map in detail. The route was longer than to Wasdale Head, Dan and Tom's destination, and involved circumnavigating Piers Gill, not everyone's preferred escape route, certainly not Dan's.

169

'The route down into Wasdale is safer and shorter,' said Tom.

'Yes, but it's at the other side of the mountain to Kermincham Hall. I have to get back there. Come on,' said Ana, full of enthusiasm. 'Let's get going. I'm ready now I've got dry socks on.'

Dan was searching for a way to explain they couldn't take the Borrowdale route, and that his choice of escape route down into Wasdale was by far the better option.

'Okay Ana,' said Dan.

He was about to begin his explanation when Olga saved him the trouble in a manner that took everyone by surprise.

'No,' said Olga. 'This may help you make the right decision?'

Olga held a Luger pistol, obscene and ugly. She was pointing it at Dan. If she pulled the trigger, she could not miss from where she stood. 'We will travel west to this grid reference.'

She handed Dan a piece of notepaper with the name *Wasdale* written on it in scrawly handwriting and a six-digit map reference, *183076*. Ana was mesmerised. She could not take her eyes off Olga's gun.

Olga stood grim faced, teeth gritted, holding the Luger in Dan's face. At first, Tom thought it was a joke. The sort of prank some reprobate at college would pull, but now he could tell by Olga's face she was deadly serious. Olga had changed.

'Olga, what do you think you are doing? demanded Ana. 'Put away the gun! Just put away the gun!'

'Okay, Olga,' said Dan, obsequiously. He'd never had to negotiate with a gun in his face before. 'I have the compass bearing you want and that's the way we're going down, but tell me, what in God's name is this all about?'

'You don't need to know that. You just need to do it and do it now!'

Olga waved the gun in Dan's face, as he checked the map and confirmed that Olga's grid reference would take them to the campsite in Wasdale.

'We can leave almost at once,' said Tom. 'It's stopped snowing and the sky is clearing. Well, at least for now. It's best we take the tent with us; in case the weather changes and we need shelter. It won't take long to pack.'

'Okay,' said Olga. 'But be quick about it.'

Ana stared back in disbelief at Olga. She suddenly realised she did not know Olga Lukic at all. All Ana knew was she had to fight. She couldn't hide, not now. Not ever. She had made a promise.

'Why are you doing this, Olga?' she asked, her voice controlled and measured.

Olga made no reply.

'Just one more thing,' added Dan politely. 'Before we make a start down.'

Olga nodded her agreement.

'Do you know there are no bullets in your gun?'

'There are eight bullets in the gun,' said Olga flatly. 'Eight.'

'No,' persisted Dan. 'None.'

'And how would you know?' asked Olga dismissively, aiming the gun at Dan.

'I opened your rucksack when I was searching for food and water, that's when I found the gun in the top zipped pocket.' Olga looked bewildered as Dan continued. 'When I was a boy my grandfather had a Luger, one he'd brought back as a souvenir from the war in Germany. He never kept it loaded, but he showed me how to take the magazine clip out where the bullets are kept and then put it back; it's pretty easy, really.'

Olga looked even more confused, uncertain as to what she should do next.

'Nice story, but why should I believe you?' she asked.

'Because all eight bullets are right here in my pocket.'

Then as Dan put his hand in his pocket, Olga pointed the Luger in Dan's face.

'I know you're bluffing,' she said.'

Then Olga pulled the trigger. Tom and Ana stood motionless on the bleak mountainside, waiting for Dan to fall. Then Tom laughed, a nervous stuttering laugh. Olga pulled the trigger again and the Luger emitted a second, rasping mechanical click, like some injured metal toy. She took a step back, took aim and pulled the trigger for a third time. Olga saw no concern on Dan's face as he stood there on the mountainside. Then he held out the eight bullets he'd removed from the Luger and Olga, without being asked, surrendered the gun, her demise confirmed.

'Now will you tell me what this is all about?' said Ana.

Olga remained silent.

'Come on guys, we need to get off this mountain before the weather breaks,' said Dan. 'We could all die up here.'

Tom packed the tent with Olga watching sullenly on, while Dan stood wondering which route they should take. He called Tom over and posed the question.

'What do think, Tom? Which route is the safe route?'

Dan left the question as open-ended as he could.

'As far as the route goes, straight down Brown Tongue and into Wasdale gives us our best chance,' suggested Tom.

'I guess the unknown revolves around Olga. What's she up to? There are too many unknowns to make a good judgement.'

'So,' said Tom. 'It's down Brown Tongue.'

'Yes,' replied Dan. 'We'll deal with Olga's problem when and if it arrives.'

In the frozen beam of his head torch, Tom rechecked the compass bearing that would take them on to the ridge of Brown Tongue. Once set, he looked up to find the others ready to descend. His father nodded, and Tom led the way out of Hollow Stones. In the hours that followed, Ana stopped several times to rest as they fought to gain the ridge. The storm had left the mountainside contorted by a melange of snowdrifts that perplexed Tom's sense of direction and denied any attempt of orientation. He followed the compass bearing unquestioningly, as he paced out the distance step by step. Several times during the descent, he fell into deep gullies hidden beneath the snow, and had to haul himself out, helped by his father.

'Well done, you're doing great, Ana. We've made the ridge. Do you need a rest?'

Breathless, Ana gave Tom her silent reply by falling face down in the snow. She lay on the frozen ridge like a burst balloon, as snowflakes again filled the sky.

'I'm okay. I'm okay.' Ana used Tom's body to pull herself up, to kneel by his side. Her face was tired and drained. 'Just give me a minute and I'll be fine.'

Dan gave Ana a sip of the remaining water and offered the bottle to Olga.

'Would you like a drink?' he asked.

Dan read Olga's muted answer chiselled in her features, her lips silent. They reached the confluence of the tributaries that fed Lingmell Beck, where they rested and shared the nuts and apples and the last of the flapjack. The breakfast cereal and milk would be kept in reserve. Ana was becoming increasingly tired. Dan gave her a helping hand over the difficult stretches, but by now he had a real concern that her strength would not hold out.

Many familiar landmarks lay hidden beneath the deep snow. Tom paused to check first their altitude and then the compass bearing.

'How can I be lost on a mountain I know so well, even in the dark? We should have reached the boundary fence at the foot of Brown Tongue. But there's no sign of it.'

A wild flurry of snow swept the night sky, as if a laggardly band of snowflakes were pursuing those that had gone before. Dan walked farther down the mountain in the direction of Keeperswood. Suddenly he tripped and went sprawling headlong in the snow, sliding down the mountain into the darkness beyond. He wrestled with his ice axe to get a purchase in the snow, hacking savagely at the icy crust, and after ten metres he was able to self-arrest. He rose unsteadily to his feet, winded but uninjured, and spat out a mouthful of icy flakes. He climbed back up the mountain towards where the others waited, and knelt down in the snow. A knob of wood, the cause of Dan's fall, punctured the snow's surface. He scraped the snow from its top with his ice axe, then followed the beam of his head torch across the steep mountainside as it picked out a line of miniature snowy cupolas disappearing into the night.

'I've found the fence, at least the fence post tops. The fence is completely buried beneath the snow.'

'We're almost down now, Ana, are you okay to go on?' asked Tom.

Ana smiled at Tom, and then without speaking, set off downhill. Olga followed.

Chapter 77

Milo looked down at his mobile phone, willing it to ring. It had remained stubbornly silent since Roman's last update two hours ago, when they'd agreed Olga's delay was simply down to the weather conditions. Milo was certain that with her mountaineering skill and experience, she would make the rendezvous eventually. Searching for her in a blizzard, on a mountain he was unfamiliar with, was not an option.

***

Milo got up and stretched his legs. He had waited in the silence of the deserted campsite for over six hours. He checked the window that looked towards Wast Water. The scene that confronted him was devoid of any light, the moon now blotted out by a dirty black sky. Milo was ready for some action. He checked his watch. The package was behind schedule. It was time to move, time to reconnoitre. He made a careful sweep of the toilet block to ensure nothing had been left that would betray his presence there, then left by the back door, into knee-deep snow.

Chapter 78

As Tom led the group through a clump of snow-laden trees, the blurred outline of a stone building emerged from the darkness that obscured any detail.

'Is that the campsite?' asked Dan.

'No. I'm avoiding the campsite. That's where Olga's compass bearing would have taken us. This is the cottage at Keeperswood. The campsite is farther down the track towards Wasdale Head, it's between here and the road.'

Dan checked the map in the restrained light of the head torch, as Ana began to shiver.

'We need to find shelter for Ana as soon as possible. Let's see if anyone's at home in Keeperswood Cottage.'

Following in Tom's tracks they waded through the snowdrifts towards the front door of the cottage. Dan knocked. There was no reply, he knocked again. Then he tried the door handle.

'No luck. It's locked.'

He placed his shoulder firmly against the door and pushed. The door was rock solid. It didn't budge. He pushed again, much harder this time, but the outcome was the same as before.

'I'll try around the back,' said Tom.

The others followed. Dan peered into the windows as they went. There were no lights visible and no sign of occupation. They arrived at the back of the cottage and Tom tried the door.

'This one's locked.'

'Here let me try.'

Dan threw all his weight against the door. There was a sound of splintering wood.

The kitchen door burst open. They were inside.

'No lights, we don't want to advertise our arrival. It's too close to the campsite.'

Ana and Olga waited in the doorway, while Dan and Tom checked out the cottage. It was empty. Then together they made their way through the kitchen and into the lounge. Resting on the settee out of the freezing mountain air, Ana began to regain her strength. After a few minutes she gave her account of how she and Olga arrived at Hollow Stones and her disbelief when Olga pulled the gun.

'So that is it,' concluded Ana. 'I can only think this concerns a business agreement my father must sign. Something to do with Bosnia and Sarajevo Steel.'

Olga had not spoken since she was shown the Luger's eight bullets in Dan's hand. Dan reckoned the chance of getting anything out of her was somewhere between nothing and zero. He didn't even try.

'When does the signing take place? Dan asked Ana.

'The agreement will be signed at eleven o'clock on Sunday morning.' Then after a moment's hesitation she added. 'That would be this morning.'

'Or not, as the case might be,' concluded Dan.

'What do you mean? Or not?' asked Ana, her voice conveying a degree of confusion.

'Kidnap or perhaps hostage?' said Dan pointing to Olga.

Dan posed the question and left it hanging there. He didn't have long to wait.

'Bitch!' screamed Ana.

In a moment she had dragged Olga off the settee and onto the floor and began to strangle the life out of her. Dan leapt forward in an attempt to release Ana's lunatic grip from Olga's throat. Ana was having none of it. She sat astride Olga and hung on. Tom saw Olga's frightened eyes were wide open, her mouth agape as she fought for breath. He knelt down beside Ana, avoiding the struggle that involved his father.

'Come on Ana, that's enough, let her up. This isn't the way.'

Ana turned to face Tom and then slowly released her grip. Tom could see the finger and thumb marks on Olga's throat, evidence of Ana's murder attempt. Olga, helped by Dan, got to her knees. Ana retreated back to the sofa.

'I'll get her a drink of water,' said Tom and went to the kitchen, as Olga got to her feet and tried to compose herself, rubbing her throat as she took huge gulps of air. Now they were down from the mountain, Dan checked his mobile phone again. This time he had a signal. He could

176

call Ted Baker and Mountain Rescue. They were safe. Tom returned from the kitchen with Olga's water.

He was not alone. Milo flicked on the light, Kalashnikov in hand. Tom instinctively knew this gun would have bullets in. Dan returned his mobile phone to his rucksack. He didn't make the call.

Chapter 79

In Kermincham Hall it was fifteen minutes to midnight and the dinner guests were beginning to drift away. Roger Arlington from the Office of the High Representative was one of the last to leave.

'Well done, Boris,' said Georg. 'The dinner was a real success. We all had a great evening.'

As Georg left the room, Leo and Stefan joined Boris.

'What about a nightcap?' asked Stefan. 'I know I could use one.'

'What a good idea,' agreed Boris. 'But I need to check on Ana first. I haven't seen her since this morning, when she left for Scafell Pike with Olga.'

'But Boris, it's after midnight, Ana will be fast asleep by now.'

Boris turned towards the stairs to Ana's room and then paused for a moment.

'Yes, yes, you're quite right Stefan, she said she might just crash out. I'll see her in the morning.'

On arrival at the Herdwick Bar, Julie Hardy served the drinks that Stefan ordered. She and Stefan seemed to be on quite friendly terms.

Chapter 80

Milo stepped forward, menacing and evil. The semantic the gun carried did not elude Dan. Its message was clear, infusing fear and trepidation in everyone except Olga. Olga felt born again. In her eyes Milo looked no different from that warm August day on the steps of Sarajevo University, when she'd taken his photo and fallen in love with him. They'd spent their winter vacations skiing at her father's chateau and long summer days climbing in the mountains. Olga had loved her life as the favourite daughter of Commissar Vladimir Lukic, a leading Communist Minister in the former Yugoslav Government. She longed for it back.

'Olga, you're down at last,' said Milo.

She crossed the room and Milo took her in his arms. He kissed her hard on the lips.

'It's so good to see you Milo. I've missed you so much.'

'We'll have plenty of time to catch up later,' he replied, keeping both the gun and his eyes trained on Dan and Tom.

'I'm much later getting down the mountain than we planned. The snow, it was very difficult.'

'I know,' said Milo. 'But Control kept me informed of progress throughout the night,' he held up his mobile phone. 'So, don't worry, you're here now and there's no harm done.'

Milo retreated to the far corner of the room and made a call on his mobile phone, before returning to where Olga stood.

'Where are the two guns you were given?'

'They were stolen from me.'

'So, who has them now?' Milo's tone had changed.

'He has the Luger,' said Olga pointing at Dan. 'The bullets have been taken out. They're in his fleece pocket.'

'Give Olga the gun,' said Milo.

Dan contemplated saying no, but not for long. He handed over the Luger. For Dan returning one gun was not a problem, but two guns? Now that could be hard to deal with. He knew nothing about a second gun. Dan began to re-plan his strategy. He had to act before Milo and Olga were firmly in control.

'Thank you,' said Milo. 'Now the bullets.'

Dan took the bullets out of his fleece pocket and laid them on the palm of his hand for Milo to see. Then he clenched them in his fist and held them out towards Olga. She hesitated for a moment in the pale light of the sitting room, and then moved towards him. Dan gripped the eight bullets tightly in his right hand. Then he slammed them down onto the stone-flagged floor as hard as he could. The bullets cannoned off the floor beneath Olga's feet, scattering in all directions. Some slid under the kitchen cupboard. Startled, Olga stepped back and as she did one of the bullets lodged beneath her left foot and she fell backwards, knocking Milo off balance and together they fell to the floor. As Milo struggled to his feet, Dan rushed forward and hit him hard from behind, sending him crashing into the wall.

For Tom, time stood still, as Dan made a grab for the Kalashnikov, sending it spinning out of Milo's hands. Both men scrambled towards where it came to rest. Milo reached it first and fired off a round in Dan's direction. In her head Ana screamed. *Oh no,* but no words came out. The bullet missed Dan by no more than a centimetre, shattering the window. Olga hovered in close attendance, unsure what to do. Ana bit her lip, almost making it bleed. She had to fight.

Chapter 81

Outside, the snow tumbled down, while in the darkness of his room, Bleiburg knelt in silent prayer. He rose and walked over to sit at the desk by the window, then as he opened his laptop, a subdued light spilt out into the room. For a moment he sat motionless, watching the rhythmic flash of the cursor, before his fingers deftly caressed the keyboard to enter his screen name: *Bleiburg 1945*. Then he logged in using his password and security code, one after the other. Any delay and the programme would time out. There was no room for error. One digit out of place would close the entire network down. The Knight of Saint Jerome submitted his report to Monsignor Bernarez. Then he read all six messages in his inbox, replied to three and immediately deleted all ten transmissions.

Chapter 82

In the sitting room at Keeperswood Cottage, Ana readied herself. She had to fight back. She couldn't let others die for her. Not this time. Milo raised his gun again, his face blighted by a sardonic sneer.

'No Milo, this is not supposed to happen,' screamed Olga. 'You gave me your word there would be no one killed. You all did.'

Milo smiled and lowered the gun to his side, and Ana's heart rate slowed.

'You're quite right, Olga. Their deaths are not included in my orders.'

Dan turned to Tom and Ana. 'Are you all right?' he asked.

'Yes Dad, I'm okay,' said Tom quietly.

Ana didn't speak. She was staring at Milo. Staring at Milo's scar. She nodded back with a fixed determined stare, as she fidgeted with the sleeve of her mountain jacket. Ana watched as Olga began rescuing the spilt bullets and reloading the Luger. The four bullets that were under the kitchen cupboard were forgotten. Now with a loaded gun Olga looked more comfortable. Milo and Olga were back in control and returned to the task of searching for the second gun.

'So, who has the other gun?' Milo demanded.

'What other gun?' begged Dan. 'There was only one.'

Ana didn't speak. Milo turned slowly to face Tom, pointing the Kalashnikov directly at his head. Tom stared back. Then Olga took the heat off him in the most bizarre way.

'Let me see your socks,' she said.'

'What?' stammered Tom, as he began to remove his gaiters in order to comply.

'Not you,' snapped Olga. 'Her.' Olga pointed the now loaded Luger at Ana.

'I remember now, back on the mountain you said you were ready to go, and that you had dry socks on. Yes?'

'Okay, so what about it?' said Ana defiantly.

'I know you didn't bring spare socks with you, so if you have dry socks on, they must be mine. Show me your socks,' demanded Olga.

Ana bent down and casually rolled up her trouser leg to reveal a pair of thick, bright blue socks. 'Yes,' declared Olga. 'My socks, you got those socks from my rucksack when I was with those two checking on the weather. The missing gun was in my rucksack with the socks, hidden in a green sponge. You have the gun. Give it to me,' she demanded.

Tom looked relieved now he was off the hook. Ana smiled sweetly at Milo. She knew an act of subservience right now might save her life.

'I don't have the gun,' she said with real conviction, her face bathed with surprise and innocence.

Confused, Olga walked over to where Milo stood.

'What are we to do? I know she has the gun!'

'Search her,' instructed Milo.

Olga moved towards Ana, brandishing the Luger. As she did, Ana pulled out a small single shot pistol from inside the sleeve of her mountain jacket.

'Here it is. You can have the gun.'

Olga turned to Milo, smiled in triumph and held out her hand to collect the gun.

'Bitch!' screamed Ana, as she discharged the gun at point blank range. The bullet hit Olga in the chest, forcing her back. She crashed hard into Milo, hitting him in the solar plexus, knocking the wind out of him. Then together they fell heavily to the floor as the Luger fell from Olga's hand and the Kalashnikov skittered to the far side of the room. Milo managed to free himself and scramble to his feet. Dan and Tom watched, while Ana viewed the scene still clutching Olga's single shot pistol. Milo looked up. Why had no one moved to overpower him?

'Good morning comrade, you look as if you could use a little help.'

Milo turned around to face a man standing in the doorway. He was well dressed and immaculately groomed. Ana recognised him at once. It was Luciano Magiera, the Front of House Manager from Kermincham Hall. Now Ana looked down the barrel of yet another gun. 'I was waiting near the campsite rendezvous in the Audi, as ordered, when I heard a gunshot,' he said breathlessly. 'I thought I should come and investigate. So I drove down. What in God's name has happened?'

He gazed at Milo, then at Olga's body.

Milo picked up the Kalashnikov and poked it into Ana's face. Ana stood defiant. She would not hide. She had to fight. She'd made a promise.

Dan crouched down to check on Olga. His search for a pulse met with failure. Olga was dead.

'I'd kill you right now, Poborski, if I didn't have orders to the contrary.' The face of an angel looked back at Milo, through the eyes of a resolute assassin. 'Just do exactly as I say and no one else will get hurt.' Milo knelt at Olga's side and gently closed her eyelids. 'Let's go.' He snapped, as he picked up Olga's Luger. 'No argument.' Dan Tom and Ana walked wearily out of Keeperswood Cottage and into the Audi, leaving their rucksacks behind. No one argued.

Chapter 83

Boris and Leo finished their drinks and made to go. Stefan had hardly touched his vodka and appeared in no hurry to leave the bar, or the company of Julie Hardy.

'See you in the morning, Boris. Goodnight, Leo.' Stefan acknowledged their departure with a smile and the wave of his hand.

'Breakfast is at seven thirty, Stefan,' Leo reminded him.

'Okay Leo, I'm coming now.'

Boris pushed open his bedroom door and switched on the light. As he turned towards the window, he noticed an envelope on the bedroom floor. Pushed under the door while he'd been at dinner. He picked it up, thinking it was some sort of last-minute instruction regarding tomorrow's signing ceremony. The envelope was handwritten in a scrawly handwriting. He opened the envelope and read the letter it contained. It was a simple message.

'We have Ana safe. You must resign your position as General Director of Sarajevo Steel. Do not sign the document to facilitate the Co-operation and Finance Agreement. Failure to comply will ensure she dies. Follow our instructions and no harm will come to her. Your every move is known to us.'

A myriad of conflicting emotions raced wildly around his head. What must he do? Could he hatch some plan to rescue Ana and save Sarajevo Steel? He stared down at the letter. For Boris the threat it carried corroded any hope of resistance. Then a thought struck him. It could be a hoax, a trick, or some kind of game. Although even as the thought was coursing through his brain, a contradictory wave of rejection sped alongside it. Boris made towards the bedroom door, intending to go to Ana's room. She could be there right now. No. They could be watching. He must avoid any action that suggested non-compliance. Boris phoned Ana's room at five minutes past one and then Olga's. There was no reply from either. He replaced the receiver, with all hope gone.

Leo was in bed when the phone rang. It was a one-way conversation. Leo listened carefully, and then replaced the receiver without speaking. He pulled on a sweatshirt and a pair of jeans, then made a phone call, before hurrying out of the room.

Stefan stared into the refrigerator, its gleaming white walls echoing their message back. The refrigerator was empty. Morosely he contemplated life without food until breakfast. He picked up the room service menu and began interrogating its pages. Then the phone rang. The refrigerator door was still open as Stefan left the room; his hunger forgotten.

Leo and Stefan arrived in Boris' room within minutes of each other. Stefan was first to arrive. He read the letter three, perhaps four times. He was still reading it when Leo arrived. Stefan handed the letter to Leo, who at first did not read the letter. When he did, it was a quick cursory glance. Leo said nothing as the silence drained in, racking up the tension, twisting it tighter. Boris broke the silence.

'I must tell you,' Boris hesitated. 'You are the first to know. I intend resigning as General Director and will not sign the agreement tomorrow.'

Silence returned. Then Leo spoke. The gravity of the situation was etched on his face, yet his voice was calm and measured.

'Why is that?' he asked.

Boris wrung his hands, his face contorted as if in physical pain.

'Is it not obvious?' demanded Boris. 'Read the letter. Read the letter,' he shouted at Leo.

'I have read the letter, and yes, I still ask why?'

'Why? You ask why? Don't make me to spell it out!'

'I must tell you resigning will have no consequence as far as Ana is concerned. No, none at all. They intend to kill Ana no matter what you do. You know this is true as well as I do.'

'But Leo, I must do something,' pleaded Boris. 'I am in danger of losing everything.'

'Absolutely,' replied Leo, placing his arm around Boris. 'First you must get a grip of yourself. We are Ana's only hope.' Leo paused. 'You cannot let her down when she needs you most.'

'What must I do?' asked Boris. Some of the anxiety in his voice had now subsided. 'I know every word you say is true.'

'Boris, yours is the hardest task of all. You must do nothing and behave normally.'

'Do nothing? You must be mad!' stormed Boris as he paced the room. 'I must find Ana.'

'Spare me the histrionics. How will you find Ana, tell me that? How?'

'I will find her. You can be sure of that.'

'How?' asked Leo.

'I don't know.' Boris felt confusion and anger welling up inside. His logic became entangled in a mass of contradictions.

'I understand how you feel, Boris, but you must stay calm.'

'Understand? What would you understand of a father's love and affection? Or for that matter the duty and obligation a father has for his child?'

'Boris,' said Leo in a voice barely above a whisper. 'It is true I have no children. But I know what it means to be a father and lose a child. The night Zara and Katerina died in Babonavic; my unborn child died too. Zara and I were to be married after the war. She was carrying my child when she was murdered. I only found out from Marija at the funeral. That night in Babonavic I lost all those I loved the most. Since that day, all I have felt is hate and the need for revenge.'

At first Boris said nothing. He couldn't find the right words.

'Forgive me, Leo. I didn't know. I'm so sorry. I didn't know.'

'Trust me,' said Leo. 'I will return with Ana. Olga may be in danger too.'

'Where will you begin?' asked Boris.

'This isn't the beginning. The beginning was back in Sarajevo. This will probably not even be the end.' Then Leo closed the door and was gone.

After Stefan left, Boris lay on the bed, completely drained. Was Ana already dead? The thought spread like an evil cancer, and as the hours passed, Boris revisited this precipice of uncertainty, as his sleepless night dissolved into a tormented dawn.

Chapter 84

Leo sat in his room with Savo, drinking strong black coffee.

'So, have you made up your mind about Olga?' asked Savo. 'Is she involved or not?'

'I can't really tell, but the company she kept back in Sarajevo makes her a suspect.'

'So that's it then, that's all the information we've been able to gather. I've been thinking about it since you rang me. Is it enough?'

At first Leo made no reply. He rose to his feet, walked over to the window and watched, as the snow drifted gracefully down and landed on the windowsill.

'I don't know. The intelligence we collected in Bosnia and the reconnaissance we've carried out here in England, gives us a chance, though not a good chance.'

'We still have one source of information we've not used.'

'You mean Room 32?'

Savo nodded.

'But if you go there, they'll know you're coming for Ana and she's as good as dead. You know what you'll have to do. Would you like me to go?'

Leo turned away from the window to face Savo.

'No Savo, this is something I need to do. Give me the key to Room 32.'

'The situation is not as we anticipated,' said Savo. 'We thought they'd come to us.'

Leo nodded. 'You're right. Now we'll have to go to them. We leave at two o'clock.'

'I'll go and get ready,' said Savo. 'I'll see you at two.'

Leo finished packing his rucksack and took the stairs two at a time, down to hotel reception.

'Good morning Mr Illic, you're up late. How can I help you?' Julie beamed.

'I need a car and driver at two o'clock prompt. I'd like Savo Stanisic and the big four-by-four he drives.'

Julie checked Savo's driver's logbook.

'Yes sir, we do have a car and Savo Stanisic is available.' Julie reserved the Mercedes ML 350 in Savo's logbook for the use of Leo Illic. 'However, due to the weather conditions, we're advising guests not to go out unless it's an emergency. Some of the Embassy drivers have yet to return from Manchester Airport. Is it a real emergency sir?'

'Yes, I guess it probably is. I'll be back at two, thank you.'

Leo took the stairs to the third floor and let himself in to Room 32 with the key that Savo had given him. He surveyed the room by the suppressed light of a small table lamp in the corner. As expected, the room was empty, its occupant delayed by the snow. He would come soon, within the hour had been Savo's estimate. Leo made himself comfortable on the bed, closed his eyes and settled down to wait.

After twenty minutes, the sound of a key turning in the lock brought Leo to his feet. One of the Embassy drivers who had brought them from Manchester Airport entered the room, a map in his hand.

'Good evening Hajji,' welcomed Leo.

Hajji was a swarthy-faced man of about thirty, with enormous hands. He walked towards Leo, his huge frame blocking out the light from the table lamp. Leo held up his hand.

'The road map if you please?' Hajji threw the map he held in his hand into Leo's face. 'Thank you. I have some questions for you, very little time and no patience at all. Do you understand?'

Hajji made a grab for his handgun from inside his jacket pocket. His next voluntary action was to pick himself up from beneath the coffee table, a splash of blood spilling from his mouth, caused by a savage smack to the face. The gun spun away towards the door. As he struggled to his feet, Hajji took another punch to the stomach and fell heavily backwards to land hard on the floor. He wiped the blood from his mouth. Clambering to his knees he took another uncompromising blow to the head. Hajji collapsed, hitting his forehead against the edge of the bedside table, splitting the soft tissue above his left eye almost to the bone. A flap of raw flesh hung over his eyebrow. More blood flowed. Leo grabbed Hajji's coat collar and hauled him to his feet, where he stood unsteadily for a moment before Leo landed another blow, dispersing his nose in an angry mess across his face. Hajji lay motionless on the floor in a sad bloody heap. Then he made a grab for the gun. Leo leapt over the coffee table and brought all his weight down on Hajji's hand with his heel, breaking Hajji's thumb and index finger. Hajji released the gun.

'My gun, I think,' said Leo, as he took it easily from Hajji's grasp. 'Now, first tell me the part Olga Lukic is to play in this?'

Hajji did not speak. Leo grabbed a great tuft of Hajji's hair and pulled his head back, almost snapping his neck. A distinct click fractured the silence, as Leo released the safety catch on the handgun. It was followed by a sharp intake of breath from Hajji. Leo forced the barrel of the gun aggressively into Hajji's bloodied mouth, splitting his tongue and tearing the skin on the roof of his mouth. Leo withdrew the barrel from Hajji's gullet to allow him to speak and thrust it hard into the bridge of his nose, gouging the skin.

'Now tell me about Olga.'

'She is to bring Ana Poborski down off the mountain to the rendezvous and on to the safe house. Then disappear.'

'And that's all?' Leo pressed.

'Yes, that is all.'

'The leather case the driver Josip Budach gave her when we arrived at the hotel. The one he so kindly 'returned' to her. What was in it?'

'A Luger 45, a single shot pistol, a mobile telephone and a tracking transmitter.'

'A tracking device? So, they know where Olga is at any time?'

'Yes,' said Hajji.

'Where is the rendezvous?'

Hajji began his valedictory speech. Bloodied dribble flowed from one corner of his mouth, while the flap of red flesh that dangled over his eyebrow seriously impaired the vision from his left eye.

'The camp site, Wasdale, in the gents shower block.'

Hajji had great difficulty talking through a mouth full of blood and broken teeth. His swollen tongue seemed to fill his mouth.

'Thank you,' said Leo, 'And the safe house?' Leo asked without a trace of emotion.

'Timbersbrook Cottage.'

'Where is that?'

'Nether Wasdale.'

'Thank you,' said Leo. 'And the time of the rendezvous?' Silence followed.

'Come on, you are doing really well, but please, I must hurry you.'

Leo allowed Hajji to prop himself up on his left elbow so he could spit out the blood and the broken teeth. Hajji sat in a puddle of his own blood that stained the carpet an anguished reddish-brown.

'It has changed because of the snow,' he spluttered. 'It is now four o'clock.'

'Thank you so much,' said Leo.

The butt of the gun was starting to hurt the heel of Leo's hand as he continued to force it into the bridge of Hajji's nose.

'It seems such a long time since your University days in Sarajevo, with Olga, and the others,' said Leo. 'But tell me, are you still climbing at Romanija? I remember seeing you the last time I was there?'

Leo grasped Hajji's head in a vice like grip and with an instinctive snap of his wrists, Hajji was silent. Leo allowed Hajji's wasted body to slump to the floor. He gazed down into Hajji's dead eyes, devoid of any feeling.

***

Savo was ready at two o'clock, as snowflakes hurried to cover the Mercedes ML 350. It was a long drive to Wasdale through the Cumbrian Mountains. They travelled south through Keswick and Ambleside before turning west over Wrynose Pass to Santon Bridge, then north to Wasdale Head. Drifting snow had sculptured icy buttresses across the narrow single-track road. As the car entered the final zigzag before the summit of Hardknott Pass, the wheels began to spin in the deep snow. Savo took his foot off the accelerator as the rear end of the car fishtailed wildly across the narrow mountain track, scattering the snow. Savo cursed under his breath as he realised his evasive action was too late. Suddenly the car pirouetted through three hundred and sixty degrees in the narrow pass. He fought with the controls, spinning the steering wheel to the left, steering the car into the skid. Savo cursed again, this time out loud, as his heart raced on. Then right on the summit he brought the car under control before they continued their long slide down the mountain, as Savo prayed.

'Well done Savo, we'd better return on the valley road, it takes much longer, but it's a lot safer. I thought you'd lost it there.'

'What do you mean, lost it?' asked Savo in an injured tone. 'There was never any problem.'

Leo consulted Hajji's map as he directed Savo to the Wast Water Inn, where the Mercedes would be inconspicuous.

'There are lights on,' said Savo. 'The place is open, perhaps it never closes?'

Leo pushed open the door, where rows of empty tables greeted them from the almost deserted bar. Several people lay asleep on the floor, some in sleeping bags. Leo guessed they were climbers, collateral damage from the storm. Ted was serving another customer as they sat down by a welcoming fire.

'Good morning, what can I get you gentlemen?'

Savo ordered for both of them.

'That's fine,' said Ted, confirming Savo's order. 'Just the two coffees.'

'Yes please, and can you make them strong and black?' asked Savo.

Leo checked Hajji's map as they drank their coffee.

'I'm done with this now,' Leo handed the map to Savo. 'You keep it, you may need it to find me, but do nothing until I send for you.'

They finished their coffee and Savo paid the bill. Leo disappeared with his rucksack, to emerge from the gent's toilet a different man. He was dressed for the mountains, ready for anything. They walked to the car and Savo handed Leo his Agram 2000 and two hundred rounds of ammunition.

'Try and get some sleep, I'll call you when I need you.'

Savo climbed into the car to sleep and await further instructions.

Leo went to get Ana.

Chapter 85

Roman woke at Timbersbrook Cottage with a jolt and rubbed his eyes. He realised he'd slept since shortly after his phone conversation with Milo, informing him the kidnap of Ana Poborski had been accomplished. On receiving Milo's call from Keeperswood, Roman had instructed Josip Budach, the Embassy driver in Kermincham Hall, to deliver the first of two hostage notes to Boris Poborski's room. The second was to be delivered on Sunday morning at nine o'clock, prior to the signing of the agreement. Everything was now going according to plan, despite Olga's unexplained delay near the summit of Scafell Pike.

He rose stiffly from the armchair, made his way into the kitchen and put on the kettle. As the kettle boiled, he could see through the cottage window that the snow had almost stopped. He made some tea and decided to finish off the last of the cheddar cheese. It was his favourite and had been impossible to buy in Bosnia during the war. A green light emitted a welcoming wink as he returned to the sitting room. He could tell from the tracking device that Olga was still at Keeperswood Cottage.

Chapter 86

Luciano powered the Audi Quattro out of the lane from Keeperswood and down the Wasdale road. Turning up the narrow lane that led to Timbersbrook Cottage, the wheels began to spin.

'I can't get any further. The last thing I need is to get stuck in the snow. We'd better walk from here.'

Milo nodded and Luciano switched off the engine and climbed out into the deep snow. Dan, Tom, and Ana sat waiting in the back of the car, reluctant to leave.

'Okay, get out.'

Milo signalled them to follow Luciano and they trudged slowly up the drive. Milo brought up the rear, his Kalashnikov trained on their backs. A grimy light dribbled out from the windows of Timbersbrook Cottage, splashing lazily on the snow-covered path, helping to show the way. Dan looked up at the night sky as finally the snow stopped. Ana Poborski chased hidden memories from the past as she followed Tom towards the cottage. The door opened and Roman waited to usher them inside.

'Take the snow off your boots before you come in.' He instructed.

Shivering, Ana kicked the snow off her boots, then entered the sitting room. The others followed suit. The room was larger than the one at Keeperswood, with big comfortable armchairs. Ana over balanced dropping her gloves on the chair as Milo pushed roughly past her to hand Olga's Luger to Roman.

'Here, you may find a use for this. It's loaded.'

Tom considered flopping down in the big armchair nearest the door but then thought better of it.

Milo's eyes followed Ana around the room, like a wolf in a sheepfold. He realised she felt no fear of death, but knew by the time he'd had his fun, she would welcome death, embrace it as a friend. Tom kept as close as he could to Ana, while Dan looked around the room for any means of escape. He saw none.

Roman welcomed Milo and Luciano. His relief they had at last arrived was evident.

'So, we have lost Olga, that is unfortunate. Her father, Commissar Vladimir Lukic, was a close friend of mine and of course Olga provided key information from inside Sarajevo Steel that has been so vital to us.' He looked over to where Ana, Tom and Dan stood. 'I see we have two extra packages to deal with,' said Roman, smoothing his salt and pepper hair.

'Yes, it is unfortunate,' said Milo, 'but it was unavoidable.'

'First we must see to our guests. This way if you would be so kind?'

Roman led them down a short passageway, followed by Luciano, to reveal a low door behind a heavy curtain.

'I'm sure you'll be comfortable in here.' He swung the door open to reveal a small storeroom.

The three of them trundled into the low, box-like room. The sound of the door slamming behind them shattered any hope of escape. It carried an undeniable finality. There was no electric light in the room; the only prospect of illumination came from a small opaque window at the back of the storeroom. It took some time for their eyes to adjust to the unlit room. They sat down on the cold stone floor.

'So, do you get it now?' asked Ana. 'These bast… these people, have kidnapped me to persuade my father that signing the agreement will seriously damage my health. But I'm not stupid, they will kill me anyway whether my father signs or not, I know they will. My father will know it too, but he will hope, and he will not sign. If I'm to live, I must escape from this blackhole.'

Dan was relieved Ana knew the truth. Both the plot, and the most probable outcome had dawned on him back at Keeperswood.

'I agree,' said Dan. 'This means we have until eleven o'clock in the morning to sort this thing out, less than seven hours.'

'We?' quizzed Ana.

'Absolutely,' said Dan. 'We're all in this together. These criminals don't take prisoners. It works like this. You're dead. We're dead. Period.'

Tom nodded. 'Together,' he confirmed, as he reached out and held Ana's hand.

Ana forced a smile, lent forward and without any thought kissed him on the cheek.

'I've no intention of hiding in here for seven hours,' she said. 'I intend to fight.'

Dan and Tom quickly assessed their chances of escape. The task did not take long. The verdict was disappointing. The door was solid wood and seemed to be bolted at both the top and bottom on the outside. The stone walls on all sides of the storeroom were of considerable thickness. The ceiling was solid and very low. Neither Tom nor Dan could stand up straight. Tom examined the stone-flagged floor.

'It's hopeless. There's no way out,' announced Dan.

'The window seems to be our only chance,' suggested Tom.

'Being no more than ten centimetres wide and twenty-five centimetres high would seem to limit the possibilities of escape,' observed his father. 'Not to mention the horizontal bars on the inside that only add to the challenge.'

They all tested the strength of the bars and concluded they would not move. It was now fifteen minutes past five. They could hear Roman briefing Luciano on the information he was to feed back to him from Kermincham Hall regarding Boris Poborski. Any sign of police involvement required immediate contact. The door to the cottage banged shut and then they listened at the window as Luciano nursed the Audi out of the lane.

Chapter 87

Milo sat down in one of the armchairs to warm himself by the fire, while Roman poured two large tumblers of whisky before joining him.

'You've had a long wait, Milo, my good friend. It's too late to return to the Wast Water Inn. Stay here tonight and return in the morning.'

'I remember waiting three days in the woods outside Visoko, while evading UN forces from Srebrenica. The good old days,' Roman reminisced.

'The good old days,' echoed Milo. 'Do you ever think about the people we killed, the victims?' Milo enquired pensively, turning the whisky glass slowly round in his hand.

'We were all victims,' replied Roman. 'We all lost Yugoslavia.'

'Yes,' reflected Milo. 'We all lost Yugoslavia.'

'Milo,' said Roman. 'I give you a toast. To the people's revolution, Operation Bosnian Dawn and the return of Tito.'

Roman emptied his glass and held it quizzically between his stubby fingers.

'To Operation Bosnian Dawn and the return of Tito,' echoed a beaming Milo. 'I'll drink to that.'

Chapter 88

Silence flooded the cottage now the wind had dropped. Dan and Tom endured a weary fight with sleep, shifting position on the hard stone floor. In the stillness, Roman and Milo's voices drifted through to where Ana lay awake, as she replayed the day's events in her head, searching for some link that would make escape possible. She looked around in the darkness. Would she die here, would this be her tomb?

'Stay here until I come for you.' She heard her mother's voice, soft and loving, wrapped in echoes from the past.

'Roman,' called out Milo. Milo had found Ana's gloves on the armchair and begun stroking his rough unshaven face with them as he drank in the essence that was Ana Poborski.

'I'm in here, Milo,' Roman called back from the kitchen. 'I'll be through in a moment.'

Ana embraced her epiphany.

Roman, Milo. Over here, Milo.

Echoes from Babonavic. Milo's scar, Roman's salt and pepper hair. Now, for Ana the game had changed. She bit her bottom lip, tasting blood. She would keep her promise. Until then, she'd share the identity of her captors with no one but her mother.

Milo made himself comfortable in one of the armchairs. Then took out his penknife and began to shred Ana's gloves.

Roman occupied the only bedroom in the cottage. He refilled his glass and sat sipping his whisky, before settling down to sleep. As he relaxed, his mind took him back forty years, back to the very beginning, to his days at the University of Belgrade.

Chapter 89
Brotherhood and Unity

Roman Drasko had decided that meeting his hero, as he promoted 'Brotherhood and Unity,' was more important than his University studies that warm September day in 1961. Roman walked the short distance from his halls of residence to the railway station in Belgrade. No part of the platform was visible below the eager faces that bobbed beneath a sea of waving arms. As 'The Blue Train' entered the station it hissed and grunted, before falling silent, and when the carriage door opened, Roman was deafened by the tumultuous cheers and applause. Roman's hero stepped onto the platform, his medals glinting in the autumn sunshine, as a broad smile escaped from behind his eyes, flooding his face. His tactile progress was slow as he laboured through the throng, shaking hands with everyone within his reach.

Roman pressed forward. Now he was so near he could almost touch him. Almost, and as their eyes met, Roman thrust his arm forwards, grasping his hero's hand in a firm, venerate handshake. Then in an instant, the ebb and flow of the molten crowd carried Roman down the platform and away from the hand of Marshall Josip Bros Tito, President of the Socialist Federal Republic of Yugoslavia and its founding father. As Roman made his way home, the cheers still ringing in his head, he knew Marsala Tita would live forever.

Chapter 90

Dan woke to the silence of his jail. He was sure their captors must be sleeping. Then he heard it for the first time. A faint tapping noise, barely audible. Could it be the wind? Then the noise stopped. He tried to sleep, but after a few seconds the distracting noise returned, louder this time, as if demanding attention. It could be the sound of stone on stone? This time it was closer. He listened at the small opaque window. Nothing? Then it came again and then twice more. Dan found a small stone on the floor and tapped a signal back. Outside, the window frame moved. At first only marginally at the bottom right hand corner. Followed by a little at the left. The opaque window disappeared, and in its place, Dan could make out two eyes. Dan held his breath. Then a face appeared. It was the face of a man. The face smiled through the bars and held an index finger to his lips, to indicate the need for silence.

'How many are holding you?'

'Two,' Dan whispered in reply.

The man smiled and looked pleased.

'Guns?' he said softly.

'At least two guns,' Dan replied, then added sotto voce, 'Kalashnikov and Luger.'

The man nodded and continued in a hushed tone.

'Diversion.'

He held up four fingers for Dan to see and mimed the word 'minutes.' Dan nodded and the face was gone. Dan pressed the button on his watch to activate the back light. It was sixteen minutes to eight. He woke Tom and Ana, explaining the need for silence, that help was outside, and that in four minutes a diversion was required. They agreed that Ana would insist she needed the toilet. Dan activated the light on his watch. Twelve minutes to eight. On Dan's signal, Ana called out, while Tom banged hard on the door. It took only a few seconds to achieve a response.

'Quiet!'

It was Milo.

'I need the toilet,' begged Ana, in a tone she judged would instil empathy. 'Please, please,' she pleaded. 'I need the lavatory.'

It worked, the door swung open and from behind a Kalashnikov, Milo beckoned. Ana had no option but to go, not because of the Kalashnikov, though that was reason enough, but because she did need the toilet. Milo held Ana by the scruff of the neck as he frogmarched her to the bathroom, demanding she keep the door open. Ana didn't mind, believing talking out loud during the diversion with the door open, served their plan. She talked incessantly, hoping their rescuer would hear her through the open door and know the diversion was in progress. She begged to go safely back to her father, begged Milo for her life, while silently she prayed for something quite different.

Milo loitered close by, staring in at Ana through the open door, his eyes darting lubriciously up her slender bare legs. He felt a wonderful sensation in his scrotum and the word fellatio floated into his head. He began to fantasise on a surge of erotica as his breathing became heavier. Ana stood up, only then did she become aware of Milo watching her and the blood drained from her cheeks. Wearily, Roman emerged from the bedroom.

'What's going on, Milo?'

'The Poborski girl needed the toilet, that's all it is. Go back to bed.'

Roman gave a lecherous, knowing grin, as he became aware of Milo indulging in his perverted voyeurism.

'Not yet,' admonished Roman with a yawn. 'You'll have to wait, but as I promised, she's all yours as soon as Poborski resigns. I'm going back to bed now, just keep the noise down, okay?'

Roman poured himself another tumbler of whisky before returning to the bedroom. As Milo pushed Ana towards the storeroom, she collided with the door and fell to the floor. Milo stood over her, legs astride.

'Don't put me back in there, please don't.'

'You're becoming a nuisance, Poborski, but later, you and I are going to have a little fun together.'

As Milo slid the last bolt across to open the storeroom door Dan and Tom pulled the door hard towards them, grabbing Milo, pulling him down into the storeroom. Then, a crash of splintering timber and breaking glass distracted Milo. He broke loose to repel what he judged to be a greater threat that was coming from the sitting room. The noise from the storeroom had already brought Roman racing out of the bedroom, Luger in hand, and into a hail of flying glass from the sitting room door. He fired a shot at nothing but his own fear, followed by a further two shots in the direction of the intruder. Neither shot found its mark. A burst of gunfire rang out, bringing Roman down, blood gushing from his chest. He fired one more shot into the air, before he slumped into the armchair at the back of the room.

Milo raced from the storeroom; the Kalashnikov hungry for its first victim. As he rounded into the sitting room, he instinctively let off two bursts of fire at nothing in particular. Milo's tactic worked, one of the bullets found its target and their rescuer crashed heavily to the floor, shot in the left shoulder. Dan raced out of the storeroom in an attempt to bring Milo down. How, he did not know. Dan recoiled in horror as he saw Milo standing menacingly over their wounded liberator, the Kalashnikov ready to conclude the task begun but not yet finished. Unarmed, Dan was unsure how best to act. He hesitated for no more than a heartbeat, and then he raced towards Milo. He was too late. Not by much, but enough to push him back into second place.

Ana tore past Dan and in one wild, fluid movement, slammed hard into Milo's back, knocking him into the armchair. Now Tom was on the scene. As Milo fell, he turned and fired off a short burst with the Kalashnikov. Tom felt the heat and then the blood as a bullet grazed his temple before continuing skywards to bury itself in the cottage's wooden beams. It knocked Tom off balance, and he tumbled into the doorway, blood spilling from the head wound. Milo got up from the armchair and threw Ana to the floor and smiling down at her he aimed the Kalashnikov in her direction.

'No,' screamed Tom as he rose to his feet and moved towards Milo.

Two shots rang out, taking down their objective. Two bullets hit home and Milo crashed headfirst into the slate-topped coffee table.

***

Dan bent down to collect Milo's Kalashnikov, laying it down on the nearby armchair. Their injured rescuer sat propped up on his right elbow, a submachine gun in his hand, still aimed where Milo lay beneath the coffee table in a broken and bloodied heap. The submachine gun dropped to the floor, as a crimson patch on their rescuer's left shoulder grew bigger by the second.

'I'm Leo Illic, he said.

'And I'm Roman Drasko.' A voice from the back of the room interrupted.

'Do forgive me if I don't get up, I only want to say goodbye to Miss Ana Poborski as she leaves for the next world.'

The barrel of the Luger pointed directly at Ana. Total silence descended on the room for a moment. Roman squeezed the trigger. Then nothing happened. Roman looked stunned. He gazed down at the gun, Olga's Luger, completely mystified. The gun was empty. Ana realised the bullets that should have been in the last four chambers were the ones Olga hadn't found; they still lay beneath the kitchen cabinet at Keeperswood. He was about to pull the trigger again, but someone beat him to it.

Ana snatched Milo's Kalashnikov from the armchair. It was much lighter than she expected. A weapon with the ability to take away a life should weigh much more. It fitted snugly into her shoulder. Somehow it made her feel complete. This was Ana's moment. She would keep her promise to her mother. She would never hide again.

Roman froze as he looked up and saw Ana with the Kalashnikov. The power of the gun gave Ana a huge adrenaline surge. She waited, but not for long. Then she squeezed the trigger, firing six bullets into Roman. His body jerked convulsively, then he lay still.

Ana held her mother in her arms, drank the fragrance that danced in her hair. Then she dropped to her knees triumphant, as she watched the life drain out of Roman Drasko. It was twenty-three minutes past eight.

Chapter 91

On Sunday morning, Boris woke from the brief escape that sleep had brought, as real-life flooded in. He knelt and prayed, trying to reach out to Ana, willing her to be all right. Somewhere a clock ticked.

Stefan came out of the lobby. He acknowledged Julie with a nod of his head and a shy smile as he entered the lift. Then he made his way to Boris' room and tapped on the door. Boris rose from his knees still chanting the mantra. 'Be all right. Be all right.' Stefan entered and then quickly closed the door.

'No news, I'm afraid,' said Stefan.

'Nothing at all?' Boris' question carried his anguish.

'No, nothing at all, but it is early yet.' Stefan tried to be reassuring but saw that his failure was visible in the face of his friend. 'Are you going to be okay?'

'Yes, I'll be fine. What time is it?' Boris asked.

'Eight twenty-five,' answered Stefan. 'We should be down for breakfast at nine. You'll have to hurry up. The last thing we need are questions or delays, they may be watching us. Anyway, you look as if you could do with a good breakfast.'

'Okay, I'll see you down there,' said Boris.

Boris went to the bathroom. He barely recognised the stranger that stared back at him from the bathroom mirror. He shaved, showered and quickly dressed before taking the lift to the ground floor. The descent of the lift seemed to correlate with his fall in optimism. He missed Ana and wanted her back. He knew he'd failed her again.

A wall of sound greeted him as he walked into the lobby. He paused for a moment and made to turn and run, but somehow managed to propel himself the last few stuttering steps into the restaurant as other delegates, including Roger Arlington, were leaving. Perfunctorily, he exchanged pleasantries before joining Stefan at a table near the window. Stefan called the waiter and ordered a full English breakfast. Boris ordered toast and coffee. He looked around at a sea of empty tables and partly eaten meals.

'This couldn't happen without collusion,' said Boris through gritted teeth, as he sipped the coffee while the toast remained untouched.

'I know, I've already worked that out,' said Stefan.

'I must have been myopically dammed,' said Boris. 'I've been such a fool.'

'You can't blame yourself. I didn't see this coming. Leo had a couple of telephone calls from Sarajevo yesterday, perhaps he had some idea.'

'It's a possibility. I've noticed he's been missing from time to time but thought nothing of it.'

'I guess we were too engrossed in securing the finance to notice anything else. Leo will get Ana back. I know he will, until then Boris, we must face this with resolve.'

'But can Leo deliver when I need him most? I've failed Ana in the past and buried the failure beneath my preoccupation with Sarajevo Steel, now that failure has simply re-emerged.'

Chapter 92

In Timbersbrook Cottage, Ana rose from her knees triumphant, and walked over to where Roman had fallen. He was no longer a dark and evil demon from her past. Just one hundred kilograms of inert human remains that made the room look untidy. Milo lay slumped, lifeless beneath the coffee table. Her nightmare was over. Ana's relief permeated through her whole body, then the impact of Leo's wounding punched in, and she turned to where he lay. Leo's eyes burnt out from an anaemic face awash with pain.

'You're hurt, Leo. Just stay still, we'll get help.' Ana held his hand. It was cold.

Dan knelt down by Leo's side.

'Tom, help me lift him up, we need to keep the wound as high as possible.'

They raised Leo into a sitting position, where he leaned against the back of one of the armchairs. 'That's better,' said Dan. 'Now we need bandages, lots of them. Find some sheets, there must be some somewhere, we have to stop the bleeding, or he'll...' Dan did not want to conclude with the obvious.

'Die.' Leo completed the sentence through a veil of pain.

Tom went to the bedroom Roman had been using and began tearing up the sheets into long thin strips. Ana came to help.

'Here Tom,' said Ana. 'You need one of these strips to bandage your head. It's bleeding quite badly.'

Dan unzipped Leo's mountain jacket and examined the shoulder wound.

'You're going to be just fine Leo, just fine.'

Leo's shirt was soaked with a great blotch of blood. Dan recoiled in horror, as the blotch grew visibly larger as he looked on.

'Hurry up with those bandages. The bullet wound has opened up a major artery,' he called, as Tom arrived.

Dan made a pad of the folded strips and pressed it firmly onto the open wound to stem the flow, as Ana looked on. At first, blood streamed through the wad of bed sheet bandage. Then it slowed and then almost stopped. Tom made a makeshift sling, and Dan held Leo up, as Tom and Ana slipped the sling over Leo's head and under his arm.

'How does that feel?' asked Ana.

'Feels good.' The words oozed out, as unannounced Leo's life was slipping away. 'I have a Mercedes four-by-four and a driver. Savo Stanisic. Wast Water Inn.' Leo's words were slow. Almost lazy.

'We need to get you to hospital as quickly as we can,' said Dan.

'No. We need to get Ana to Kermincham Hall before eleven o'clock.' Leo's voice trailed off as he sat grey-faced on the floor. 'Eleven o'clock, before the signing takes place.'

'I think we can do both,' said Dan. 'If we can only find a phone, mine's back at Keeperswood still in my rucksack.'

Tom and Ana searched the cottage for a phone.

'Here,' called Tom.

Dan dialled up the number while Ana nursed Leo to make him as comfortable as she could, then she applied a makeshift bandage to Tom's head wound. The phone rang at the other end.

'Come on. Come on, pick up,' encouraged Dan.

'Good morning Wast Water Inn,' said Ted Baker.

'Hi Ted,' Dan tried to iron out the anxiety in his voice without losing the urgency. 'I need your help. You'll find a Mercedes four-by-four waiting in your car park. The driver is Savo Stanisic.'

'What about him?' asked Ted quizzically.

'Tell Savo to pick Leo Illic up from Timbersbrook Cottage, in Nether Wasdale. You know the one. Tell him it's urgent. You may need to give him directions.'

'Who is Leo Illic?' asked Ted somewhat bewildered.

Dan ignored the question and continued. 'Leo has been shot, Savo will understand. Leo is badly hurt. He needs to get to hospital. Got that?'

'Yes,' confirmed Ted as the seriousness of the situation hit home.

'Secondly, ring Greg Childs at Air Ambulance. I need a helicopter up to Wasdale Head to take Leo to hospital at Keswick via Kermincham Hall. Greg owes me a favour. Tell him how urgent it is and ask him to send his best medics along. Leo really needs one. I know they can't land a helicopter at Nether Wasdale, there are too many trees. That's why we need Savo to come to Timbersbrook Cottage to collect us. Get Wasdale Mountain Rescue to stand by in case the road is blocked and Savo can't get through. Did you get all that?' asked Dan.

'Yes,' replied Ted.

'Any problems ring me back on this number.'

Dan read the number written on the telephone dial and Ted repeated it back to him.

'Take care,' said Ted.

'It's a bit late for that…,' but before Dan finished speaking there was a sharp click, and the line went dead. When he returned to the sitting room, Ana's concern for Leo was intense. He lay there without moving, so still.

'Leo, I know you're tired, but you must fight the urge to fall asleep. Talk to him, Ana,' said Dan. 'You seem to know him.'

'Leo, wake up, we'll soon be at Kermincham Hall and my father will sign the agreement, and then everything will be okay. How bad is the pain? Is it really bad?'

Ana knelt down beside him, kissed him gently on the cheek and held his hand.

***

Leo tried to smile. He lay there watching patches of coloured light as they burst all around him. He was back home in Babonavic with Zara. Leo felt Zara's kiss on his cheek. He held her hand and for the first time in six years he was happy. Then Leo slipped away, embracing sleep.

PART THREE

Chapter 93

Paula Amanda Medrith, BL PhD, reread the security brief she'd just received, but it still made no sense. She tried to get her head around the possibility that a Soviet agent may be at Kermincham Hall. This was a low-key security assignment. A diplomatic mission populated by bankers and bureaucrats. Only the presence of two Ambassadors, Joe Brown and Ivan Bobic justified the modest MI6 involvement. She turned back to the subject of the security brief. He was a possible candidate. He had recent military experience, he had killed before and even though that was under military command, Paula knew it was highly relevant. The question Paula had to address early on that Sunday morning was a simple one. Was he here to kill again? It was her call.

A doting father had mapped out Paula's career. She would read law at Oxford, which she did, she would pass out at the very top of her year, which she did, and she would join her father's legal firm as a junior partner, which she did not. A lifetime of repetition, interspersed with skiing in Aspen and summer breaks in St. Kitts, was not the life Paula was searching for. Same old, same old wasn't Paula's style. She really didn't have the figure for a straitjacket. At five feet eleven she could mix it with the larger ladettes and hold her own with the Knightsbridge set. Either way, wherever she went male eyes invariably followed her mop of blonde hair, nice arse and firm breasts.

Then at one of the many Oxford dinner parties sponsored by law firms looking for fresh talent, she was approached by the intelligence service. She'd never imagined joining MI6. That was more than ten years ago. She'd never looked back, and her father had never forgiven her. Not even now.

She sat in her executive suit that served as a control centre in Kermincham Hall rechecking the profiling criteria, but she couldn't fault it, there was no doubt Dalibor Tesak fitted the profile like a glove. There was a tap on the door. Paula replaced the security brief in her case, secured the lock and closed down her laptop. She opened the door and Jon White entered the room. They'd seen service together before, Jon with the CIA or The Company, as he liked to call it, Paula with MI6. This was Jon's last tour of duty before he hung up his gun. He was not sorry to be leaving. He was looking forward to becoming a full-time family man. Paula dug out the security brief and Jon scrutinised it, while she fired up her laptop, bringing up a mug shot of Tesak.

'This is our suspect,' said Paula as Jon viewed the screen.

'Sure does seem that way,' Jon agreed.

'He doesn't look like your everyday hit man, but he certainly has all the right credentials. The problem is, if we pull him in and we're wrong, we expose our vulnerability and if we're right, they simply replace Tesak with the operative next in line. Someone we don't know.'

'No worries, Tesak is my problem now, he won't be able to pass wind inside this hotel without Jon White knowing.'

'Are you okay with this, as well as caretaking Joe Brown?' asked Paula. 'I know the American Ambassador is your number one priority.'

'Sure thing, but I figure any threat to Joe could come from this direction, and I have quality cover on call twenty-four seven.'

Paula printed off a photo of Tesak and passed it to Jon.

'Something for your album,' said Paula.

He held the print strangled in his giant fist as he left the room. Paula picked through the rest of the day's security briefings relating to incidents that were outside her current theatre of operation. One brief in particular caught her attention. It announced that the Chinese were threatening to withdraw from the XXVII Olympiad, which was to be staged in Sydney in 2000. The Chinese had tabled no official explanation and insider speculation failed to suggest any credible reason for their action. The Cubans were expected to follow in the next twenty-four hours and other Communist countries were making unhelpful noises. The situation had placed the games on the brink of collapse. To Paula it all sounded like handbags at twelve paces.

Chapter 94

Ted Baker replaced the receiver as the line went dead, then dashed out into knee-deep snow. A big Mercedes four by four stood in the far corner of the car park. Ted banged hard on the driver's door. The door opened at once, covering Ted with snow as it slid from the roof. Savo jumped out of the car.

'What is it?

'Are you Savo Stanisic?' Savo nodded. 'I have a message from Leo Illic.'

'Ana. Has he got Ana?'

'I don't know, but he's been shot. It sounds pretty bad. He's not alone though. Leo has help, but he needs you to bring him back here.'

'So where is he?'

'Timbersbrook Cottage, Nether Wasdale.'

'How do I get there?' Savo wrestled with the map. 'Come on. I need directions.'

'Okay, okay. You go down to the far end of Wast Water. Then take the first turning on the left. It's signposted Stanton Bridge. You'll find Timbersbrook Cottage on your right. It's the first cottage you come to, set back a little way from the road. Be careful, the road from High Birkhow through to Nether Wasdale could be blocked.'

Ted's words trailed away, as Savo slammed the car door, started up the engine and floored the accelerator, sending the wheels spinning wildly. Leaving the car park, the rear of the Mercedes slid sideways taking out the gatepost and two metres of wall.

***

Savo coaxed the big four-by-four up past the Youth Hostel, and with care climbed High Birkhow, the wheels starting to spin as he cleared the summit. When Savo arrived and made himself known, Tom and Dan were holding Leo upright. Leo was unconscious. The concern on Ana's face conveyed more than any hospital communiqué ever could.

Savo checked out Leo when he arrived.

'I think he can make it, but we have to be quick,' said Dan. 'Time is crucial.'

'What about the other two?' asked Savo.

'Roman's well dead,' said Tom, 'and Milo has no chance, he's got a serious head wound where he crashed into the coffee table, as well as being shot twice.'

'Give me a minute, let me check,' said Dan. Dan knelt down to where Milo lay beneath the coffee table and searched for a pulse.

'Just forget it, leave him,' snapped Savo. 'Leo's the one we should be looking after, not Milo.'

Together they carried Leo to the waiting car. Savo guided the Mercedes down the snowbound road to the Wast Water Inn, while Dan and Ana sat either side of Leo, supporting him, in the back of the car. Tom sat in the front peering out, helping to determine the path the road took in the snow-choked lane. At High Birkhow a fallen branch from an ancient oak tree had brought down the telephone lines.

Ted Baker was there when they arrived, waiting at the helicopter pad with five members of Wasdale Mountain Rescue. He checked Leo's wound. It was bleeding again.

'We need to stop the bleeding or we're going to lose him.' Ted's voice projected a calmness that contradicted the medical evidence. He applied direct pressure to the wound and managed to stem the flow of blood from Leo's shoulder to a trickle. Ted looked at Ana and shook his head. He called over to the Mountain Rescue Team.

'Bill, Tim, help me wrap a couple of these blankets round him.' They helped envelope Leo in a cocoon of blankets as Dan and Ted held Leo upright in the back of the Mercedes.

'Hold on, Leo, there's a helicopter on its way, you're going to be okay,' Dan promised. They waited, bathed in the headlights of the Mountain Rescue Land Rover as Ted applied a temporary dressing to the wound on Tom's head.

Chapter 95

After Stefan finished his breakfast, he and Boris left the dining room. Boris' toast was left untouched. Stefan had managed three cups of black coffee; Boris barely a sip. Oblivious to the presence of others in the lobby, they took the lift to Boris' room. Stefan searched for any sign of an intruder. The room appeared to be as they'd left it no more than forty minutes earlier. Then Boris found a note on the dressing table. He glared at it from a distance, as if it spread its evil by contagion. He reached forward, picked up the envelope and tore it open. The now familiar handwriting crawled maliciously across the page.

We have Ana safe. If you wish her to remain alive, you must refuse to sign the Co-operation and Finance Agreement and resign publicly from your position as General Director of Sarajevo Steel, at eleven o'clock today. This is the only way you can guarantee no harm will come to her. Failure to comply will of course also put your own life in danger. As before, we know your every move.'

Boris gazed down at the letter, the jangle of his thoughts competing with the silence. He handed the letter to Stefan, then paced the room, tracing a pattern on the carpet. Stefan looked at his watch.

'It's still only twenty minutes to ten. There is still time.'

'I don't think so. Time is running out.'

Chapter 96

The familiar, thwack, thwack, thwack of the Sea King's rotor blades filled Dan's head, as Greg Childs struggled to bring the chopper down squarely onto the helipad at Wasdale Head in a strong wind. Dan and the others sheltered behind the Mercedes. Two medics jumped from the cargo hold just before the landing wheels touched the ground and with torsos bent, sped over to where Dan, Ted and Leo waited. The first carried a stretcher, the second carried medical equipment. Together they lifted Leo from the car and on to the stretcher, still covered in blankets. He was still unconscious. Still bleeding.

'Where's he hit?' demanded the first medic. His voice carried an urgency that demanded an immediate reply.

'Left shoulder, he's lost a lot of blood.' Ted responded even before the medic had finished speaking.

'Get a saline drip in,' barked the lead medic.

Dan watched as the needle punctured Leo's white flesh and the life-saving fluid began to flow. Savo's concern showed on his face, as he willed Leo to hold on. The noise from the helicopter was deafening.

'Is he going to be all right?' shouted Ana at the top of her voice.

The scream from the helicopter drowned out her words and the wind swept them away into the cold winter sky. Mountain Rescue, helped by Dan and Savo, lifted Leo into the helicopter, then Savo pushed Ana and Tom up into the cargo hold, before Dan scrambled in. Then the helicopter took off. There was no room for Savo. He would have to make his own way back.

As they gained height to clear the saddle at Sty Head, a violent gust of wind sideswiped the Westland. It spiralled down out of control towards the tarn, the rotors thrashing wildly in the early morning light. Then the icy waters of Sty Head Tarn raced up towards them as Ana prayed and held on to Tom.

Chapter 97

In a world without colour, Boris left his bedroom, followed by Stefan, to attend the signing ceremony. He abandoned the malignant scrap of paper on the dressing table, though he didn't fail to take its message with him. They presented their passes to the uniformed security officers and were given clearance to enter the conference hall, where rows of grey-suited bureaucrats confronted them. Boris caught a flash of azure blue near the stage. It was Bernadeta, the one speck of colour in an ocean of anorak grey. She waved over to him and Boris returned something he hoped resembled a smile.

A colony of manic reporters, with their television crews, were camped at the front of the stage, ready to beam the signing ceremony around the world. A waiter placed eight drinking glasses on a table next to the lectern from where each delegate was to speak. Boris couldn't understand why everything looked so normal. Georg was meticulously positioning each signatory in a straight line across the stage. The flags of the nations they represented hung behind each delegate.

'Please Stefan, could you just check one last time with reception for any news of Ana and Olga? Or if Leo has made contact in some way. You never know.'

'No problem, Boris. I'm on my way.' Stefan left the conference hall as Georg approached.

'Good morning, Boris.' Georg as usual was immaculate, nothing out of place.

'Good morning, Georg. Will I be okay sat here?'

'Yes, that's good. You are of course centre stage.'

Boris sat next to Herr Becker, who was beaming broadly. Jon White sat near the door on the front row, directly opposite Joe Brown, the American Ambassador. A few more days and Jon would be going home for good. The other delegates fidgeted nervously, unsure if the cameras were running. Everything was ready. There was one small problem. Only one. Boris Poborski would not be signing.

Boris felt someone touch his arm and he spun quickly round, hoping to see Stefan. It was Georg.

'It is precisely two minutes to eleven o'clock,' he advised smiling. 'I think we're ready to commence.'

Boris hesitated for a moment.

'I don't think we're quite ready yet.' A voice from behind Georg contested. 'There is something Boris needs to attend to first.'

It was Stefan.

'Is it Ana? Is Ana safe? Please, please.' Boris prayed out loud. 'Let Ana be safe!'

He pushed past Stefan and barged the two security officers out of his way, to emerge into the hotel lobby. Several members of the Bosnian administrative team entered the lobby from the direction of the restaurant and made their way to join the long queue already waiting at reception. But Ana, where was Ana? The question screamed around his head, as tears piled up behind his eyes. Those who had concluded their business at the reception desk drifted away, and for a moment the queue thinned out just enough for Boris to glimpse a cluster of people at the far end of the lobby. They appeared incongruous, out of place in the smart surroundings of an internationally renowned conference venue. Where was Ana? As Boris hurried towards reception the space between those waiting widened, framing a girl. At that moment the girl turned to face Boris. It was Ana. She was safe. Boris held Ana in his arms as the tears he'd been holding back, dissipated in a great surge of relief.

'I'm fine, Dad, go and sign the agreement. I'm safe now.'

Boris kissed her on the cheek.

'Where's Olga. Where's Leo. Is that blood on your coat?' He looked at Dan and Tom, then turned back to Ana. 'Who are these people, where have you been all this time. Are you hurt?'

'Everything is fine now, I'm tired and I'm hungry, but I'm all right. Go and sign the agreement, I'll be waiting here when you're finished.'

A huge smile lit up Boris' face. Ana kissed him and he left with Georg snapping at his heels. Stefan followed in their wake. Dan, Tom, and Ana stood alone in the lobby. Dan pulled Tom towards him and held him in a long and loving embrace.

'You did great up there, son. I'm really proud of you.'

'You save it till you need it,' said Tom and then added with a smile. 'You weren't so bad yourself.'

'You too, Ana, you were marvellous,' praised Dan, as he hugged her. 'Your dad will be proud of you too.'

Ana stood in a daze, trying to piece together the disconnected events that had invaded her life over the past twenty-four hours. There was the death of Olga, someone she had considered a friend. Then the anguish created by the return of Roman and Milo, and the euphoria at their demise. Finally, there was the pain in Leo's eyes as she held his hand while waiting for the helicopter at Wasdale Head. For a few seconds all the pieces fitted together. Then they didn't. Somewhere a piece of the jigsaw was missing. Ana's thoughts were an emotional nightmare. She tried to think clearly.

'Well Tom, I suppose we should tell the police about our Chamonix training programme,' ventured Dan.

'If that was the training programme for Chamonix you can go on your own!'

'There's something missing,' said Ana.

'We need to use the phone to call the police, but it's not easy to know where to start,' Dan continued.

'Try, three dead and one wounded and work your way back,' suggested Tom. 'Along with my head wound. That should get their attention.'

'You're right there, if that doesn't work, nothing will.'

They joined the throng in reception to make the call, where a number of guests were milling around waiting for attention. The blood on Dan's mountain jacket and Tom's head generated anxious looks.

'Something is missing,' Ana repeated.

'Seems to be a bit of a hold up,' observed Tom.

There was only one receptionist on the desk trying to handle a variety of enquires.

'They appear a little short staffed,' Dan suggested.

Then, for Ana, the missing piece fell into place, filling the void. The impact was vivid, acute and dramatically violent.

'It's not something that's missing. It's someone! Luciano! Find Luciano, we must find him, my father is in danger!' Ana's voice, stabbed through with anxiety, drew the attention of other guests waiting in reception. All three scanned both reception and the lobby. There was no sign of Luciano.

'The conference hall, he must be in the conference hall!' shouted Ana.

They raced down to the conference hall, sidestepping those in their way. They arrived to find the doors closed and guarded by two

218

uninformed security officers. Dan tried to compose himself as he approached the first officer, while the second officer became embroiled in a heated argument with a camera crew who had arrived late.

'It's essential we speak to Boris Poborski at once, you must let us through!'

'Could I see your security pass please sir?'

'I don't have a pass.'

The security officer dwarfed Dan.

'I do.' Ana dug in her pocket to retrieve her security pass.

'Access all areas, that seems to be in order, Miss Poborski.' He looked down at Ana as he scrutinised the photograph on the pass, comparing it with the battered scrap of a girl that stood before him. 'Okay, but its only you I can allow in.'

As Ana walked into the conference hall, she deliberately dropped the security pass at the officer's feet. The officer bent down to pick it up for her. Dan and Tom quickly slipped past before he had time to react.

Georg was concluding the introductions as they arrived in the conference room. Ana scoured the sea of faces for Luciano. He was nowhere. She searched again but couldn't see him.

'Now I would like to call upon Boris Poborski to sign the agreement on behalf of Sarajevo Steel,' Georg announced with a flourish.

Accompanied by applause, a smiling Boris Poborski rose from his seat and stepped forward to the lectern where the agreement lay in wait of his signature. Cameras flashed. Georg smiled.

One of the waiters moved towards the stage with a jug of water and a napkin folded over his right arm. Everyone ignored him. He approached unchallenged, as conspicuous as the wallpaper.

Ana saw him first and let out a cry, and being closest, raced towards the waiter. Jon White was there first and without ceremony brought the unaware assassin to the ground. The jug of water crashed at Boris' feet. The napkin fell from Luciano's arm and the gun it concealed slithered towards Ana. She bent deftly down and picked it up. There was a sharp intake of breath from the seated delegates in the room. Ana turned the gun towards Luciano as she stared down at him. Sweat burst out across his brow, as he looked down the barrel of his own gun. Ana closed one eye for a better aim, as the tendons stiffened in her trigger finger, and then slowly, very slowly, she handed the gun to Jon White. Georg rose coolly from his seat.

'Will someone please call security?' he asked without raising his voice. A nervous ripple raced through the audience, and then realising the danger was over, they breathed a collective sigh of relief. On the trail of Dan and Tom, security arrived seconds later and together with Jon White they escorted Dalibor Tesak, aka Luciano Magiera, robustly from the room and immediately increased the security cordon around the conference room. Paula Medrith took Jon's seat at the front of the audience, directly opposite Joe Brown.

Boris stepped forward to the lectern and signed the agreement, accompanied by loud applause. Cameras flashed and film crews manoeuvred to secure the best angle. Boris stood in a blaze of light, as Ana and the whole world looked on.

'Ladies and gentlemen, I am here today representing the dreams and aspirations of Bosnia. The Co-operation and Finance Agreement will provide the funding to breathe life into Sarajevo Steel, and it is the hard work and the love of our country that will make this a successful venture for each and every one of us. Too many nations have lost good futures by living in the past and by scratching at old wounds. Our wounds are deep, but our love for Bosnia is deeper. Today sees new hope, new opportunity, a new Bosnia. Ladies and gentlemen, I thank you.'

Ivan Bobic, the Bosnian Ambassador, was next to sign. He stumbled over his speech, as if the rigours of his diplomatic life had prevented sufficient time for rehearsal. Then Herr Becker, on behalf of the Deutsche Bank Consortium made his speech before the remaining signatories stepped forward in the required order, ably orchestrated by Georg. In their speech, each one squeezed the maximum amount of political mileage from the occasion. The impromptu overture had guaranteed worldwide media exposure. Boris sat surrounded by well-wishes as he anxiously plotted his escape. He missed Ana.

***

Dan, Tom, and Ana left the conference room and made their way into reception, where Dan dialled 999. A girl's voice, crisp to the point of impatience, snapped back at him.

'What service do you require?'

'Police please.'

After two rings the call was answered. A grudging drone drained lazily down the line and into the telephone receiver. It had clearly been one of those shifts.

'Police, how can I help you?'

'Good morning, my name is Dan Kennedy. I'm at Kermincham Hall, Bassenthwaite Lake, Keswick and I want to report a shooting.'

'A shooting at Kermincham Hall. Is the gunman still on the premises?'

'Err. No, it's complicated. We don't require an armed response unit, just an officer to take down the details.'

'Let me be the judge of that, sir.' The police constable intoned. 'Did anyone sustain any injuries during this, umm, alleged shooting?'

'Three dead and one wounded,' replied Dan. 'There's one body at Keeperswood and two at Timbersbrook Cottage in Wasdale. The casualty is on his way by helicopter to Keswick Cottage Hospital with a gunshot wound. The injury appears to be life-threatening.'

Tom was right, that got their attention.

'I'll put you straight through to a senior officer,' said the constable.

Detective Sergeant Jack Fletcher introduced himself. His assured tone gave Dan confidence. Dan repeated his story in a little more detail, including the attempted murder of Boris Poborski. Jack Fletcher summarised the information Dan had given him.

'Okay, I've got all that now, thank you, just stay at Kermincham Hall and keep safe. We'll attend to everything.'

Jack Fletcher replaced the receiver. Then the phone rang again. It was the manager of Kermincham Hall. One of the cleaners had discovered a body in Room 32. The circumstances appeared suspicious.

Next Dan telephoned Jane, as Tom and Ana waited. He was unsure how much he should divulge, especially over the telephone. Jane answered on the second ring. She must have been sitting by the phone.

'Well done, you. You're just in time with your call. I was about to get worried. Another ten minutes and I would have been there,' she laughed.

'We're safely down,' said Dan. 'Though not without some unforeseen drama.'

'I know,' said Jane calmly. 'I phoned Ted earlier about the trip to Chamonix. He thought I knew what had happened. I'm afraid he rather spilled the beans. Please don't tell him, he'll be upset if he knows. As long you and Tom are all right, that's all that matters.'

'I'm fine, and so is Tom. There are formalities to go through up here, so we won't be leaving anytime soon. I'll ring again when we know more, but we won't arrive home before Tuesday at the earliest. Could you let the office know in the morning and ask them to rearrange my appointment in New York with Maynard's?'

'Sure, I'll ring Alice and let her know. I've so many questions.'

'Tom wants a word before you go, love you lots. I can't wait to see you when I get home.'

'Me too,' said Jane. Dan handed the phone to Tom.

'Hi Mum, and yes before you ask, I am fine. It was a bit scary at times, everything happened so fast. Still, we're down now and we're okay.'

'Thank God you're safe, I don't know what I'd do if anything happened to you. I love you Tom.'

'Love you too, Mum. I'll see you soon. Bye.'

Jane replaced the receiver, unaware of Tom's head wound. Finally, Dan phoned Keswick Cottage Hospital to enquire after Leo. On police advice the hospital refused to release any information.

As Dan replaced the receiver, a man and a woman appeared at his shoulder. The man had a physical presence that Dan found both threatening and reassuring at the same time. He recognised him as the big guy who had taken out Luciano in such style. The woman, tall and elegant, displayed an assertiveness Dan associated with the legal profession.

'Can I help you?' asked Dan.

'I guess I'd better introduce myself. My name is Paula Medrith. I'm the Senior Diplomatic Officer attached to this delegation, and this is Jon White. Jon's with the US Diplomatic Service.'

Dan checked Paula and Jon's credentials as she continued. 'We need to get you three somewhere safe as quickly as possible. I have a team establishing the integrity of the whole area, but until I get the all-clear I need you where I can take care of you. Come on, we're going to my suite.'

All five took the stairs to the first floor and arrived without incident at Paula's suite, where a medic from her team attended to Tom's head wound. The medic removed the emergency dressing Ted Baker had applied back at Wasdale Head. As he did the wound started bleeding again.

'I've got some good news and some bad news,' quipped the medic. 'The bad news is you need a stitch.'

'And the good news?' asked Tom.

'If the bullet had been a centimetre to the right, you'd need a coffin. But as it is, you're going to be as good as new. Be careful when you shower. Any problems or heavy bleeding, call me. I'm Will, you can reach me through reception. In the meantime, here are two wound dressings just in case you spring a slight leak.'

Dan's nerves had been on a knife-edge for twenty-four hours, but after the incident with Luciano, he relaxed a little. A knock at the door brought Dan's attention sharply back into focus. Jon White opened the door, and Boris walked into the room.

Ana sprang up from the settee and sped over to hug her father, as the images from Babonavic and Jesus on the cross faded and finally disappeared. Ana had kept her promise.

***

Monsignor Bernarez opened his email and moved the cursor to cover Bleiburg 1945. He doubled clicked. The news was disappointing.

Chapter 98

Detective Chief Inspector Mat Coulthard opened his bedroom curtains to find a thick blanket of snow outside his bedroom window. At first, he was afraid the road conditions meant an abandonment of his lunch date with Patricia. He drove out to join the main valley road and waited as a giant snowplough thundered past, dispersing the snow high into the air. In the distance, white mountain peaks pierced the winter sky. Mat picked Patricia up from her cottage in Applethwaite at eleven thirty and drove to The Swan in Grasmere. Patricia wore the new blouse she'd bought last week in Keswick and her hair, freshly styled, was in keeping with the latest trends. They enjoyed a glass of wine as they waited for their meal to arrive. The waiter placed two bowls of carrot and coriander soup and freshly-baked bread rolls down in front of them.

'Enjoy your meals,' he said as he left.

Mat broke his bread roll in two as his mobile phone rang. It was Detective Sergeant Jack Fletcher.

'Hi, Mat Coulthard speaking,' Mat listened for a moment, a suffusion of surprise and disbelief transforming his features. 'Sorry,' apologised Mat. 'Run that past me again. Yes, yes, the line is fine. I just don't believe what I'm hearing. Okay, I've got that now, Jack. Have we set up roadblocks at Gosforth and Santon Bridge? Well done, that's good. We've not had a shooting on our patch for months, now this. Okay I'll see you at Kermincham Hall.'

He turned to Patricia, 'Sorry Patricia, I was really looking forward to our lunch.'

'I know you were, I was too,' she smiled. 'This is not a new experience for me. Remember I was married to a copper. I'll be fine, I can make my own way back.'

'You sure?' asked Mat. They shared a kiss. 'I'll ring you later, when I'm through.'

Mat paid the bill and made his way to Kermincham Hall.

Chapter 99

Boris released Ana from his arms, and taking his handkerchief, wiped a tear from his cheek, as Paula waited.

'Listen up,' she announced. 'The news from the hospital is good. Leo Illic, as you know, was shot earlier this morning. I sent my top medic to Keswick, a guy who knows about ballistic trauma. He reports Leo has sustained a significant, but clean wound to his left shoulder. The bullet entered low down, rupturing a significant artery but missing the shoulder blade and anything else of importance. He lost a considerable amount of blood, but there's nothing life-threatening, nothing permanent. He will be in hospital two, maybe three days, with an armed guard as company, then they'll discharge him. He's one lucky man.' She looked across at Boris and Ana. 'He's asking to see you both.'

A cheer of relief went up from Dan and Tom, as Ana hugged her father.

'Secondly, we've completed a three-sixty-degree sweep of the surrounding area, as well as a room-by-room search, and I'm satisfied it's now clear of any combatants. However, an incident in Room 32 continues to be investigated. Jon and I have briefly questioned Luciano, but he's saying nothing. Nothing at all. In addition, we've moved in some heavy backup to guarantee the security of any vulnerable targets.' Paula paused and looked at Ana and Boris. 'That obviously means you two. Right now, though, we need to understand what you guys have been through in the last twenty-four hours or so. Can you help?'

Paula and her number two, Sam, listened patiently and without interruption, while Dan and Tom relayed their account. Sam traced the route they took on two Ordnance Survey Maps.

'So you saw no one else in the mountains, until you met up with Ana and Olga at Hollow Stones?'

'No,' Dan replied. 'We saw no one.'

Ana related her story up to the time she and Olga met up with Dan and Tom. Boris sat open-mouthed, as all three confirmed the part that Olga played. Dan concluded with the events at Keeperswood and the shooting of their two abductors at Timbersbrook Cottage that led to their rescue. Boris reached across to where Ana sat and squeezed her hand.

'You're okay now,' he said, shaking his head as he spoke.

Ana reminded her father of the incident the night they arrived at Kermincham Hall during which an Embassy driver had given Olga a small leather case. 'You remember the driver, Josip Budach. He said Olga had forgotten the case. She'd left it in his car. Well that's when I think she got the guns. She got them from the driver Josip Budach.'

Paula nodded. 'Thanks for that. We know Budach played a part in all this. He was the driver who took you and Olga to Seathwaite. We have him safe already. We're waiting to question him.'

There was a knock at the door and Sam answered. Rob, another of Paula's team, entered and signalled his need to speak to her.

'Thank you,' said Paula, as Rob left the room. Paula turned to Boris and Dan. 'The police have arrived. I think we should see them in here together, if that's okay with you.' Dan and Boris both agreed.

Detective Chief Inspector Mat Coulthard and his Sergeant, Jack Fletcher, entered the room, introduced themselves and produced their warrant cards. Paula returned the cards with a smile. Paula, Sam and Jon offered their I.D. for inspection. The DCI thoroughly checked their credentials and painstakingly made a note of all the details. Paula, amused at his diligence, wrestled with a smirk as it fought to spread across her face.

Dan, Tom, and Ana went over their story again. This time it took much longer, as Mat Coulthard continually asked for more information to aid his understanding of the issues involved. Jack Fletcher did his best to take notes but struggled to keep up. Dan clarified a couple of points regarding Savo's involvement in the rescue and Boris gave a full description.

'We've picked up one male IC1 fitting that description at the roadblock at Eskdale Green driving a Mercedes Benz ML 350. We're holding him at Keswick Police Station, but he won't answer any questions. At first we thought he must be deaf and dumb. He hasn't spoken a word since we picked him up.'

A wry smile spread across Boris' face.

'That's Savo Stanisic, all right. We were together during the Sarajevo Siege. Leo saved his life. He'll not say a word if he thinks it might affect Leo. He worships him.'

Mat turned to Jack. 'It seems our mystery man is one of us. You can make a call to Keswick nick to release him now, update him on Leo Illic's status, and let him know the agreements have been signed and Ana and her father are both okay.' Mat turned to speak to Ana as Jack made the call. 'It appears on this evidence, that the death of Olga Lukic and the man you know as Roman, at Timbersbrook Cottage could be self-defence. So don't worry at the moment, Ana, you may yet have no need for concern.'

The discovery of the body in Room 32 still mystified everyone. The incident appeared to have no link to Ana's abduction. The only connection was like Budach: Hajji was an Embassy Driver.

***

Mat began to write up his notes, as Paula left with Boris, and Ana for Keswick Cottage Hospital. Sam arranged two rooms for Dan and Tom. He guessed they might be staying for a while. Sam escorted them to their rooms, while Rob followed.

'I've sent out to Keswick for a change of clothes for both of you. They should arrive anytime now.'

'Thanks for that,' said Dan. 'We'd really appreciate a shower and to change out of these bloodstained clothes.'

Sam carried out a second security check on both rooms.

'See you after your shower,' he said. 'We'll be in Paula's room, Room 110. You can sign your statements then.'

Chapter 100

On arrival at Keswick Cottage Hospital, Paula confirmed Boris and Ana's security status. Then she went to grab a coffee and catch up with her calls. An armed guard admitted Boris and Ana into Leo's room. Leo looked pale and drawn, as he lay motionless in bed. Ana sat on the chair next to Leo and held his hand. Leo opened his eyes.

'How's it going, Leo?' Boris asked.

'I'm pretty good now, pretty good.'

'You did it, Leo, you saved Ana. You brought her back to me. I should never have doubted you.'

Helped by Ana, Leo took a sip of water from a paper cup at his bedside. He forced a smile.

'Thank you for trusting me, I know it must have been hard for you.'

Boris pulled up his chair close to Ana. The strain of the last twenty-four hours had taken its toll. 'Ana,' Boris began, 'I have something to tell you.' He paused; afraid he would bring the memories of Babonavic flooding back. Then for the first time he realised the memories had never gone away. 'Your Aunt Zara was expecting Leo's child when she and your mother died that night in Babonavic. I didn't know.' Ana held her father's hand as the tears filled his eyes. 'I put my hate behind me, and I never sought revenge for what happened that night, but Ana, if I'd lost you, nothing would have prevented me from seeking retribution to the full.'

'Trust me,' said Leo beneath his pain. 'I seek revenge. My life has been filled with a passion to kill those who murdered Zara and my unborn child. We were to be married after the war. Zara wore my wedding ring on a chain round her neck. I lost everything I loved that night. You still have Ana. All I have is hate.' His tone changed, laced with bitterness and regret. 'I can't find peace until I have my revenge.'

Ana stood up and faced Leo.

'At the cottage where Olga died, I counted the bullets from her Luger as Dan held them in his hand. There were eight. Then I watched her reload the pistol with four bullets. Only four. They were all she could find after Dan threw them to the floor.' She paused for a moment and then continued coldly. 'When Leo came to our rescue, I could see into the room. I watched as Roman fired Olga's Luger at nothing more than an old man's fear. One shot. Then I saw two more fired at Leo as he burst into the sitting room. So that was three shots altogether. Roman fired a fourth shot into the air, before he collapsed onto the settee. When Roman aimed Olga's Luger at me, he must have thought there were four bullets left.' She smiled. 'I knew there were none.' Ana turned to Leo. 'Last night I recognised Roman and Milo as the two soldiers liable for Babonavic. You have your revenge.'

Chapter 101

When Tom returned to his room, his new clothes from Keswick were in a black holdall on the bed. He showered, letting the water flow over his body as he reran the day's events in his head. As he dried himself, he saw a splash of blood on the white towel. He checked in the mirror and saw the wound on his head was bleeding. Using one of the dressings the medic had given him, he stemmed the flow. Tom wondered how much closer he could get to death without dying. The answer came to him at once. A centimetre, the medic had said. The thought occupied his mind as he switched on the television and flopped down on the bed, hopping from channel to channel, documentary to drama, cartoon to culture, watching but not seeing. He thought about Ana and realised after recent events he'd changed. He had a new belief in himself. A new confidence. Tom had always wanted to fly in a helicopter and now he had, but it was not as he'd imagined. He'd seen himself returning after conquering K2 or Lhotse. And soaring between white Himalayan peaks after proving himself to his father. But having survived last night's events, Tom finally knew he was good enough.

Chapter 102

Paula returned to Kermincham Hall with Boris and Ana and took them straight to her suite on the second floor. Mat Coulthard was still there writing up his notes, with the help of Jack Fletcher.

'You are very meticulous,' observed Paula, as she sat impassively waiting for him to finish.

'Sorry, it's the Crown Prosecution Service. The CPS. No evidence, no crime, seems to be their guiding principle. Even if we do have a gunshot victim in Keswick Hospital and four bodies.'

'I don't have that problem in Sarajevo. I'm based out there with my team. We're attached to NATO. I don't usually bring outsiders into a case, but I could use some local knowledge on this one. Can we work together on this thing?'

'Sure, that's fine by me,' Mat smiled and held out his hand.

Paula shook his hand, and then looked across to Boris and Ana, to include them in the conversation.

'Provisionally we're holding Luciano Magiera, aka Dalibor Tesak, in Lancaster Prison. It's only a category C prison, so transport is on the way to move him down to Strangeways. It's a category A in Manchester. We've no idea why he's involved with this Bosnian affair. It doesn't make any sense. I have HQ on the case; they seem to think some kind of a pattern may be emerging. Something involving several major Communist countries.'

Dan and Tom arrived to sign their statements and sat down as Mat's mobile phone burst into life, making Ana jump.

'Hi, where are you now?' he asked. 'You've already been to Keeperswood? What have you found that's new?' Mat weighed up the information from the Scene of Crime Officer, as his brow furrowed. 'You found four live bullets for the Luger under the cupboards in the kitchen. Nothing else new.' Mat made some notes. 'Okay, what about

Timbersbrook Cottage?' Mat listened carefully as he received the report. Finally, the DCI looked up at Dan.

'We seem to be a body missing.'

Dan looked puzzled. 'I don't understand. The body of Olga was at Keeperswood when we left. She had no pulse.'

'We still have the body of Olga Lukic. It's at Timbersbrook Cottage. We're one missing. We only have one body.'

'There was definitely two there. We all saw them,' confirmed Ana. 'There has to be two at Timbersbrook, there must be some mistake.'

'There's no I.D. on the body we have at Timbersbrook, but from the description you gave us earlier, we're pretty sure the body is the man you know as Roman. Milo has disappeared.'

***

Ana undressed in the sanctuary of her bedroom. At first she hardly recognised the image that reflected back in the bedroom mirror. A mosaic of yellow and purple contusions covered her body. She sat in her dressing gown as her mind went back to the fall down the steep snow gully with Olga. It seemed so long ago. Now Olga was dead, but Milo could still be out there. Still watching. Still waiting. The possibility filled her with alarm and foreboding.

Chapter 103

As Mat drove away from Kermincham Hall, he analysed the evidence against Ana Poborski in his head. Then he re-examined the circumstances leading up to the shootings at Keeperswood and then Timbersbrook Cottage. At Keeperswood, Olga Lukic was unarmed when she was shot at point blank range, though Ana Poborski could contend that her life was endangered. At Timbersbrook, Roman had a weapon and had declared his intention to use it. That would make it a clear case of self-defence. Except that the Luger had no ammunition. Had Ana known the Luger's ammunition was on the floor at Keeperswood? Mat tried to second-guess the decision of the CPS based on this evidence. It was not looking good for Ana Poborski. Finally, he addressed his real dilemma. Should he uphold the law or deliver justice?

Chapter 104

Bleiburg made his way out of the lobby at Kermincham Hall and along the corridor to the stairs. He took the stairs two at a time and hurried to his room. He checked his watch. It was one-minute to six. He must log on at six. He locked the door and drew the curtains in his room. It made him feel safe, secure. He unlocked his briefcase, took out his laptop and punched in his screen name, Bleiburg 1945. Then he logged in using his password and the security code. An electronic voice announced, 'You have email.' The Knight of the Holy Order of the Sword of Saint Jerome opened the only email he had received that day. The message took his breath away and left him with a strange and unaccustomed sensation in his bowels.

It was the shortest message he'd ever received. *'Revelation 16:16.'*

He understood the message and knew its consequence. Revelation 16:16 heralded Armageddon, the Day of Judgement; the battle between good and evil had begun. The Knight immediately summoned his Longa Manus, his 'long arm,' to drive him to the house of Charles Borromeo.

Chapter 105

On Monday morning, Georg rescheduled Sarajevo Steel's journey home for the following day. He telephoned Boris and suggested they meet with Stefan in Georg's room for an update.

'Thank you for coming at such short notice, I do appreciate it,' intoned Georg. 'It's good to see you both looking so well after your ordeal,' he said, smiling at Boris. 'DCI Coulthard has confirmed no charges are to be brought against any member of our delegation. We are all free to leave tomorrow. Regrettably, I will not be in a position to travel with you. I must leave first thing in the morning, for a meeting with our High Representative in Sarajevo. He requires a full report on the implications of the Finance Agreement, and the events that have taken place here in England.' Georg paused to hand out typed travel itineraries. 'For clarity and the avoidance of doubt, I will be happy to take you through the details line by line.' Georg paused for breath and smiled. Stefan scowled back.

'The flight leaves Manchester Airport at six thirty-five tomorrow evening, and you should present yourselves at the diplomatic lounge inside the airport terminal, no later than five thirty. The cars will leave Kermincham Hall at precisely three thirty tomorrow afternoon. This gives you two hours to reach the airport. Please make sure you travel to the airport in the car I have arranged for you. Don't be late, we cannot risk missing the flight. No mistakes, do you both understand?' Pleasingly they understood. 'I have arranged a farewell dinner for you both, along with Mr Dan Kennedy and his son Tom, and of course Ana, in a private suite, tonight at eight o'clock. I hope you will all be able to accept my invitation?' Boris nodded a muted acceptance. Georg continued unabated. 'Unfortunately, I am unavailable to attend, I have too much paperwork, I hope you will forgive me?' They forgave him. 'So remember, pack early and whatever you do, don't be late.'

'What about Leo, how will he be travelling home?' asked Boris.

'I have arranged for Savo Stanisic to accompany our friend Leo when he is fit and well. You may be assured Savo will take excellent care of him.'

Chapter 106

Milo lay in the back of the BMW X5 that had brought him down from Cumbria the night before. His call to *'Escape'* on the mobile phone had initiated an immediate response from his handlers. They had dispatched their field team to snatch him from Timbersbrook Cottage and instructed Dalibor Tesak to eliminate Boris Poborski, at whatever cost.

Milo's bandages applied at Timbersbrook had been replaced by sterile dressings and a saline drip attached to his left arm. One of the two bullet wounds was superficial and the bleeding from the other had been stemmed. His head was covered in bandages, only his eyes peeped out. The concussion he suffered after contact with the slate topped coffee table was receding, but the migraine still pounded in his head.

The BMW entered the cargo area at Birmingham International Airport and a doctor checked Milo's breathing, pulse, and blood pressure. Then he was sedated, before being zipped into a black body bag and loaded onto a Russian military Antonov An-12 bound for Zhukovsky International Airport, Moscow. Milo was accompanied by the doctor and the two paramedics for the eight-hour journey. The medical prognosis suggested he may not survive the flight to Moscow.

***

In the hours that followed, Milo drifted between semiconsciousness and periods of lucidity, never sure if he was awake or asleep. Twice when he dreamt that he'd woken up, he was in a different place, a different time. When he did wake up, he realised he'd been dreaming and discovered he was still zipped in the body bag. Milo's eyes closed again, and he blacked out, surrendering to his drug-induced coma.

***

In his dreams, Milo was eight years old. He was home again. He could feel the biting wind, as it blew in through the broken windowpane. The room was so cold, with nowhere left to hide. His mother lay on the bare, shabby floor, as the blows rained down on her. This was her punishment, for trying to prevent the ritual abuse that left a red stain on Milo's underpants. Eight-year-old Milo cowered by the window, watching his stepfather kick his mother. He searched for proof of life and tried to find some way to deliver a measure of relief.

'No'.... Milo's distress erupted in a despairing cry. Instantly the kicking stopped, then brutish hands clawed at his body, tearing him from where he lay. Milo's world spun crazily round, and as quickly as he left the floor, he returned to it, arriving in a crumpled heap in the far corner of the kitchen. Warm blood gushed from a large gash above his right eye, flooding down his tear stained face. The seed of a scream gathered in his throat, but before it could bear fruit, he was on the move again. Wrenched up by his broken arm and his left leg, Milo's stepfather threw him across the kitchen, to land headfirst in the open doorway. He made an effort to stand, but nothing functioned, nothing seemed connected. Milo heard his mother crying, and relieved that she still lived, he lost his grip on consciousness and descended into a pool of midnight black.

Chapter 107

Boris left Georg's room feeling reassured, now their return to Sarajevo had been confirmed. As he passed the lift, Bernadeta stepped out.

'Hello Boris, I've been seeing Herr Becker off. He's flying out tonight, I won't see him now for a few days.'

'So you're on your own. You must join us for dinner, I'll not take no for an answer.'

'Oh, thank you, that would be really nice.'

'Georg has arranged a private room, for dinner at eight o'clock. There will be Stefan, Dan Kennedy and Tom, his son, the two people who rescued Ana on the mountain, and of course Ana.'

'I'd love to come, if you're sure that's all right?'

'That's agreed then, I'll come by your room at eight.'

***

Boris tapped on Bernadeta's bedroom door at eight, and it opened almost at once.

'That's good, you're ready on time,' smiled Boris. He so wanted to complement Bernadeta on her appearance, to tell her how nice she looked, but Boris was unable to find the right words. 'Ana was nowhere near ready when I called earlier. She said she would meet us there.'

Chapter 108

Ana filled the bath, and lay soaking in the hot soothing water. As she relaxed, her thoughts waltzed around her head. Finally, they dwelt on Tom. She realised she liked him. She liked him quite a lot. Perhaps Tom was the friend she'd been looking for. An intimate friend; someone she'd be able to hold on to and not lose, like Dagma. A confidant?

Ana had been hoping for a chance to wear her new little black dress, the one she'd bought on the shopping trip, with Bernadeta in Sarajevo. Tonight, she'd have that chance. She brushed her hair and applied a little of the lipstick Bernadeta had helped her choose. She gave a giggle, as she pulled on her new sling back shoes. Ana was ready.

Dan and Tom were there first. They welcomed Boris and Bernadeta on their arrival. Stefan joined them moments later. The waiter took their order for drinks.

'I'd like a beer, please,' said Tom. 'I think I've earned one.' In her absence, Boris ordered a lemonade for Ana. The door swung open, and there in the doorway, stood a stunning enchantress in a little black dress. Boris turned and stared, as his mouth fell open.

'I'm sorry, I've only ordered you a lemonade,' he blurted out.

'That's fine,' said Ana. 'I'm really quite thirsty.'

Tom looked at Ana like a complete loon, as he tried to find a tone of voice that wouldn't show it.

'You look absolutely beautiful,' he said.

At the sound of Tom's voice, something quickened inside her.

'Well you've scrubbed up pretty good yourself,' she laughed.

Boris wished he'd been able to find the right words for Bernadeta, but the memory of Katerina held him back.

Stefan scrutinised the menu. 'What,' he cried in mock dismay. 'No porridge?'

Boris played the perfect host. He refilled Bernadeta's wine glass and picked up her napkin when she dropped it. Stefan smiled a knowing smile. He thought he saw something of the Boris he used to know shining through again. At around ten o'clock, Boris called the waiter to order more drinks.

'Another lemonade, Ana, or would you like some wine this time? It's very good!'

'No thank you, I'm quite tired, I think I'll go to bed.'

She kissed her father and said goodnight to them all. Tom left shortly afterwards. It seemed he was tired too.

Ana opened her bedroom door to Tom. 'Do you want to come in?' she asked.

'Yes please,' he smiled. 'If that's all right?'

Boris saw Bernadeta safely back to her room. He wished her goodnight and turned to go. Then he stopped and gave her a goodnight kiss on the cheek.

'I've really enjoyed this evening. Enjoyed being with you,' he said in barely a whisper.

Bernadeta waited in the doorway, her heart raced as Boris moved towards her. Then Boris stopped.

'I'm so sorry, I don't think I can do this.' Boris apologised.

Boris had never been with another woman. He and Katerina had been childhood sweethearts. He'd never dreamt there would be anyone else.

'I know, I don't think I'm ready for this either, but I would like to try again, perhaps when we get back to Sarajevo.'

Boris nodded and kissed her again.

'Yes, I'd like that too,' he said, as he lingered, enjoying the moment. Bernadeta closed the door, a big smile spreading across her face. Boris' kiss had encouraged hope to grow. Buried deep inside her, Bernadeta knew she had a woman's passion unopened and untouched.

Chapter 109

On Tuesday morning Savo Stanisic arrived at Keswick Cottage Hospital in the Mercedes ML 350, and after security clearance, a nurse took him to Leo's room.

'Leo's making a remarkable recovery. He'll be discharged in a day or two. Don't stay too long, I don't want him to get tired and I need to change the wound dressing on his shoulder.'

The nurse closed the door as she left.

'You're looking good,' said Savo. 'A lot better than when I saw you last. How do you feel?'

'The last time I heard those words the roles were reversed. We were in Sarajevo and it was you who'd been shot. But I'm fine, I feel pretty good now they've stopped the leak and I'm full of blood. What's happening at Kermincham?'

'Nothing much, there's no sign of Milo Tolja or should I say, Angelo Moretti. According to the police, that's the name he used to register at the Wast Water Inn. His handlers will have snatched him. I don't expect we'll see him again this side of Moscow.'

Leo got up from his chair.

'Did you bring the clothes from my room as I asked?'

Savo opened the bag he'd brought from Kermincham and handed Leo the clothes.

'Are you sure you're okay?' he said as Leo dressed.

'Come on Savo, we're out of here.'

Before leaving, Savo arranged to have Leo's wound dressed at Kermincham Hall. The nurse was not well pleased.

Chapter 110

Tom browsed the gift shop in the lobby at Kermincham Hall. He picked up a small black-faced Lakeland sheep, and then rejected it as inappropriate. There were hand painted cards of Derwent Water and Blencathra, blank on the inside so you could write your own message. Tom couldn't find the words to say goodbye, never mind write them down. The assistant looked at him askance. He'd been in the shop for ages.

He turned to leave empty-handed. It had been a stupid idea anyway. Then he saw them laid out on a red velvet cushion. They looked expensive. Tom turned the price tag over, they were expensive, but he had to buy one. He made his purchase and left, just as Ana was coming in.

Dan knocked on Tom's bedroom door and Tom opened it at once.

'Are you ready to go? Dan asked. 'I thought we'd see Ted at the Wast Water Inn on the way home. I see you're packed.'

Tom had packed his mountaineering clothes and boots into the holdall Sam Chadderton had bought in Keswick. It stood on the floor, by the door, evidence of his readiness to leave.

'Well, yes and no,' replied Tom. 'Yes. I am packed, but no, I'm not ready to leave, I just need ten minutes. There's something I have to do.'

With that, Tom left his father standing in the bedroom no wiser than before.

***

Ana sat on the corner of the bed, reluctant to finish packing. Unwilling to accept it was time to go. In the past she'd lost all the friends she'd made in Babonavic, and in Banja Luka, Dagma could have become a good friend. Now she was saying goodbye to Tom. But this was different. Tom had already become more than a friend. She placed her little black dress in the suitcase and zipped it up. Only one small gift lay on the bed. There was a knock on her bedroom door, and Ana raced to open it. It was her father.

'I'm ready now,' he said. 'Good, I see you are too. We need to leave the cases outside the bedroom door for the porter to collect.' Boris lifted Ana's suitcase off the bed and made for the door. 'Come on, slow coach, the cars will be here soon. We cannot afford to miss the plane. We've got strict instructions and timings to adhere to. We must not be late.'

With that, Boris strode down the corridor to the lift. Ana sat on the bed, uncertain what to do next. She moved towards the door and as she did, she heard footsteps coming down the corridor. Ana listened as they came closer and then her heart sank as they stopped before reaching her room. Holding her small gift in her hand she walked towards the door. The gift was unwanted, irrelevant. She pulled open the door. Tom was there, waiting just outside the doorway, unsure if he should knock. Ana didn't hold back. She threw her arms around him.

'I thought you weren't going to come.'

'I bought you a present,' said Tom tenderly. 'I hope you like it.'

Ana sat on the bed and took the gift-wrapped package from Tom and opened it. A small heart shaped locket on a silver chain fell out into her hand. Ana put it on.

'It's really beautiful,' said Ana. 'I really love it and I love you.'

Tom put his arm around her shoulders.

'I love you too,' he said.

'Look, I've bought you a present,' Ana said brightly.

Tom opened Ana's gift. It was a small heart shaped locket on a silver chain. Ana's gift was identical to his. She opened the clasp and put the locket around Tom's neck.

'Is this goodbye?' she asked.

***

Tom met his father as he returned to his room.

'I'm on my way to see Leo before we go. It seems he decided to discharge himself. He's back in his room.'

Tom followed his father down the corridor to Leo's room. Will, the medic from Paula's team was just leaving.

'Hello, I've just finished changing the dressing on Leo's wound. You can go in now, Mr Poborski and Ana are in there too.'

Will held the door open and Dan and Tom stepped inside.

Leo sat in an armchair. Ana sat on the bed next to him.

245

'Good to see you, Leo. You look really good,' said Dan.

'Thanks, I'm feeling pretty good.'

'Leo's doing exceptionally well,' said Boris. 'Must be the mountain air. We had DCI Coulthard in earlier. Leo's cleared up the mystery of the body in Room 32, much to the Chief Inspector's relief. It was just another case of self-defence after the driver Hajji pulled a gun on Leo.'

Dan, Boris and Ana waited as Tom collected his holdall, and then all four walked downstairs together. Stefan and Bernadeta were waiting in the lobby. Most of the delegates had already left for various parts of the financial and political world, and a cathedral like silence had descended on Kermincham Hall. Tom glanced towards their rucksacks. The police had collected them from Keeperswood Cottage, returning them to Kermincham Hall after forensic examination.

'Dan,' said Boris. 'We're ready to leave now and I need to thank you for what you've done for us.' He smiled at Ana as he continued. 'My deepest regret is that once again, I was not there when Ana needed me.'

'Tom and I were happy to help.'

'I know I can never repay you, but I say truly I will never forget what you have done for us. Thank you.'

Boris released Dan from an emotional embrace as Paula Medrith walked towards them.

'Boris and I are just saying our goodbyes and then we're off home,' said Dan.

'So I see,' smiled Paula. 'I've just arranged for your account to be forwarded to my office, it's the least we can do.'

'Thank you,' said Dan.

'Oh, and by the way, Boris,' Paula continued. 'There will be no problem with the visas you requested. The High Representative's Office in Sarajevo will be attending to everything. You'll receive the visas direct from the French Embassy in Paris.'

Dan turned to go, but Ana's outstretched hand diverted him.

'Wait,' Ana said, as she put her arms around Dan's neck and held him close. She kissed him hard on the cheek. 'Thank you,' she said. 'It's good to feel safe again.'

Dan and Tom lifted their rucksacks onto their backs and walked out into the car park, where Ratko Kartic, an Embassy driver, waited to give them the car keys after he'd collected their Range Rover from the Wast Water Inn. Tom gave a final wave to Ana. Then they were gone.

Boris looked anxiously at his watch as their suitcases were loaded into the first Mercedes.

'Come on Ana, you know we can't be late. This is our car.'

Ana scrambled into the car and fastened her seat belt as the car moved off down the wide gravel drive.

'Stop. Stop the car. I need to go to the toilet before I go. I'll be as quick as I can.'

'I do not believe it. Go on then, Ana, but be quick.'

Ana jumped out of the car as it came to a standstill and dashed off to the toilet.

'I'll only be a minute,' she called back, as Stefan and Bernadeta climbed into their car. 'You go on ahead, Dad. I'll go with Stefan and Bernadeta in their car.'

As Boris' car pulled out onto the main road, he began to relax in the comfort of the Mercedes E500 saloon as the Lakeland vista flashed by. Ana was safe. Perhaps now he could forgive himself for the death of Katerina and with the finance for Sarajevo Steel in place, he could build a new life. A life in which Bernadeta could play a part.

Chapter 111

Dan and Tom Kennedy drove through Keswick in the Range Rover and on to the A591, in complete silence, heading towards Ambleside. Dan looked across to check if Tom was awake and he was, wide awake. Dan broke the silence.

'You okay, son?'

'Sure,' Tom replied. 'I'm just thinking about Ana and what she's been through. Not just in the last few days, but back in Bosnia. We talked last night about the war and what it's like in Sarajevo. Her mother was murdered, and she was there.' Tom fell silent for a moment. 'Will I ever see Ana again?' he asked.

'Did you hear Paula mention visas, when Boris and I were talking in the lobby?'

'Yes, I guess. Something about the Embassy in Paris. What's that got to do with Ana?'

'Ana needs a visa to fly to Chamonix. They're all coming with us, if that's okay with you? It was agreed last night after dinner.'

Chapter 112

Boris watched the little stone cottages whizz by as the Mercedes Benz E500 saloon pulled out of Keswick and onto the A66. Soon through Threlkeld, the winter sun setting in the west, they began the steady climb around the flank of Blencathra. As the car breached the skyline near Scales Farm, a massive explosion ripped through the belly of the Mercedes, catapulting it into the air. It cartwheeled in a ball of fire, landing on its roof. Still travelling at fifty miles an hour, it sledged along the tarmac for forty metres, as sparks and broken glass showered the road. It came to rest upside down in a ditch, a maimed and twisted wreck.

Chapter 113

With the assistance of Paula Medrith and her team, Mat Coulthard was getting on top of the paperwork. Mat needed a break, and with their abandoned lunch date fresh in his mind, he summoned up the courage to ask Patricia out for a drink and perhaps a bite to eat. He arranged to pick her up at four, and then the call came through from Traffic at Threlkeld, and the inevitable apology followed. Mat knew Patricia understood; the question was, did she care?

Paula was on the scene when Mat arrived. Jack Fletcher arrived moments later. He was still in his yellow golf jersey. With the course closed, he'd been having a drink in the bar with friends and the club captain, when the station telephoned. Paula walked briskly towards them. Her breath was clearly visible in the cold, sharp air.

'Both of them', she said angrily. 'They died instantly. Boris Poborski wouldn't have felt a thing. The forensic pathologist is going to have difficulty identifying all the body parts. But after such a major explosion, there's really not much left. Limbs have been found on both sides of the carriageway. We're not sure who the driver was, there's some confusion at Kermincham Hall. Ana Poborski needed the loo, so she got into the second car. She had a lucky escape. She was following in the car behind. Ana witnessed the explosion. The whole dammed thing. So did Bernadeta and Stefan. They're on their way back to Kermincham now.'

'I hope nothing's been moved,' said Mat as he took in the sombre scene. 'Are forensics on their way?'

'Yes,' confirmed Paula. 'They'll be here inside the hour, along with a couple of people from Jon White's team. But we already have a suspect, or at least an organisation, if you can call a bunch of Communist twats an organisation. Having failed the first time, they were taking no chances the second time around.'

Mat shook his head. 'Isn't that a little premature? The MO bears no resemblance to the previous attempt. None at all.'

'What about the victim? Don't forget the failed attempt on Poborski's life at Kermincham, as well as the kidnap. Come on plod, try and keep up.'

'I am an old-style copper. I want evidence, lots of it, and not just forensic. Can you finish up here, Jack? I'll need to get a statement released. The press is going to have a field day. Then I'm going to Kermincham.'

'I need to re-interview Luciano,' said Paula. 'Perhaps Jack could come to Lancaster Prison with me?'

Chapter 114

After over an hour with Ted at Wasdale Inn, making arrangements for their Chamonix trip, Dan and Tom headed south, passing Keeperswood and Timbersbrook Cottage. In Stanton Bridge, he turned on the radio to catch the news.

'Good evening. I'm Jeannette Tremlett. This is the six o'clock news from the BBC. Reports of an incident near Keswick in Cumbria are just coming in. A car bomb has exploded, killing the occupants.'

Dan and Tom listened as the story of the A66 tragedy unfolded. Dan spun the Range Rover round in the narrow lane and thrashed it up through Gosforth. Then north up the A595 towards Kermincham, as the news continued.

'All UK political parties, along with the leaders of the Western world condemned the outrage unreservedly. They expressed their continued commitment to halting the scourge of global terrorism. Communist countries, however, have yet to respond. And now for the rest of the news.'

'At the Climate Change Conference, hopes of making progress on global warming received a severe blow when the Russian and Chinese delegations withdrew from negotiations just as a formal agreement appeared close. The leader of the Russian delegation, Yuri Zapatoka, gave no reasons for the withdrawal and no date for the resumption of talks has been agreed. The Chinese delegation also left without comment. Insiders believe other Communist Bloc countries including North Korea will follow.'

Chapter 115

Mat Coulthard arrived at Kermincham Hall and made his way to reception. Julie was on duty, her tear stained face clear evidence that the news had already reached her.

'Hello, how can I help you?' she asked.

'DCI Coulthard, I'd like to have a word with Leo Illic if he's available, please?'

'Certainly, I'll ring through to his room for you.'

Ana sat alone in a private lounge on the second floor, traumatised by the death of her father. The police guard outside only intensified her feeling of vulnerability. The door opened and Bernadeta returned with some magazines.

'I've brought someone to see you.' Bernadeta tried to smile.

Ana looked up to the open doorway, to where Tom stood with his father. She got up and walked towards Tom holding back the tears.

'I'm so sorry, Ana,' Tom said, as he held her close. 'I'm so very, very sorry.'

Bernadeta turned to Dan and indicated her intention to leave the room.

'I think we need to give Ana some time with Tom,' she whispered as she and Dan turned and left the room.

'What will I do now?' Ana asked Tom, as the door closed.

'I don't know, but you will always have me.'

'Bernadeta and Leo have been telling me everything will be all right, but how can it be?'

'It can't be all right, it can never be the same again, but it will get better.'

'I knew you wouldn't lie to me. After all this time I'm still trying to deal with the death of my mother,' she paused. 'Now I've lost my father.'

'There'll be people around you, trying to help. All meaning well. But remember most of them will be grieving too. This is not just about the death of your mother and father. It's about you and the sort of person you are. I know you can fight back. I saw that in the mountains. It will be hard, but you can do it.'

'I still see my mother, even now. I see her face most nights before I go to sleep. I think I'm psychotic.'

'That's not psychotic, that's wonderful. I love my mother absolutely loads. I know if my mother died, I'd see her face all the time. I'd talk to her too. The same goes for my dad. Anyone who wouldn't must be mental.'

Ana forced a smile.

'Will you come to see me in Sarajevo?'

'Yes. I'll come to Sarajevo.'

Chapter 116

Leo came down as soon as he received the message from Julie. His left arm was supported by a bright blue sling.

'I'm really sorry about what's happened, really sorry,' said Mat.

'I know. It's not your fault.'

The only outward sign of sorrow Mat could detect was in Leo's eyes; they were dead, lifeless.

'You knew him well?'

'Since childhood. Boris and I have been friends for almost thirty years. It's my fault Boris is dead. I should have seen this coming. I'm the one to blame.'

'Perhaps the security service should carry some of the responsibility, you can't blame yourself, but you can help bring his killers to justice.'

'I'll do whatever it takes to find who did this.'

'Have you any idea who could be involved, any clue, is there anything that doesn't sit right? Your sound intel from Sarajevo gave you a good handle on the kidnap. Is there anything that might give us a lead now?'

'Only Milo. His injuries may not have been fatal, but they were pretty serious, I'm sure he'd be unable to take any part in this. The only other obvious beneficiary could be Zelejezara Steel; Boris had to hold the position of General Director, for the finance to be released.'

'So could it be another terrorist group that's involved, not necessarily a Communist cell? What do you think?'

'It's a question I've never even considered. The Communists seem to be the only possibility.'

'I think you're right, my question is, where's the evidence that implicates the Communists? I'm so used to working with a pedantic bunch of CPS arseholes, I can't assume anything, even when there are no obvious alternatives.'

Mat's mobile phone truncated his train of thought.

'Excuse me, it could be important, do you mind if I take this call?'

'No, not at all, go ahead.'

'Hi Jack, how's it going?'

Mat's face took on a solemn expression as he ended the call.

'That was my sergeant, Jack Fletcher. There's been some uncertainty about the driver involved in the fatality. Jack's just confirmed it was Savo Stanisic. I'm sorry, I know you and he were friends.'

Leo sat for a moment without speaking.

'We survived the Sarajevo Siege together. How could I lose Savo now, here in England? But Savo shouldn't have been driving that Mercedes. It wasn't his car. Ratko Kartic should have driven that diplomatic car to Manchester Airport. Why did they change drivers?'

'Would anyone know at reception?'

They walked over to reception where Julie offered a sad, injured smile.

'I'm sorry about this,' said Mat, 'but I need to ask some questions about the drivers of the diplomatic cars. We now believe Savo Stanisic was driving the car. The one that was involved in the tragedy. Leo thinks Ratko Kartic should have been the driver, how can we determine if the drivers were changed for some reason?'

'You could try the driver's logbook,' suggested Julie. 'Each car and its allocated driver has its own logbook. It seems it's standard Embassy procedure. I think it's to do with parking and speeding tickets. We used them to reserve the cars for diplomats and delegates. The drivers completed the logbook for every run. Time out, distance travelled, time of return, you know, that sort of thing. The logbooks were all here this morning, waiting for the Embassy to collect them. I saw Ratko looking at them.'

'Is it possible we could see them? It could help.'

Julie searched reception and then the back office; she returned empty handed.

'No, sorry, Ratko must have taken them with him. I can't think why. There is another way.'

'Anything.'

'Well, reception was given the job of booking the cars by entering the reservation into the logbook when instructed by Embassy staff. The problem was we had disputes because the drivers would keep the logbooks in the car when they were out driving, so when we got reservations they couldn't be logged in the books. Double booking of cars became a big problem. Mr. Komikosovitch would go berserk, he was such a stickler for the rules. Is any of this making sense?' Mat was unsure, but he nodded back. 'So, to cut a long story short, Mr. Komikosovitch insisted we took a photocopy of the logbooks so we could make a provisional booking and then update the proper logbook when the driver returned with it. The system worked perfectly. I guess this doesn't help, I'm just wasting your time, aren't I?'

'No not at all, you could have provided the solution we need. Could we see the photocopies?'

'Oh certainly, they're in here, we keep them locked in this drawer so the drivers couldn't make changes to them.'

Mat looked through the photocopied logbook for the Mercedes E500 Saloon involved in the A66 tragedy. It showed that the driver's name, Ratko Kartic, had been neatly crossed out and the name of Savo Stanisic substituted.

Mat turned to Leo. 'The change of driver seems strangely fortuitous for Mr Kartic.'

'Where's Kartic now?' Leo asked Julie picking up the scent.

'I can't say, he left this morning driving Savo's car, I haven't seen him since.'

Chapter 117

At seven thirty, after completing security formalities, Paula Medrith and Detective Sergeant Jack Fletcher stood in Lancaster Prison, waiting for the arrival of Luciano Magiera aka Dalibor Tesak. Jack's mobile phone burst into life.

'Could you excuse me while I take this call?' Paula nodded.

'Hi Mat, how's it going?'

'Okay, I guess. Dan Kennedy and Tom have returned to Kermincham. I'm still with Leo Illic. How are things with you?'

'Paula and I are still waiting to talk to Luciano in Lancaster Prison. She's hoping she can pin some involvement in Poborski's death on him. She thinks he may talk, if he's looking at a murder charge.'

'Don't hold your breath. But listen up, I need to locate a car that may have been abandoned. It shouldn't be too hard to find; it's a black Mercedes Benz ML 350, one of the Embassy cars. Probably driven by Ratko Kartic.' Mat read out the Merc's licence plate details. 'It should stand out like a sore thumb. Get Traffic and our beat boys to keep an eye out for it, do a sweep of all the hotels and public car parks, the usual stuff, my guess is it's somewhere in Keswick.'

'No problem. I'll get onto it right away.'

'Good luck with Magiera. Oh, and do me a favour. Watch his reaction when you tell him what happened on the A66. He's been banged up since Sunday morning, with Josip Budach one of the other drivers, so he can't have been directly involved.'

Jack Fletcher concluded his conversation and switched off his mobile as Luciano Magiera made his appearance under armed guard. His penal blue ensemble was accessorised by a warm smile and a firm handshake.

'My dear Miss Medrith, how well you look, please do take a seat. I apologise for these somewhat austere surroundings. I'm not accustomed to entertaining my guests in such grim surroundings as these.'

Paula smiled back. 'Hi Luciano, I hope you're going to be more helpful than the last time we talked, with Jon White at Kermincham.'

'Ah, sorry Miss Medrith, I'm afraid I can't help, but I'm always delighted to converse with such a sophisticated young lady as you.'

'Thank you, Luciano. You are as ever the perfect gentleman. Let me introduce my colleague Detective Jack Fletcher, he's a Sergeant with Cumbria Police.'

'A policeman? And I thought this was a social call.'

Jack Fletcher didn't smile. Good cop, bad cop was an old routine, but it had worked for him and Mat Coulthard so many times before; why shouldn't it work now? Jack went straight into his bad cop routine.

'This is not a social occasion, Magiera, or should I say Dalibor Tesak. We're here to ask questions and you're here to answer them. Got it?'

'Tut, tut, manners maketh the man, there's no need to be so rude.'

Luciano responded with such a hurt and injured tone, that Jack almost apologised. Almost. Undeterred, Jack continued with his bad cop role. He needed to know if Luciano had any involvement in the deaths on the A66.

'You really need to start talking, you scumbag. Tell us what you know.'

Luciano said nothing.

'We just thought you might want to help yourself a little, you know, reduce your sentence from life imprisonment to ten or twelve years, maybe less,' intoned good cop Paula, turning on the charm.

'Life in prison, on a charge of kidnap and attempted murder? I do not think so.' A smirk spread over Luciano's face. 'I am of course innocent until proven guilty, am I not? Charging me is one thing, getting a conviction is entirely another.'

'Why don't we just cut the bullshit,' said Jack. 'We're talking murder here, and after the failed attempt at Kermincham Hall, your name is at the top of the leader board.'

Luciano's mask of duplicity shattered with the announcement that a murder had been committed. He quickly regained his composure, to continue his game of charades.

'Nice golfing connection there, Detective Sergeant.' Luciano pointed to the Keswick Golf Club badge on Jack's sweater. 'But if you don't mind me saying so, primrose yellow does absolutely nothing for you. Wrong skin tone. I see you more in, now let me see, a dark blue, even mauve but definitely not the yellow.'

'I'm sure you're right, your dress sense is impeccable,' soothed Paula.

'But if you've someone to pin a murder charge on,' Luciano paused as if thinking. 'Then there must have been a murder. My, now who could it be? Not Poborski? Are you seriously telling me Poborski is dead?'

The look on Luciano's face told Jack Fletcher all he needed to know. Before they left Preston Prison, Paula received a call from Jon White. She immediately telephoned Mat Coulthard.

'Hi Mat, well you were right. Luciano Magiera had no idea that Boris Poborski died this afternoon on the A66. Absolutely none at all.'

'Well the reports we gathered from Keeperswood and Timbersbrook indicate conclusively that the munitions deployed were of East European origin, the kind of kit much favoured by Communist countries. Luciano's revolver and Olga's two pistols, along with the Kalashnikov, definitely originated from that source. We also found Josip Budach's fingerprints on the leather case that concealed Olga's weapons. All this seems to tidy up the kidnap and the murder attempt at Kermincham Hall, leaving the Communists the only ones in the frame. But we've nothing to connect them with the murder of Boris Poborski. No evidence at all. Perhaps we need to consider another explanation for the A66 explosion? We just need some evidence.'

'Well this could help. I've just received the latest from our American colleague, Jon White, on the explosive device deployed, and it will surprise even you. Although it's early days, the report just in from the CIA indicates that the detonator employed on the A66 explosion is high tech. I mean really high tech. It's from the latest U.S. ballistics programme, the CIA are confident there is no way the Communists could have got their hands on this piece of kit. The Americans haven't even passed it for final trials yet, and according to Jon, their top brass are spitting feathers, they want answers and they want them yesterday. This incident has caused a major security scare in the Pentagon. Someone, as yet unknown at the very highest level, is divulging classified intelligence. I guess you could be right, this does put the Communists in the clear.

Chapter 118

Mat and Leo sat in reception at Kermincham Hall with coffee and biscuits, and the photocopied logbooks, one for each of the eight Embassy cars.

'We need to check the rest of the logbook copies for any changes, or inconsistencies. They all cover the time the delegates were picked up at Manchester Airport, right up to an hour ago. Here, you check Savo's. I'll look through the copy for Kartic's car.'

Mat handed Leo the copy logbook for Savo's Mercedes Benz ML 350, as he began to scrutinise Kartic's. Leo finished checking Savo's logbook first.

'There's nothing in Savo's log that raises any questions. What about Kartic's?'

At first Mat made no reply as he carefully rechecked the entries.

'The last run Kartic completed in the Mercedes E500 was Monday evening. According to the log it was a return trip to Manchester Airport.'

'So that was yesterday?'

'Yes. The time out was five forty-three. The time of return was eight twenty, a total trip time of two hours thirty-seven minutes. But that can't be right. The journey would take five hours minimum.'

'So, where had Kartic been all that time?' asked Leo.

'It can't have been to Manchester Airport. The mileage in was logged at twenty-one thousand and thirty-nine. The mileage out was twenty thousand nine hundred and seventy-seven. A round trip of sixty-two miles to a destination I know is a journey of over two hundred miles. Even the thickest Plod could detect it doesn't add up. Or is it subtract? I'm not sure.'

'So, there was adequate time for Kartic to conceal an explosive device in his Mercedes Benz, before he changed cars with Savo.'

'Kartic's previous trip, on the Sunday night, was a trip into Keswick at seven fifteen, returning to Kermincham Hall at nine fifty-eight. The mileage on this trip looks about right.' Leo checked the entries. 'His passenger was the same individual on both occasions.'

Leo's eyes were brighter now, life was returning. Mat made a note of Kartic's passenger, and then rang Security at Manchester Airport.

***

Paula Medrith and Jack Fletcher drove the next ten miles to Kermincham in silence.

'Well Jack, that's blown my theory out of the water. Luciano had no idea Boris Poborski was dead. He showed total surprise. It looks like your boss Plod may be right, it may not be the Communists after all; but if not the Communists, then who?'

'If you're not convinced, why don't you take a leaf out of Mat's book?'

'How do you mean, a leaf?'

'Find the evidence. No evidence, no crime; that's the CPS credo.'

Paula thought for a moment.

'You're right, let's make a fresh start. Let's go back to Timbersbrook Cottage.'

'Fine, we can go straight there from here and go back to Kermincham via Cockermouth.'

It was dark when they turned off the A595 in Gosforth and headed toward Nether Wasdale. Paula slowed to a crawl as she eased the Range Rover up the icy gradient to Timbersbrook Cottage, where they were greeted by two police officers from the firearms unit.

'Evening Jack, this is a rum do. What do you make of it all?' asked the constable.

'It's early days yet. How are things up here?'

'All very quiet, you're the only living thing we've seen since SOCO left an hour ago. Things are pretty much as they were. Apart from a big slate-topped coffee table that's been taken back to the lab.'

'Are we okay to go in?' asked Jack.

'I couldn't stop you, Jack. Even if I wanted to. Which of course I don't.'

The snow had been cleared from the path and Jack and Paula ducked beneath the police barrier tape and made their way up the stone steps to the cottage door. The sitting room bore the marks of the SOCO boys. Yellow tape indicated the final resting place of more than a dozen spent cartridges. Blood patches had been highlighted in several areas of the sitting room. After examining the bedroom together, Jack searched the kitchen while Paula carefully picked over the sitting room.

'There's nothing in the kitchen, anything in the sitting room?'

Paula struggled to pull her hand from between the cushion and the side of one of the armchairs.

'There's something down here, I can see it and I can just touch it, but I can't quite get hold of it to get it out. It's too far down.'

Jack Fletcher knelt down and took the chair's cushion out. Paula tried again, pushing her hand deep into the space between the chair's side and the base.

'That's better. It's a long way down. Yes, that's got it.' She pulled out her hand. 'It's a pocket diary, there are initials on the front. R. D.'

Paula leafed through the diary. 'There are several recent entries, all written in scrawly handwriting. Well here's one appointment Roman Drasko can't keep. Even if he was alive.'

"Marsala Tita. Charles de Gaulle International Airport, Paris at 10.00."

'You could be right, Paula. I guess Tito's been dead for what, almost twenty years?'

'Not quite, he died in May nineteen eighty. The trouble is half the population of the former Yugoslavia are still praying for his return.'

'What about the other half, how do they feel about the second coming?'

'None too pleased. The Catholics in particular were glad to see the back of Tito. I'll courier this diary to HQ in Vauxhall, we'll see what they can make of it.'

Chapter 119

Mat Coulthard had endured more TV dinners than he cared to remember. Invariably beans on toast accompanied by an episode of some soap opera or a nondescript documentary. He usually woke up in time to go to bed, but not always. Tonight, Mat's TV viewing was to be different. He grabbed a couple of cheese rolls and two coffees, as he made his way through the concourse of Manchester Airport, where Dick Carroll welcomed him with a friendly greeting. It was fast approaching ten o'clock.

Dick and Mat had worked together last year on a major credit card fraud that blighted the northwest, just two months before Dick left the Manchester Force to take up his new post as Head of Airport Security.

'How's it going,' Mat asked as they sipped their coffee. 'Have you made any progress so far?'

'We've completed several discrete sweeps of the airport since you called. Both with CCTV and foot patrols, there's no sign of your suspect, not based on the description you gave me. I think we must have missed him, though no one has boarded a flight using a passport in that name. So perhaps you'd better take me through the time frame again, just to make sure that I've pulled out all the tapes you need?'

Mat took out his notebook to check before replying.

'The explosion occurred at five minutes past four this afternoon. It would take at least two hours to drive to the airport. I timed it on the way down. So, I'm looking at a time frame between, say seventeen thirty and twenty-one thirty, to be on the safe side. Yes, that should more than cover it.'

Dick slotted in the first tape and switched on the monitor.

'Enjoy your TV dinner, my supervisor will ring me if you need any help. I'll catch up with you later.'

Mat ran the tapes covering the taxi rank and the main entrance to departure for Terminals One, Two and Three, as he tucked into his cheese roll. By now his coffee was cold, no change there. Regardless, he took a sip. The first two tapes drew a blank, but on the third tape, he hit the jackpot. He recognised a man emerging from a taxi at Terminal One. At first, he wasn't certain. Then the passenger turned around to face the camera.

Dick Carroll came at once, checked the tape and confirmed the time had been twenty thirty-two.

'I need a list of all Terminal One flights from twenty thirty until twenty-two thirty, if you can arrange that?'

Dick waved over his supervisor from the control desk. He walked over to Dick and Mat, bringing a sheaf of computer printouts.

'Already done,' smiled Dick.

Mat browsed through the list of departure times for the flights from Terminal One, discounting those before twenty thirty.

'I need to scratch out any flights to intercontinental destinations, as well as anything tinged with a holiday feeling. I don't think my suspect is in a holiday mood right now. That leaves three possibilities that fit the time scale. Munich, Milan and Geneva.'

'Right, I'll get the security tapes covering all three boarding gates. You can grab us both a hot coffee.'

Mat returned with the coffee, and Dick ran the Munich tape first. Nothing. The Milan tape was next. At first, they had difficulty in getting the tape to deliver a clear picture. They tried successfully using a different monitor. Still nothing. Finally, Geneva. They watched as the passengers filed through the boarding gate for the twenty-one fifty-five flight to Geneva. Watched and resigned themselves to failure as the air stewardesses closed the gate. Dick shrugged his shoulders. Then, out of camera, a late arrival attracted the Flight Attendant's attention. As he came into view, Mat recognised him. He'd been the passenger on Kartic's last two trips. Mat finished his coffee, it was cold, but he didn't care.

***

Mat wasn't out of the airport complex, when his mobile phone rang.

'Hi Mat, it's Paula Medrith. Jack and I are coming into Keswick. Jack's had an update on Savo's missing Mercedes Benz ML 350 from Traffic. They've located it in the car park on High Hill, up near the Church of Saint Charles Borromeo, the Catholic Church. He says you'll know the one. Does that mean anything to you? It doesn't to Jack.'

Mat thought for a moment.

'Beats me, I can't think straight at the moment, my head's still buzzing from watching too much television.'

Paula laughed; she had stopped laughing long before Mat concluded his report.

'He's an improbable suspect,' Paula growled. 'Are you sure?'

'Looks that way. He flew to Geneva, using the passport of a Robert Nova at twenty-one fifty-five. Flight 1751.The question is, can you find out where he went to from Geneva?'

'I'll get our people in Geneva onto it straight away. I think you've done a fantastic job. You must teach me the secret of your detective work sometime.'

'Sorry, school's out. I'll speak to you tomorrow, perhaps we can all meet up at Kermincham Hall with Leo, and I'll bring Jack, at, say, four o'clock?'

Chapter 120

Luka stepped off the tram and walked slowly home through the streets of Sarajevo. Every building she passed had suffered some sort of war damage during the siege and the road and pavements were peppered with craters left by the shelling. She went directly to her room while her grandmother prepared the evening meal. She changed her clothes and hung her suit and blouse in the wardrobe. Luka sat on the bed for almost an hour, her head in her hands.

'Luka, it's seven o'clock, your meal is ready.'

Luka took her seat at the kitchen table, staring out at nothing in particular, before pushing away her plate.

'What's the matter, aren't you hungry? Are you ill?' Her grandmother asked.

'No, I'm not ill.' A tear hovered at the cusp of her eyelid. 'Mr Illic has been hurt and now Mr Poborski has been murdered, blown up by a car bomb in England.'

'Oh, but that's terrible.' Her grandmother's hands rose involuntarily and covered her face to restrain a gasp of disbelief. 'How will this affect you?'

'I don't know for certain. They say Mr Poborski had to be our General Director for the money to be paid. It's something to do with the Finance Agreement. The money will go to Split in Croatia, instead of Sarajevo Steel.'

'So, will you go to work tomorrow or stay at home until you know what's to happen?'

'For certain I'll go to work. There's a meeting tomorrow to elect an action committee. I may be able to help in some way, though I don't know how. Anyway, I have to be there. I need to make my telephone call to Mr Illic at the usual time.'

Chapter 121

Paula's medic changed the wound dressing on Leo's left shoulder in his room. Then checked his blood pressure, heart rate and temperature before leaving. All were okay. Leo went downstairs at four o'clock. DCI Mat Coulthard and Sergeant Jack Fletcher were waiting. He looked out of the window before helping himself to a strong black coffee. The snow had turned a dirty grey at either side of the drive, a sight he always hated. Leo sat down opposite Mat and sipped his coffee as Jack offered Mat a refill.

***

Mat sat juggling the information from last night's visit to Manchester Airport in his head, but nothing made any sense.

'That's better,' said Mat.

'What's better?' asked Paula as she pushed open the door, followed by Jon White.

'Hot coffee. I seem to spend my life drinking it cold. Would you and Jon like one?'

Mat opened the meeting as Jack served up more coffee.

'I need some help to get my head round what we've scraped up so far. I can't see how it fits together, or even if it does.'

'Well, Milo Tolja, aka Angelo Moretti, is out of the frame,' began Jack. 'He'd be in no fit state to assassinate anyone. Apart from the blood found on the floor from the gunshot wounds, the headlong fall onto the slate-topped coffee table would have rendered him unconscious for some time, probably resulting in a brain bleed and possible death. The lab found a significant amount of skin tissue on the corner of the coffee table.'

'You're probably right, Jack, but we've no body yet. He could be anywhere. We need to check out his room at the Wast Water Inn again, can you see to that?' asked Mat.

'This doesn't help much either,' said Paula. 'I found a diary at Timbersbrook Cottage. The initials on the diary are R D and the handwriting checks out with the scrawly writing on the ransom notes, so we believe the diary belongs to Roman Drasko. It seems he has an appointment with Marsala Tita next week, but Marshal Tito has been dead for eighteen years. The diary's being analysed by HQ boffins as we speak. So that means we have two main suspects,' continued Paula. 'First there is Ratko Kartic who was supposed to be driving the Mercedes E500 when Boris died. He appears to have gone missing on High Hill near the Catholic Church of Saint Charles Borromeo, where he dumped Savo's Mercedes. Then there's Mat's new suspect. A man in his position does seem to be an unlikely candidate, but he was AWOL when Boris and Savo were blown up. Then he flew to Geneva using the alias Robert Nova.'

'Do we know where he went from Geneva?' asked Mat.

'Yes, he flew to Rome's Leonardo Di Vinci Airport,' Paula replied.

'Where did he go from there, did he meet anyone? What's the story?'

'He was first seen on CCTV monitors as he took the train to the Stazione Termini and then he took a taxi to an address in the city. We only have the street address, no number. He went to Via Tomacelli, it's down near the River Tiber. Does that mean anything to anyone?'

Paula's question bounced back from a stonewall of blank faces.

'What kind of area is it, you know, residential, commercial, retail?' asked Mat.

'Mainly commercial; it's an important business quarter,' she added.

'Okay, it's clear we have more work to do in Wasdale and Keswick. Jack and I will get onto it.'

'Yes, and there's some digging I can do in Sarajevo,' suggested Leo 'We need to find Kartic, and have a word with our new suspect, alias Robert Nova.'

'Tread carefully, Leo, our suspect is a highly respected member of the Bosnian administration. He has connections with influence, and our latest intelligence suggests there is some sort of global Communist undercurrent at the moment,' added Paula.

Jon White looked across at her and nodded.

'Will you be going to Sarajevo for Boris' funeral?' Paula asked Mat.

'Yes,' said Mat. 'The Chief Constable wants me off the case, but he's agreed I can go to the funeral.'

Leo sat deep in thought.

'I expect I'll see you there?' said Mat.

'Boris was my closest friend, so it will be good to see you.'

Chapter 122

Milo lay in the Burdenko Main Military Clinic in Moscow. He was only half aware of his surroundings as he stumbled in and out of consciousness. As he drifted into nightmares from the past, the strong smell of antiseptic filled his head like a drug, teasing out memories of hospital visits he'd made as a child—visits that would live with him forever. The beatings and sexual violation had increased over the years, becoming a ritual. His mother had suffered too.

***

Milo was alone at home with his stepfather.

'Will you help me with the potato patch?' Milo asked as they finished their evening meal.

'What help do you want?'

'It's the depth of the trench. I'm just not sure.'

As the sun set and shadows lengthened, they walked to the rear of the house. A heap of fresh manure stood in readiness, steaming beneath the low bruised sky. Last year Milo had sold a few sacks of potatoes, and kept a little of the proceeds as pocket money, most of which he'd spent on the penknife he now clutched in his hand.

'Could you just mark the depth with this stick please?'

Milo put the penknife in his trouser pocket. His stepfather knelt down to reach into the pit. Milo looked all around him. There was nothing. He looked again. There was no one.

He raised the spade high above his twelve-year-old frame, bringing it down on the back of his stepfather's head, rendering him unconscious. For how long, Milo was unsure. Milo kicked the comatose body into the pit, and it fell face upward beneath the darkening skies. Now his fun could begin. Milo drove the spade deep into his stepfather's outstretched arm.

Blood flowed. Milo looked down at the result and smiled. He gave the arm a kick to confirm it was broken. He screamed with delight. This was paradise. He raised the spade again, directing the blow just above his stepfather's right eye. The spade found its target. Milo checked—there was a deep, angry gash from which more blood flowed. Milo watched, fascinated as his stepfather's left eye flickered, then slowly opened and he began to scream out, and as he did, Milo hit him hard in the face with the spade, and then again. Harder the second time to make sure. Milo tried to control his excitement as his stepfather lost consciousness once more. Then using his penknife, Milo made certain his stepfather's days as an abuser were over.

'How does that feel?' Milo asked quizzically, gazing down at his stepfather, as if waiting for an answer. His stepfather stirred and gave a muffled inhuman cry. He was beginning to regain consciousness. 'I have waited for this a long time, waited for you to share my fun for a change.' His stepfather gave a guttural cry and then lay still.

'No! No! You can't go yet,' Milo screamed. 'I'm not finished with you.' He began to sob. 'Not finished... There's so much more I need to share, please.'

Waves of hysteria roared through his head, colliding with a wall of anger and frustration. He looked down at his stepfather. His fun was over, yet his need for more remained. As he turned to go, he felt a hand grip his ankle, pulling him into the pit, down into his stepfather's grave. Milo lay prostrate in the soft moist earth, as his stepfather raised himself, to tower above him, his broken arm hanging limply by his side. Milo stared up at his stepfather's disfigured face and bloodied groin and watched as the grotesque figure stood covered in blood, before collapsing unconscious on top of him in the makeshift grave. He felt the weight of the mutilated body pressing down on him, forcing him into the earth. Milo couldn't move as the wet earth began to fill his mouth and nostrils. Clawing frantically at the earth, Milo managed to break free. He climbed from the pit breathing hard and wiped the bloodied earth from his face. He cleaned the penknife on his stepfather's shirt and began to fill in the pit. It was only then he realised he was soaked with his own urine.

***

A male nurse entered the room as Milo slowly escaped from his nightmare and drifted back to the real world. 'You have a visitor, a very important visitor.'

The nurse bowed his head as a sign of respect as the visitor entered, then he closed the door and left.

'I am told you are recovering well.'

'Yes, I feel much better, even my headache has gone. The shoulder wound was superficial. It was the concussion caused by the blow to the head when I hit the coffee table that caused the problem, but everything is healing well. This morning I took a walk.'

'Good. That is good news. But I've have had more good news since I saw you in Birmingham Airport. Poborski is dead. Blown up in a car bomb. We have no idea who our co-conspirator might be. Poborski's daughter had a fortuitous escape. It appears classified reports signed off by the CIA have eliminated us from any possible involvement and absolved us from all blame. Poborski was required under clause 83.1 to hold the position of General Director before the finance could be released. Therefore, no payment can be made. It also means that back in Sarajevo, as we cannot be implicated in the death of Poborski, we will suffer no adverse effect. Operation Bosnian Dawn is now back on track. You need to instigate the armed insurrection in support of the People's Revolution we have planned in Sarajevo. You have the guns ready?'

'Yes, the guns are ready. They are stored in the Zetra Arena.'

'I will be in Paris later today where I will make the final arrangements and set the wheels in motion. I'll let you know the details. You will need to fulfil Roman's part in this matter. I'm told he didn't make it. Your role is now crucial. The next time we meet, it will be in Sarajevo.'

The visitor left the room.

'So, Ana lives?' said Milo out loud to the empty room. Then he lay back on his pillow and fantasised over his next meeting with Ana.

Chapter 123

On Thursday morning in the production office of Sarajevo Steel, Dragan looked up at the office clock, and then over to where Luka sat. It was ten o'clock, coffee time. Luka worked on. He looked at the clock again.

'It's no good looking at the clock. We don't have time for coffee anymore. We need to work twice as hard now. If the money isn't going to come from the Deutsche Bank Consortium, we have to find it from somewhere else.'

The door opened and one of the men from the foundry walked in.

'Are you coming to the meeting? It's been moved back to three o'clock. Can you two make it okay?'

'Sure, we'll be there,' said Dragan. Luka nodded in agreement.

***

All of Sarajevo's workers filed into the canteen as three o'clock neared. Luka and Dragan were among the last to arrive. A small group stood at the front in a huddle, engaged in conversation around a well-dressed man. Luka knew most of the men, at least by sight, and all of the women. Yet she had never seen this man before. Dragan recognised him at once from the days before the siege, during the time Communism presided over the former Bratsvo Steel. The group at the front of the canteen dispersed, to leave the man standing alone. At once he began to speak.

'Comrades, first I would like to add my condolences for the death of Boris Poborski. The legacy his death condemns you to is not one I would have wished for the workers of Sarajevo Steel. It leaves you without finance, without jobs and without a future. It leaves you at the mercy of Capital exploitation. There is, however, a solution. It is the return of

Communism and our beloved Marsala Tita. It is the rebirth of Brotherhood and Unity. This Western backed Interim Government must be shown their interference in our country is no longer required. We must take to the streets of Sarajevo. A People's Revolution. What is it to be? Protest or penury? Will you join me in the People's Revolution?'

Silence seeped in from beneath the canteen tables and filled the room, as Bosnian worker stood shoulder to shoulder with Serb, and Serb with Croat.

'No.'

A single word fractured the silence. One word escaped from the far corner of the canteen and dribbled out to where Lenord Stanislav stood.

'What? What was that, speak up?'

Everyone moved aside to see who had spoken, opening up a corridor in the centre of those present at the meeting. A girl stepped out from the back of the canteen, into the breach and walked to stand face to face with Lenord Stanislav, the former General Director of the Bratsvo Steel.

'No. I won't join you. I'm going back to work. The legacy of Mr Poborski goes on. It is a legacy of hard work, honest work, and I know these things have value.' Luka stood toe to toe with Stanislav, poking her index finger in his face as she continued. 'This will be recognised by other banks. We will find the finance we need from them. We have worked so hard to get this far. I won't throw it away for Brotherhood and Unity or Marsala Tita.'

'You are too young to remember the good old days. You don't remember Tito and the comfort and success that Communism brought to the people of Yugoslavia. But these things will return when a Communist Government is firmly in control. When Tito returns.'

Luka stood alone as the silence engulfed her. She made to leave.

'Communism. Comfort and success, excuse me.'

It was Dragan. He walked purposefully forward to stand at Luka's side. 'Is that why we built Yugo cars and the Swedes had Volvos? Or why the East Germans had the Berlin wall and the Americans had Disney World? It may have been comfort and success for the oligarchy, up there in the clouds where you were, but down here in our world, it got pretty grim at times, watching the corruption and fraud. We have a chance now, maybe not a good chance, but a chance. I'm going to take mine. I'm going back to work. You can go to hell.'

Most of the men followed Luka and Dragan, filing slowly out of the canteen, leaving Stanislav standing with only three men. None of the women stayed. His reputation as a sexual deviant had not been forgotten.

Luka sat in the silence of Leo's office as she waited for her telephone call to be answered.

'Hello, Leo Illic speaking.'

'Mr Illic, it's me, Luka. Can you hear me all right?'

'Yes Luka, I can hear you.'

'How is your shoulder, how are you keeping?'

'I'm fine. Has everything been okay since we spoke yesterday?'

'Someone called Lenord Stanislav talked to the workers in the canteen. There's been some kind of a leak from the Interim Government. They say the finance will be forfeited. It's making headline news. A few of the men want to lobby the Parliament Buildings. Others are saying there will be a People's Revolution. The news of Mr Poborski's death has been greeted with a great deal of sadness and dismay.' Leo waited while Luka fought back a sob. 'But I won't give in. What do you want me to do?'

'Stay calm and stay safe. Find out as much as you can, but don't put yourself in any danger. Telephone me as usual at the same time tomorrow. I'll be back for Mr Poborski's funeral on Tuesday. Be careful.'

'Okay, I will. Goodbye, Mr Illic.'

Chapter 124

Dan Kennedy poured two glasses of white wine, as Jane finished serving up the pasta bake.

'Is that enough pasta? There's plenty left, Tom's had his meal. He's in his room.'

'Yes thanks. A little more salad would be good, though.'

Dan helped himself to more salad, as Jane sat down.

'I've got to ask this. Is Tom up to it? I know how much he wants to go to Sarajevo and attend the funeral, but should we let him go, considering everything that's happened?'

'He's not going on his own. I've kept my work schedule to a minimum for that reason. I only have one appointment next week, but it is crucial. It's with Maynard's in New York. The one I had to cancel. I'm flying out on Sunday, for a Monday morning breakfast meeting, at eight o'clock. Then in the afternoon I'm flying via Munich, to meet up with Tom in Sarajevo. I'll be there for the funeral. Jet lagged and knackered, but I'll be there.'

'That's fine, but you didn't answer my question.'

'Yes absolutely, Tom needs to go.'

Tom stood in the hallway listening to the discussion that so engrossed his parents. He pushed open the kitchen door and went in.

'Dad's right. I do need to go. I need to be there for Ana. We went through a lot together, and we survived because of each other. I'm going to Sarajevo next week. On my own if I have to. Walking if I have to, but trust on me on this. I am going.'

Chapter 125

At nine o'clock, Paula and Sam arrived at the UN offices in Sarajevo for their Monday morning briefing with her boss. The damage to the building from the shelling during the siege was still evident. The mood in the office seemed sombre and hyper at the same time.

'Good morning.' Douglas Freeman greeted them. 'Come on through to my office.'

'Okay. You're here this morning to take on board the latest intelligence about major Communist activity, centred right here on the city of Sarajevo. We've been monitoring the situation for some time now, but nothing fitted together. The diary you turned up at Timbersbrook Cottage changed all that. It means we'll be turning up the heat on a number of major political players, and one in particular. So, well done, you.

'Individually, each stand-alone event appeared unconnected as if the boys from Eastern Europe were just getting a bit puerile. Except it's not restricted to Eastern Europe. It's the whole dammed Communist world. At first, they seemed random events, but when we cut and pasted them together, we had to wonder what was going on. Too many dice were rolling up six. I know you are aware of some of this. But there's a shed load more. This morning a Russian naval battle force was picked up on satellite leaving the warm water port of Sebastopol and heading through the Bosporus. Destination unknown. All this is leading up to the big one. A People's Revolution, the code name for the coup d'état is Operation Bosnian Dawn.

'The Communists believe the western powers are becoming bored with the Balkans situation and want to move on. Providing all military hostilities can be avoided, the Communists are convinced opposition to any power shift will be merely diplomatic. They think there are too many issues requiring global co-operation for a local problem like the Balkans to get in the way. Confirmed intelligence shows they intend to force a Communist regime on Bosnia. The catalyst for this is to be the failure of the Western backed Sarajevo Steel. The entries in the Timbersbrook diary provided the last piece of the jigsaw that solved the puzzle. It pinpoints the individual who is orchestrating the whole show and the architect behind Operation Bosnian Dawn.'

'The only name in the diary was Tito's and he's not in good shape right now to orchestrate anything.'

'You're right, Paula. It seems it's a case of like father, like son. There's no more I can share with you at this time.'

'So where do Sam and I come in?'

'Listen up. The downfall of Sarajevo Steel cannot be allowed to occur. It would bring the Interim Government crashing down. Sam first. Sam will meet Herr Becker, off his flight from Frankfurt, at Sarajevo Airport at ten thirty-two, Central European Time. Herr Becker is attending a meeting with Joe Brown, the American Ambassador. Sam will take him directly to the meeting and see he arrives without incident. He will be accompanied by an armed guard from the UN. Is that clear, Sam?'

Sam nodded.

'Okay, so now for you, Paula. You too will go to Sarajevo Airport when you leave this office and meet a passenger on Austrian Airlines flight 1260 from Charles de Gaul Airport, Paris, at eleven hundred hours C.E.T. Be gentle with him. He's a VIP. Here are the details.' Freeman handed Paula a red file. 'His arrest will not be made public for forty-eight hours. We can't afford to alarm his fellow conspirators. We have plans for them. You'll have backup from the UN Protection Force to deal with his aides and members of his reception party. Do this discreetly. It's essential we avoid any drama at the airport. Softly, softly does it, we want to avoid drawing attention to an event that officially isn't taking place.'

Chapter 126

NATO's Bosnian headquarters, at Camp Butmir in Sarajevo, was the venue for the hastily arranged meeting between Herr Becker from the Consortium and Joe Brown.

'Good morning, Herr Becker, I appreciate you coming at such short notice, but I know you understand the importance and the urgency.'

'Of course. I too am in the process of trying to find a solution to the problem Boris Poborski's death has created.'

'Both of us mourn the sad loss, but the US Government is not prepared to let Poborski die in vain. We understand your Consortium's concern regarding the advance of such a significant amount of finance, especially now that Boris cannot take up his General Directorship in accordance with clause 83.1. I would propose therefore, that Leo Illic be appointed General Director as from today, with Stefan Matic as a Director. I met both these men in England and was impressed with both their business acumen and their vision.' Herr Becker nodded in agreement as Joe Brown continued.

'I am empowered to inform you that when these appointments take place, the US will underwrite the balance of all unsecured funds. This means that one hundred percent of the loan is underwritten, every dime; you people have nothing to lose. So, let's hear it. You don't have a problem now, am I right?'

'I'm absolutely certain that you are. However, I am not mandated to sanction the finance without full board approval. Zelejezara Steel, from Split in Croatia are lobbying hard for the same funds. However, I still favour Sarajevo's proposal.'

'I see, but how soon could you get the mandate you require? Could you get it today?'

'No. That will not be possible. When I received your call late yesterday, for a meeting today, I knew your motive.' Herr Becker paused and gave Joe Brown a knowing smile. 'I've been doing my job for as long as you have been doing yours.'

Joe Brown smiled back.

'Okay so what's the deal?'

'I've already arranged a full board meeting for nine o'clock tomorrow morning, in order to request the mandate I require.'

'But will you get it?'

'I don't know.'

Joe Brown got up from his seat and shook Herr Becker's hand.

'Thank you for your help. I owe you a great deal.'

'Don't thank me. I haven't won the mandate yet. If all goes to plan, I'll know one way or the other by twelve thirty tomorrow.'

Chapter 127
New York

Dan Kennedy sat in the departure lounge at JFK staring out at the fog as it swirled around the service trucks and the aircraft on the runway. His breakfast meeting with Maynards had gone well, now he was waiting for his Lufthansa flight to Munich, then on to Sarajevo to meet Tom for Boris' funeral. He looked at his watch. It was just turning two fifteen. Picking up his case and newspaper, he walked through the busy concourse towards the departure lounge, checking the status of his flight as he went. The information board showed his flight was boarding on time, at gate twenty-seven. Then it changed. The destination at the top of the board began to flash and a rhythmic pulse of green light flashed alongside it, spelling out the word, delayed. Dan was relieved to see Rio de Janeiro flashing next to it. As he turned to go, the letters spelling out 'delayed' spilled down to the bottom of the giant information board. JFK was fog bound. All flights were cancelled. Dan telephoned home.

'Hi Jane, bad news. I'm afraid JFK is fog bound.'

'Tom's expecting to meet you tomorrow for the funeral. He's already in Sarajevo.'

'I simply can't get there. I've checked, nothing's getting in or out of JFK until tomorrow morning at the earliest. It's a real pea souper. I won't be able to make the funeral after all. Can you call Tom and explain?'

'Yes. I'll ring now. Will Tom be all right?'

'Yes, of course he will. Tom will be just fine.'

Chapter 128
Sarajevo

Austrian Airlines Flight 1260 from Paris to Sarajevo taxied to a standstill and the last passenger prepared to disembark. He had waited for this day for as long as he could remember. His mother had promised his time would come, and he must be ready for it. He must be worthy of it. This was his right and his destiny. He stepped down from the aircraft, princely, regal. In his head he heard the band begin to play. He paused for a moment at the top of the steps and prepared to accept the accolades of his adoring subjects as they waited in the falling rain. He was ready, he was worthy, but as he descended the aircraft steps to meet his destiny, the dream evaporated.

There was no band and no accolade, only Paula Amanda Medrith B.L., Ph.D. and six UN Marines, detailed to arrest the major protagonist of Operation Bosnian Dawn. Ivan Bobic, the Bosnian Ambassador to the UK and illegitimate son of the former President of the Social Federal Republic of Yugoslavia, Marshall Josip Broz Tito, would be escorted into custody. The coup d'état had failed. The dream was over.

Chapter 129

Paula's billet was in the Holiday Inn, Sarajevo. Leo and Ana checked in there on their arrival back. Ana couldn't face the apartment across the park from the Café Paris. She preferred the anonymity of the hotel and the company of friends.

Tom Kennedy and Mat checked in there too. It was from this hotel that Serbian snipers fired on Sarajevans, as they gathered in front of the Parliament Buildings, at the start of the war. It was the only hotel to remain open throughout the siege.

During breakfast on the morning of the funeral, Paula suggested they should meet up for lunch after the funeral, before she caught her flight to Geneva. This was to be the last day of service for Jon White. After lunch he was leaving for the States.

Chapter 130

Ana Poborski looked up at the dungeon-grey sky that smothered the village of Babonavic as the private funeral of her father took place in the Church of Saint Mary and Saint Stephen. Ana and her grandparents entered the church together. Tom Kennedy followed close behind. Ana needed to say goodbye to her father away from the eyes of the world.

Flowers now transformed the church after its recent restoration, but to Ana it was a place of great sorrow and distress. It was in this church more than five years ago, that she'd made the promise to her mother. It was still vivid in her memory. Powerful and compelling. Infinitely dominating. As the pall-bears carried her father's coffin shoulder-high into the church, Ana looked up at Jesus on the cross and made a second promise—a promise to avenge the murder of her father. Leo and Tom placed their floral tributes beside Ana's bouquet of winter pansies. Leo had already dispensed with his sling. Jan and Marija laid their flowers on the grave Boris now shared with Ana's mother, Katerina. Then, together they drove from Babonavic to the commemorative service at the Old Orthodox Church in Sarajevo.

*****

Ana arrived to find many of her father's colleagues waiting in the church. She knew their futures were uncertain with the withdrawal of the Consortium finance. They sat in silence as Ana and her grandparents took their seats in the front of the church. Mira Kucsan and her daughter Ena, Ana's school friend, sat close by.

*****

Luka entered the church alone, scouring the pews for a vacant seat in the crowded church.

'Luka, over here, there's a seat over here,' whispered Bernadeta. Luka squeezed in to sit beside her, near the front of the church. Bernadeta introduced Herr Becker and pointed out Tom, who sat in the row in front of her, directly behind Jan and Marija. Bernadeta could see Ana sitting beside her grandparents. Leo sat next to Boris' mother, his arm wrapped around her shoulders, as if trying to prevent her from falling apart.

Towards the back of the church, at the end of the row, Georg Komikosovitch watched and analysed the congregation, taking everything in, while giving nothing away. As usual, he had come alone. Mat and Dragan sat two rows behind him. The service began with a song of love and forgiveness. Herr Becker delivered his tribute on behalf of the Consortium, and Luka read a short passage from the Bible, as a tribute from the employees. Ana and Bernadeta had helped her choose an appropriate passage when they met the day before at Sarajevo Steel with Leo.

***

Georg sat and contemplated his own life and his own mortality. At the end of the second hymn, Georg left the church and walked quickly away through the graveyard, towards the Latin Bridge and the Miljacka River. As he reached the centre of the bridge, he glanced back over his shoulder to see Mat Coulthard someway behind him. He made to run, but as he turned, a car pulled up in front of him. A familiar figure stepped out and approached him from the other side of the bridge. Georg recognised the man at once. He had no doubt. It was Leo Illic.

Looking down at the dirty water of the Miljacka River, Georg watched as the current ripped at the rocks below. He had to do it. He had to do it now. Bleiberg, Knight of the Holy Order of the Sword of St Jerome, could not be instrumental in bringing police scrutiny to bear on the Order. He had to preserve the secrets of St Jerome. He had to deliver against his oath. Georg surveyed the pavement, and finding a place he considered the cleanest, brushed the debris away with the back of his hand, before kneeling down. He took out a pistol from his inside coat pocket, crossed himself, put the pistol to his head and pulled the trigger.

Georg slumped to the pavement, as a flock of startled pigeons burst into the air with a clatter of wings. Blood flowed from the bullet exit wound in the side of his head, canalising the cracks between the dirty pavement slabs. Mat was first on the scene, as the passenger he'd observed boarding Flight 1751 to Geneva in Manchester Airport, stared up at him through dead eyes. Seconds later Leo arrived. Finally, from out of nowhere, Paula Medrith was a good third. Paula stooped down to take the pistol from Georg's right hand and make it safe, as Mat carefully examined the body and the pavement slabs.

Lenord Stanislav did not attend the service. He stood some distance away in Mula Mustafe Bašeskije, and as the mourners arrived, he scribbled the names of those known to him on his notepad. He knew Milo would want to know every name, every detail.

Chapter 131

Mat and Paula waited on the bridge for the Sarajevo Canton Police to arrive, while Leo returned to the church as the commemorative service was ending. Leo met Luka and Bernadeta on the steps as they came out of the church. He made no mention of the tragedy that had unfolded on the Latin Bridge.

'Thank you for reading the passage from the Bible Luka, you read it beautifully.'

'I was just proud to read it Mr Illic, it was no problem.'

Leo turned to Bernadeta.

'We're having lunch together at the Holiday Inn. Would you and Luka like to join us?' asked Leo.

'That would be nice, I'd like to come,' replied Bernadeta.

'What about you, Luka?'

'Oh no thank you, Mr Illic, my grandmother will have my lunch ready when I get home. Thank you for asking me.'

'You could meet Tom, and I know Ana would welcome your company.'

Bernadeta smiled at Luka. 'You can sit with me. I'd like you to come.'

'All right, what time do I need to be there?'

'One o'clock is fine,' said Leo. 'Just come into the hotel reception and ask for me.'

Chapter 132

Lenord Stanislav and Boris Poborski had worked together at Bratsvo Steel for five years. They'd known each other well during the time Stanislav was General Director of Bratsvo Steel. After being summarily replaced by Boris, Stanislav's vitriol knew no bounds.

Stanislav saw Boris Poborski's death as both just and gratifying. He completed the list of mourners from his vantage point on Mula Mustafe Bašeskije, then he instructed his driver to follow Ana's car when she left the church.

***

After the funeral one of the cars drove Boris' mother and father home to Kobilja Glavia. Ana went with them, before returning to the Holiday Inn. As their car wound its way from the church, the traffic slowed, and for a moment, the car was stationary on the busy road that skirted the Zetra Arena.

Ana's grandmother sat gazing pensively out of the window at the dozens of abandoned aid containers that littered the car park. She looked up at the Arena with its buckled steel girders and twisted copper roof. Then, as the traffic moved forward, she saw a man walking towards the service entrance at the back of the building. There was something about him. Something sinister.

***

Grandmother Poborski considered for a moment. Was it his hard, granite-like features, the broad brow, or the jet-black, piercing eyes?

No, she finally decided. It was the deep scar above his right eye.

Chapter 133

Before lunch, Paula outlined the events on the Latin Bridge, and congratulated Leo on his appointment as General Director of Sarajevo Steel. She shared the latest news on the whereabouts of Milo, and held out little hope of ever bringing him to justice. Leo was still coming to terms with his new position as General Director and stunned by the arrest of Ivan Bobic. Lunch concluded in quiet and sad reflection, as they mulled over the morning's events. It was Tom who ventured an opinion first.

'My dad is very sorry he couldn't be here with us today. His flight from New York was delayed, but I'm pleased I came.' He looked at Ana sitting next to him. 'It was nice to meet your grandparents and talk to Jan and Marija.'

Ana squeezed his hand under the table.

'I hope you can all make it work.'

Luka picked up the thread of Tom's thoughts.

'I know we'll make it work. We have a life and a cause. Mr Poborski has not deserted us, even now.'

'He was such a good man,' said Bernadeta. 'He worked so hard. What kind of person would want to kill someone like Boris?'

'We don't know,' replied Mat. 'What we do know is Georg Komikosovitch was involved in some way, along with the Bosnian Embassy driver Ratko Kartic.'

'Then Georg turned up in Rome using a passport in the name of Robert Nova,' added Paula.

'But why did he take his own life on the bridge today?' asked Ana.

'I'm sorry Ana, we just don't know. I wish we did,' said Leo.

'Kartic disappeared from Kermincham Hall, dumping Savo's Mercedes ML350 outside the Catholic Church of Charles Borromeo in Keswick, and Georg ended up in Rome via Geneva,' said Mat. 'Both Georg and Kartic were AWOL at the time of the tragedy on the A66.

Neither were where they should have been when your father died, but it doesn't prove collusion. There's not a shred of evidence to connect them.'

'Mat's right. We've run extensive background checks on both of them. They've all come back blank,' Paula continued. 'One point of interest, it seems Kartic worked in pharmaceuticals. He spent years working in Rome, though not with Georg.'

'There is this. Not that it makes any sense.'

The others watched, as Mat extracted something quite small from his jacket pocket. He held it in his hand for a moment, before rolling it out across the table. 'I found it in Georg's fist after he shot himself. There seems to be the letter 'J' intricately carved on one side. Could be some sort of talisman? Does anyone know what it means?'

Paula held it up and examined it, shaking her head. She passed it around the table.

'I know what it is and what it means.' It was Bernadeta who spoke. She picked up the small Val Susa, blue-green pebble and held it between her thumb and forefinger, before continuing. 'I was a novice nun in Susa, in Italy, and this is where the blue green pebble comes from. I'll share with you what I know, but before I do, tell me, did Georg go to The Monastery of Saint Jerome, in Via Tomacelli when he went to Rome?'

'I'm sorry,' said Paula, 'I just don't have an answer to that.'

Leo poured Bernadeta a glass of water, as she began to tell her story.

'I left Mala Buna, my village in Croatia, and joined the convent in Susa, when I was sixteen. My father encouraged me to follow my sister and become a nun. It always seemed my family had a debt to repay. Atonement for a service rendered in the past.'

'On my eighteenth birthday my mother told me of the events in the fields outside the town of Bleiburg, Austria in 1945. Croatia, a Catholic country, had sided with the Nazis during the Second World War, setting up a puppet state, and after the fall of Hitler, Tito took revenge. Thousands of Croats tried to escape to Austria. My grandparents were among them. Tito hated the Catholics. His National Liberation Army murdered thousands of unarmed soldiers and civilians. They raped the women before stoning them to death. My grandparents were saved from the Bleiburg Massacre, by The Knights of the Holy Order of the Sword of Saint Jerome. I know it was to the Knights my family owed the debt. The Vatican stood by and did nothing. The cardinals were conscious of their failure, though they never acknowledged the fact.'

'When did you leave the church? What caused your change of heart?' asked Ana.

'After being in service for two years in the convent at Susa, I was sent on secondment to a convent in Rome, where I worked in the hospital. The work was hard but rewarding, and I felt I was making a difference. The nearby Monastery of Saint Jerome had a staff shortage in their hospital, and my Mother Superior asked if I would help out.

Monsignor Bernarez ran the monastery with an iron fist. I remember he drank a great deal of red wine made with grapes from the monastery's own vineyard. He was a very powerful man. He's still there now. If Georg or Ratko were involved in Boris' death, you can be certain it was on the orders of the Monsignor. My sister serves in the convent in Mala Buna, she thought Ratko Kartic may be moving nearby.'

Bernadeta took a drink of water, and Leo refilled her glass. 'A terminally ill Knight in the hospital was waiting to travel to the Monastery of Saint Florian, a hospice in Linz, Upper Austria. He said he needed to confess his sins before he died.

He never made it to Saint Florian. The Knight died in my arms. He held a pebble like this one in his hand. He said it was the sign of the Holy Order of the Knights of the Sword of St Jerome, a secret army safeguarding Catholicism throughout the world. Saint Jerome was the founder of the Order. He was the guardian of Catholic purity. The Knights defended his teachings for more than five centuries. Of course, I could never tell you what the Knight confessed, but I realised the Order were violent and cruel, no better than Tito's National Liberation Army. The experience destroyed my faith in the church. I had to leave.'

Ana had not missed a single word.

Chapter 134

During lunch Tom and Ana made plans to meet in her room. Leo and Mat went down to the hotel lobby. Mat hoped to hitch a lift to the airport in Paula's car. Paula and Sam were already waiting in the lobby. Their car pulled up as Leo and Mat arrived. Leo shook Mat's hand.

'Goodbye Mat, thanks for your help,' said Leo.

'No problem. I'd love to stay, but I've already ignored eight texts from my Chief Constable. I guess I'll reply to the ninth. I've got the message; he needs me back.'

'Take care,' said Paula as she gave Leo a hug. 'Perhaps we can meet up when I get back from Geneva.'

'Sounds good, yes I'd like that.'

Paula and Sam picked up their bags as the driver took Mat's case. Sam shook Leo's hand and climbed into the front of the car.

Leo watched the car pull away, and then returning to his room, he found the telephone ringing.

'Hello, it's Bernadeta. I'm in my room with Luka, if you want to come along now. Luka is just about to leave.'

Leo left at once and made straight for Bernadeta's room.

Chapter 135

Ana waited for Tom to arrive. She was unsure where her life would take her now. Her father's funeral had left her feeling empty. Drained. She needed to talk. Tom would understand.

Ana went into the bathroom to freshen up. She brushed her hair and put some lipstick on. There was a tap on the door and forcing a smile, she opened the door to welcome Tom. Tom wasn't there. A man stood in the corridor with his back towards her.

'Can I help you?' she asked. 'Is there something you want?'

He made no answer and before Ana could speak again, he turned to face her. It was Milo.

Ana tried to slam the door, but Milo's foot prevented her from closing it. She pushed hard against the door desperately trying to force him back. Slowly, Milo's strength told. Ana couldn't prevent him from forcing his way in. She let the door go and raced towards the bathroom. The sudden withdrawal of Ana's resistance sent Milo sprawling across the bedroom floor. He made a grab for her foot as she sped away, tripping her up, sending her crashing. She scrambled to her feet and managed to make it into the bathroom, as Milo lunged headlong into the wall. Ana bolted the bathroom door and looked for some way of escape, or at least some means of defence, but there was nothing, all she had was a lipstick. Milo got to his feet and attacked the bathroom door. His first kick burst a gaping hole in the door panel. He peeped through at Ana and smiled.

'Are you coming out to play, Poborski?' he asked. Ana switched off the bathroom light. 'The last time we played together I lost my two friends. Do you remember Olga and Roman? Now it's my turn to have some fun,' he sneered, holding up his penknife for Ana to see. 'Come on. Let's go where we can have some real fun. Somewhere we won't be disturbed. The Zetra Arena is nearby and is really cosy, you'll like it there.'

Milo kicked the door a second time and then a third. The final assault was enough to send the door panel splintering wildly across the bathroom floor. Ana struggled to escape from Milo's hold as he pinned her down, but she couldn't move. He reached inside her blouse and squeezed her small breasts, then thrust his hand between her legs. Milo lifted Ana bodily from the bathroom floor and out of the bedroom. Then, making for the fire escape, he dragged her down the deserted corridor. She tried to shout out for Tom or Leo, but Milo's hand was clamped hard over her mouth, strangling her cries for help.

***

Tom closed his bedroom door and made for Ana's room. He wondered what he could say to make her feel better. Saying he was sorry about her father's death was not enough. The door to Ana's room stood invitingly open and he stepped inside.

'Ana, its Tom, are you there?'

Then he saw the pile of timber splinters from the door panel and looked inside the bathroom. There was nothing but the shattered bathroom door. He checked inside the wardrobe, even looked under the bed. Ana was not there. He looked again in the bathroom and this time something grabbed his attention. He switched on the light and gasped.

***

Leo finished his coffee as he sat on the bed in Bernadeta's room, deep in thought.

'So, no one you've spoken to knows the whereabouts of Monsignor Bernarez?' he asked.

'No, I still have friends at the Monastery of Saint Jerome. They would tell me if they knew. I know they would. Francesca his housekeeper would know. I'm sure of it. She's in Sicily visiting her family. I can ask her when she goes back to Rome tomorrow.'

'What about the driver, Ratko Kartic? He could have been involved in Boris' death. You said your sister still knows him.'

'Yes, I have just spoken to her again. As I thought, she does still know him. He's gone home, to Okuje, a village near Mala Buna. He's given up his driving job with the Bosnian Embassy and changed his name. He has a new identity; he's tried to change his appearance. She knows the village; even knows the church he goes to. He's joined the choir.'

'This is the church you say has connections with the Holy Order of the Sword of the Knights of Saint Jerome?'

'Yes. I know it. He will be safe there. The church will be his guarantee of anonymity. They'd never give him up.'

'Kartic could be the link I need to find Bernarez.'

'So you are still intent on revenge?'

'Yes.' Leo thought for a moment. 'Yes, I still seek revenge.'

'Boris has found his peace, but I see in your eyes you still search for yours. I know it's like Luka says, peace never comes from revenge. Peace only comes from forgiveness. Can you not forgive?'

Leo made no reply. His attention was drawn to the hammering from across the corridor. They rushed outside to find Luka banging on Leo's door.

'What is it Luka? What is it?'

Leo stood waiting for a reply.

'It's Ana. Ana's gone! I went to her room to say goodbye, the door was open, but she's gone.'

Leo led the way to Ana's room followed by Bernadeta and Luka.

'The mirror! Look at the mirror in the bathroom,' said Luka.

All three stared at the bathroom mirror. The message on the mirror contained two words. Only two, but they were enough for Leo to fear the worst. Bernadeta suppressed a cry as she read out Ana's message scribbled in lipstick.

'Milo, Zetra.'

***

Tom had raced from Ana's room to the far end of the corridor, to see the door to the fire escape slowly closing. He dropped down the stairway three steps at a time, slipping once to crash hard into the metal handrail. He picked himself up and ran on. Two flights below, he caught sight of a blur of colour racing down the stairs. Encouraged, Tom picked up speed. He was gaining.

'Ana, hold on, I'm coming!'

Ana struggled to free herself from Milo's grip, she grabbed hold of the handrail, but Milo wrenched her away with a violent tug of her hair, pushing her outside into the street. Tom sped down the final flight of stairs. He was almost there. He reached the foot of the fire escape and then through the exit door, crashing headfirst into Milo, sending him to the ground. Ana was free.

'Run Ana! Run!'

Ana remained motionless. Tom could not understand why. Then he felt the barrel of a pistol jab him in the back. Lenord Stanislav, gun in hand, forced Tom into his car, as Milo grabbed Ana and pushed her roughly inside.

Milo drove away from the hotel, making for the Zetra Arena, while Lenord Stanislav sat in the passenger seat, pointing the gun in the direction of Ana and Tom. As they made their way along Maršala Tita, their car became caught up in a mob of chanting protesters heading for the Parliament Building. Two shots rang out close by as the crowd brought the traffic to a standstill. A protester jumped on the roof of the car, as an accomplice tried to force open the door. Stanislav aimed the gun in his direction and the protester backed off, pulling the other from the roof. Milo smiled; the People's Revolution was under way sooner than they'd planned. Operation Bosnian Dawn had begun.

***

Milo forced the car through the crowd and into Tešanjska. Minutes later they arrived at the rear of the Zetra Arena and concealed the car among the shipping containers. Ana and Tom followed Milo into the rear of the building, Stanislav following behind, his Glock pistol ensuring their compliance.

***

In the darkness Milo navigated the confusion of service passages with practiced ease. They arrived at the bottom of an unlit stairway that led up to the areas not open to the public and quickly climbed the first four flights of stairs.

Milo stopped. He listened carefully to confirm they'd not been followed. When satisfied, he pushed open the door and turned on the lights. Stanislav pointed towards the double doors on his right.

'In you go,' he said.

Ana and Tom entered one of the locker rooms and Stanislav left, locking the door behind him. 'They'll be okay in there for a few minutes, there's no way out.'

'What now, Milo?' asked Stanislav. 'What if Illic comes, what then?'

'If Illic comes, we'll be ready for him.'

Milo led Stanislav down the passage to a storeroom that had been used for equipment storage. It was filled with heavy packing cases.

'I see Helmut Jorgen has delivered our guns on time, as usual,' said Stanislav. 'There's quite an arsenal here.'

Milo lifted the lid from one of the packing cases nearest the door, to reveal ten Kalashnikov submachine guns.

'These will help to arrange a little armed insurrection around the Parliament Building,' he said. Next, Milo opened two of the cases at the far end of the room. From the first he took two German sniper rifles, like the ones the Serbs had used so effectively during the siege.

'Here, Lenord, I know how much you enjoyed shooting Bosnians during the Siege, now you have a few more to kill.' The second case held over a thousand rounds of ammunition. 'How much ammunition do you need? Are two boxes enough?'

Stanislav nodded and took the ammunition as Milo stuffed two boxes into his jacket pocket. He split open a third box and he and Stanislav loaded their rifles. 'We've just over two hours before our friends from the SDP arrive to collect the Kalashnikovs and the rifles. They will give us all the backup for the People's Revolution we'll need. Until then, I'll have some fun with Miss Poborski and her boyfriend. You go and watch out for Illic in case he comes.'

'Can I have Ana after you've finished with her? You know, before you kill her,' asked Stanislav. 'I enjoyed her mother so much and I know you did you too.'

'Of course you can, Lenord.'

Chapter 136

Leo and Luka climbed into a taxi in front of the Holiday Inn, as the noisy crowd surged around them, banging on the windscreen and doors.

'Zetra Arena, as quick as you can,' barked Leo.

One of the protesters pointed a gun at the driver. The driver turned to Leo, his face awash with fear.

'I don't think so,' he stammered. 'I'm going nowhere.'

Leo jumped out of the taxi and for a moment the pressure of the mob swept him down the street and away from the car. He fought his way back, opened the car door and threw the driver out onto the road.

Chapter 137

Tom and Ana explored the locker room. There was a window high up in the far corner. Its presence gave them hope. Tom lifted Ana onto his shoulders, and she peered out through the grimy windowpane.

'There's nothing there, just the twisted steel girders on the outside of the building that supported the roof before the bombing.'

'Can you see the catch? Can you open the window?'

Standing on Tom's shoulders, Ana grappled with the window catch.

'Yes. I've found the catch. It looks straightforward enough; I just can't move the thing.'

'Don't worry. Let me try,' said Tom.

Tom helped Ana down and waited until she had her breath back.

Then Milo returned. He held several short lengths of rope in his hand.

'Lie down on your stomach,' he demanded, pointing his rifle at Tom.

In Ana's head, Milo's voice echoed around the chancel of Saint Mary and Saint Stephen in Babonavic. She had to keep her promise.

'No, don't do it, we have to fight.'

There was calmness in her voice that surprised Tom and intrigued Milo.

'Fine by me, I'll shoot him now.'

Milo stuck the barrel hard into Tom's chest. Tom knelt and then lay face down on the floor as Milo threw the rope to Ana. 'Now tie his hands behind his back. And make it tight.' Ana did as she was told. 'Thank you, that's very neat. Now his ankles, come on quickly!' snarled Milo, a growing excitement rising in his voice. With the rifle close to hand, Milo knelt down beside Tom and took out his penknife. 'I've something very special in mind for you, when I've finished with your girlfriend.' He smiled as he opened his penknife. Then taking a great tuft of Tom's hair he cut through it with ease.

'I always keep it razor sharp,' he confided. Picking up the rifle, Milo walked over towards Ana and laid the rifle down. She raised her fists to fight. Her reaction only triggered a dismissive laugh, as Milo threw her roughly to the ground. 'Can you see all right from where you are?' he called over to Tom. 'I love watching almost as much as I love taking part. You can watch if you like.' Milo straddled Ana's slender body and pinned her arms to the floor. She tried to raise her head, but Milo forced her back as he kissed her hard on the lips, then he bit her neck, drawing blood. 'What no tears, no plea to be spared?' Milo clawed at her white blouse, ripping it open to the waist. 'Now, where shall I start?' Milo considered carefully, and then sank his teeth deep into her shoulder and then into her naked breast. Milo unfastened his belt and fumbled with the buttons on his trousers.

Chapter 138

Leo and Luka arrived at the front of the Zetra Arena, only minutes after leaving the hotel. Debris littered the car park and glass from the broken windows covered the steps. All the doors were locked. There was no sign of life. Rising vertically above the entrance, stood a solitary flagpole. The top had been splintered by flying shrapnel from Serbian mortars during the siege. It stood like a jagged finger pointing to the sky. Tied halfway up the shattered pole, the flag of Bosnia hung limply in the freshening breeze.

'There's no one here,' said Luka. 'Perhaps there's some a mistake?'

Leo made no reply. They started to cross the deserted car park, making for the service entrance at the back of the building, when a gunshot broke the silence.

'Down! Get down!' Leo and Luka scrambled for cover. 'Stay here and keep down, you understand?' asked Leo.

Luka nodded. Leo squirmed along on his belly to squint around the side of a jumble of old packing cases, to determine the sniper's location. Instantly a wooden box above his head exploded, sending packing case fragments rocketing in every direction. A thought entered Leo's head. Like Boris and Savo, had he survived the war only to die in the peace? Leo retreated deep into the forest of packing cases and containers. Then, keeping out of the sniper's line of sight, he pulled himself up on top of a Red Cross container and surveyed the car park. The containers were laid out like giant stepping-stones on some surreal game board. Suddenly the barricade that had been his shield disintegrated into a thousand splinters, as it took a direct hit. Leo pinpointed the location of the sniper and dropped silently to the ground. Picking out a path through the labyrinth of containers, he made off on a one eighty-degree arc, for his rendezvous with the hidden marksman.

He moved round behind the sniper and waited silently. Then another shot rang out. It hit a metal oil drum thirty metres over to Leo's left and ricocheted down the container alley. It told Leo the sniper had no idea where he was. Leo moved forward, treading soundlessly amongst the debris. His target knelt concealed at the other side of the packing case wall, two metres away. Leo moved closer to the sniper; he could hear his laboured breathing. He recognised Lenord Stanislav immediately. Leo locked his hands tightly around Stanislav's head. He gave a sharp jerk and Stanislav's rifle rattled noisily to the concrete. Leo released his hold and let him fall to the ground. Stanislav twitched twice before lying still, and then Leo returned with the rifle to find Luka crouched where he'd left her.

'Are you okay? Did you find who was shooting at us? Was it Milo, is he dead?'

'I'm fine, but no, it wasn't Milo.'

Chapter 139

Milo heard the gunshots and got to his feet. His fun had been interrupted just as it was about to begin.

'Don't go away, you two, I'll be right back.'

He tied Ana's hands behind her back as she lay on the concrete floor. Then he left and locked the door. Ana struggled to her feet and walked unsteadily to where Tom lay. She was bleeding.

'I'm sorry I couldn't help,' he said as they sat back to back and Tom struggled to untie Ana's hands.

'Never mind that now. We need to get out of here before Milo comes back. I hope the shots we heard was Leo bringing help.'

Ana untied the rope that held Tom's hands and then he untied his feet.

'Here, take this,' he said. Taking off his sweatshirt and handing it to Ana, he waited while she pulled it on and then he tried the door. 'It's no use, it won't open.' Tom went over and stood beneath the window. 'Can you hold me on your shoulders, and I'll try to open the window?'

Tom stood on Ana's shoulders and pushed hard at the obstinate catch. It moved, Tom pushed again, and the catch slid open. To Tom's surprise, the small window opened outwards with ease. Then squeezing his head and shoulders through, he looked out across the buckled remains of the roof supports. He sat astride the windowsill as the wind blustered around him and then he pulled Ana up to sit beside him. For a moment Tom balanced precariously on the edge before slithering out of the open window and dropping down onto the narrow-exposed girder, followed by Ana. She gave a sigh of relief.

'There's no way back now, but we're free.'

Chapter 140

Milo made his way out onto a service gantry high above the front of the building, overlooking the car park. Far below him, the Bosnian flag flapped wildly in the gathering breeze on the splintered flagpole. Milo watched as Leo and Luka forfeited the security of their packing case barricade and made their way between the containers, towards the rear service entrance. He tucked the rifle butt into his shoulder and steadied his hand on the top rail of the gantry. Then he tried to pick out Leo in the cross hairs of the gun's night sight.

Chapter 141

With no access back into the building Tom and Ana edged their way along the girder. They now seemed trapped up on the roof supports four stories above the car park.

'If we can make it to the end of this girder, we might be able to climb onto what remains of the roof.' Tom looked down at the ground below. So did Ana.

'It's a long way down,' she replied. 'But it's better than facing Milo.'

Chapter 142

Leo paused for a moment, listening for any sound that may indicate Milo's presence, but he could hear nothing above the groan of the wind. This was Milo's chance to take Leo down. The tendons in his trigger finger slowly contracted as a smile spread across his face. Luka saw him first but failed to make the connection between Milo and the threat of impending death.

'There he is, over to your left.'

Luka pointed towards the service gantry, as the realisation that their situation was critical hit home. Milo squeezed the trigger as Luka moved forward to better direct Leo's attention, standing between the sniper and Leo. Luka fell backwards, she died instantly, cradled in Leo's arms.

Chapter 143

As Tom and Ana moved slowly along the narrow, twisted girder, they heard the shot and their imagination dragged out their worst fears. Then without warning, the girder ended abruptly in a tangled knot. Their perilous pathway recommenced more than four metres from where they stood.

'Now what do we do? There's no escape!' said Ana. Tom thought there might be. High above them, just below the roofline, a small ledge threaded its way around the top of the building. Attaining the roof could bring them to safety. Tom looked up, as the wind danced round his head. The ledge could be reached, but only by executing a dynamic move, reminiscent of the technique he'd used on 'Misdemeanour,' his college gymnasium route.

'We need to get on the roof. I think I can climb up, if I can reach that ledge.'

Ana looked up, in the fading light. At first, she didn't see the tiny ledge that squirmed around the edge of the roof.

'You'll never pull yourself up on that. It's far too narrow, even if you can reach it. And what if you fall?'

'I know,' he said. 'But I have to try.'

Balancing carefully on the narrow girder, Tom slowly lowered his weight to squat down on his haunches and then concentrated all his strength on his next move. He waited until the wind had dropped and his mind was still. He took three big breaths before unleashing an explosion of energy, springing upward, his arms reaching out as the ledge came ever closer. Then the abyss below him beckoned as he hung on to the ledge with his fingertips, but not for long. Strength expended resting in this way was strength lost for the final move. With a great heave, Tom swung his right foot up to make contact with the roof edge. Then, digging his fingertips into the ledge, he pulled himself up onto the roof. He was safe.

'Now you. Come on Ana, you can do this.'

Tom lay belly down on the rooftop and reached down towards Ana, as she stretched up and prepared to jump. She reached upward as her feet left the safety of the girder, fighting to reach the ledge. Ana didn't make it. Her fingertips barely brushed the underside of the ledge as gravity applied its force to pull her down. In an instant, Tom snatched Ana's left wrist, her weight dragging him towards the roof's edge. Tom dug his elbows and toes into the twisted metal and held on, then he grabbed Ana's right hand. Tom rested for a moment before pulling Ana up towards him and the safety of the roof.

Chapter 144

Milo raced up two flights of stairs to secure a dominant view of the car park. He emerged onto the front roof of the Zetra Arena. Leo was nowhere to be seen. Milo knew he would have to break cover soon. All he had to do was wait. A noise distracted him over to his right and turning he saw Tom and Ana high on the main roof, silhouetted in the half light. Milo took aim. He had Ana in his sights. He never missed from this range.

***

Hands and fingers moist with sweat and blood, Leo caressed the rifle. He squeezed the trigger and felt the recoil stab his shoulder. Milo stumbled backwards as the bullet hit home, somersaulting down towards the front of the building. Milo didn't make it to the ground. Impaled on the splintered pole carrying the Bosnian flag, he died twenty minutes later, the flag stained by his blood.

Chapter 145

Detective Chief Inspector Mat Coulthard's flight landed at Manchester Airport, precisely on time. He waited alone in the baggage collection hall, as the carousel grumbled its way round, carrying nothing at all. He knew he'd lost any chance he may have had with Patricia.

***

A buzz went around the baggage hall, like the rustle of autumn leaves, as the first jumble of luggage was dumped at the far end of the carousel. Mat's case was one of the first to escape. He loaded the bag on the trolley and pushed his way slowly in the direction of passport control and customs, finally emerging into the airport concourse.

A multitude of people confronted him, mingling round the exit. Happy, expectant faces. Families met families, lovers kissed lovers and friends met friends. No one met Mat. He made his way out towards the taxi rank as dawn broke over the City of Manchester, and he contemplated Saturday evenings watching Match of the Day, with beans on toast and his own company.

'Hi, any chance of a lift on your trolley?'

Mat heard the voice, but in his flight-induced daze, not everything had switched to full power. He ignored the voice and kept on pushing. 'Hey you!' The voice demanded attention. 'What's a girl got to do to hitch a lift around here?' A hand reached out and touched Mat on the shoulder. It was Patricia Robinson.

Chapter 146

The Consortium's announcement that the finance for Sarajevo Steel was still in place, Ivan Bobic's arrest, and Roman and Milo's failure to orchestrate an armed People's Revolution, had left the streets around the Parliament Building deserted. Sarajevo was calm. Operation Bosnian Dawn was dead.

***

After Luka's funeral, Leo drove to the graveyard of Saint Mary and Saint Stephen in Babonavic. He knelt at the grave of Zara and his unborn child, and laid two small bouquets. He tried to picture the child who he would never see and never know, but the image would not come.

He saw Boris and Katerina climbing together at Romanija. Leo tried to hold the vision, but it faded and was replaced by others. He saw Roman Drasko and Milo Tolja, then his former General Director, Lenord Stanislav and Olga Lukic. Their images were quickly replaced by the images of Markovitch and Hajji, as others without names flooded in. Others whose lives he had taken during the Sarajevo Siege. Then as Leo's thoughts returned to Zara, he heard the Luka's voice, soft and low, as it filled his head.

'You must now live your life for them, for their memory. You must be happy for both of them, especially for your child. You must forgive them. You must forgive them all. Can you not forgive?'

Did he still seek revenge? Luka had sacrificed her life for him, giving him the chance to save Ana. He saw Luka's face again as he watched her life drain away. Then slowly, Luka's innocence changed his understanding. Revenge would never bring him peace. In that moment, he forgave them, and his pain began to fade. He looked up and saw Zara. The sunlight was shining in her hair. She held the hand of a child as she walked towards him. Leo recognised his own features in the face of his unborn son. He felt her lips on his as he held his son in his arms, and in his heart, like Luka, he forgave them. He forgave them all.

Chapter 147

Rather than go back to live in the apartment or return to Banja Luka with Maria and Jan, Ana decided to stay with Bernadeta in Sarajevo. At least for now. She loved the city. It was her home, it was where she belonged, a place to build a new life and exorcise her ghosts. Tom stayed on for a few days before Leo and Ana drove him to Sarajevo Airport for his flight home. There were no tears when Tom and Ana parted. They knew they would be together again soon.

Ana arrived back from the airport and sat with Bernadeta in the kitchen of her apartment.

'You know you can stay with me for as long as you want. I could do with the company. I really could,' said Bernadeta.

'I know. I'd like that. I just need some time. There are things I have to do. I guess I'll have to think about university in a month or two, but not just yet.'

'What will you study at University, or are you undecided?'

'Oh, Chemistry for sure. I want to be a chemist, nothing else will do.'

'I'll make some more space in the wardrobe in your room. I've been meaning to do it for ages. Do you know I still have my novice's habit in there, from more than twenty years ago?'

Ana unpacked her clothes and hung them up in the vacant part of the wardrobe. A stack of religious textbooks, old pamphlets and letters were piled up in one corner of the wardrobe floor. Ana moved them to one side to make room for her shoes. Finally, she laid out her hairbrush and makeup on the dressing table and went down to lunch. She waited before entering the kitchen while Bernadeta finished her telephone call to Sister Francesca, the Monsignor's housekeeper. Bernadeta prepared the meal while Ana set the table.

'Tell me about Mala Buna, your village in Croatia. Is it far from Sarajevo?'

'Mala Buna is just outside Zagreb. I used to go from Sarajevo on the train, but it must be more than ten years since I've been back.'

'And your time as a novice nun, where did you say you went after Susa? Was it somewhere in Rome?'

By the time lunch was over Ana knew a great deal about Bernadeta's early years in Mala Buna and the life of Ratko Kartic. As well as her time spent in Rome as a novice. Bernadeta had talked for well over an hour and said a great deal more than she'd intended too. Now Ana was ready.

EPILOGUE

Chapter 148
Florian, Austria

The sun was setting over Horsching Airport in Upper Austria as the plane landed and the thoughts of Monsignor Bernarez turned to his first days at St Florian Monastery as a young man. He made his way through the arrival hall to the exit, where his driver waited. It was the sixth canonical hour. The time for Vespers. He would pray during the twenty-five-kilometre drive to the monastery.

Monsignor Bernarez had left Saint Jerome discreetly and travelled alone from Rome's Fumicino Airport. Bleiburg had delivered on his oath and there was nothing to connect him to Bernarez, the Holy Order, or Poborski's death. Even so, he did not wish to draw attention to either his departure or his arrival at Florian. The flight to Linz had been uneventful, punctuated only by a twenty-five-minute stopover at Vienna.

Offering sanctuary was a role the St Florian Monastery was accustomed to. In the past it afforded anonymity to others fleeing justice. Leading Croat supporters of the vanquished Nazi puppet government had made it their refuge after the fall of the Third Reich in 1945. All were anxious to evade the attention of war crime investigators and the retribution sought by the liberators of Yugoslavia, Tito's National Liberation Army.

Bernarez had not chosen the location for this reason alone. His interest was also in the historic library. It held one of Austria's oldest and most impressive collections of medieval manuscripts, all housed in oversized bookshelves in the baroque main hall.

***

The novice returned to the refectory after prayer and filled a decanter with a carefully measured amount of red wine. Since arriving at the monastery only three days after the Monsignor, she had been anxious to make a good first impression. Sister Beatrice had duly noted her enthusiasm. The way she was the earliest to rise each morning and always the last to retire after prayers. Her work ethic in the monastery kitchen had been exceptional, especially for one so young. Sister Beatrice knew that with discipline and training her latest recruit would do well. Her practice of only engaging novices from personal recommendation of others from the order, had always worked well for her in the past. Sister Beatrice looked up at the big clock hanging on the far wall. The pendulum swung to and fro as the clock ticked away the minutes. The time was two o'clock in the afternoon.

'Have you prepared the wine?' Sister Beatrice asked.

The novice bowed deferentially.

'Yes, Sister.'

'Then you may take it through now.'

The novice placed the decanter of red wine on a silver tray with a clean glass and a napkin and then left the refectory. Her non-regulation Nike trainers, concealed beneath her habit, made no sound on the polished wooden floor.

Monsignor Bernarez sat reading in the silence of the library. Having arrived two weeks ago, he was now comfortably ensconced in his private apartment. His intention was to stay for the rest of the year to avoid any unwelcome attention from the authorities. He looked up from the Latin text he was reading as the young novice placed a tray on the table next to him.

'Some much needed refreshment. I thank you. This is indeed thirsty work.'

The novice filled the glass almost to the brim with heavy red wine and Monsignor Bernarez drank down a full draught of the thick rich liquid. The novice handed him the napkin and he dabbed his lips as the beginning of a smile of satisfaction spread across his face. The Monsignor's smile fell away to be replaced by a grimace of distaste as the wine washed the back of his mouth and descended down his throat.

'What is this?'

'The wine is from the Monastery of Saint Jerome, the grapes come from the monastery's own vineyard. But you would know that Monsignor. There is an added ingredient, the presence of which I believe you may have detected.'

'The added ingredient, how exactly did you come by this knowledge?'

'It was a friend of yours, Ratko Kartic. I last saw him in Okuje, a village near Mala Buna. Kartic told me about it, just before he died. I met him first at Kermincham Hall in England. He was a driver with the Bosnian Embassy. He was one of your Longa Manus. We shared a common interest in Robert Doyle, the seventeenth-century alchemist, an early scientist with a love of chemistry. It seems chemistry and pharmaceuticals were subjects Ratko specialised in when he worked with you in Rome.'

'Who are you? What do you want?'

'I am Ana Poborski. I want to fulfil the promise I made to my father, and to watch you die. You see, I'm not like the others. I can't forgive. I know you of all people will understand that. I made a promise to my mother that I would never again hide and that I would always fight. I've done that. And I promised my father I'd take revenge for his murder and now I've done that. Well, almost. Just before he died, Ratko said the barbiturate would take five minutes to kill you.' Ana looked at her watch. 'So you've two minutes left.'

Ana sat down on the chair opposite Bernarez and made herself comfortable. She brushed an errant wisp of hair behind her ear. Bernarez tried to focus on Ana but his vision was blurred.

'You are evil. You will be consumed by your own hate.'

'Oh no, life's too short to waste hating anyone. I learned that from my father. I don't hate you, but for me revenge helps me make peace with the past, so it won't mess up the future.'

Monsignor Bernarez slumped forward and fell heavily to the floor. The volume he'd been reading fell open to reveal an elaborate illustration of Jesus on the cross. Ana picked up the book and gazed down at the ornate iconography. The Crucifixion, such a powerful image of a cruel death, yet a path to heaven. Ana's ghosts flooded in. For a moment she embraced her mother, drank the fragrance that danced in her hair. She held her father in her arms, and then sank to her knees, her ghosts exorcized forever.

'That's it.' Ana whispered as she rose to her feet. 'It's over, I've kept my promise.'

Ana made her way out of the library, and through the cloisters, to the novice's dormitory. She took off Bernadeta's habit and laid it on the chair. Then, taking out a small brass key from her jeans pocket, she opened the wooden locker at the side of her bed, and recovered her rucksack, into which she packed Bernadeta's habit. She slid a manila envelope into the side pocket of the rucksack and zipped it up. The envelope contained her passport, a visa issued by the French Embassy in Paris, and an airline ticket to Chamonix.

***

Finally, Ana put a small heart-shaped locket on a silver chain around her neck. She was done here. Then she cried.

ACKNOWLEDGEMENTS

Many thanks to the Vale Royal Writing Group for constructive and helpful feedback and to Richard Leslie for his help and advice with the editing the manuscript.

Thanks also to Tracey Oultram for designing the cover of this book.

To my wife Maureen, who has been a valuable support in proof reading, typing and supplying endless cups of coffee.

ABOUT THE AUTHOR

Peter Dyson was born and brought up in Wolsingham, in Weardale, County Durham. He worked in automotive distribution before retiring. This is his third self-published work. He lives in Cheshire with his wife Maureen and eight bicycles.

Other books by the same author:
Poppy Tears
a collection of short stories

Eight Days in May
a compelling story of family intrigue

Follow @PeterVaneDyson on Twitter
Or visit
www.peterdysonauthor.co.uk to find out more

AUTHOR'S NOTE

remember watching the television news broadcasts during the Bosnian War and the Siege of Sarajevo, the longest siege of a capital city in the history of modern warfare. It seemed to be a war like no other. As the conflict persisted, the media briefings became less frequent and my attempt to under it diminished. Even now, a European war during which so many died, is poorly understood.

I spent some time in Bosnia after the war. I met a lot of people. Nice people. Just like you and me.

While there, I tried to make sense of what had happened and why. I still have many unanswered questions.

Although the characters in Bosnian Dawn belong to different faiths, as well as holding different political views, it is important to say that wrongdoing is a human behavioural trait in people of all religions and all political persuasions, and all are equally capable of the kinds of deeds that are set out in this book. Therefore, no offence or slight is intended towards anyone.

Printed in Great Britain
by Amazon

37133295R00183